Beastie

Jack O'Donnell

SpellBound Books

Chapter 1

Grimms

PIZZA FACE IS SMALLER THAN EVAN, BUT WITH A BIG SQUARE head, so they figure they're really the same size. Blinkered by duffel-coat hoods, battered by hailstones, they work as splay-footed partners raking the middens for treasure. An icy wind funnels up the River Clyde and steals through soot-blackened tenement walls stirring bedroom curtains. Blows through the gaps of a rusty fence parked against the grey wall of a disused wash-house. On the washing line jiggles a windblown print-dress, a yellowing bra and outsized woman's pants. They take a breather. Cup their hands over their mouths to warm them.

'Nothing but rubbish here.' Pizza Face lobs a blue detergent bottle from a bin against the wash-house wall. He drags out a woman's shoe with no heel and lets it tumble to the muck. Boots the bin next to Evan's in frustration.

The lid marked *No Hot Ashes* clatters to the ground. Pizza Face pounces and grabs an Irn Bru bottle, holding it up in triumph. He rubs grit with one hand and wipes clean his fingers and palm on his grey school shorts. 'Jist shows yeh, eh? That's thrupence. Some folk are jist fucking made of money.'

1

When he glances over to share his triumph, he gets the picture. 'Whit happened tae yeh?'

Evan grins lopsidedly. He hooks a finger into the corner of his mouth to better show his split top lip, but winces. An incisor knocked off-kilter.

Pizza Face boots the nearest bin, making it jump. Skin pigment in his birthmark turns woad-like before one of his berkies. The din echoes around the quadrangle of windows and walls. A dog howls in the back court nearby. 'Bastard! When I grow up I'm gonnae—'

The tip of Evan's tongue probes his cut lip. He studies his wellies and blinks away tears. 'He didnae mean it. It was my fault for no paying attention. Dropping a good plate. Getting him aw worked up.'

Pizza Face's mouth twists like a yarn winder, but he holds aloft the glory of the gingy bottle. 'Don't worry, I'll go halfers and buy yeh a sweetie.'

Thumbs and fingers gnawed to the quick, his hand plunges into the ragged pile of paper nesting on the bin. Careful to avoid potato peelings and crumpled fag packets, he jouks around to attack from another angle, checking for other treasure. He pulls out a tatty scud book.

Pizza Face plays the big man. He upturns a bin lid, sticks *Playboy* on top of it and peels open a page. Heads bowed, with their backs to watching windows, studying what their bodies are hiding with the intense absorption of divers running low on oxygen.

Big hair and pouting lips and humongous tits and hairy fannies and bare bums flash before their eyes.

Pizza Face sniggers. 'I'd ride the whole lot of them.'

Evan giggles, tugging *Playboy* away from Pizza Face. He hoiks it back, and part of a woman's mouldy breast comes away in his hand.

'The only girlfriend yeh'd ever get is Claudine Legat,' cries Evan.

'Junior said he'd poked her.' Pizza Face sprays saliva and laughs until his eyes squint. 'But yeh know how oor Chaz always tries to get the better of him. And he said she was so fat that he stuck his hand up inside her fanny. Then he was sucked up inside her hole and it was a couple of days before he could figure a way oot.'

Pizza Face grabs the bottle and they meander towards Maisie's. Rain lances their faces and they make a run for it.

They shelter in their close, next to the sweetie shop. Pizza Face slurps a penny lollipop, squinting at the traffic. Above his head, scrawled in red paint and disjointed lettering: *BUnDy Ya BA*.

Evan leans against the opposite wall and nibbles sweet cigarettes.

Housewives with hats pulled low on their heads push prams which jolt along the wide pavement. A blue anorak hood bobs along between them as he dribbles a ball past the close mouth. The ball escapes, rolls into the gutter. The boy spots Pizza Face and Evan eyeing him.

Pizza Face growls, 'Whit yeh gawking at four eyes?'

An Auchenshuggle double-decker bus cuts into the side of the road, puddling water onto the pavement. He picks up the ball and leaps aside before he gets soaked. 'But I don't wear specs,' he says.

Pizza Face leaps off the top stair and runs at him. 'Yeh will when I fucking finish wae yeh.'

Ball tight under his arm, the footballer sprints and weaves in and out of pedestrians. Pizza Face clatters behind him, Evan in tow.

Chapter 2

That old thing

Evan's mum's clothes aren't empty, but a luminous living relic. He comes here to listen. To hear her talking and laughing with neighbours. Dolled up in the green dress and sheer silk scarf she liked so much—she's like a movie star gone offscreen.

Weekends, they would take off on an adventure and ride the red SMT bus to the top of the hill. She loved The La Scala. She loved Westerns. Her deep-set blue eyes glinting brighter than any house lights. They smuggled pic"n'mix from Woolies, high on the hog of velour chairs. She'd hoot with laughter at cherry polished B-movie actors playing American Indians. Chew over them lining up to get gut shot, and tumbling down-and-out, scowling, but with their eyes shut.

When it was over, when it was really over, they'd come out and blink in daylight. His mum would take his clammy hand. 'Insurance, in case she lost him,' she said.

He bestows a kiss on that old thing she liked to wear when nipping downstairs to the Kippen Dairy. Tan tights stuffed into a

4

pocket, as if she'd be reaching back for them—threadbare memories no needles can sew or unpick.

He bows before a line of undressed costumes hung in the wardrobe. Swirl of blues and greens, the darkness of browns and blues, but never black. The bounty bag of her missing body, and the incense of her cheap perfume and lavender that grabs at his throat.

Higgledy-piggledy shoes at the bottom of the wardrobe. No left or right, no swish of crossed legs as she sat comfy in her chair by the fire. Dream-catching, crooked smile, when he'd tried her shoes on, and paraded about the room with pointy toes, crying. A door opens inside him. He steals, nimbly, from the living room and the dying room.

Chapter 3

Fairies

SEATED SIDE-SADDLE ON HIS UNMADE BED, EVAN'S imagination soars. He enters a world where witches were likely to dupe you unless you quickly lop their heads off. The thirty-watt bulb hangs crooked and illuminates the well-thumbed pages of *Grimms' Fairy Tales*. An escape plan he'd got free from Dalmuir library.

Dermot's stocky frame fills the doorway. He hawks up phlegm and coal dust, spitting blackened saliva into the palm of his hand and wiping it on the backside of his work jacket. 'Someone tae see yeh,' he croaks, leaving him with his charge.

Evan grins. 'Angel,' he cries in a familiar and teasing manner.

Angela bristles with impatience, her flowery frock torn at the shoulder, and grubby at the hems. Purple grab marks wax yellow on the skin above her elbow, and a scab on her kneecap shows signs of previous battles. Sticky fingers tug at his wrist and hand. 'Come and see.'

The book bounces off the bed, forgotten on the floor. A turn of the handle and front-door key. They stand on the threshold of their third-floor kingdom.

She clatters onto the stone steps, thinned and buckled in the middle by communal footfall. Crouched on the lip of the stair, she points a wavy finger. 'See?' her bulb of face and blonde hair aglow.

He takes a few steps and squats beside her. 'That's magic. How many dae yeh think there ur?'

They gawk at black worker ants cascading over the brick from their stronghold in the hunched and broken limestone.

'Fucking millions,' she charges them. Shows she means business by stamping hundreds into speckled gore, scarlet dotting the hard soles of her unbuckled summer-sandals. Her greenish eyes sparkle. Mass murder suits her.

Ants are terrible gossips. It's in their blood. They jitterbug and change their invasion plans. Their inhuman tormentor shrieks and flees to stand beside Evan on the landing. 'We'll need tae get boiling water. That's what yeh dae.' She takes the measure of him. 'If there was a war, us against aw the animals, who'd win?'

'Yeh'd win, Angel. Yeh'd always win.'

'Jist wait.' She goes into battle with strategic stomping on ants, her tongue tucked into the side of her mouth, jumping from one stair to another and back to the landing. 'Wee bastards.' Her face pinks with laughter, glancing at him with long lashes.

The smile disappears when she spies her mum standing with the door open. Kerry-Ann, an Embassy Regal in her nicotined fingers.

'In,' Kerry-Ann motions with a smoky sweep of her hand towards the lobby at her back. 'Whit did I tell yeh about fucking sneaking oot?'

Evan becomes invisible to her.

Kerry-Ann's stringy hair, parted in the middle and loosely gathered in twisted braids was once spun gold as Angela's. Dark baggy blouses and long skirts disguise the sudden leap from youth to obscurity. A big mole near her left ear is home to three luxuriant whiskers. She's a witch, if ever he's seen one.

Chapter 4

Blodger

PIZZA FACE SKULKS WHEN HE TAKES A DRAG ON A FAG AND smuggles it behind his leg when he isn't smoking. He'd stolen a dout, almost a full Regal King Size, from the ashtray in his house last night and planked it. He stands inside the close with Evan and they wait for the rain to give them a chance. They weigh the merits of a Norton motorbike parked behind a green van at the kerb.

'Yeh want twosies?' Pizza Face holds out the butt-end of a fag.

'Nah,' Evan shrugs. 'Yeh ur alright, no after yeh've been slabbering aw o'er it.'

Pizza Face purses his lips, sucks his cheeks in like an old man taking a few last drags, before flicking it out onto the pavement.

They hear a door slamming. The staccato of running feet, pausing at the landings above, drums louder. Angela appears ghost-like, glimmering in the close's dark corners in her dirty white print-dress, hurdling off the steps and landing with a thud.

'Hi Evan,' she chants in her sing-song voice. Her smile is for him, blanking Pizza Face. She peels off towards the backcourt, hamstrung because of a broken sandal buckle. Her left leg scrapes her heel along the ground to keep shuffling feet on course.

Evan sprints and gets in front of her, near the jagged remains of a wall. He grabs her shoulder and hauls her backwards. 'Where yeh goin? It's bloody freezing and yeh've nae jacket.'

'I seen a dog fae the windae.'

Evan has a quick dekko. 'No yeh didnae. Yeh've got dogs in the heid.' She's shivering, but her face is pinkish with excitement. She loves petting dogs in the way other wains loved ice-cream cones. Any mention of a stray and she was off and running down the stairs to rescue it.

Pizza Face creeps up beside them. He turns his head to whisper, 'That's Blodger's dog. Yeh better no go near it. He eats cats for a living and snacks on rats.'

Blodger's dog gives them a lazy-eyed once over, before sniffing the buckled wash-house door and following a trail of broken bricks. It lifts its muscled head like a connoisseur of bin-to-bin dining, pausing to claw its arse with a thumping sound like the beating of a carpet. Mud splattered and uneven cobbles. In the rain, their backcourt glimmers a deep shade of shale blue. The mongrel's scabby legs are like stilts. The reek from it makes Evan itch. A beast with bloated belly and more foul teeth showing than the front row of a geriatric's funeral. When its head whips round and it growls, Evan and Pizza Face retreat to the safety of the close mouth, but Angela stays put.

'No. No,' she says. 'Blodger likes me.' She makes a beeline towards it with the flat of her hand out, as if to pet it. 'C'mon son. I'll no let them hurt yeh.'

Pizza Face, for once, does the right thing. He rushes and picks her up like a goose. 'Nobody likes yeh. Not even yer ma.' He doubles back towards the close with her struggling in his arms. 'Yeh ur a cheeky wee bastard.'

'Put me doon,' she howls. And when that doesn't work, 'Yer hurting me.'

Blodger's dog is already upon its prey. When Evan comes to the rescue, it snaps at his ankles, his flared denim blanketing it, saving his leg from being gnawed. He squeals, kicks out, catching it a lucky blow in the mouth and it lets go. It glances at him before cutting off his retreat by circling in front of him and making another foray. Evan feints one way and goes the other. The mongrel snaps at his heels. He runs faster than he did in the school race, overtaking, but dunting into Pizza Face.

Pizza Face stumbles and they fall. He twists his body so his shoulder gets the worst of it, but he's kept a grip of her. She seems unhurt, first to recover her feet and bounce up. The dog loses interest in Evan, and about faces to make a dishrag out of Angela. Its snout thrusts forward and it angles its head to get a grip of her skirt or bite into her bare leg.

Evan, nearly greeting, prays that a neighbour might appear to save them. He hesitates before turning back to the fray. Pizza Face scrambles to his feet, the back of his duffle-coat bogging, he dances around the fracas of Angela and the dog, his eyes darting and searching for something to defend himself.

'Stop it, Blodger.' Angela slaps the dog hard on the snout. 'Behave! Be a good dog and stop yer carry on.' She holds out the flat of her hand. Blodger's dog sniffs, its wormy tongue licks her palm, holding its neck up as she strokes matted fur.

Evan side-steps and cuts towards them. The mongrel whirls around and growls. Evan backs off sharpish. Pizza Face cuts towards the bins, returns with a bin-lid shield and a piece of fence for a sword. Angela kisses the dog on the nose. It tucks in at her side, tail wagging, until Pizza Face comes closer. It lunges towards him. The bin lid clatters as he runs and uses one of the bins to vault onto the wash-house wall.

Chapter 5

Slavering

EVAN LIES COSY IN BED. JAMMIES WORN OVER DAY CLOTHES and two pairs of socks keep his feet toasty warm. Fairy stories are inscribed on his heart. He turns pages and worlds turn. He imagines what would happen if the prince didn't kiss the princess because he fancied Rose Doyle, and would rather kiss her, or some other frog, instead.

A kerfuffle on the outside landing. He hears shouting and somebody battling up the stairs. He slides across the bed and edges his feet onto the cold linoleum. Sneaking into the lobby, he pokes open the letterbox and peeks out.

Kerry-Ann is slavering drunk. She has no coat, dressed as a fashion-plate with hooped gold earrings. Her cheesecloth blouse shows a patch of bare stomach over yellow bell-bottoms. She is swaying, tottering.

Chaz models an imitation black Crombie, narrow lapels sweep to the elevated heels of his suede two-toned shoes, peeking out under the flared turn-ups on his jeans, which lift him to the height of five-feet nothing. He strokes her arm, bracing her body.

Two other long black coats are back a bit, chain smoking. Plukey face Rab with greasy hair lives in the next close and Podge, his pal, with blonde hair in a bouffant and a dimple on his chin.

Her eyes frosty circles, trying to focus on something, or someone, and the mumbled spiel around her stops.

'Let's get yeh inside.' Chaz grabs her by the elbow, trying to direct her from the landing to the front door. She staggers forward and sideways, bumping against him.

'Fuck off,' she howls. 'Aw of yehs. I'm fucking sick of it. I'm fucking sick of yeh. Fuck off.'

'C'mon, don't be like that.' Chaz skims his fingertips along her arm. 'We ur gonnae huv a wee party. You, me, and a few of my mates.' The plastic bag rustles against his leg. 'Yeh'll like that.'

Rab and Podge snigger, taking a step forward, bottles clinking.

Kerry-Ann is swaying, undecided. Her front door flies open and she stumbles inside, past Angela, the lobby light a halo in her daughter's golden hair. Blodger slinks beneath Kerry-Ann's gaze.

Blodger torpedoes out of the door and wraps its jaws around Chaz's leg. The mongrel punctures flared denim and meaty flesh below the knee. He shrieks like a wee lassie and tries hopping, leg outstretched, to pull away. Angela's dog bites him again, higher on the thigh. Snarling, it gets a better grip. Chaz screams even louder.

Podge and Rab bunny hop with the ruffling of plastic bags beside man and beast. Podge, on the front foot, tries to give the dog's flank a fly boot. Blodger's hackles rise higher. It lets go of Chaz and snaps at Podge's balls, but its snout slides away from his long coat.

Rab scrambles down the stairs, Podge behind him, kicking at the dog, fending it off. 'Fuck off, ya evil bastard,' he bawls.

14

Rab scurries out of sight.

Chaz clambers over the banister and railings. His hair hangs over his face. He hesitates, looking at the crash-landing, but when Blodger, loops back up the stairs, growling, he jumps.

Evan hears the thud of his platform shoes.

'That dog's getting it,' rings round the walls.

Blodger dukes back and pitter-patters into the lobby. Angela puckers a kiss on the dog's nose. It tucks into her side, tail wagging.

Evan opens the front door, on guard, and steps into dim light. 'Whit happened?' he asks Angela.

'Blodger bit Chaz because he's bad.'

Evan sticks his index finger over his lips, and whispers, 'Shush, he might be listening.' And he points downstairs.

'I don't care. I hate him, and next time I hope he dies.'

Evan eases the door shut and tiptoes back to his room and his bed. He picks up the book of Grimms' stories.

Chapter 6

Black hole to the outside world

EVAN SPRAWLS BEFORE THE COAL FIRE, HIS BACK RESTING against his da's armchair. He's waiting for *Doctor Who* on the telly.

Dermot breezes past him and into the kitchen. His workie jacket hung on a shoogly nail pegged to the front door, like a black hole to the outside world. He fills the sink with cold water. He lacks patience to heat pots as his wife did.

He strips his soiled jersey, shirt and vest and slaps water against his body with worker's hands hard as pumice. Carbolic soap, dunked in cold water, the smell alone a Lourdes cure for aches and pains. He kicks off his boots and steps out of trousers on to the stone floor, washing quickly down below. It takes the shine off engrained dirt.

Murky water drains grey. He refills the sink, gives himself a final scrub.

Ratty towel in his fist, he stumbles through to the living room. His best clobber lies on the arm of the chair. White shirt and tartan-green tie, dark Sunday suit and polished brown brogues. He combs his hair, leaning over the hearth, till it clings to both sides of his head like wing mirrors. His face ruddy and rude with health. Hailstones batter windowpanes like the handful of change thrown at his wedding.

He picks up the poker and drives it into the smouldering coals. Shadows surge and flames leap wilder than the special effects in *Doctor Who.*

He gets dressed in weekend finery and eases himself, with a grunt, into the chair by the fire.

His eyes open and he sniffs, snorts, and hawks into the flames. 'Whit happened?'

'Cybermen ur chasing Doctor Who.'

'Oh, aye, that's right.' He acts as if he's forgotten and not fallen asleep. Eyes glittering, a bit of a bead from earlier still in him.

Let's get some dinner, boy.' He digs deep into his back pockets for notes and coins. Sorting the money from his wages from his tips. 'Chips?' He ruffles his son's hair.

Evan ignores him, until he's sure Doctor Who is a gonner, has no chance of escape, and he is going to die. The theme music blares and Evan relaxes, knows it's only a hoax. Doctor Who is no mug. He'll find a way.

A Woodbine dout appears in Dermot's hand, ash falling onto the cracked linoleum. He sucks in his cheeks in, takes another drag. 'It's always chips, innit?'

And the way he smacks his lips together makes Evan know he's flush.

'Aye.' Evan turns around to look at his da's face, grinning.

'Get me a fish supper then.' He hands Evan a crisp pound note and the added weight of guilt money. 'Get whatever yeh want—and get yerself some ginger and some sweets.' He turns his head away and stares deep into the embers, cigarette burning to his fingertips.

Evan dresses up warm in his duffle coat and woolly hat. Welly boots on his feet, he skitters down the stairs.

Snow follows hail and drifts, setting the world to white. Dumbarton Road, like the Tardis, smaller and larger, in the blink of an eye, crisp and clean as the world stops. Light shimmers, the fuzzy orange glow of the lampposts captures closed shops and latticed-metal grills grey the windows.

No need to test his feet on the pavement. Snow to kick through, traffic slows and older people skitter and skate, but with money in his pocket, Evan is late and on home turf. He gallops, lopping aside other pedestrians and hunting crouching old dodderers in long coats.

Mario's chippy isn't far enough to work up a sweat, just over the canal at the bottom of a tenement building. Maggie Scott's pub next door. The smell of vinegar and chips, a Pied Piper that brings all kinds of rats marching in line from the back courts.

Evan's mouth fills with saliva at the thought of warm food. As usual, on a Friday the chippy is jumping, a queue outside the door. Evan doesn't mind standing invisible in the heat of other larger bodies.

Mario, behind the counter, has a tonsured head, a woebegone expression, and acts dumb. He leaves talking gibberish to the two women working alongside him. They wear the same chippy uniform as their gaffer, white coats nicotine-yellow with grease from fish, pies, black pudding, or other jewels kept warm at eye-height, under the hotbox lights.

'Whit yeh wanting, pet?' A Players No.6 gives a jaunty angle to the thin red line of the chippy woman's tight lips.

Evan smiles shyly. She knows his dad, who delivers her coal. He rhymes off his order.

With a conspiratorial wink, she sprinkles salt and an extra-large dollop of vinegar. 'Anything else?' Her tired eyes flicker away from him, waving her cigarette at another customer.

Evan toys with the money in his jacket, not to be hurried. He tells her he also needs ginger and sweets off the shelves as well.

Parcelled in newsprint—with the headline, 'Gas explosion Destroys Shops at Clarkston Toll'—warm chips pressed against his stomach are carried like a newborn. He scampers across the road at the canal. Snow has turned to rain, the streets run to slush, but he is content with his booty.

He races up the stairs and wangles a chip or two out of the parcel for his troubles. The riches of a CurlyWurly sticks out of a duffle-coat pocket. A bottle of Irn Bru hangs lopsided in the other.

He hears clipped coughing climbing up the walls. Hand clutching the banister, he peers into the darkness of the close mouth. The coughing reaches a crescendo and begins anew.

'I'm no feert,' he mutters, sliding his shoulder against the wall, and ghosting down the stairs.

It is darker than he likes, but enough light to see his feet and the slippy flagstones of the bottom landing. The hacking coughing continues. He slowly pulls open the door of the derelict toilet.

Blodger capers out, nipping his heels, chasing him away. The fish supper slips from his hands. As he bats the dog's snapping jaws and teeth, the bottle falls out of his pocket and smashes. The mongrel pounces on the grub.

Evan gets within kicking distance and it growls. Rubbing his back against the wall, he gives the dog a wide berth and takes a better look inside the slanted open door and hanging cobwebs.

Underneath a dripping cistern, Angela crouches, drookit and dirty, among building debris. Her eyes are stuck so far in her head, she's like a wild cat keeking out of a hole. She stares back at Evan, her body bent with coughing and sobbing.

'Whit ur yeh daeing here?' Evan says. 'It's fucking freezing.'

Blodger slobbers newsprints before it slinks past Evan. He steps back, just in case, but it ignores him and pushes its snout into Angela's midriff. She cuddles the dog, shivering. Her nose runs, and she dabs at snotters with her sleeve as she splutters a disjointed explanation. 'Cause she says she hates me, grabbed my arm and flung me oot the door.'

Angela holds out her right arm, peels back the print dress to show the tinge of blue and yellow bruising.

Evan leans to get a better view. Blodger growls and he jumps backward.

He tries to cajole her out. 'Don't be daft. Yer mum doesnae hate yeh. C'mon I'll take yeh up the stairs myself. If yeh stay oot here any longer, yeh'll get yer death of cold.'

Angela shakes her head and slumps on to the dog. 'My mum hates me. She said she wishes I hadnae been born cause that was the only time she was ever happy.' She coughs even harder. 'She wishes I was deid.'

Evan pulls the Curly Wurly out of his pocket. Holds it out and waves it in front of her face, hypnotising her with a chocolate delight. 'C'mon don't be daft. She's only kidding yeh on Yer mum loves yeh.' A kink in his throat and he stands a little straighter, choking. 'The same as my mum loved me.' And he ends in an emphatic, aggrieved tone. 'At least yeh've got a mum.'

Angela springs and snatches the Curly Wurly out of his hand. She rips the wrapper open with her teeth and chews a bit, which stalls her coughing. Tearing off more chocolate-caramel, she holds it over Blodger's mouth.

'Yer no supposed tae feed animals Curly Wurlies.'

Blodger snaffles the chocolate. Angela looks equally unimpressed. 'How no? He likes it.'

'Member, yeh cannae bring that thing up the stairs with yeh,' says Evan.

Angela feeds the mongrel the remainder of the chocolate and kisses its cold nose. Evan takes off his jacket and droops it over Angela's shoulders and leads the way. The dog pitter-patters behind Angela to the first landing with its tongue hanging out.

She kisses its nose again. 'Go on, son.' She gives the dog a cuddle and shoves its flank.

Evan expects it to ignore her, but the dog scampers downstairs.

Angela grabs his hand. He swings her arm to-and-fro in the way she likes as they climb the stairs.

Evan chaps Angela's front door, but her mum doesn't answer. Angela waits and watches, shivering and coughing, and sheltering behind him. 'Yeh can come tae mines for a minute,' he suggests.

Angela perks up. 'Will yeh read me the story about the princess?'

'Aye, course.'

Angela hangs back outside his front door. 'But whit about yer da? Won't he be angry? He's always angry.'

Evan chuckles like an adult. 'Don't worry, he doesnae wait mair than five minutes for anybody, or anything, but booze. Nae cauld chips for him. He'll be gone. And yeh'll be long gone by the time he gets in. He'll be pissed.'

A kiss-curl over her right eye makes her seem suddenly shy.

'C'mon pet, yeh'll be alright.' He crouches and takes her hand, but she jerks away. A racking cough brings her closer. He lifts her from under her oxters. She throws her bare legs around his waist. Carrying her through the hall, he back heels the front door shut and ploughs into his room.

He drops her like a mucky moonstone on top of the candlewick bedspread. Wind whistles in the lum and the blocked fireplace, bringing the sickly sweet taste of soot. He knows it would be warmer in the big room beside the fire, but that's da's place, his space.

Under his unmade bed, he lifts his book of fairy stories. 'Get cosy,' he tells her, peeling off her plastic sandals and dropping them with a thud. He edges blankets from underneath her. She's still got his duffle coat on, but he wraps her inside a homemade cocoon.

Shivering, he kicks off his wellies. He picks up the book and tucks his body in beside her warmth. The worn binding falls open at a familiar story. He starts reading, more from memory than the page. 'Once upon a time...' but already her eyelids are closing and so are his. The book falls from his fingertips.

Chapter 7

One Pope of Rome

LUMBERING FEET, FALLING UP THE STAIRS, A BRAYING VOICE chanting a Celtic song. 'Wan Pope of Rome,' echoing in the cavities of the stairwell. Dermot pushes the door open and slams it shut, flops against the lobby wall and lurches towards the big room.

Angela nuzzles into Evan's shoulder and neck. Her coughing doesn't waken her. Dermot stands black, swaying on the threshold of his son's bedroom, peeinginto the gloom. He staggers across to the bed and stumbles on the fallen book. Whisky breath, he bends and gawps at Angela's blonde fizz.

Dermot bawls, 'Whit's she daeing here?'

Evan mutters, 'We fell asleep.'

Dermot reels and sticks a hand on the bed but stumbles backwards. 'Well, get her up and into her ain house. She shouldnae be here.'

Evan scrambles out of bed. He puts on his wellies. 'I chapped her door hunners of times, but naebody answered. There was naebody in.'

He nudges Angela awake, but she squirms from his grasp to the side of the bed facing the wall. When she sits up, the silhouette of blankets place a shroud over her head. They listen to coughing and her mewing cry.

Dermot glares at his son, and the lumpen form of the wee girl. Evan follows his da into the lobby and watches from their door. Angela slips in beside him, clutching his leg and reaching for his hand. Her hand feels sticky, her cheeks pink blodges, and her forehead sweaty from the heat of the bed.

Dermot chaps the door. He chaps louder. The palm of his hand batters against wooden panels. Shouting, 'C'mon, I know yer in there. Stop fucking about and answer this fucking door this fucking minute.'

Kerry-Ann flings open the door. Boudoir materials, pink and soft on her body, almost see-through—if a man looked very hard. A figure not rich with curves. The sweetness of long neck, of jaunty hips and the honk of eau de toilette. Mussy hair gathers at the nape, showing off her tits. By a jerk of the corner of her mouth, and a flash of the wet tip of her tongue on her lips, she contrives to look outraged and pleased with the attention she is getting. 'Whit is it noo?'

Dermot's expression dithers between disbelief and fury. He blurts out, 'Yer wee lassie!' He points at her standing in the doorway beside his son.

'Aye, whit's she done, noo?'

Chaz swaggers out of the lobby behind her and into the landing. His hair slicked back with Brylcreem.

'We were jist huving a wee drink, Dermot. Yeh'd know aw about that, eh?' He holds Dermot's gaze before clattering downstairs.

Kerry-Ann screeches at Angela, 'Yer grounded. Whit did I tell yeh about sneaking oot?'

Chapter 8

Doolally

PIZZA FACE AND EVAN PLAY WALLIE. DUFFLE-COAT HOODS protect them against driving rain. Evan catches the dimpled size-4 Mitre sweetly with the toe of his wellie, but groans, because the orange ball hits a washing pole, ricochets sideways and trundles towards the miry cobblestones and the close.

Pizza Face wallops the ball off the washhouse wall to start another game. 'How come yeh werenae at school yesterday?'

Dalmuir School offers a comprehensive enough education. Evan and Pizza Face sit close together at a front-row desk. But Pizza Face melds into Graham Sweeney, Monday to Friday, when Mrs Thompson, their Primary Five teacher, shouts him into existence, marks him down on the school register as being in and, briefly, looks up to check. His face two-tone, like a new-born's fist, dominated by the purple-ink splash of his birth.

She can never be sure with him. Classroom experience has taught her his type never learn. A strapping woman, with fleshy arms, good at the belt, Mrs Thompson is not to be trifled with.

'Slept in. And I'd a bit of a cough.' Evan chokes on a fake cough and grogs against a wonky bin lid. He nudges Pizza Face's shoulder to make his legs buckle and miss the ball.

'Fuck off,' Pizza Face grunts. He blooters the ball against the wall and grins.

They tramp shoulder to shoulder, and Evan picks the dripping ball out of an oily puddle. He lifts a bin lid, but they've already checked it for goodies. Evan hands Pizza Face the ball to restart the game.

'But I heard whit happened tae yeh,' says Evan. 'Fucking hell!'

Pizza Face shrugs as if he's not bothered. 'I stuck him wae the compass,' and there's gallusness in the timbre of his voice. 'But yeh should huv heard him squealing as if I'd shot him. Greeting, like a wain. His leg stuck tae the chair. Aw that noise and it wasnae my fault. Aw I did was ask tae borrow a pencil aff him. And he said, "NO", even though he'd two, jist sitting there, daeing nothing. And he wears specs, and he's looking at me as if I'm the doolally wan.

'"You should be black ashamed of yourself," that fat cow, Mrs Thompson said. "You're nothing but a thug."

'And she grabs me by the neck, hauling me oot in front of the class. And everything in an uproar. Chairs pushed back, necks bottling, wanting tae see whit happens next.

'Yeh know Rosie Doyle is in the seat behind us. She stands up, as if yeh get a gold star for swanning about. Practically leaning o'er my shoulder. And she's alright. She knows I like her, so I smile. And she squeals when she sees the compass stuck into Martin Monaghan's leg and falls back doon on her chair.

'"Oh my god, I think he's killed him!" Rosie Doyle screams and goes into a mock faint.

'Mrs Thompson stuck me outside the door, where there's nothing tae dae. Then sent me tae the headie.

'I hands McMurtie the note fae her. And I can see him eating it up. Next thing he's got me by the ear. Baldy cunt!

'"I think there's something seriously wrong with you," McMurtie said. "And we need to send you to a school for mental defectives. It most definitely runs in your family."

'And he lets up wae the ear twisting. He dives into his desk and pulls out his belt. He grips it as if he means business. "I'm going to make an example of you. The only cure I know is to whip it out of you." He's fuming. "Hands up," he said. "I'm not going to let you leave here until you apologise for everything."

'"Ninety-nine is ninety-nine," I said. "Fuck off."

'"Yer long-division. Fuck off. Fuck off."

'"Primary 5b, Fuck off. Fuck off."

'And I've got my hands o'er my ears. "Listen, I'm not listening. Fuck off. Fuck off. Fuck off."

'And he's trying tae pull my hands doon. And get me tae haud them up so he can gi'e me the belt. But he can't.

'As soon as he lets go, I stick my hands back o'er my ears.

'And that drives him mair nuts. He gi'es up. And starts whipping me wae the belt round the legs and bum.

'And I'm shouting at him, "Fuck off. Fuck off, Baldy. Yeh cannae hurt me. Primary 5b. Primary 5b, Baldy. Fucking cunt. 5b. Prick. Clydebank Bundy ya Bass. Ninety-nine is ninety-nine".

'Then he starts smacking me on the back of the head and telling me tae shut up. I'm an embarrassment. And how he'll need tae get my da tae the school.

'But my da would knock him oot wae wan punch.

'Then he yips some shite about getting my mum up tae the school.

'But he's that daft. He cannae, cause she's no well. She's in hospital. Ward Nine. Ward Nine. She made a mistake and tried tae take some tablets she shouldnae huv. Baldy cunt. And he's trying tae make me greet. But he'll never dae it. Never. He cannae hurt us.

'"Yeh're jist a Baldy fucker," I tell him.'

He flicks up the ball, playing keepie-up. He's good at it but showing off takes a mid-air swipe.

Evan tells him, 'Yer nothing but a stupid cunt.'

'Aye, so ur yeh.'

Evan nudges the ball with the edge of his boot and passes it against the wall with his instep.

'Yeh know whit, he's nothing but a fucking dobber.'

'Who?'

'That baldy old cunt, McMurtie.'

'Aye,' Evan's not going to start disagreeing with him.

Chapter 9

Statues

EVAN'S STARTING POINT IN THE LOBBY IS OFTEN CONFUSED with Angela's finishing point. Heels together, upright as a plinth, he stands rigid with his back against the front door. He tries to sneak up, unstatuelike, on Angela, who has her back to him.

Kerry-Ann has come into some money, with a big Provident-cheque loan. She splurged on an expensive new outfit for Angela, so she looks smart for her fifth birthday. A natty lime-green nylon blouse with a red bow at the neck. Although her barking cough is largely gone, she swipes her snotty nose on her sleeve. Her blue pleated skirt mostly covers her grimy knees and white socks her legs, but they worm around her ankles. Black shoes and silver buckles have lost their burnished shine but are a rare treat and make her seem more like a proper wee girl ready to go to school after the summer.

Halfway up the hall, a scuttled Silver Cross pram with its hood up from when Angela was a baby. It reduces foot slog to a thin lane. Dirty floorboards squeak and with every step Evan takes, Blodger growls.

Angela turns and shrieks, 'Caught yeh!'

He staggers as if gut shot and knocks against faded roses wallpaper. But he warns her to keep the noise down. Her mum is—he thinks—sleeping in the living room.

He freezes and starts again. When Blodger lets him pass, he taps her shoulder. Close enough to whiff shampoo and hear the panting of her shallow breath. Her eyes big as a panther's. 'Whit's the matter, pet?'

'Nothing.'

'That's it then.' He slaps his hands around her waist, picks her up and bounds across the lobby. Blodger barks at his, wagging its stumpy tail. She knows where he's going, but he warns her anyway. 'I'm sticking yeh in the smelly cupboard.'

The smelly cupboard, once used for coal, chock-a-block with unwashed washings. It charts Angela through the ages: her growth from shitty nappies to discarded duffles waiting to die.

She giggles when Evan puts her down, and he's laughing too. Angela tugs at the door handle. Only Blodger takes a step forward. Evan pinches his nostrils with thumb and forefinger and talks funny with a nasal twang, 'Oh, no. Pongo!'

He kicks the door shut. They gulp in fresh air and blow out chubby cheeks in cartoonish masks of each other.

She shrieks and grabs the cuff of his shirt sleeve and pulls him sideways towards the door. 'I'll put yeh in the smelly cupboard.'

He plays along, sinking down on one knee, and raising his fingers in a steeple of mock prayer. 'Oh, no, pretty Angel, I beg yeh, don't put me in the smelly, smelly cupboard. I'll be a good boy. I promise.'

Angela beckons so she can whisper in his ear. He grins and angles the side of his face closer to her solemn wee mouth.

'Chaz hurts me,' she whispers.

'How?'

Angela pulls her blouse out of her skirt and hooks her thumb under her stained pants. 'He put his fingers inside me.' She shakes her head, her hair hiding her red face. 'Aw the way tae my stomach and made me bleed. He said I was tae put his thing in my mouth and it would taste like ice cream.'

The living-room door handle rattles. Angela's mum marches into the hall, negotiating the chicane of the pram with practiced ease. Kerry-Ann loops the cloth belt in her nightgown and ties it together. She steps over Blodger.

'Move!' She grabs the hem of Angela's blouse and drags her backwards. 'Can't get a minute's peace tae myself.'

Her speed and strength wrong-foots Evan. She hoiks him one-handed by the hood of his jacket and hauls him into her orbit. With the other hand, she pulls open the cupboard door and shoves him inside, slamming it shut.

He flings out his hands, which feel sticky. Reekit clothes fizz in his face, choke his throat. He recoils, bounces against the blackness and starts screaming for his mum. Kerry-Ann guards him with her back pressed against the door until he's blubbering.

When a slanting light shows, he crawls out, sobbing. He slaps his hand against his mouth to stop himself boaking. But he's sick on the bare floorboards at her brown slippered feet.

Blodger barks when she slaps him with a hard, stinging smack across his cheek, knocking his head against the wall. 'Yeh'll clean that up, ya clatty wee cunt.'

Blodger nips in, lapping and supping the sick from the floor.

'Ugh, that's disgusting.' She turns away, and her robe flashes open. Her tits and baby-pink nipples are visible, aureoles dark as spent pennies. She has a vivid scratch on her stomach. Smudged eyeshadow meets his gaze. She ties the belt on her nightgown.

'Jist like aw the rest.' Weariness in her tone. 'Beat it.'

On hands and knees, he scrambles across the lobby and stands only when he pulls open the door.

'Yeh'll soon learn,' she chides him, her words turning into a smoker's cough.

'He's my friend, no yers,' he hears Angela bawling, before slamming the door shut behind him.

Chapter 10

Eldorado

CHAZ, PODGE AND RAB ARE NECKING BOTTLES OF ELDORADO, and messing about on the canal. They hollow a shallow boat out of Styrofoam and wedge the packaging into the reeds at the side of the embankment. They test their manhood by standing on it. Laughing, they take turns wobbling and almost falling into the canal.

Rab goes one better. He balances on the boat, sits and pushes away from the marshy ground and out on to the open water of duck land. His hands act as oars, and he splashes to the other side of the canal.

On the bridge across Dumbarton Road, Angela gawks at them through the railings, Blodger nuzzling her side to be petted.

'Ya daft cunt,' shouts Chaz.

He holds up the green bottle. 'Yeh forgot something?'

That brings another round of jeering. Chaz takes a slug, wipes his mouth and passes the Eldorado to Podge.

Beastie

'Hi, keep some for me,' hollers Rab. His boat dips low in the water as he turns his craft, hand paddling, churning water to get back across the canal. He makes it to the reedbeds when the polystyrene raft turns turtle and his foot gets caught and he goes under.

Podge and Chaz watch him kicking and flapping, unable to get air. And Podge panics, 'Yeh think we should jump in and save him?'

Chaz swigs a quick uppie and downie of wine. 'Fuck off. I've got my good jacket on. Let the cunt drown.'

Rab raises his head above the scummy water and gulps air. He grabs a handful of reeds, and using them for leverage, claws his way onto the bank. Styrofoam remains entangled like a giant plaster-cast boot encasing his heel and leg. He kicks the raft off. Water runs off his hair, his face, his coat and his denims. He looks up at Chaz and Podge. 'Fucking great. Noo, I'll need tae go up the road and get changed.'

Chaz hands Rab the bottle as he sloshes onto the path. 'Here, take a drink of that tae warm yeh up, ya nugget.'

'Hi, Hi, don't finish it,' shouts Podge, but it's too late.

'I needed that.' Rab smacks his lips and flings the empty bottle into the canal with a splash.

Podge says, 'I thought we were goin up the toon anyway.'

'We ur,' Chaz laughs. 'When I'm good and fucking ready. We've got a bit of business tae dae first.'

Chapter 11

Heave-ho

A HALF-COLLIE BITCH WANDERS TOWARDS THE SEWERAGE works.

'Blodger come back,' cries Angela. 'Heel, Blodger, heel.'

She chases after her dog, dodging Chaz and his mates. They're going the other way, but her attention wanders.

Angela uses a stick to bring the Styrofoam closer to the embankment. She edges a heel onto the polystyrene. It bobbles but holds steady. She eases more weight onto her standing foot. Risks both feet and balances between canal and shore.

She clutches the sides and turns to check if Chaz can see her from the road and hears Blodger's distant barking. The canal water and the stench from the sewerage works turn her stomach. A pair of dragonflies dart through the toxic halo lower in the water.

She twists sideways and pushes off the embankment, but the craft tilts deep to one side and she almost falls out. Scared to move, she grasps the sides. Through her tears, she sees Blodger lolloping back towards her. But she feels someone else is watching her. She slowly turns her head and twists her body, sure it's Chaz come back to hurt her, and that's enough to put her under the Styrofoam. Her hair spreading out, Rapunzelian gold, becoming part of the water, becoming part of the air.

Chapter 12

Christenings

EVAN WEARS HIS NORMAL CLOTHES. PIZZA FACE SPORTS A home-made Rangers strip with a white number 11 chalked on his back. Life-and-death challenge. Older boys from Dalmuir West, who think they are something. A massive side-off on the gravel park at the back of the derelict Regal Cinema. The nylon studs of George Best football boots add an inch to Pizza Face's height. He clacks along the pavement and gives wings to his bigger dreams. With the instep of his left foot, he knocks his ball against the bridge stanchions.

Blodger's barking mad antics draws their attention towards a piece of polystyrene drifting in the gunk near the bank. Immersed beside it are towheaded tendrils and a familiar face.

Evan bumps against Pizza Face's shoulder and registers his baffled expression when he sprints away from him. The ball rolls from underneath Pizza Face's magical left foot.

Blodger belly flops into the water just before they get there. It doggy paddles circles around Angela's head. Her underwater face is whiter than her hair and her mouth gapes fishlike.

Pizza Face howls to God. Somehow they're holding hands and leaning on each other at the edge of the embankment.

'We need tae get help,' cries Evan.

'Nae time.' Pizza Face glares at the thing underwater. 'And I cannae really swim...Fuckit.'

He leaps over the reeds and splashes into the water. A brutal sight, he clings onto Blodger, who being dragged underwater bites him on the cheek. Head tilted, mouth hovering air above the marine life, he grabs Angela's anorak hood. He goes under and up and works his way into a standing position but doesn't let go. He pulls and tows her behind him.

Blodger bounds onto the grass and shakes his head and body, splashing Evan.

Pizza Face drags Angela to shore.

'Yer bleeding,' says Evan.

'Um I?' He doesn't seem bothered. 'Yeh'll need tae help.'

Evan jumps into the mire beside them. Foul-smelling muck fills his sannies and a glaze of ooze at his knees makes him shiver.

The dog cocks its head, watching Evan. He hugs Angela's droopy body to his chest. She is heavier than he has prepared himself for, heavier than he's used to. He slips, almost dropping her.

Pizza Face sticks a helping hand on Evan's back and shoves him forward until he regains his feet.

Pizza Face tucks his hands under Angela's legs and Evan under her arms. They lift and roll the parcel of her sodden body over the lip of the grass.

Evan pulls himself out. Pizza Face hugs himself, he chitters with the cold. He takes two tries to get onto the embankment.

Evan grabs Angela's jacket. He rolls her onto her back and kneels before her wee body.

Blodger scoots in and licks Angela's nose and mouth with a rough tongue and lapping sounds.

'She's deid,' says Evan. Her inanimate face and eye sockets sink-holes lost in a blank glacial stare.

'Aye.'

Blodger stops licking her face and slumps beside her body.

Evan's voice flutes upward. 'We could try gi'eing her the kiss of life?' He'd seen it on *Nationwide*. They'd used hard plastic dolls. But he'd got red faced when they started kissing them and groping their chests.

Pizza Face squelches away from them through the downpour. 'We'll jist need tae leave her.'

'No, we cannae,' Evan cries. Lifting her lolling head, her lips are stiff and unresponsive. But he kisses her so hard his teeth buckle. The bitter-green scum of the canal leaves an aftertaste.

Pizza Face comes sloshing back towards them and stands at his back. 'That's no the way yeh dae it. Yeh need tae spit intae her mouth and breathe in her, like a vampire in reverse.'

Evan won't give up. He slaps his hands against her cheeks, jerks her jaw open and grogs inside her mouth. He clamps his lips over hers and blows as hard as he can. Stopping and starting again, as if he's filling his bedroom with bright red balloons. His vision goes hazy. He splutters and sobs. Begins anew, spitting into her mouth and trying again. Each time, he runs out of breath quicker.

Blodger growls, and Pizza Face pats his shoulder. Evan turns to look at him. His cheek is bleeding where the dog bit him and his eye swollen. The port-wine stain blooms a plumper purple and his face resembles a comic-mask villain.

'Here, gi'e me a shot.'

Evan changes places with Pizza Face. And he does a strange thing. He gawps at Angela's face and then kisses her lightly on the forehead. He eases her mouth open and spits a good one, then holds her mouth shut as if allowing time for his potion to work. His lips flattened on hers, breathing through his nose, rocking back and forward and lying on top of her body, like a doomed helicopter with flailing elbows.

Evan tells God he'll be good. Her chest, or stomach, twitches. She's greeting. All the spit he must have put in her stomach comes up. She boaks up again and again.

Evan and Pizza Face no longer feel the cold, drenching rain. They dance and Blodger barks and licks her face.

She says in a wee grown-up voice, 'Whit were yeh kissing me for?'

Evan scoops her into his arms and smacks his lips against her cold cheek. She seems lighter now she's no longer filled with canal water. Allowing him to hug and carry her with her arms around his neck. 'I had tae kiss yeh because yer a princess and yeh were sleeping.'

'Oh, that's aw right then.'

Pizza Face's eye socket has stopped bleeding, and the wound looks clean. Shivering, he ambles along beside them with his head down. He searches for his ball he left in the gutter. 'Thieving bastards.'

Blodger trails behind Angela, her face wedged into Evan's neck. His steps shorten and as they trudge past the church he stumbles, almost falling, and dropping her. 'I'll need tae put yeh doon, pet. I'm knackered.'

Blodger splurges his body in the middle of the pavement, pedestrians shuffle around him.

Her grip loosens, and her bum slides onto his chest, but she grabs him in a choke hold around the neck. She whispers in his ear, 'I need tae tell yeh a secret, first.'

Pizza Face slumps against the wall and sits puddled on the pavement, but he's smiling.

'Yeh know when I was under the water, sleeping?' says Angela. 'And aw the church bells were ringing and everybody cheering?'

Evan nods, humouring her. 'Aye.'

'Well,' says Angela, 'Yer mum came tae see me and she was awful smiley and happy. And she kissed me too, but I didn't wake up, because she wasn't a prince, but it was funny, because I could see her and hear whit she was saying.'

Evan loses his grip on her. 'Whit did she say?'

'She said she loves yeh forever, but yeh've got tae watch out or—or —or—'

He grips her wrist, shaking her arm. 'Or whit?'

Blodger gets to its feet and growls, before drooping with its head down.

'Nothing else. That was it. But something else.' Angela frowns and cries as she tries to remember. 'Nah, that was it—'

Pizza Face groans, gets to his feet and shuffles towards them. 'C'mon Toots, I'll carry yeh?'

Angela shakes her head in an adult and deliberate way. 'Nah, I'm no a baby. I'll walk.' Blodger nudges her hand with its nose and she pats it on the head and caresses under its throat. She puts her cold hand in Evan's.

'Is that whit she said?' Evan tests the idea, speaking aloud what Angela had told them.

They walk a couple of hundred yards, then they are home.

Evan says, 'That's brilliant. I'm sure she said I'll end up like Superman being able tae fly through the air. Or seeing people nudie through their clothes wae X-ray vision. Or Spiderman.' He pretends to spray webs from his wrists onto the dingy windows of the buildings above them.

Pizza Face sniggers, 'Mair likely turn yeh into fucking Scooby Doo or Thelma or a flying turd.'

'Nah,' says Angela. 'It was something bad. Really bad.'

Chapter 13

Hates

Chaz hates hats. He doesn't wear one, even when it's raining, because he thinks it makes you bald. None of them do. 'Look at John F Kennedy,' he tells Podge and Rab, 'he wasn't bald, and if he had a bullet-proof heid, he'd still be alive.'

With too much mucking about for his liking, they get nearer the job. It's close to Albert Road, one of the big corner houses off Second Avenue.

He reluctantly pulls a pair of women's tights over his head, gawks through tan, denier-number thirty, and straying strands of lilac.

Rab got close enough to touch the flaking green paint of the back door. He said it was open-sesame season.

They wore their work and leisure gear, imitation black crombies. The broken streetlight made them as difficult as gorillas to pick out from the bushes.

The Council put geriatrics on the ground level for easy pickings. It was a version of their childhood game of knock, knock—trying the door handle—and not running away. The boys didn't want to get caught in the second-storey houses. An architectural design fault meant it was too much like grunt work with steep stairs and tight railings. Three bodies made it a squeeze and they made too much of a racket when they were half-pissed.

The living rooms, farthest from the front door, had the best pickings. Bedrooms to the right of the hall were most likely to spring a surprise. A hard landing if anybody woke and challenged them.

Podge had to put one on some old dear the week before. The flat smelled rank of cat's pee, without the cat. She didn't even have a telly, just some old radiogram with Bakelite knobs perched on spindly legs near the window. All they'd got for their troubles was a half- packet of Dunhill and an imitation gold lighter, which didn't even work—it was criminal.

The fancy catalogue of a two-storey house they'd targeted promised richer pickings. Rickety sashes that begged a poor man to pull the window up and step inside for a rummage. An overgrown garden with a wain's swing at the back and Ford Capri out the front. Child's play, hide-and-seek, bicycles with dinging bells, healthy long walks, and cold red apples to suck on.

Chaz guesses a faint light on in one of the top windows near the slanting roof is a spare visitor's bedroom. And they're the callers.

Podge, with a dancer's nimble toes, darts towards the back door and into the kitchen. Rab shadows him.

Chaz hangs back. He lets his eyes adjust to unlit virgin territory. A dripping tap plays a familiar tune. Jumpy, he turns to check nobody is about. He listens for the scream of police sirens, a dog barking, or the knock of somebody's foot as they get up from the bedroom and come wandering downstairs. It's his turn to play lookout, his back against the door, holding it open for his mates to run through.

Chaz pulls open the nearest cutlery drawer and picks out from underneath the trays a black, bone-handled knife. The blade is about nine inches and he flicks a finger over it to test the sharpness. He leaves it on top of the unit. The drawer further along has a false front. A wire hangs with an orange-coloured curtain hiding cleaning stuff under the sink.

Podge stumbles into the kitchen, a colour telly wedged to his chest, plug trailing and bumping behind him. The sour smell of spent booze has worn off, but his sister's tights sit like a jobby on top of his head. He cackles, 'There's fucking hunners of good stuff in there.'

He puts the telly on the overgrown path for collection later and, grinning, comes back into the kitchen.

Chaz and Podge freeze as they hear a knocking sound. Rab comes slinking out of the hall and into the kitchen. A navy-blue Adidas bag clinks in one hand and a pair of sannies in the other. 'Fucking brilliant,' he says.

Rab clocks Podge isn't wearing his mask and peels the nylon skin his from his face. 'Adidas,' he giggles, nipping outside. 'Jist my size tae.'

Chaz takes off his mask, stuffs it into his coat pocket, and rifles his fingers through his hair until it feels just right. Podge and Rab have already darted in and out with even more goodies, including a record player, set of speakers, and a guitar. 'Keep the fucking noise doon,' mutters Chaz, but there was no holding the lads back when they got to work.

Chaz becomes distracted by a set of fishing rods standing waiting for him in a cupboard next to the fridge. The last time he'd been fishing was with his brother, Junior. They'd been wheeling a bamboo pole with a round metal hangar and a green nylon sleeve for catching tiddlers in the Dalmuir burn.

The weight of a cork-handle feels good in his hand. He swishes the rod about for a practice run below the high ceiling. Leans it against the table and dives back into the cupboard. Wellington boots sit ready for service and the green camouflage of Barbour jacket, smelling fishy. Another two smaller rods lean against the wall, a landing net beside them.

A gleam of cobalt-blue metal. He can't quite believe it until he's pulled it out and has it in his hands. He ages it by the heft, the elaborate scroll of decoration on the barrel and the polished oily feel of rosewood, as if many hands have worn it clean. 'Fucking hell,' he mutters.

The barrel opens with a smooth clicking action. He places the twenty-bore on the work surface. He opens and bangs shut cabinet drawers that climb the wall, ignoring leather gloves, fishing hooks, reels and a variety of rainbow coloured flights with feathers attached. At the back of the cupboard, he finds boxes and boxes of shells. He hauls the drawer out, putting it on the floor.

He breaks open white cardboard sheathes, breathes in cordite packed into shells with brass-coloured heads, like a ten pack of Benson and Hedges. He can't resist plucking two out, hearing the satisfying click as he pins the stock to his knee to break the barrel, and loads the gun.

A light throws its beam from the hall and he hears the clatter of someone on the stairs. 'I've phoned the police,' a male voice warbles.

Rab and Podge appear like ferrets from a hole and bundle into the kitchen. They barge into each other near the backdoor.

Podge drops a bottle of white wine on the stone floor and it smashes at his feet, as he looks into a barrel of a gun. He hisses at Chaz, 'Hurry up, bring that wae yeh. He's phoned the police.'

'No, he hasnae, ya stupid cunt.' Chaz lets the arc of the barrel fall. 'There's the phone there.' He points to a phone underneath the cabinet and a black knife beside it. 'And I've cut the line.'

There's no time to argue. The quicksilver movements of a pale boy, determined to be a man, springs through the door.

Chaz fires.

Chapter 14

Bark and bite

'Ya fucking stupid cow,' Chaz lies groggy in his cosy bed, but sits up and growls at his sister, Peggy, who has stepped on him. She is big and slow, dressed in tent-like material and follows her mum about.

Senga knocks crumbs off the linoleum against the wall and brandishes a sweeping brush, the veins in her neck bulging blue. Fierce grey eyes squint at his face. Ginger hair hovers above him. 'Get up, ya lazy bastard! It's almost gone eleven! Why don't yeh go oot and get a job like aw the rest of them?'

Four makeshift bed sheets beside him haven't yet been tidied away. Stray spittle spots his face. Chaz grips the underside of the blankets as she tries to haul them off the bed. She whacks the side of his cheek. 'Get up and let me get on wae the cleaning, won't yeh?'

'Ach, shut up, will yeh.' Chaz leaps out of bed with only his Y-fronts on and grabs at the brush handle. 'Everything's dirty wae yeh. Yeh undress in a cupboard wae the door shut in case yer shadow sees yeh bollocks and as for her.' He stares at Peggy and chuckles like a crow.

Senga holds on with a clenched-fist determination. 'If I had my way, I'd wash yer dirty mouth oot wae carbolic soap.'

'C'mon Ma,' he jockeys. 'Always shouting. Always moaning. Ne'er happy. Yeh'll hurt yerself and end up back in the loony bin.'

Chaz lets go of the brush, his mother stumbles backwards and into his sister behind her. He steps over a clay pot, overflowing with blackened douts, where his brother's share an ashtray. 'I need a pish, anyway. Put me on some scran.'

His shirt, socks and trousers lie heaped on a chair ingrained with smoke. He lifts them and pulls on a damp reminder of the blaze from the night before. His bare feet grow cold. Edging the curtains open, he glances at the traffic and at the bite of frost on the roofs.

Senga scurries around a lop-sided chair into the strip of linoleum in the kitchen. Chaz hears her petulant banging and the wheeze of gas as she sticks the kettle on. He ponders going into the kitchen for a quick cold-water wash and shave. Bread, margarine and stewed tea for breakfast hold little attraction.

'I'm no wanting tea,' he shouts, running his fingers through his hair and nipping behind her back into the lobby.

He checks his coat for fags and finds none. His luck picks up as he rakes through the lining of his pockets. A cigarette stub inside a box of Swan Vesta. Hustling into his coat, he's got it in his gob and has lit up even before he's outside the front door. The realisation that he'd be in the news, perhaps on the front page, cheers him up. He laughs out loud, like a loony, but stands on the bottom landing, checking to see if anybody heard him.

He lopes forward without thinking about direction, or traffic, and is outside Maggie Scott's bar. As he pushes the swing doors, he hopes the boys will be there to meet him, because with ten pence in coppers jiggling in his pocket, he has only enough for a half-pint.

There is nobody much in. A half-scooped punter pesters Drew, the heavy-set barman. 'Jist wan mair pint,' the regular says in a wheedling tone, and calls him, 'my good friend,' hands knitted in prayer.

Podge scrambles out of the corner seat. He orders a round for himself and Chaz. Rab is nowhere to be seen.

Chaz nips into the toilet. When he comes out, he squints at a dart player at the end of the bar. A glass of whisky in one hand, his arrows in the other.

The pub smells musty as if it has sunk into the canal. The walls show uneven patches of mud brown. Dust rises as he falls into a musty seat at the end of the table beside Podge. Nicotine-stained windows above them, the dull hum of traffic percolates through and they sit snug with knees almost touching.

Podge, bleary-eyed, stares blankly across at him. Before Chaz finishes his pint, Podge swallows a half-and-half chaser and stumbles to the bar for more. He comes back with another round gabbing about some Rangers player and who the club must sign.

Chaz picks up Podge's fags from the table and sticks a Senior Service in his gob and lights it.

Podge sniffs and tugs at his earlobe and takes a deep breath. A choking noise coming from the back of his throat. 'About last night—'

'Aye?' Chaz sups a mouthful of lager and blows cigarette smoke in Podge's direction.

'The thing is, I want oot. I mean, I didnae really dae anything.' His head drops to his chest. His sobs shake his torso.

Chaz grabs Podge by the coat lapels, wrestling him halfway across the table. A half-pint of lager tumbles and creates a puddle beside the seat.

'Hi,' Drew shouts, lifting the hatch. 'Whit's yer game!'

Chaz holds his hands up in mock surrender, picks up the glass and puts it upright on the table. 'It's alright Drew, he's jist drunk. I'll get him safely up the road.'

Drew lets the hatch fall and retreats behind the bar, watching the dart player pitching his darts into cork with a hollow thump.

Chaz's chair scrapes against broken tiles as he pulls it in closer to the table and his head drops to the same level as his companion.

'Nah, nah,' Podge mumbles, shaking his head. 'I want oot. I want oot, scoot.'

'Listen ya stupid cunt, yeh were there, and yeh were jist as involved as the rest of us.'

'Nah, nah, nah,' Podge's mantra changes: 'I need another fucking drink.' Blinking rapidly, he avoids meeting Chaz's gaze. He pushes up from the chair without waiting for an answer. 'Yeh want another drink?'

Chaz tugs his elbow, pulls him backwards. The seat creaks as he slumps into it.

Podge sounds sober and defiant. 'I don't fucking care. I'm turning myself in. I didnae really dae anything.'

Chaz takes a swig of lager and flings his arm around his neck pulling him closer. 'Podge, Podge, Podge.'

Drew rings the bell and shouts, 'That's yer last orders. Last orders at the bar.'

'Let me tell yeh something Podge, yeh gi'e yerself up and the game's a bogey. Yeh don't want tae be a grass. And the police will roll me and Rab up like an old mat. But think about this, pal. I'll put my haunds up and say, "Aye, I did it. I might huv shot the boy, the wee bastard was getting lippy."'

Chaz leans in closer. Podge's forehead is damp and shiny. 'The boys in blue will be delighted wae that. "Result," they'll be saying tae themselves. "Cut and dried." And I'll be making it easy for the cunts tae. Singing like a linty.'

He slaps Podge on the back. 'But I'll be having a wee word wae Rab first. And we'll get our stories straight. We'll tell them we didnae use petrol and rags tae set the hoose on fire because we ur professionals, and yeh showed us how tae fake it. It was yeh that raped and suffocated they two wee lassies. Yeh that made that wee boy dae things we don't want tae mention. Yeh that did aw of these things. And yeh know whit, the police don't gi'e a fuck who they get as long as they've got a body, anybody. And it will be yeh that get caught het. And yeh know whit they dae tae nonces in prison, pal?'

He squeezes his knee under the table. 'Think about that pal.' Chaz stands and pulls an open razor out of his inside breast pocket. He slashes Podge in a wavy line from his left ear, across his cheek and the blade bumping at his chin. He steps out of the way to stop blood splashing on the cuff of his coat.

Chaz points at him as he's holding his cheek together. 'Be warned!'

On his long swagger across empty tables and chairs, made shorter by the shot of adrenalin, he looks across at Drew behind the bar. 'Yeh didnae see anything, mate,' he advises him and pauses near the door.

He reaches for the bloodied razor. The dart player is giving him the eye, but the guy plays along, because he saves himself with a funny, 'I'm blind. I cannae even hit double twenty wae my nose.'

Chaz tucks the blade into the nylon lining of his coat pocket and keeps walking along Dumbarton Road. He knows he'll need to catch Rab before opening times that night.

Chapter 15

King Billy on his charger

THE CLAMOUR OF MEN'S CHATTER DISSIPATES FROM MAC'S
pub with early closing, but the miasma of booze seeps into the
dark close, and the metal hatch of the pub covers a subterranean
world beneath Chaz's feet.

An ambulance, with sirens and flashing lights, weaves through the
traffic. He doesn't look round, but his fingers feel for the ivory
handle of his razor in the same way other men would stroke the
fur of a rabbit's paw.

Sammy answers the door with the stub of a roll-up in his mouth.
He looks like a cannier version of his son, Rab. Faded dress
trousers with a boozer belly and a stained yellow vest, reeking of
sweat and fags. His pitted bald head blocks the light from the
lobby. He peers short-sightedly at Chaz. 'Yeh'll be lucky, he's still
in his scratcher, but yeh can try yer luck.' Big hands that once
worked in the yards wave him inside.

His wife jumps from her chair beside the fire when he comes in.
'Yeh'll be wanting tea, son.' Her housecoat a popular catalogue
choice for redeemed Embassy coupons, dainty flowers withered

with wear over a polyester brown dress. She doesn't bother waiting for an answer, sliding away from the men's talk.

Chaz spots Rab's feet outside the blankets. A made-up bed, in an inshot beside the window, his transistor radio turned low. As he gets up, he makes a show of yawning and stretching. He bends his head and body into the curtains to pull his shirt and trousers on with his back to them, but with his bum wiggling like a burlesque show.

'Take a seat son.' Sammy waves Chaz into the armchair vacated by his wife and slumps into the seat opposite, staring into the fire and flicking his fag into the lum.

They sit under a luminous portrait of King Billy, his ectoplasm hovers above matching wally dogs on the mantelpiece. He's prancing on his charger, ready to right all wrongs, with gold-trim tricorn hat and a better perm than Rab's mum.

Sammy spits into the embers. 'Whit yeh up tae noo, son, anyway?'

Chaz unbuttons his coat and stretches out his legs. 'Nothing much.'

Sammy shouts to his wife, 'Can yeh no hurry up wae that boy's tea,' and apologises, 'Sorry I cannae offer yeh something stronger.'

'Och, nae problem.'

Rab sneaks in between them, warming his hands at the fire and nods at Chaz.

Rab's mum ducks her head in. 'Whit dae yeh take in yer tea, son?'

'Four sugars.' Chaz speaks to Rab, knowing his dad is within earshot. 'I'd a bit of trouble there with Podge, had tae sort out.'

Rab laughs through his nose, 'Aye, whit's the daft bastard done noo?'

'It's no funny. Caught him red-handed tampering wae my sister, Peggy.'

'Yon wee spastic lassie,' Sammy blurts out. 'I mean, whit's the world coming tae? I'd soon put a stop tae that.'

Rab's mum disrupted their pondering by stumbling through with a brown glazed teapot and a tea tray.

Sammy leans on his elbow and stares at his wife as she serves Chaz his tea first. 'Did yeh hear that woman? That bastard has been kiddy-fiddling.' His anger belts up a notch and his cheeks go red as Santa's.

Chaz sips at dishwater tea as Rab's mum serves Sammy's brew from the pot.

Rab dances away from the fire to give her room. 'Any bread, Ma? For a wee bit of toast.'

'Nah son, we're aw oot. I'd need tae go doon tae the Kippen Dairy.'

'Well, get us a packet of fags when yer doon there.' Rab takes his cup out of his ma's hands to help her along.

Chaz blinks and smiles boyishly at her. 'Yeh want me tae go doon tae the shop for yeh, Mrs Burrows?'

'Och, no son, I couldnae ask yeh tae dae that.' Mrs Burrows retrieves her battered purse from her piny pocket but looks and sounds pleased. 'Go tae aw that bother.'

'It's only fair,' Chaz takes another swig of tea. 'After aw the hassle last night, when the pubs closed, and me and Rab had tae come up the stairs and tap yeh for a fag—member?'

Her hands and fingers knit together. 'Oh, aye! That's right,' she looks at him askance. 'That's no any bother, son.' And instinctively searches through her pockets for her ten packet of cigarettes.

'Hurry up, Ma,' says Rab. 'I'm starving.'

Sammy's knuckles whiten around his chipped mug. 'I know whit I'd dae wae him.'

Chaz sniffs. 'Whit can yeh expect fae a Catholic?'

Sammy spits into the fire and bangs his mug on the fireside tiles. His ire directed at his son. 'Whit dae yeh mean bringing a Taig into this fucking house? Sitting on my fucking furniture. Sitting on that very chair there.'

His pointed finger hovers over Chaz, but he shouts at his wife, who is standing in the lobby with her coat on. 'Get a cloth and some of that spray stuff and get in here noo and clean that chair.'

Mrs Burrows scuttles from the hall into the kitchen. Sammy slaps Rab a crack on the back of the head. 'I thought yeh'd huv mair sense than that, bringing those white fucking Pakis here. Taking oor jobs. Monkeys that'll sleep wae any cunt, they ur. Look whit he did tae that poor wee spastic lassie.'

He motions towards Chaz, 'Yeh'll need tae move son, while she cleans the chair. And yeh'll need tae get that coat off yer back and gee it a good clean wash.'

Rab rubs the back of his head, and answers in a wee boy's voice. 'I didnae know he was Catholic, he's always going on about Rangers. That's aw he ever goes on about.'

Rab and Chaz lean into the heat of the fire, their heads bowed in conclave in front of King Billy. Chaz laughs and flings in his tuppence worth. 'Aye, that's true, but his ma is a Catholic—never away from that chapel.'

'Jesus,' Sammy growls. 'If yeh lie wae dogs, yeh get fleas.' He inspects his wife's work. 'That'll dae,' he waves her away. 'Goin and get that chair o'er there,' he instructs her with a nod. 'And there's a seat in the kitchen. Bring that through.'

Chaz holds his hands up, 'Oh, no, I'm jist goin Mrs. But that's no even the half of it. Wee Benny was saying that he heard Podge broke into an old woman's house and half killed her, tried tae rape her. And the bastard was boasting about it, as if he was the big man.'

There isn't enough space to hold Sammy's anger. He whacks the side of the seat and rolls his shoulders, ready to unpack a fight. 'I wasnae gonnae tae say anything. I'm sworn tae the greatest secrecy. But I huv it on very good authority that of the sixty-six glorious dead, men and boys, killed in the so called Ibrox disaster, at least ten had bullet wounds. Shot by the Fenians.'

He spits into the fire, and it hisses. 'Covered up, of course, by the high, fucking heid yins. But noo that the British army has tae roll o'er the border and take Dublin tae stop those mad fucking Paddies bombing everybody, and everything. We need tae dae our bit here. We'll be getting rifles. Shiploads of them. There'll be internment here and there. And yeh boys ur jist the kind of boys we need. And the first thing we'll dae is take care of that dirty wee Fenian toerag. First name on the list. So fucking help me God, we'll cut his balls off and string him up. The only thing worse than a Fenian is a white Paki. In fact, if yeh gave me the choice, I know which wan I'd pick.'

'Nane of them,' Rab chuckles.

Chaz joins in their laughter.

Chapter 16

Hunting

Wind scours the back courts. Rab set a bin on fire to warm his hands, Chaz beside him. Smoke clings to their clothes and the taste of burning plastic lodges on the back of their throats.

Wandering back into the shelter of the close, coats buttoned high around the neck. The glow of a fag in their mouths. They chug a bottle of Eldorado to warm their insides.

Chaz kills time by boasting again about slashing Podge. 'I didnae dae it hard enough. I should huv cut the cunt's heid off.' He pulls the hatchet out of his coat pocket. 'And I would huv if I'd this baby. I'd huv finished the cunt.'

Chaz takes a drag and flicks the dout out into the rain. 'Yeh got the sack and the rope ready?'

Rab's cigarette drops from his lips and he grinds the stub out with black platform shoes. 'Aye, I'm fucking ready. I'm gonnae hit the cunt a dillion.' He reaches for the spade handle resting against the wall. 'My da's been getting ontae me. Yeh still interested in joining up?'

Chaz smirks. 'Nah, I'm no really interested in that shite.'

'But yeh said—'

'Aye, but jist stringing him alang, buttering him up. Yeh know the score. Noo if anybody asks yer ma will be able tae say that she'd seen us that night. Jist me and you. Not that Fenian bastard, Podge. If things go tits up, we've got an alibi, and we can finger him. Say we split up wae him earlier that night.'

'I never thought of that.'

'That's cause yeh never think.' Chaz taps his finger against the side of his forehead. 'Oor word against his and we've got witnesses. Every cunt hates him noo anyway, after whit they heard about him, kiddy-fiddling. It's jist a matter of time—'

A door opens. Wheezing coming from the stairs, the lavvy door opens and bangs shut, which tells Chaz it is his neighbour, old Mrs Lynch.

Rab's grip of the shovel slackens. He leans it against the wall and blows into his hands to warm them.

'I wish yeh'd join up.' Rab witters on as if he's not heard a word Chaz said. 'Da says it's aw gonnae blow up noo and we need tae be ready. Need tae strike first when the iron's hot. And that's why we're getting a consignment of rifles from o'er the water tae train wae.'

'Rifles?' Chaz shows a flickering interest.

The toilet flushes and they hear Mrs Lynch, huffing and puffing, her weight knocking against the banister, making the rails ring as she returns home.

Chaz pees against the wall. 'Fucking need tae go for a slash myself.'

A door lock clicks above them. He pulls up his zip and his coat tails swish as he positions himself at the bottom of the stairs. He digs into his pocket for the hatchet.

Rab stands at his elbow, the shovel in his hand raised like a bat.

Blodger skitters downstairs. Angela and Evan trail behind it, unbuttoned duffle coats over their clothes. They hold hands, sneaking out of his house to let the dog pee.

She hums, 'Hickory, Dickory, Dock, the cat ran up the clock—'

Blodger growls, teeth bared, hackles raised, as it leaps off the last few steps. The wallop against its head knocks the dog against the wall. The mongrel scrambles to its feet. A ringing thud bites deep into its nostrils. Bleeding, a blurry of thwacks. Its back legs hang limp. A hood waxes its head. Tied tightly, Chaz drags Blodger sideways, like a bloodied butcher's carcase.

Angela shrieks, 'That's my dog!'

Rab comes up the stairs to cut her off. He sniggers, gives her a playful dunt on the forehead as she tries to kick him.

Evan piles in, but Rab's coat smothers his punch. Knocked against the wall by a backhander, he loses his footing and tumbles down the last few stairs, his lip bleeding.

He focuses on Angela's screeching and her torn white dress. Chaz, giggling, with a hand over her throat, pins her to the ground like a struggling moth.

Rab does the grunt work of dragging Blodger to the landing above. Chaz eases off tormenting Angela and races up to help him. It takes both of them to tie the knots and fling the sack over.

The dog hangs with its neck broken and its bowels open.

Angela, shit splattered, shock and silence shake her.

'Dirty bastard,' Chaz snorts. 'That's minging.'

Chapter 17

Last round

DERMOT DROWNS A COUPLE OF GOLDIES, WHISKY FLOWS AND warms him. He basks in pub nostalgia for better days. Pushing through the doors, he's sorry the night has ended.

The wind loses its cutting edge inside the close and his eyes take time to readjust.

'Hi smartalec,' the boy with the glaikit and plukey face crows. 'Who dae yeh think yer looking at?'

Fly men are always mouthy. His shuffling feet come fast towards Dermot, carrying a shovel.

Dermot's swift jab knuckles his eye. The boy staggers back. Dermot follows through mashing his nose and hits him four times, whacks to the chin and cheeks, before he goes horizontal, trying to get a handle on pinstripe.

'Watch oot Da!' his son shouts.

Dermot drops his shoulder, and an axe blade flickers past his face. He punches Chaz in the gut. Winded, the boy steps back, and that's all the opening Dermot needs. A flurry of smashes to face and lips has him drowning, and he falls against the pockmarked wall. The hatchet drops, clanging. Dermot holds him level with his coat lapel, hitting with a ferocity he rarely uses, his feet, head, knee smacking against soft flesh, cartilage and bone. No Marquis of Queensberry rules. Chaz's head smashing against the wall, with every punch given counting as two.

The plukey-faced boy struggles to his feet and comes lurching towards Dermot, but seeing the state of his pal's face, he skulks away. Dermot lets Chaz fall and kicks him in the ribs.

'Da,' his son shouts. 'Don't, yeh'll kill him.'

Dermot nods in faint recognition. Evan comes flying across, clings to his legs, greeting. He pats his shoulder. 'C'mon son, we'll get yeh up the stairs and into yer bed. It'll aw be alright in the morning.'

Angela, hypnotised, stares at the dog. 'Maybe we could give Blodger the kiss of life, like yeh gave tae me?' Her face is snotty and strawberry-cheeked from crying.

'Nah hen, that's no the way it works.' Dermot steps over Chaz, gathers her in his arms. She weighs little more than a wrap of coal. He carries her up the stairs, his son ahead of them.

Angela lifts her head from Dermot's shoulder. 'Whit about Blodger?'

Dermot asks, 'Who's Blodger?'

'Blodger's her dog,' his son chimes in.

Dermot shoogles Angela, 'Oh, aye, don't yeh worry pet. I'll make sure he gets a good burial.' He searches his pockets for house keys and holds them out so his son can open the door. He remembers when the one with the spade got up and came towards him, it caught him out. Chaz had moved his head when he went to punch him again, and he'd punched the wall. The knuckles in his right hand feel busted.

Evan turns the handle. 'The door's already open, Da.'

Dermot slaps Kerry-Ann's letterbox with his good hand. He waits and listens for movement inside and slaps it again and again.

'Where's yer mum?' he asks Angela.

'Dunno,' she sucks on her thumb.

Dermot admits defeat. He follows his son inside the lobby and into the warmth of the living room. He plonks Angela down on his chair. Gripping the poker, cack-handed, he stirs the embers in the fireplace.

He rushes through to the kitchen, running his louping hand under the cold tap. Evan lurks at his stooped shoulder. He snaps at him, 'Make yerself useful. Put some coal on the fire.'

'But Da, whit ur we gonnae dae wae Angela?' Evan pegs his nose with his fingers. 'She's minging.'

'We'll clean her up and gi'e her a warm bed.' That becomes Dermot's plan, diving beneath the sink for a basin and looking for pots to heat water.

He arms himself with a damp flannel facecloth, a block of green Sunlight soap and sloshing hot water.

Dermot returns to the living room. Angela has her face pressed into the cushion. His son perches on the chair opposite him.

'Goin and get ready for bed,' Dermot mumbles. 'And bring another pair of yer jammies for the wee lassie.'

'They'll be far too big.'

'That doesnae matter.' His hand gives him gyp, but he ignores the pain, lifting Angela and peeling her clothes off. She slumps, half-drunk with sleep, helping him by moving her arms and legs like a marionette. Dermot can't manage the buttons and she whimpers but refuses to open her eyes when he tugs her dress over her head. He nips the elastic and peels off her dirty pants.

His son comes back cradling a set of pyjamas, gawping. Dermot winces as he sponge-bathes her. He knows it's not the secret of her vagina his son is looking at, but the starburst-purples, blues and yellows of bruising at the top of hers leg and stomach. The scratches on her chest.

She doesn't cry as he washes her, but pouts with a petted lip.

His son's chest heaves and he starts bawling. 'Who did that?' He points to the marks.

Dermot feels his eyes moistening. 'Dunno.' He's got his suspicions. 'We'll need tae let the cruelty man decide.' He dips the cloth into the water and rinses it out. Rubs it against her feet and in between her tiny toes.

Angela shivers, 'It's cauld.'

'Sorry.'

'Whit's the cruelty man?' asks his son.

'That's when a man comes tae see who's been bad and hitting children. And he comes tae help them.' He tries to make it sound pleasant. 'Sometimes taking them away. Getting them somewhere better tae stay, wae a new mum and da.'

'But yeh hit me.'

Dermot drops the cloth into dirty water. 'Aye, son, but it's no like that... yer right... I swear on yer mum's grave, I'll never hit yeh again—unless, unless I really huv tae.'

Dermot wraps Angela in a clean towel. He follows his son into his bedroom carrying her. Evan picks up his book of fairy stories and peels back the blankets. Dermot tucks her into the bed, facing the wall, and leaves them to settle. He flicks the light off on his way out.

Undressing isn't easy with one hand. His clothes lie higgledy-piggledy on the wooden chair. Bed is more a gloomy destination than sitting alone. Slumber and sleep churn dark hours in a portion of night pains.

Fog outside, drifting, cotton wool against the window, colours his dreams. It carries hammering harmonies over the shifting tides on the Clyde.

No lights show when he gets up. In the silences of the close, the creaking groan of his bare feet on floorboards as he tiptoes is like a haunting. He rummages in the back of the kitchen cupboard where Maggie kept the medicines: the calamine lotions and potions and strips of bandages that covered childhood sunburn, but never her dying.

His hand knocks against a striped, heavy brown bottle crusted at the top. He has trouble opening it, sniffs it and takes a slug. Cough mixture. About a third of a bottle. He swallows it in one go, figuring it might not help the pain, but it might help him sleep and if it doesn't, he'll not have a cough to contend with for a while.

A blanket wrapped around his shoulders, he sits by the grey embers of the fireplace. He stokes and builds the flames, adding coal with the eye of a stonemason building a dry-stone dyke. He warms his feet and nurses his hand, the night empty.

His eyelids flutter when he thinks he hears a scratching at the front door. He picks up the poker and pushes it deep into the coal, waiting until the tip is hot enough to sizzle in his hand before pulling it out. The letterbox raps and he swiftly makes his way to the door, hugging the wall.

With his injured hand he can't hold the poker and pull the door open, so leans it against the facing. The smell of burning linoleum harries him. He turns the key and pulls the door, reaching for the poker.

Kerry-Ann stands gawping at him, her eyes thick with more black eyeliner than Cleopatra at her weddings. Nightgown and slippers are her night attire. Her voice is low and husky. 'Is my wee lassie there?'

'Aye,' replies Dermot.

'Well, can I speak tae her?'

'No, yeh cannae. She's sleeping. After whit yeh done tae her, I wouldnae let yeh keep a budgie.'

'Angela,' she shouts, twisting her head and looking past him. 'It's yer mum. Ur yeh in there, hen?'

'Hi, I've already told yeh.' He leans forward, in into her face, breathing cheap perfume. 'I've seen the marks on her wee body. Ya, cruel, fucking cow, yeh.'

Her head drops and she looks at him through straggles of loose hair. 'Look, sometimes things get oot of haun. She can be helluva cheeky and I admit I sometimes dae go o'erboard. But I cannae get back tae sleep in that big bed, myself.'

'Well, yeh should huv thought of that before.'

'Nae need for yeh getting aw high-and-mighty on me. They're thin walls yeh know. Don't think I didnae hear yeh blowing up wae yer wife. And I heard every blow and her screaming and begging for yeh tae stop.'

Angela appears and stands beside Dermot, her bush of golden hair making her seem taller, almost up to his hip. She looks at her mum, sleepy-eyed.

'C'mon hen,' Kerry-Ann trills in a soft voice. 'I'll take yeh away fae the bad man.' And she holds her arms out.

Angela brushes past Dermot. Clutched tight against her mother's breasts, she looks angelic.

He moseys towards the landing below, keeping an eye out and listening. Satisfied that the dog is no longer hanging from the bars, he returns upstairs. There's little point going to bed. He sits on the chair waiting for morning.

Chapter 18

Fog

DERMOT WAKES WITH A START. HIS HAND FEELS AS IF HE'S pushed it into the coal fire. He has a wash, shaves awkwardly with his left hand and puts on clean dress trousers and a white shirt. He drenches in Old Spice to finish.

He calls into Maise's at the bottom of the stair. It's not really a shop, more a place where old women gather like cobwebs in the corner of a dingy room to natter. Maisie, wee and squat, lives behind the counter where she sells tobacco, newspaper, sweets and bottles of ginger for the kids.

'A pack of Senior Service and a box of Swan Vestas.' Dermot scratches in his pocket for fifty pence.

'That's 27d and 2 and 1/2 d for the matches.' Maisie has not quite mastered decimal currency. Although she doesn't wear glasses, she dispels rumours she is going blind, between ringing up the change and passing his cigarettes and matches by remarking on the way Dermot is dressed. 'Where you off to the day? Down the water to Rothesay?'

'No, the doctors.'

Dermot holds up his hand and she squints at it.

'That's terrible.' She waits for more—gossip is a big part of her business.

'Aye, I hurt my haun at work.'

'What doctor's that son?'

'Dr Fleming's practice, jist beside the plots.'

'Oh, aye, he's a great doctor. Very clean. Smokes a nice cigar. And the nap of his suits. Great quality.'

The shop bell dings and an old woman wearing a hat bustles in. 'Ena,' Maisie addresses her as an old friend. The medical panegyric ends. Dermot slopes out of the shop— yesterday's news.

Mist and fog outside claim him and make what he looks like as irrelevant as curtains on a brick wall. There's motion in the haze and he recognises the noise and looming car lights. Smudges of people pass him on the pavement and float in different directions. His feet know the way and filling his lungs with misty air is a salve to sore fingers.

Dermot becomes part of the drift. If he flung a stone, it wouldn't land, but simply disappear. Fog floats the church steeple then it stands still. When he gets back to his close, passers-by veer towards him and the flash of a green and gold Corporation bus spotlight the middle of the road.

Climbing the stairs, it seems strange to him that there's awkwardness in his legs because of his hand. A front door jerks open when he draws near the second-floor landing. Wee John, Chaz's da, eyeballs him from the doorway. A wedge of receding hair, and

Zapata moustache, he wears a vest, trousers and working boots. A belly, like a chip pan, sits on his buckled belt. He gesticulates toward Dermot, his arm tattooed with an anchor and RFC graffiti scrawl below it in Indian ink, and growls, 'My boy's in hospital cause of yeh. Concussion. His mum, Senga's up tae high doh about it.'

They glower at each other. His son appears covering wee John's back. Older brothers of Chaz congregate beside him, with similar hair and etch-a-sketch faces.

Dermot thinks of them as silly wee boys, but dangerous as snakes, unless defanged. John's eyes flicker, waiting for an answer.

'Away tae fuck, John,' Dermot says. 'Did yeh see the dog? And member he's got haunners. And he's tooled up. Hit my boy. And he beat up a wee lassie that's no even at the school yet. Whit the fuck yeh want me tae dae, kiss his forehead?'

His son in an open-necked blue shirt wanders away. His brother, in a denim jacket, swaggers up the hall behind him.

'Aye, I'm heart sorry about that.' John plays at sounding contrite. 'I'll huv a word wae him. It's that other boy, Rab. Every time he goes oot wae him he seems tae get into some kind of trouble. He's a good boy, really.'

Dermot nods. 'Ah, well, John, we've aw got our crosses tae bear.'

He lifts the pint of milk from the doorstep. The splash of milk left on the windowsill overnight in the bottle has soured. He drinks it rather than waste it, knowing his son wouldn't. A cup of tea for himself. He doles out a bowl of cornflakes for the boy.

Befuddled by Dermot leaning over him, Evan asks. 'Whit is it?' And his hand searches for Angela. 'Where is she?'

'Kerry-Ann came for her last night.'

'But yeh said yeh'd need tae get the cruelty man in. She'd get a new da and mum.'

'Aye, but sometimes it's no as simple as that. She said she was sorry and it wouldnae happen again.'

Evan's forehead kinks in disbelief. Dermot reasons with him. 'The wee lassie wanted tae go hame. Yeh cannae keep a child fae its mother.'

He slaps the side of the bed. 'Hurry up and get up. I've made yeh breakfast.'

'Yeh made me breakfast! How come yer no at work?'

Dermot holds up his arm. 'Sore haun, I need tae go tae the doctors.'

Evan gives it a cursory glance and lurches out of bed. He shivers and gets dressed in his school clothes and hauls on his wellies. The door left ajar as he nips downstairs to the toilet.

Dermot waits in the living room and sits in the chair opposite, watching him eat cornflakes weighed with sugar and fresh milk.

His son glances over at him, chewing and swallowing and talking with his mouth full. 'Whit happened tae Blodger?'

Dermot turns and glances out the window. 'The cruelty man came and took him away.'

Evan's face shows belief and disbelief.

'Hurry up, or yeh'll be late for school,' Dermot leaves loose change on the mantelpiece for school dinner. He adds an extra bob for sweets.

Evan abandons his plate and counts his money. 'Thanks Da.' He offers a cheeky grin. And he's running, clatters towards the front door.

Chapter 19

Kittens

Snow mixes with rain and gusts into their close, Angela trails behind Pizza Face and Evan. Duffle coat hoods keep their ears warm and the boys stamp their feet and face each other.

'Scram,' Pizza Face tells Angela. 'Yeh're too wee and yer a girl. Go and play wae other wee lassies.'

'I'm no too wee.' She chases after them, across the back court. 'I'm nearly five. And they won't play wae me. They call me smellybelly.'

The boys mock her with laughter. Ankle-strap shoes are no match for their wellies. They've entered a world in which bins and walls and rone-pipes become climbing frames to greater things.

Pizza Face is acrobatic and fearless. Even the bigger boys from Swindon Street watched him climb a drainpipe and shuffle along to the kitchen window of his house, three storeys up. He sat on the windowsill as if he was squatting on the lavvy pan.

Pizza Face kicks off a bin and leaps across to the washhouse wall.

Evan comes at the roof from the next washhouse, where the broken door frame acts as a makeshift ladder. He clutches the concrete parapet, dangles, clambers against the underside of the wall and uses his elbows to crawl along the flat surface. His knees are soaked and cold. The side of his duffle coat is sopping, but the heat of conquest warms him.

They leap washhouse roof to roof and conquer old worlds. Below them Angela follows their route, weaving through puddles, stampeding bins and stomps aside household junk, but they soar, leaving her orphaned.

Bricked doors, smashed chimney pots leave a rectangular-sized hole in each block, a boy's own entrance into the darkness of empty rooms.

Pizza Face rattles a box of matches and scratches one. Their eyes take that bit longer to acclimatise than their noses to the stench of cat piss. They search for scraps to burn for a more lasting light.

Eyes shimmer and watch them from the corners of walls. The pitter-patter of feet in hollow space swirls, marks their orbit, and awakens darkness. They came to explore the hidden depths of cement walls but are more explored.

The light dies and they become blind. Another match, Evan sees the kittens. He nudges Pizza Face, but he's spotted them too in the rubble.

Evan creeps by touch into the inky darkness. Another scratch of light. Kittens raise their heads from their nest, soft bellied and slack. Pizza Face picks one up, and his touch flattens its head and ears. The match burns out.

'Stick wan in each of yer jacket pockets.' Pizza Face pulls at the back of his coat, tugs his makeshift poacher's pockets forward.

'And we'll take them ootside tae play wae.' He holds out the kitten. 'Hurry up. I'm running oot of matches.'

Evan cradles the kitten in the palm of his hand. A hiss and the queen cat calls. He places the kitten back into the nest with its brothers and sisters, whispers into the golden orb of eyes and reassures the maternal presence, 'It's OK, we wouldnae take yer wee baby.'

Pizza Face drops the kitten he's holding as he tries to scoop up another. 'I'm taking a couple of them tae play wae.'

'No yeh urnae.'

'I'm ur.'

Evan shoves him, hears him stumble. The mother cat yowls, but he's more concerned that Pizza Face has breenged into and hurt the kittens. He peers into blackness. Pizza Face catches him side on and he topples. They roll together. Pizza Face is on top of Evan and he punches his cheek. Evan wrestles on top of Pizza Face, punching blindly, and his knees pinning his arms. His thumb hooks his cheek, scared and excited that he'll rip his mouth open.

'Gi'e in, and don't touch the kittens. And I'll let yeh up.'

'Awwwight.'

Evan shifts the weight on his knees, scared he'll be betrayed and the promise of truce broken.

A match strikes. They stand glaring at each other.

'I wouldn't huv hurt them.' Pizza Face's nose trickles blood. 'I jist wanted tae play wae them.'

'I know, but they need their mum.'

Pizza Face climbs up ahead of Evan into the light. He tells him, 'Chaz says I was tae batter yeh every time I seen yeh, cause yeh ur a Papish wee bastard.'

Evan crouches and peers into the gloom, wiggles his fingers at the kittens in farewell. 'I'm no a Papish bastard and I go tae the same school as yeh. No my fault, I don't support Rangers. I don't support Celtic. I'm no fussed about fitba.' He climbs on to the roof, but Pizza Face is already away.

Chapter 20

Puppy eyes

SATURDAY MEANT NO SCHOOL, AND A LONG LIE. BUT EVAN hears his da arguing with Geordie the milkman outside the front door.

'For God's sake Geordie, I jist paid yeh last week and noo yer wanting mair money?'

'Aye, you paid me, but that was four weeks ago, and that's—'

'Yeh sure?'

'I can show you the book. I wouldn't fiddle you!'

'Well, I can only gee yeh half the noo. And yeh'll need tae come back for the rest.'

He hears the cling of coins. 'There yeh go.'

'Cheers.'

'Wan mair thing. I'll need tae cancel yeh. I can get the milk in the morning myself.' Dermot gives a defiant shout. 'It's cheaper in the Kippen Dairy.'

Evan turns over in bed and wills himself back to sleep. There's little hope of pocket money, or sweets. He wears wellies to school regardless of the weather. Even Pizza Face has sannies for gym and doesn't go barefoot. His duffle coat is too small and has lost all but two toggles.

His da is either stoshus drunk, or tries to make out everything is great, like a sick man with a watering can slinking back from the graveyard.

Evan knows about being sick, his ma unspooling cough by cough in front of his eyes. It tutored him in grief and pain. It taught him about dying. But it's too late to get back to sleep. He trails through to the living room.

Dermot sits in old work clothes, reading form in yesterday's paper. Unshaven, nursing a Woodbine, an overflowing ashtray beside his chair, he rouses himself to stick a match to the kindling. No need for the metal guard. Flames no longer leap. Even coal is rationed. Breakfast is an empty place. They are struck dumb with each other.

Evan gallops to answer the door. Angela has taken to calling in whenever she's nowhere better to go. Whenever she likes. She enjoys watching Saturday-morning telly. *The Flashing Blade* with Evan, jockeying on his knee, or an armchair. She matches the action on the screen with her screams.

Angela, in bare feet and nightdress, brightens their morning with her chatter. 'Chaz says he's gonnae buy me a dog, cause Blodger got lost. A wee puppy.'

Evan sniggers, 'That'll be right.'

'Aye, he is.' She grabs his pyjama leg and tugs. 'An Alsatian. And I've tae walk it and feed it and train it—and everything.'

Evan tunes the telly, waiting for the on-screen dot to become more real than white noise, a wavy line and echoic voices. Turning the dials until magic happens and other people, happy people, crowd the room. Sometimes an early-morning film. Lassie the dog, rescuing some tousled and stranded all-American boy in terrible danger. Evan bats the top of the telly and twists the aerial, backing away to check for a watchable picture.

'Hi pet,' Dermot lets the *Daily Record* slide into the side of the chair. He gives her a real, and not counterfeit smile, bends over and kisses her on the cheek and asks with mock solemnity, 'How ur yeh?'

Angela rattles on about getting a dog. Dermot nods, half-smiling, and teases her. 'Where ur yeh gonnae get this wee dog fae?'

'My da's getting it.'

Dermot coughs and chokes. 'Yer da?'

'Aye, Chaz.'

Evan whips around. 'Chaz isnae yer da.' Lassie barks a warning on the telly.

'Aye he is.' She flounces in a hissy fit. 'He says he is noo, cause he lives wae my ma. And I've got tae dae whit I'm telt.'

'Fat chance of that.' Evan looks back at the screen and Lassie beside the rapids. But it's no surprise. Although he's tried to avoid him, he's spotted Chaz had a key for next door. His left eye was bruised as a fried egg slipping from a plate, but he seems back to his normal swagger and dagger eyes.

Dermot stubs out his fag before he gets up from the chair with a gasp. He runs the water in the sink before brushing his teeth and gargling with salt. 'Jist nipping oot.'

Evan doesn't bother looking round. He knows what that means.

Chapter 21

Masonic Brotherhood

RAB SITS IN MAGGIE SCOTT'S WEARING A BORROWED BLACK interview suit, without the tie, or court date. Sammy's finger drums on the wooden table beside the door.

Sammy gets up when he pushes through the doors. 'Whit yeh wanting son?' He adds in a note of commiseration, 'We've only got time for a quick wan, afore we go.'

'Lager mate.' Chaz hasn't bothered getting formally dressed. He slides into a seat beside Rab.

Men and an older woman from the next table look over. They are all collar and neck and faces picked from God's potato sack, surprised that somebody has spoken. A younger man sits at the bar quaffing pints, listening to the tinny radio on the gantry playing top-ten hits. Behind him Drew runs a dirty rag over the bar.

'Whit's aw this pish about?' Chaz mutters to Rab.

'Och, nothing. Yer jist joining the Masons. But yer no tae tell any cunt, or yeh get excommunicated or some shite.'

Chaz laughs on cue, 'Geez a fag.'

Rab picks up his pack of ten Regal from the table and holds it out. 'I've no got that many. I'm pink lint.'

Sammy gathers the drinks at the bar into a triangle of pints in his big hands.

'I meant,' Chaz glares at him. 'Whit huv I got tae dae here?'

'Nothing and agree tae everything.'

Chaz waits until Sammy pushed between them and quaffed a drink before he repeats his question. 'I was jist asking whit I need tae dae when I join the Masons.'

Sammy checks that nobody is in earshot. 'Yer very privileged tae be asked. Jist remember that. And it's muggins here that's sticking his neck oot and sponsoring yeh.'

Rab quickly responds because his da glares at him as if he's unsure he should be sponsoring his son. 'Aye, right Da.'

Chaz takes a mouthful of his pint and grunts assent.

'Yeh'll be tested separately. Child's play. Jist bear it oot.' Sammy quaffs his pint of heavy and comes up for air. 'And when yer asked if yeh want tae join the Brotherhood, nae prevarication like the noo. There'll be a lot of good folk watching yeh. Yer answer is aye. Always aye. Nae backing doon. And then, after that, there's nae turning back.'

Chaz purses his lips and puts on his serious face. 'Right.'

Sammy changes the subject, hits a lighter note. 'Sorry tae hear about yer bit of bother.'

Chaz chokes on his drink. But Rab slaps him on the knee, in warning. 'Aye, it was four or five of those big Papish bastards, came at us wae pickaxe handles from aw angles. We didnae stand a chance.'

Sammy leans across the table, black chest hair sprouting out of his grubby, open-necked, white shirt. 'Did yeh get a good look at them?'

'Nah, no, it was dark. And it happened that quick.' Chaz makes a joke of it, so they can relax. 'And yeh know whit they say, aw Catholics look the fucking same.'

Sammy gives an exaggerated wink. 'That other thing yeh were talking about... I've got a few folk looking into that matter, right noo.'

Chaz cottons on he's referring to Podge. 'Aye, that's great.'

Chapter 22

The 543

A couple of hundred yards from the pub, hidden behind a block of tenements on Dumbarton Road, The 543 Masonic squats toad-like beside the canal and functions as a municipal hall.

Sammy leads them away from the main entrance to a side entrance. He knocks on the door three times. And it opens into a well-lit room. They pass into another darker room. Their coats are taken from them and hung alongside ceremonial robes. But Chaz and Rab are separated.

Sammy takes a handkerchief from the cupboard and stands behind Chaz. He ties it in a tight knot around his head that catches in his hair, but he keeps his mouth shut and doesn't squeal. He stumbles forward, lets himself be led by the hand Having gone about ten feet, he comes to an abrupt stop. Blind, he tries to squint out of the side of the bandage.

'Whatever happens tae yeh,' he recognises Sammy's voice. 'Yeh must bear it aw like a man. Are yeh firmly resolved tae join our Brotherhood?'

'Aye.' Chaz remains on edge, unsure who else he is talking to or who is listening.

A plummy accent instructs him, 'When you hear a knock at the door, uncover your eyes. I wish you success and courage.'

The tread of feet disappears. Chaz holds his breath and waits for the knock. After about five minutes, the fear he's being watched makes his fingers tingle. His legs almost give way. He hesitates, peels back the kerchief, before he hears loud knocks on the door, as if the edge of a rod is being used, but the room remains in darkness, which he's glad of because he jerks backward in fright.

When his eyes adjust, he sees an old-fashioned lamp burning inside something white. As he gets closer, he sees a human skull. It stands centrepiece on a raven-black table, on which lies open the pages of the Gospel, and he reads, 'In the beginning was the word, and the word was made God.'

Chapter 23

The C-word

'YEH'LL NEVER GUESS WHO THE RHETOR WAS?' CHAZ STANDS next to Rab in the crowded public bar of the 543 having a pint.

Despite the dimmed lamp light of the ceremonial room, Chaz had recognised Chief Inspector Collins. He was a tall man, thin as chewed grass. His ungainly gait would have given him away. But he'd a policeman's kisser, more nose than face. He'd loped towards the table and picked up a pair of leather gloves and put them on. He wore a different uniform. A white leather apron covered most of his chest and part of his legs. A necklace with strange symbols hung around his neck, but it was difficult to focus on it because an antique white ruffle lit up his long chin.

'Fuck knows.' Rab turns and perches on a bar stool, a half-finished pint of Tennent's lager at his elbow, an Embassy Regal dangling from his bottom lip. He chuckles and tries to go one better by picking a more ridiculous figure. 'I got wee McGrorty.'

They'd known him years ago in his day job of school janitor and he was never off their back for fighting, or spitting, or defacing school property.

Chaz peers through layers of winding fag smoke drifting into the lights and high ceiling. Everything in the hall, the carpet on the floor, the tables and chairs merge into funeral grey tones. He feels the spreading warmth of three pints and whisky chasers spreading through his body. Colour comes from the two barmaids laughing behind the bar. A matronly woman, not worth looking at. The other sparkles with red hair, robin-red lips painted on and a ready smile that catches the eye. It's the saucy one he wants to serve them when some other mug orders them a round of drinks.

The bar extends into a larger hall, separated by a plasterboard walls. Chaz is drunker than Rab and he sniggers. 'That stupid cunt Collins asked me, "Whit dae yeh seek fae us? Wisdom? Virtue or enlightenment?" I mean, I didnae know what he was on about. I jist said, "Aye, mate," which worked a treat. And aw that shite about having tae roll yer trouser leg up. Whit's that about?'

'Fucking hell, man. That bastard wee McGrorty gave me it tight. It was as if we were back at school and he was accusing me of having pulled the sinks fae the toilet wall. "Whit is yer conception of Freemasonry?" he asked. I nearly burst out laughing, because all I could think of was The Three Musketeers and I said, "Wan for wan, and wan for aw". The wee cunt quite liked that. But never cracked a light. Gave a big spiel about the chief aim of the Order. How the foundation of something rested on something, but the fate of mankind depended on something else.'

Chaz slaps his pal on the back and takes a spill of his pint, drinking it to the dregs. 'That's the last fucking thing I need, is the fate of fucking mankind depending on Mongos like yeh.' He picks up another pint from the bar.

The stout barmaid touches his arm and points to two old men playing dominoes a few tables away. 'They bought you a round,' she says.

Chaz grins and holds his pint up in acknowledgement when the old guy wearing a rain mac looks over. He turns to Rab, 'Collins whittered on some shite about seven virtues corresponding tae the seven steps of Solomon's temple. And he told me them, but I forgot them right away. But come tae think of it, he did mention "generosity". The only virtues I know ur getting bevvied and getting my hole.'

'C'mon, yeh must remember, "The Love of Death."' Rab utters a strangulated sound. 'Even I remember that wan.'

'Oh, aye, I remember that alright. But it wisnae my death I was thinking about.' Chaz glances sideways. 'Yeh know whit I mean?'

'Aye.'

Chaz bumps against Rab's shoulder and mumbles, 'Whit about they guns yer da was talking about?'

Rab splutters into his pint. 'Shush, don't talk about it here. Walls huv ears.'

'Fuck off. Yeh've been watching too much fucking *Dad's Army*. Walls huv fucking ears!'

They chaff at the barmaid's singing, 'Last orders. Do your talking, while you're walking.' The pretty barmaid deftly nicking the glass out of their hands before they finish their pints.

A chargehand, in a black-suede jacket, stands behind them, jingles keys ready to lock up. Chaz and Rab are herded and pushed out the door with other stragglers.

Chaz pulls up the collar of his coat. Rab tucks his hands into his jacket pocket. They sway out into the main drag on Dumbarton Road.

Rab staggers and stops near Maggie Scott's pub. Next door, the gleam of tropical green inside two glass jars on display in Lamont's, the chemist-shop window, hypnotise him. He searches through his pockets for his cigarette packet.

Chaz stands a few steps away, gazing at The Linen Bank's facade the way he'd look at a naked girl. It dated to an industrial era when there was a connection between making things and saving money. 'If we'd a gun, we could jist walk in there and take whit we wanted.' His lips purse and break into a fierce grin. 'We might no even need a gun.'

Rab crumples the carton of his ten packet and flings it into the gutter. He takes a long drag of his fag before passing it on. 'We'll need tae share. I've only got wan.'

The tobacco burns in Chaz's hand, but he isn't really listening.

'Hi, Hi,' Rab makes a grab for it. 'Yeh'll be leaving fuck aw for me. And it's my fag.'

'Fucking shut up.' Chaz takes a quick draw. He hands it to his pal. 'I was jist thinking if we put on a couple of masks and stuff. And if we had something that looked like a gun. That might be enough.'

Rab takes a last drag, flicks the dout away. 'Fuck off. That's mad. Whit if somebody challenged yeh?'

'Well, yeh jist smash them. The way yeh would normally.'

'Nah,' Rab makes a face. 'That wouldnae work. Yeh always get some old stupid cunt.'

'Whit if—' Chaz's hair falls from his forehead, clouding his eyes, and he claws at the back of his neck. 'Whit if... yeh put on an Irish accent.' He mimics an accent he's heard on telly. 'Put the fucking money in the bag and you won't get hurt!'

'That's fucking rubbish.' Rab staggers sideways, laughing.

'Yeh dae it then.'

Rab sniggers all the way through his recital. 'Put the money in the bag or we'll fucking blow you up. We're the fucking IRA Bhoys.'

'Yer absolutely shite at that. Yeh sound mair Paki than Irish. They'd probably end up hauning yeh a Mother's Pride loaf and a pint of milk.'

'That's a good yin.'

They stand together heads almost touching, shaking with laughter.

Rab puts his serious face on when they step apart. 'I'm no sure, anymair. My da says he'll get me an apprenticeship in Brown's when it reopens. Welder. I'd be pretty good at that.' He checks out his fuzzy silhouette in the window.

'Ach, don't talk shite. Yer fucking nearly eighteen. Far too auld. Think about it. Yeh and some pimply faced kids gi'eing yeh snash.' He lets it sink in. 'Nah, who wants the hassle of being involved in endless strikes? Nae pay and nae bevvying. I'd much rather huv a lie-in.' He glances at Rab's face. 'We've got o'er things tae think about.' He blows out his cheeks in exasperation, 'Besides, working's for fools and mules.'

'Aye, yer probably right.'

'Yeh know we wouldnae huv this problem if we could a haud of some decent firepower.'

They walk towards the canal bridge and a pretty young girl wearing a mini-skirt approaches them. They peel apart and brush against the shoulder of her leather coat and breathe in perfume, as she slips between them.

Scooting across the road, Chaz has another idea. 'We'd need a driver, whit about that daft cousin of yers?'

'Arnie?'

'Aye, Arnie.'

'No sure. Arnie can be a bit funny. Yeh know whit he's like wae that car of his. Yeh'd need tae put mair oil than petrol in it. Aw the police would jist need tae dae was follow the oil slick.'

'Aye, but we can jist steal a car. Well, I couldnae, but yeh know whit I mean?'

'Aye,' Rab holds his hand up in a farewell salute. He stops and doubles back, whispers, 'Whit about that cunt up the close wae yeh?'

'Don't worry about him. We've got a kinda truce—until next time. Then I willnae be so slow.'

Chapter 24

Funny buggers

CHAZ CAN'T FIND HIS KEYS AND HAMMERS ON THE FRONT door, flipping the letter box with an untimely rat-a-tat-tat, echoing through the close. Kerry-Ann's playing funny buggers, and not answering. He boots the panels, shouting her name and bawls what he's going to do to her unless she does answer the door and hurries up about it.

'Sorry,' Kerry-Ann opens the door in her polyester pink nightdress with an old pair of shoes on her feet. She holds her hand over her mouth with an unconvincing yawn. 'I was sleeping.'

Chaz slams past her into the lobby. She trots behind him. Angela, sleeping sideways across their bed in the living room, annoys him. A muggy miasma, mixed with the faint stink of pee, comes from their sheets irks him more. 'Put some breakfast on. Some ham and eggs.'

'We've nae ham. Nae eggs.'

He takes a few steps into the cupboard-sized kitchen. The sink is awash, dishes in greasy water and pots rusting like scuttled ships. He trails the sole of his shoe back and forth, measuring the stickiness of the floor. The blackness of the empty houses across the way mirrors his mood. 'Toast, then.'

'Nae bread.'

He raises his arm to give her a back-handed slap, but she steps away. 'Ya, fucking lazy, good-for-nothing cow.'

'We've nae money. Yeh took it aw. Never thought tae leave a penny.'

'Fucking lying cow,' his voice rises. He follows her retreat into the living room and the courage on her face crumbles like a child's den. She stumbles backwards, falling onto the bed. Angela groans in her sleep.

'But I get my money the morra.' Her voice flutes upward as her head drops. She holds out her hands in appeasement.

She scoops Angela and lifts her floppy marionette body from the centre of the bed, and her daughter's eyes open and close. Kerry-Ann slides off her shoes, and she slips her unshaven legs under the sheets.

Chaz hangs his coat on the kitchen door and unzips his denims. He stands peeing into the kitchen sink, washing the pots. A light flicks on in the house opposite. He shakes his foreskin, a few droplets, and he's getting a semi-hard-on. He tugs his shirt out of the back of his trousers.

He breezes into the room and flings his shirt on to the bed, exposing his skinny torso and light-yellow bruising on the ribs. He sits on the top blanket to untie his shoes, her hand wandering across and patting his warm right hip.

She waits for him, her legs open and the smell of her need hanging in the air like a crayoned note. His prick raises a flag of convenience, and her hand plucks at his Y-fronts. Tugs and teases his cock out of his pants, bringing him crawling towards her.

He pinches the strap of her nightie and she smiles and slinks her shoulders, showing her breasts, as she slips it off. She gasps as he enters her.

The bed thuds against the plaster wall. Sweat mixing, skin on skin, her hand on the small of his back, guiding and encouraging as he rides her hard and tries to master the glint in her eyes.

'Stop hurting my mum.' Angela glares at Chaz with wide-awake eyes. His rhythm slows and stops. His wet cock shrinks and slips out of Kerry-Ann.

'It's OK, pet, he's jist tickling me.' Kerry-Ann's hips scoot forward towards him and her bum lifts from the wet and crumpled under-sheet, trying to keep him inside her. 'Jist go back tae sleep.'

Angela studies the burst of scarlet on her mum's cheeks, the slick of sweat on her forehead and breasts. Her mum sits up and covers her nipples and torso with a sheet. Angela feels the heat of their bodies and hears a car gunning along the road, like a faraway wasp, and it drifts away inside her head. 'I'm no tired.' She untangles her feet from the blanket to get up. 'And I need a drink.'

Kerry-Ann tut-tuts. Her hand darts and explodes against her daughter's ear.

Angela squeals. She is going to cry, but when she looks at Chaz, freezes, tucks herself in and turns her back on them, tugging a cover over her ears.

Kerry-Ann reaches for his cock, still wet and slippery from her cunt.

He pulls away from her, creating a sticky gap in the sheets. 'Yeh got a fag?'

'Nah, nothing, but I could make yeh wan up fae whit I've got in the ashtrays. That's whit I usually dae until payday.'

'Alright.' He takes his flaccid cock in his hand. Wanking it, until it grows a bit of bone. 'Gi'e me a bit of heid first. Finish me—'

She does as she's told. Puts her lips over his shrinking cock, pulls and jerks the foreskin, and wanks him with her mouth and tongue. His cock mushrooms, and he grabs her hair, jerking her head backwards and forwards, hard onto him. She breathes through her nose, until she comes to the surface for air, and thinks she is going to gag, but tries again. His cock shrinks and she knows she's lost him.

'Yer nae fucking use,' Chaz is ready to hit out. 'Why ur yeh so fucking useless?'

She scoots out of their bed. Her eyes accustomed to the gloom, she drags an ashtray from under the bed. Picks apart blackened tobacco carcasses and lipstick smudged douts to wrap in Rizla paper, she makes healthy and whole cigarettes.

To keep him sweet, she cups in her left hand as a paltry offering two Rizla smokes. The sweat on her body has dried and she shivers.

He's wanking, fingering his prostrate cock. She squeezes her left breast, rubs her nipple and licks her lips, longing to be warm in bed. The remaining douts are chucked in the ashtray for later.

He grunts as she takes him into her mouth. He holds the base of his cock, wanking and jerking into her mouth in a renewed frenzy. She tastes pre-cum when he slaps the back of her head.

'It's nae use,' he says. 'Let Bridget the Midget dae it.'

'But she's only wee. She doesnae know how.'

'She's got tae learn. Noo is as good a time as any.'

'Whit if she's sick?'

'Then yeh get her tae clean it up. Simple.'

Chapter 25

Nests

THE SCHOOL NURSE MOUES AS SHE READS THE NOTE FROM HIS teacher. A calor-gas heater hisses, and colour posters climb the wooden and lime-green panels of the walls, promising all kinds of dangers. Evan wipes sweat from his forehead.

Slats of a box-white hat checked her grey hair. Her belly overflows her white uniform and the dinky polyester chair moulded to her. Absentmindedly, she hits the tarnished gold button on the ashtray on the table. Her menthol cigarette leaves only lingering smoke.

She pinches his school jersey at the shoulder and drags him across to where the electric light hangs lopsided on a cord from the ceiling. Her glasses hang precariously on the fleshy part of her bulbous nose hiding hazel eyes behind thick magnifying lenses. He winces. Bony fingers drag his scalp, and part it into hedges for beasties to leap over. She takes a jolting step backwards, knocks her bum against the desk, and the digits on her fingers grow kind and human. He feels—rather than sees—a fine-tooth comb plying its trade, paying particular attention to the places around his ears. She has him tilt his head to probe the shoal of shiny skin, where

101

the itch is greatest and grows legs under the hair at the nape of his neck.

'Let's see your hands,' she instructs him.

Her thumb and forefinger encircle his wrist and uncurl his fingers. She leans over him, peers at the bitten flesh around his nails. The sigh that escapes her thin lips needs no lipstick coating. Index and middle finger tap the base of his thumb and wrist. She frowns at the numbers on the upside-down watch pinned to the lapel above the shelf of her left breast.

'Right,' she seems satisfied, takes off her specs and rubs her eye. 'Take off your wellies, will you?' She wrestles the seat away from the desk to encourage him, and yawns, without covering her mouth.

Cringeworthy, cavorting feet, creeping things best hidden inside the stink of rubber, and he has no socks to cover his shame. He glances sideways at her as she gawps at them, notes skin discolouration, and black stretches on long, white bones, like Indian ink and graffiti.

She points at the runway of linoleum near the door. 'Stand over there.'

He sticks his wellies back on.

She sits behind her desk. Turning to a shelf behind her head, she reaches for lined paper and a shatterproof ruler. She yanks open a drawer and grabs a biro. Taking off her glasses, she rubs her eyes. She licks the brown envelopes, sealing them shut by pressing with the ruler.

'One of these I'll put on file. And I'll give a copy to your teacher,' she tells him in a bored tone. 'Explaining your absence. You've not to go back to class. You've to go home.'

She lets the thought settle. 'The other letter is for your mum, advising her to take you to the chemist—'

'I've no got a mum,' he cuts in.

'Right,' her tone softens. 'Give the letter to your dad. It tells him what kind of head-lice powder to get, and shampoo and soap. But don't worry, the chemist will be able to advise you, if you're stuck.'

She scratches at the back of her head but stops when she sees him watching her. 'I need to see you back here twice a week before I sign you off, because there'll be eggs left over no one can see. You understand?'

'Aye.'

'Where is it you stay, again?' She makes it sound like a throwaway remark.

'726 Dumbarton Road.'

'And what landing is that?'

Evan sticks out his chest. 'The top.'

'Will there by anybody in if I send you home now?'

'Aye, my da.'

'What's his name, again?'

'Dermot.'

'OK then,' she jots in a lined pad and waves him away. 'Mind and give him that letter. It's very important. And I'll give the other letter to your teacher. Don't forget!'

'I need tae go back tae the classroom for my jacket.'

She looks at her paperwork and picks up the remaining brown envelope. 'In that case, you might as well give this envelope to Mrs Thompson. But don't hang about. Straight home. I'll have a word with her in the staffroom. I'm sure I'll be seeing a few of your classmates later.'

He grabs the envelope out of her hand, glad to escape, but she throws a final query at him.

'Who do you sit beside in class?'

'Pizza Face,' he blurts out and gets red in the face. 'I mean Graham Sweeney.'

Chapter 26

Feuds

'I'm Marie.' A soft hand floats up for Dermot to shake. 'I'm a social worker. Here to see you about your son, Evan.'

The social worker's Bearsden accent speaks of elocution classes and private education. Dermot doubts whether he'd properly heard her say what her name was. Marie or Maria, not that it matters.

'Hing on.'

He pays court to his visitor by disappearing for a few moments and flings on a clean shirt and a brown cardigan.

Evan pops his head out of the room. Her expensive pearl-white blouse and matching coloured jacket and skirt are not a uniform they are used to. And her perfume mugs them like incense and makes other women seem coarse, as if they've dragged their bodies out of the nearest stank.

The social worker is so genteel Dermot feels he and his son are in the wrong house, the workhouse, and mucking up the tight schedules of her life. She follows him into the living room without wiping her feet.

'Yeh want tea?' Dermot asks.

'No thanks,' she smiles apologetically.

'I've nae coffee.' He stretches out an arm and guides her into the chair across from his own beside the fireplace.

'This is nice and cosy.' Her pale blue eyes fix on the black-and-white wedding photo on the mantelpiece, propping up a stack of unopened brown envelopes. The social worker's smile flashes brighter than the dampened flames in the fireplace.

Dermot scratches the back of his neck. He flings himself into the seat across from her and speaks bluntly. 'Look hen, I'm sure yer awful nice. But we ur daeing alright. And I don't want yeh telling me whit tae dae, or sticking us in yer notebook—for consideration later.' He uses his elbows and gets up from his chair. 'We'll gee it a miss, thanks.'

She looks steadily across at him. 'You've not heard what I'm here for yet.'

'I know whit yer here for. I got letters oot fae the school. The wee yins no well and that's the end of it. I used tae get covered in tics and lice and bites when I was carrying the coal. It's no the end of the world. Toughens yeh up. I could tell yeh stories that would make the Pied Piper sound like a bit of a pansy poofter. But I thought they'd send oot a child catcher, or truant officer or something, no a—'

'Social worker,' she pips in.

'Aye,' with a wave of his hand, he invites her to leave. 'So if yeh please.'

'But maybe I can help you.'

'Help me,' he snorts. 'Look hen, nae offence, I wouldnae trust yeh tae haud a pokey-hat up the right way withoot a daft dog stealing a lick.'

'I've got a statutory duty.'

Evan and Angela appear at the door. He's barefoot, in grubby pyjamas. Angela wears a pair of boy's shorts and an oversized Rangers top.

Dermot adopts a military bearing. 'Well, statutory duty yerself oot of here then.'

Marie lifts her bag. 'I'm sorry, I've caught you at a bad time. I didn't know you had another little boy.'

'I'm no a wee boy,' bawls Angela. 'I'm a wee girl.'

'She's fae next door,' Dermot laughs, shaking his head, exchanging a smile with the social worker.

'I'm sorry too, Mr Connelly, I've just started this new job and I don't really know what I'm doing. And I was really hoping to get something on paper.'

'Och, why didnae yeh say that.' Dermot thinks the daft wee thing is going to cry. 'Sit doon. I'm my ain worst enemy, sometimes. I'll get yeh a cup of tea and we'll work something oot. Milk and how many sugars?'

'Just black, please.'

Chapter 27

Old dinosaurs

EVAN NUDGES ANGELA AWAKE. THEY HEAR THE FRONT DOOR closing. Dermot chiming 'Cheerio,' and they know the nice lady is away. They're sick of hiding from a giant dinosaur under the bed and crawl out dusty and uneaten.

'I guess that's it,' Evan snorts. 'I'll need tae go back tae school noo.'

Angela stands at the window coughing and stares into the driving rain. 'I'll huv naebody tae play wae.' A sulk grieves her face and lips.

Evan goes over and pats her on the shoulder, but she flicks his hand away. 'Don't worry, yeh'll be at school yerself soon.'

'Don't want tae go tae school. It's jist stupid.'

'Too bad. Yeh'll jist huv tae.' Darkness sweeps in with overcast clouds like the tails of a pantomime villain's cloak. Doors and windows rattle. Grey stone on the back courts turning pebble blue. Rainwater prattling gutters and clears the air.

'Read me a story.'

A snotty-nosed request, but something more. A need he recognises to lose yourself. The made-up world of books being better than the real world.

'Okay-dokey.'

He picks up their book. She lies on top of his legs under the covers. Her finger scroll along the page as he reads, her mouth forms the highs and lows of words. He stops mouthing when they get to the bit about the wicked witch and the poison apple, but she continues pointing and reading.

'See, yeh can read.' He pulls her into a hug. 'School is gonnae be really easy for yeh. And everybody will love yeh. The teacher is gonnae think yer jist the bee's knees—unless yeh get Mrs Thompson.'

Angela wipes her nose on the stripes in his pyjamas. She perks up, chuffed. 'See the wicked witch, I mean, I know she doesnae really like Snow White, but she doesnae really want tae kill her, does she?'

Evan taps the page as evidence. 'Aye, she does. She poisons her wae an apple.'

Angela's jaw clenches, and she grinds her teeth. 'Yeh cannae get a real poison apple, can yeh?'

Evan shakes his head. 'Nah.' But reconsiders. 'Aye, yeh can get poison, though.'

He pats Angela's back absentmindedly and carries on talking. 'But it's nae use, cause yeh always get caught. It's like Sherlock Holmes wae *The Hound of the Baskervilles*. I mean, they dogs werenae even real dogs, and Sherlock Holmes jist knew it.'

She wipes her nose with the back of her hand. 'Who's Sherlock Holmes?'

'He's like a guy that wears a funny hat, a deerstalker, and smokes a big pipe and he jist needs tae look at yeh. And he knows everything. He'll point his finger at yeh, and says, "Yeh had egg and toast for breakfast this morning." And he's always right.'

'I'd nothing for breakfast this morning.' Angela scrambles from the bed. 'And I'm starving. Yeh got any biscuits?'

'Nah, don't think so. We could go through and see.'

Dermot worked his way through the last of a pack of Senior Service, which he flicks into the coals. A slow-burn smile is more for Angela than Evan. 'Hello pet.'

The glint in her green eyes impales him. 'Yeh got any biscuits?'

He rouses himself from the chair. 'Nah, I wouldnae think so. Biscuits don't last that long in here.' He swoops and picks her up, holding her tight in his arms. He looks across at Evan and winks, 'especially of the chocolate variety. But I'll show yeh a wee trick.'

He saunters into the kitchen, after leaving her in his warm seat. *Ernie, The Fastest Milkman in the West* blares from the radio at his back.

'Can I turn the telly on?' Evan asks.

'Aye,' says Dermot. 'Fire in.'

'Can I turn yer radio off?'

'Aye, that song's a lot of shite. Drives yeh bonkers. I'd rather listen tae *The Sash*.'

Evan turns on the telly and squeezes into the seat beside Angela. They watch *Jackanory*, with such intense concentration they're transported.

Angela's eyes stray from the screen. The slap and smell of hot coals spitting on the fire. Dermot, with the metallic short-handled shovel in his hand, grabs her attention more than the story of *The Wise Owl*.

'Whit yeh daeing?' She shifts forward and covers her mouth because she's going to cough.

Evan looks over her shoulder at his dad.

Dermot lobs a few potatoes into the flames, using the poker to cover them with coals and ashes. 'Best meal in the world. Potatoes still in their skins, burnt black by the flames.' He makes smacking and kissing noises with puckered lips.

'And for the young lady.' He takes a slice of white bread from the wrapper, spears it with the poker, and holds it over the flames. It singes and browns almost immediately. 'Homemade toast. Em. Nothing better.'

Angela slips from her seat. 'Can I get a shot?'

Slices of white bread drop from the poker as casualties, turn black and curl into the flames. Whooping laughter. Dermot teaches them how to turn Mothers Pride and Stork Margarine into a feast.

The potatoes take longer. Dermot bats coals aside and picks tatties out with the pincer of tongs.

He hands an overcooked spud to Angela and another to Evan. They swish them in hand-to-hand combat and juggle them to keep them from burning fingers and the palms of their hands.

'They need a bit of salt,' Dermot splutters. 'Wait a wee minute.' He nips through to the kitchen and comes back with the salt cellar. He picks the shell of a spud left cooling near the grate. Angela and Evan gawp at him so intently it makes him chuckle. 'Right, bite the heid aff.' He snaps his teeth together and munches potato, leaving a body of white flesh.

Evan nips at the skin of his potato with his teeth. Angela licks her blackened potato skin, undecided.

Dermot taps a little more salt and swallows his jacket-potato whole. 'Lovely,' he smacks his lips when he finishes chewing.

'Gee me that,' Dermot play-grabs, as if to steal the potato out of her hand.

'No,' she shrieks, turns sideways, hiding away from him. She takes a bite out of it.

Evan does the same. 'Em, I think it needs a bit mair salt,' he pronounces. Checks his dad's expression. He receives a pat of benediction on the top of his head.

Angela snuggles into the armchair with Dermot. *Nationwide* on the telly, but as a background noise. She strokes his unshaved chin and runs a finger over his bruised cheek.

'Whit's that?' she asks.

'Nothing for a wee nosey-pokes like yeh tae worry about, hen.' He plants the smacker of a kiss on her forehead. 'Sometimes yeh only know there's trouble when trouble comes tae get yeh.'

Her body slackens and face glows. She makes murmuring noises in a deep sleep.

'Jesus.' Dermot springs from the chair and holds Angela away from his body like an unwanted parcel. He places her on her feet in front of the fireplace.

Angela ripped from the warmth of Dermot's lap, screams and cries.

Evan bolts from his seat. 'Whit's the matter Da?'

'Nothing tae worry about. The wee lassie's no well. That's aw.' Evan notices the wet map of pee on his Da's semmit.

'It's alright hen, nae harm done,' Dermot woos Angela with a soothing voice. 'Don't yeh worry about it, pet.'

Dermot whispers to Evan, 'Better go next door and get her ma.' He adds, 'If that asshole boyfriend of her gi'es yeh any snash, yeh let me know. Got it?'

'Aye, Da.'

'I don't want tae go hame,' Angela screams. 'I want tae stay here wae you. And for yeh tae be my dad.'

Chapter 28

Going soft

CHAZ TREATS EVAN AS IF HE'S INVISIBLE WHILE SEARCHING in his coat pockets for his cigarette packet. He whacks Pizza Face a slap on the back of the head. He caught him smoking a roll-up at the bottom of the stairs. 'Get up tae Rab's and tell him tae meet me in Maggie Scott's.'

Pizza Face rubs his head. 'Whit's in it for me.'

'A boot in the baws, if yeh don't.'

They stare at each other until Pizza Face's head drops. 'Alright,' he mutters to his sannies.

Chaz tosses a Silk Cut to Pizza Face as payment. 'Here, ya wee cunt, don't let anybody know I'm goin soft.'

Coat collar up, shoulders thrown forward like cutlasses at war with each other, Chaz shuffles out of the close to Maggie Scott's.

Chaz takes a table under the blacked-out windows, sparks a Silk Cut and sits toying with the Tennent's place-mat, tearing it into strips. He gives the door a fleeting glance when someone with wavy hair comes in. Chaz is on his third pint by the time Rab arrives and he shouts a greeting. 'Better late than never.'

Rab stands beside Wee Dan, away from the wash of the crowd at the bar. Chaz bursts out laughing when he totters across carrying two pints. He sniffs the air. 'Yeh've got the poof juice on. Looks as if yeh've had a wee bath.'

Rab flings his denim jacket over the chair frame. His white open-necked shirt is ironed, his flared trousers are clean and pressed and his shoes polished enough to satisfy a Sergeant Major on parade.

'Aye, got a date the night,' Rab admits. 'Goin tae the Park Bar.' He takes a drink of his pint. 'Don't want tae get too pissed.'

Chaz shakes his head. 'Pissed! They take a photo of yeh in the Park Bar and compare it tae later in case yer mugshot cracks a smile. They'll no even let yeh in if yeh look like a Catholic, or if yer gonnae fart at some point in yer short life, laugh too loud, or enjoy yerself.' His diatribe gets louder. Others at nearby tables glance over and smile. 'And if the bar staff hear yeh fucking swearing. Fuck sake. They get aw upset, demand counselling, phone the police and bar yeh for life.'

'Away yeh tae fuck! Aye, well, it's jist wan of these things. The barmaids ur tasty, though, eh?'

'Who's the bird?'

'Och, yeh don't know her.' Rab's right hand circles in explanation. 'She's my mum's, sister's pal's, sister's daughter, or some shite like that.'

Coughing and spluttering, Chaz slaps his chest to get his breath back and takes a mouthful of beer. 'Whit's her name?'

'Myra Winton.'

'I know her,' whoops Chaz. 'Went tae school wae oor Julie. Binger. Fat. Face like an old trout.'

'She's no that fat.'

'Aye, and Pinocchio isnae really made of wood.'

A man in a soft hat shuffles past, whistling through his teeth, and Rab turns to stare at him. His eyes flicker back to Chaz and he gulps a mouthful of lager. 'Aye, well, she's got nice big tits. And we urnae aw like yeh, loved up. Any port in a storm.'

Chaz finishes his pint, stands up to get another. 'Same again.' He picks up his cigarette packet and shakes it. Sticks a fag in his gob. 'Bit of news there myself. She's up the duff.'

His tentative admission puts a smug look on Rab's face. He shoots out of his seat. 'Yeh sit doon pal. I'll get this wan. No often we get tae be a daddy.'

'Fuck off,' Chaz's face beaming. 'Runs in the family. My auld man jist needed tae sniff my ma's drawers and she was pregnant again.'

Rab giggles. 'Yer secret's safe wae me.'

When Rab comes back from the bar, he dumps a couple of double whiskies on the table with two pints. 'If we're gonnae celebrate, we need tae celebrate right.' He picks up his half and holds it up in salute. 'Who's like us?' he roars, and flings it back, banging the glass on the table.

Chaz picks up his measure and looks through the sun coloured glass, savours the whisky, before quaffing it. 'Yeh hear about Podge?'

'Aye, heard the bastard got a good haul.' The opening bars of *Summertime*, an Ella Fitzgerald number, plays on the jukebox. Rab tilts his head to listen. 'Who put that shite on?' He shakes himself out of it. 'Aye, boasting he bagged a brand-new stereo, colour telly, and about a thousand LPs. Lying cunt. He'd need a car. And naebody in Kimberly Street owns a colour telly. He cannae keep his fat mouth shut for a minute. Telling everybody whit he's gonnae dae tae yeh.'

'That right?' Chaz's arm sprawls casually over the backrest of the seat. But Rab knows he's needled him. 'Where's the cunt drinking noo?'

'Up the Atlantis.'

Chaz picks up his pint and chugs what's left in a oner. Stands up. 'Mon then. We'll get a taxi up there, noo.'

'Hing on.' Rab takes a drink of his pint, to give him time to think. 'Member, I've got a big date the night. Besides, by the time we get up there it'll be near closing time. And he might no be there.'

Chaz slumps back into the seat. 'OK then, get another wan in then. We can get that cunt anytime, but it'll need tae be soon. He's daeing too much fucking yakking for my liking.'

Rab picks up the empties to take them back to the bar. He leans across, glances over his shoulder to check nobody is listening. 'My da wants us tae meet a few boys o'er fae the Falls Road. Yeh know whit he's like, thinks he's getting too auld and we need fresh blood.'

'Whereabouts?'

'The Orange Hall.'

'Shouldn't yeh be heading up the road, about noo? To get ready for yer massive date.'

Rab's bottom lip droops. 'Nah, fuck it. I've got mair important things tae dae.' He glances around at the other punters in the pub, drinking and glowering. He swills lager around his glass, swallows it, and stands up to go to the bar. 'Besides, I'm enjoying myself here.'

Chaz's right eyebrow rises and he adopts a mocking expression. 'Suppose we could get another wan before we go.'

Rab turns to go to the bar, but he steps back to the table. 'Go where?'

'The Orange Halls, of course.' Chaz acts surprised. 'If a couple of boys came tae see me aw the way fae Ulster, I don't want tae let them doon. I'm no like some people. She'll be standing outside the Park Bar the noo, on her todd, modelling her white wedding dress, greeting her wee piggy eyes oot.'

'Fuck right off.' Rab's cheeks and ears glow. 'Sometimes I wonder whit fucking planet yer on. Yeh jist think yer too smart for yer ain good.'

Chapter 29

God Save the Queen

They get an Auchenshuggle 64 bus to the Orange Hall in Clydebank, less than a ten-minute journey. Chaz squeezes like a schoolboy into the window seat in the smoking section upstairs. Chapping the window as the bus runs parallel with the Park Bar, he nudges Rab in the ribs and chortles, 'Did yeh see her there? Big white blimp of a balloon, standing ootside, waiting for yeh?'

Rab stares ahead, moving with the sway of the bus, smoking a fag and keeping his mouth shut.

They parachute off the back step of the bus, timing their jump to when it slows, but before it stops. Stepping into the void, and rain-swept beat of Dumbarton Road. Knock-kneed laughter fills them as the brakes squeal and the double-decker comes to a juddering stop. The headlights of passing cars, like flash photography, pick them out. A car horn sounds. An old woman wearing a plastic rain hat carefully steps off the platform at the designated bus stop.

The Orange Hall is nearby, across the road from the closed front gates of John Brown's shipyard, Titan cranes tower above the tenements, once a thumping heartbeat of metal on metal marking the dreich night. Rab's da was forever telling him that was no accident. You had to check into the Orange Hall first before you got a job in Brown's, in the good old days.

Chaz follows Rab down the stone steps because he's been inside the Hall. He remembers being shunted off to a side room. Ash colours. An absence of green, apart from the baize on the pool table. They hid it away and covered with a cloth at Christmas. Santa's white beard knocked askew, smelling of booze, with a sack of goodies, yodels, 'Yo-ho-ho,' dressed in a bright orange suit with a hundredweight of cotton wool for white trims and Council surplus wellies.

Music drones from the lounge, Elvis Presley's *Heartbreak Hotel* wooing woodchip walls. Tacky floor tiles. The toilets at the entrance and the foyer whiffs of pee.

'Yeh a member?' asks a big tired-looking man, curly hair peppered with streaks of grey and eyes that once twinkled like Santa's. His shirt is open-necked, his sleeves rolled up, showing hairy forearms. He sits on a bucket chair too small for him, behind a desk, a pint of heavy beside him for company. The open pages of a register lie in front of him, with a pen attached to it by a red elastic band.

Rab picks up the pen. 'Nah, but my da will sign us in.'

'Who's yer da?'

'Sammy Burrows.'

'Gi'es a minute.' The doorman looks past Rab, checking out Chaz. He pushes open the lounge door and has a confab with a shirt on the other side.

As the beat of the music gets louder, Sammy appears.

Sammy escorts them through the big hall to tables near the bar. Rab and Chaz hear the raised voices and Irish accents before they get seated.

A bulky man with a crew cut, about Sammy's age, stands and blocks their path. 'Anything yeh need, Sammy, yeh let me know.'

Sammy slaps him on the shoulder and winks. 'Will dae, Tommy, yer a good man. And the first man we'll need when things get rough.'

Sammy commandeers chairs and puts a pint of lager in front of them. Rab starts a funny story that fizzles and dies with frowns. Chaz says nothing and listens.

The two Irish boys hold court. Del does the talking and most of the laughing. He's big the way bison are big, pink faced with blond hair, but it's the twinkle of an earring in his left ear, a gold bar, that makes him stand out. Chaz has never seen a man wearing an earring. For all his bluster, he's not the one in charge.

He addresses himself to Dougie, his travelling companion. He's unremarkability in a faded suit jacket and feather-cut brown hair that tends to hide his eyes. Firm build but not fat, aged about thirty-five, around ten years older than Del.

The barman hovers within touching distance of the five-foot mark with gangly arms. When Chaz glances over towards the bar, he notices Dougie watching and follows his gaze. A tall man with a braying voice, a beer belly and fat arse is giving the bar staff a hard time. The barman ducks and dives around the stout barmaid behind the bar with a rictus grin.

Del's chair scrapes across the floor. Dougie jumps up at his back and follows him to the bar. Chaz's fingers dip into his jacket, hanging on the back of his chair, and clutch the bone handle of his razor. But it's all over before Chaz can get involved. A man sprawls on the ground, his head bleeding after being cracked against the bar, Del with his foot on his throat, finger pointing like a gun as the disgruntled customer is lectured on manners.

People from other tables steal a look. *Penny Arcade* plays on the jukebox. A drunken woman clambers from her seat, clapping her hands. She sashays her bony hips as she draws her aged beau towards the dance floor.

Dougie squeezes in beside Chaz at the table, leans across, lifts his pint and takes a swig, before sitting down. 'I heard about your wee bit trouble with your wee sister.'

Del passes them, his hand scrunched on the blazered neck of the unmannerly. The man being ushered out of the hall.

'Aye.' Chaz's hand trembles a little as he sculls a drink of lager. 'But I dealt wae it the best I could.'

'How?' It's spoken quietly, amid hi-jinks on the dance floor, where women and men gather to relive their youth. But Dougie's gaze scrutinises him, making what is happening over his shoulder a sideshow.

Chaz smirks, 'I took a razor tae him.'

Rab turns his head to listen.

'Fae here tae here,' Chaz draws a line across his own cheek with his index finger. 'But he got off lightly. I really wanted tae kill the cunt.'

'How did you not?'

Chaz shrugs, 'No sure, I didnae huv time.' He knows he's played it right, casual, something that can be picked up again. 'But I'll no be so slow the next time.'

'We can help with that.'

'Aye, that'd be good, but I'd want tae dae the job myself.' Chaz sits motionless after his declaration, only searching for his cigarette packet when he gets a nod of affirmation.

'I want tae dae the cunt tae,' slobbers Rab, his shoulder nudges against Chaz's.

'God Save the Queen', marked the last bells and closing time. And God help anybody daft enough not to line up and hold themselves upright, Even the drunken woman with the headband grows sober for Her Majesty before falling backwards, her body splashing into the chairs and knocks drinks off her table with a smash.

Chapter 30

Safari

When Chaz wakes the next morning his head is like the match ball used in the Old Firm game. The lump of flesh in a frilly orange nighty beside him thwarts his attempt at burrowing back into the pillows. He kicks Kerry-Ann's leg under the blankets and her eyes blink open.

'Any Irn Bru?' he asks.

'Nah. Yeh should know better than that. Angela drank it. I tried telling her.'

Angela sleeps hockey-stick horizontal at the bottom of the bed, blankets over her head. Chaz forgot she was there until Kerry-Ann mentioned her. His eyes flicker to the broken settee and telly, trying to work out what time it is. A light hum of traffic makes him think it's still early.

He lifts a bum cheek and farts loudly.

'That's minging!' She slides out of bed.

Listening to the water running and waiting for her coming back, he shuts his eyes. But he gives up and flings himself out of bed and pulls on his Y-fronts. He tackles the front-door lock and the cold stairs on the landing, barefoot, two at a time.

Perched on the lavvy pan, he realises his mistake. No toilet roll. No scraps of newspaper. His stomach playing rodeo. He uses his Y-fronts to wipe his arse and flings the stinking mess into the toilet bowl. When he flushes, the water rises and keeps rising. He doesn't hang about and skips naked up the stairs.

He stumbles through to the kitchen, his feet cold, anger rising at the stench from the sink and because he can't find a clean cup for water. The tap left running.

His bell-bottom denims are still damp. Loose change acts as ballast as he pulls them on. A sock is in one shoe, the other one giving him the run-around. He pokes about under the bed before giving up. His polyester shirt lies on the floor. He glances at his softening belly. Dressed, he doesn't feel any better, but doesn't feel any worse.

He lifts Kerry-Ann's bag from the side of the sofa and takes it through the kitchen. Drinking a mug of water, he roots about. Less than a quid, and snash in her purse. Better than nothing.

He pokes about in the cupboard by the sink, searching for her tablets. The bottom shelf is a place where spiders hide. A heavy soup pot, with a metal lid on it, sits big as a wishing well.

Kerry-Ann's predictable that way. A child that hides behind a curtain and forgets you can see her feet. He pops a tablet out for luck and swallows it with a mouthful of tepid water. Another two to quell the knot in his head, and he thinks about hiding them to teach Kerry-Ann a lesson. He did that with his mum's Mogadon. But she'd cried for a week and they'd taken her to the loony bin. It wasn't worth thinking about the hassle that caused.

Chapter 31

Buroo

CHAZ STANDS FREEZING AT THE BUS STOP OUTSIDE RAMSAY'S Fruit and Veg. A beige Morris Marina sweeps through the puddles. Dougie, in the passenger seat, winds down the window. He gazes at Chaz and his mouth twitches into a smile. 'Where you going to?' his accent seems sharper out in the streets.

'Och, naewhere, jist intae Clydebank.' A bus lumbers into view. Chaz points, but he's not sure Dougie will see it unless he looks in the rear-view mirror, but he reckons the Irishman pays little heed to public transport.

Dougie clicks the back-door lock. 'Get in.'

'Nah, it's alright,' says Chaz. 'Honest, it's no far.'

'What, you think we're going to kidnap you?' Dougie laughs, 'I mean, we've nowhere to keep you, the boot is already full of Taigs.'

Chaz takes the hint and pulls the door open and flings himself into the back seat. The windscreen wipers squeak out of time as they pull out into the traffic. His shirt feels damp with sweat before they get to the canal bridge. Children play balancing tricks on the horizontal of the bars. Del drops his fag out of the window onto the road before it's half-finished and reaches for another from his packet. Checking the rearview mirror, he flips one to Chaz.

Dougie turns and hands him his cigarette lighter, and yawns, showing a mouthful of yellow teeth and black fillings. 'Where we dropping you?'

'Jist along at the buroo. No far.' He looks out the window as they pass the windblown plots, huts painted in cheery colours. 'Straight on,' he adds.

'That pal of yours—' says Dougie

'—Rab.' Chaz lights his fag and passes him back his lighter, noting the heft in it and the fancy engravings.

'Yeh, that fellah. Seems a bit of a bawhead.'

'Nah, he's alright,' says Chaz.

Eyes turning in unison as they pass the Town Hall clock and Police Station.

'You'd vouch for him?' Dougie asks.

'Aye, Aye, I would.'

The car slows as they come to the traffic lights at Kilbowie Road. 'With your life?'

The Marina jerks forward, but Dougie's gaze doesn't leave Chaz's face. When he keeps schtum, Dougie changes the subject. He turns around, staring at the road and the car in front. He talks out of the side of his mouth. 'That other matter.'

'Aye.' Chaz knows he's talking about Podge. He winds his window a tad and his dout gets caught in the slipstream.

Dougie swivels to check if he's listening, suddenly worked up. 'You need to tell us exactly where to get him. So we can have a quiet word in his ear. You got that? You know what to do there, don't you? We're not a comedy act. We're not your usual Chic fucking Murray or Benny fucking Hill.'

'Aye,' Chaz looks past Dougie at the road.

'We're jist in here, tae yer left,' he instructs Del, but the car is already turning.

Even for a visitor it's a familiar sight, the braille of a former industrial city. A gathering of men hanging about. Smoking and waiting. Hard men. They look at them parking through squinted eyes. Jokers and jesters who bounce from group to group, waiting for the call. And those ghosts of themselves, standing with their mouths hanging open, sucking exhaust fumes, a bit of paper in their limp hand that reminds them of who they were.

'You want us to wait for you?' Dougie laughs.

'Nah, it's alright. They'll probably make me hing about for being late or something. Stupid bastards, yeh'd think it was their money. Whit difference does it make tae them?'

The car door sticks, Chaz jerks it open. The icy wind bites, even with his thick coat on.

Dougie speaks to him through the half-open window. 'I'm thinking we might find a bit of work for you. Half goes to the cause. And we split the other half between us, three ways, for expenses. Mind, don't be a stranger.'

The Marina does a U-turn into the traffic. Chaz ponders what he meant. Dougie was saying he could be somebody or he could be nobody. The choice is his.

He barges into an older guy with a moustache and chapped lips, who clicks his tongue impatiently, but makes a joke out of it. 'Who the fuck was that? Yer boss? I wouldnae like tae work for that cunt.'

Chaz reaches into his pocket for his razor. 'Whit the fuck's it got tae dae wae you?'

'Easy pal,' the man with the moustache shrugs without moving his shoulders. 'Nothing tae dae wae me. Jist a joke, man. We aw got tae eat a bit of humble pie sometimes.'

Chaz knows what the skinny wee clerk who makes him queue to sign on and babbles on will get. His humble-pie days are over.

Chapter 32

Playing away from home

Rab remains stranded on the pavement on the other side of the road. He is unwilling to commit his body to holding up the traffic. Chaz negotiates the tooting horns of cars and buses with the absent-mindedness of a toddler and seems startled he stands outside the Atlantis bar.

The two-storey pub is a white lighthouse added to the gable ends of tenements. Glasgow crime-lord Arthur Thompson, allegedly, offered a hundred grand for it, but the owner refused his offer. The sight of it guides drinkers from Singer's factory in such numbers that the bar staff pull pints before tea breaks and lunch-breaks and clocking-off time and stack glasses on beer mats on top of each other like a Crystal Palace.

As well as his razor, Chaz hides an axe deep inside his coat pocket. Rab has a butcher's boning knife, a thing of beauty.

Rab ventures across the road and smiles wearily at Chaz. 'I'm choking for a pint. After aw that walking.'

A drunken man stumbles out of the door beside the off sales. His Oxfam suit rumpled, but shoes are black and shiny. He holds the door open, a courtesy, when he spots them outside waiting. The noise of the bar grows dim as he lets go and the door shuts over, sealing stale cigarette smoke and flat beer. 'I think I know you, son,' he points at Chaz.

'Don't think so, pal.'

'Aye, I dae.' He tilts his head. 'Yer wee Danny McCann's boy, urn't yeh?'

Rab's mouth hangs open. Chaz nudges him aside, a beamer of a smile on his face. 'Aye, that's right enough,' he says. 'How yeh getting on, anyway?'

'Aye, no bad son. Never forget a face. Yeh tell him I was asking for him, eh?'

'Will dae,' Chaz pats his shoulder. 'Jist wondering if wan of my mates was in there. Cannae really miss him, about my height, but wae blonde hair and a couple of scars on his coupon.'

The drunk man wheezes. 'Aye, he's no there. I would huv noticed.'

'Ah, well, that's that.' Rab sounds relieved.

'Hing on,' the drunk man screws his face up to help him think. 'Blonde hair, did yeh say, like a poof?'

'Aye,' Chaz slaps him on the back.

'Aye, stupid bastard, never away fae that one-armed puggy. Probably put about a fiver in it! Some people huv mair money than the sense God gave them.' He coughs, holds his hand in salute, before staggering away. 'Mind tell yer da I was asking for him.'

Chaz watches him totter down the hill. Rab is first to speak. 'Whit dae yeh want tae dae noo? The place is louping wae folk.'

'Mon then, we'll go upstairs and huv a pint while we think about it.'

Rab turns around as someone spins out the door of the bar, but it's nobody they know. 'I jist want tae get it o'er and done wae.'

'I'll dae it myself then. If yer shitting yerself.'

'Nah it's no that.' Rab's voice rises, 'It's jist the place is mobbed and whit happens if somebody knows oor faces?'

'Well, if they know us, then they'll know no tae say anything then, won't they?'

They trek upstairs to the lounge. The lounge is fancy in the way the bar is spartan. McGregor tartan on the walls, plush seats of ersatz leather, small tables with clean ashtrays and a few padded stools and an arrangement of booths.

Chaz and Rab lift their pints from the bar and trail across an empty room to find a booth. From their eyrie by the window, they survey the comings and goings of the streets below.

Rab sparks a fag and nudges his cigarette packet towards Chaz, 'They'll probably think we're a pair of benders sitting here the gether.' He takes a mouthful of lager and nods towards the squat barmaid.

'Speak for yerself.' Chaz helps himself to a cigarette from his packet. He claws at his head and seems unsatisfied with the resultant dandruff storm. 'Here's whit I want yeh tae dae.' He points past an older couple sitting close together at the door. 'I want yeh tae go oot and kid on yer goin tae the toilet—'

Rab cuts in, 'I dae need a pish.' He honks with laughter.

'Alright,' Chaz rides the interruption. 'When yeh come oot, go tae the phone in the hall. And kid on yer speaking, but leave it hinging, as if someone is on the other end. Yeh got that?'

'Aye, but whit am I daeing that for?'

'Listen up.' Chaz's tone is sharp. 'After that I want yeh tae come in here and go tae the bar.' Dean Martin's slushy love song plays in the background. He leans closer. 'See that wee Munchkin,' he nods at the barmaid. 'I want yeh tae tell her somebody phoned for somebody called Podge, and they're pretty sure he's in this pub. And they need tae get in touch wae him because his ma has had a very bad accident. Very bad. I want yeh tae emphasise that. Yeh can say it's a heart attack.'

Rab takes a drink of his pint. 'Has she had an accident?'

'Nah, ya fucking idiot. But the barmaid doesnae know that. She'll shout oot for him. And when she doesnae get any answer, she'll phone the bar doonstairs... And Podge will come upstairs tae answer the phone.'

'Then we dae him?' Rab splutters into his pint.

Chaz shakes his head. 'Nah, then we don't dae him. After yeh've been tae the bar and told Munchkin heid about somebody being on the phone, I want yeh tae go outside and wait for me at the snooker club. If I chase Podge oot and he runs towards yeh, I want yeh tae chase him back towards me. Got it?'

'Aye. Can I finish my pint first?' He necks it in three gulps, rifts loudly, and knocks into a chair as he hurries towards the bar.

Chaz stares into the mirrored reflection of the window. Takes a deep breath before he turns to check that the Munchkin is on the phone. Flings back his pint, tugs and checks his zip before standing. His feet slow as he comes to the double doors. He looks through the glass shell of the lounge to the stairs and glances at the receiver bobbing on its cord.

Podge dashes up the steps and grabs for the phone. He mouths 'Hallo, Hallo,' into the receiver. When he spots Chaz watching him, Podge turns and leaps. His feet rattle the steps and he crashes out the door. Chaz follows, but he can't keep up with him.

Rab gets talking to a young thing outside. But then glimpses Podge's blonde hair way up the hill on Second Avenue. He gives chases but slows and wheezes as he trudges parallel with the waste ground sloping towards Singer's train station.

Del quicksteps from behind a beige Morris Marina with the boot open. He punches Podge, a short jab to his throat. Struggling for breath, carried in a bear hug, and flung into the boot, it closes with a clunk on Podge's head.

Del locks the boot, strides forward, and opens the driver-side door near the pavement. He swings his long legs in and cocks his head to listen as he starts the engine. Dougie sits in the front passenger seat and acts as lookout.

When Chaz gets closer, Dougie gets out of the car and holds open the back door for him. The dull thumps beneath Chaz's cushioned seat play out on his body. Del turns on the Morris's headlights.

Dougie cuts off Rab as he lumbers up the hill.

'No son,' Dougie stands in the bright lights like a bouncer on the door of Clatty Pat's nightclub. 'Just you go home.'

Rab twists his neck. He leans sideways as if to look behind him for Chaz, who'll vouch for him. He mumbles something.

With a glower and shake of Dougie's head, he's put in place. 'No son! Not tonight.'

Del fiddles with the radio and turns the volume way up. The babbling disc jockey fills the car interior with cheerful gobbledygook. By the time it morphs into a T.Rex, *Get it On*, Del has a lit fag held between his lips at a jaunty angle. Dougie makes a quip which Chaz can't quite make out. The car splashes through puddles, getting the green light, taking a left-hand turn and speeds up Kilbowie Road. The bumping from the boot lessens and grows feebler.

'Where do we go from here?' Dougie asks Chaz.

'No sure,' Chaz looks through the window at the La Scala cinema for inspiration. He thought the UDA boys would have somewhere they could take punters, but he didn't want them taking the huff.

'Yeh could go up the hills.' He leans his elbows on the headrest of the front seat as he gives them directions. 'Straight ahead,' as they pass Clydebank College and the Hub. 'Jist keep goin and when yeh get tae the roundabout, yeh go hauf way around it and take a left up the hill.'

A lime-green Jaguar cuts them off at the roundabout, tooting its horn and overtakes them. 'Fucking wanker,' Del spits out, but he keeps the car steady, within the speed limits, indicates, and takes the slip road.

It had been years since Chaz had been up the hills, swimming in the reservoirs. A bottle of Irn Bru and a packet of sweeties shared between his mates. Cochino Road is little more than a glazed track crunching under the tyres, the sound of traffic left behind.

Del slows and turns the headlights full beam, picking out trees, bushes and overgrown grass. When they could go no further, they park the Marina. Del turns the radio off with a quiver at the corner of his lips, and delayed silence.

Dougie gets out of the car, the others follow his lead. He limbers up, stretching the kinks out of his legs and arms. 'Time we were getting properly acquainted.'

His eyes rove around the car, Chaz standing opposite, Del shuffling behind him and the makings of a dry-stone wall in the distance.

The bumping coming from the boot makes Chaz jerk backwards, unsettling him, and his slack grip on the axe handle tightens. He's glad of dull cloud and no moonlight.

'Aye, well,' Del takes things in his stride. 'No surrender,' he quips and steps around Chaz. He springs the lock and a bouffant of hair shines in the darkness, and Podge's eyes glitter like a child's.

Del grunts as he picks him up by the collar and neck and lifts him out of the boot.

'I didnae dae anything.' Podge pleads with them before his feet touch the ground. His gaze fixes on Chaz. 'Tell them I didnae dae anything. It was yeh and Rab that did it. No me.'

The smash to his face knocks him off his feet. Del's knee to the groin has him writhing. He tries to cover his head and body and screams, 'Tell them Chaz, tell them, it wasnae me.'

His head ricochets as Dougie boots him flat and hard against cheek and jaw. And he splatters blood and front teeth.

Chaz comes from behind Del and the axe slices through the air and cleaves Podge's forehead and makes a sucking sound as he pulls it sideways out of his nose and eye socket.

'Tell 'im I didnae dae it, Chaz,' begs Podge.

Chaz swings the axe until he's sure he's struck dumb.

'That's enough, son,' Dougie slaps Chaz lightly on the shoulder. 'You're making hell of a mess of my clothes.' He extends the left arm of his pinstripe and shows him flecks of blood.

'Aye, sorry about that.' He wipes the blade of the axe on Podge's shirt and looks around for a place to toss it.

'No son,' Dougie shakes his head. 'Put it back in your pocket. You've done a good job here but wait till you get home and put it somewhere where nobody will ever find it.' He stares over his shoulder, listening, but it's only the wind in the trees. 'And get a gallon of petrol and burn your coat and everything you've got on.'

'But it's my good coat,' says Chaz. 'I've no got another wan.'

Del laughs. 'Fucking shut up.'

He rummages in his back pockets. Chaz is ready to run, sure it's a gun, but he pulls out his wallet and peels ten tenners from a wad of notes. 'A hundred quid.' He hands it to him. 'Treat yourself. Get yourself a fucking new wardrobe. But hang on a minute.'

His feet slip on mud and blood as he steps around the side of the car and pulls open the driver's door. He comes back flourishing a *Daily Record*. 'Drag the Papish bastard over there, behind a bush, but make it quick.' He motions a general direction with a nod of his head. 'When you come back, sit on this till we get you home, we don't want to get the seat dirty. Makes sense, don't it?'

'Aye,' Chaz holds the newspaper in his hand. 'Perfect sense.'

Chapter 33

Out of order

ANGELA NIPS ACROSS THE LANDING AND RATTLES THE letterbox. Dermot opens the door. He's wearing his work gear. 'Where yeh goin?' she asks.

He laughs, 'Jist oot tae see a man about a dog.'

'Whit kinda dog?'

'A dog wae blonde hair and big floppy ears like yeh.'

'Up,' she commands.

Dermot scoops her up and holds her tight in his arms. She glances over his head at Evan standing in the lobby.

With scratchy, unshaved, chin and mouth, he blows a farting raspberry on the soft skin of her face and plonks her feet safely inside the lobby.

Sour faced, she follows Evan through to the living room. 'This place is minging.'

'That's him!' Evan picks up the poker and digs into clunkers. 'He said it's his stomach, but I cannae smell anything anymair.'

'How come yeh've no got the telly on?'

'No working.' Evan lets the poker fall with a clatter and a puff on ash on the ceramic tiles.

'But we'll miss *Champion the Wonder Horse*.'

'Well, there's nothing we can dae about that.' Evan mimics his da's dour delivery, but jinks in front of her, plugging the telly into the socket and presses the button.

'It's working,' she shouts, pointing. 'There's the dot.'

'Aye, but yeh cannae get any channels.' He twiddles the knob, hoping a humming sound can pick up stations. Pictures appear and disappear into the ether like a ghostly imprint. He bangs the dust on top of the cabinet. He repeats with parental authority, what his dad said, 'It's probably the valve.'

'Let me dae it.' Angela takes her turn, bashing the top of the telly with the palm of her hand, while instructing Evan to whir through the channels. 'Nah, that's rubbish, it doesnae work,' she loses interest.

Evan pulls the plug. 'Yeh need tae turn it off at the wall or yeh could start a fire. We could go doon for Pizza Face?'

Her face lights into a smile. 'Look, I've got fifty pence.' She holds out the coin in the palm of her right hand.

'Where d' yeh get that?'

'Pocket money.'

'I didnae know yeh got pocket money.'

'Neither did I.' Her fingers close over the coin and she shoves it back in her anorak pocket, with a smirk on her face, satisfied that he believes her. 'We could get sweets and ginger.'

Evan darts away from her. 'Wait till I get my jacket,'

The bell dings in Maise's shop. They stand at the back of the queue of one person. Evan snatches a *Dandy* and *Beano* from the wall rack, Maisie's eyes gleaning the movement and tabbing up the transaction.

When the old woman finally leaves, Maisie is a step ahead, whipping out the half-penny and penny tray from beneath the counter for them to feast their eyes on.

Evan plonks his comics on the counter and picks at the tray, Sherbet dabs, flying saucers, Highland Toffee, MB bar and a giant gobstopper.

Maisie bobs her head to get a better look. 'Whit does your wee sister want?'

'I'm no his wee sister.' Angela points at the jars of Kola Kubes. 'I want them and them.' She points at Soor Plooms. 'And them and them.' She's not sure what they're called, but Maisie knows.

'Does your wee sister want quarter bags?' Maisie reaches and lifts the nearest jar, opens the lid and tipping the glass. Sweets cascade into the scales. She lifts one, and then another Kola Kube, checks the weight, and puts them back in the jar.

'Are you sure your wee sister has got enough money?' She gives Evan a sly look before she nestles the paper bag beside sweets and comics. His purchases spread out, taking counter space, and balance unevenly on newspapers and the headlines of the day.

Angela hands Evan the fifty pence and he sticks it flat on the counter. She whispers a list to Evan, suddenly shy. 'And I want a Whopper and Toffos and a Fry's Cream and a Caramac and a Jubilee and a packet of chewing gum and a bottle of limeade.' She reconsiders. 'And a Jubilee and Blackjacks.'

The thought mortifies Evan. 'We maybe no huv enough money.'

'That's all right, dear.' Maisie has been weighing and measuring and counting ahead.

Angela slips the pennies into her anorak pocket and crams in bags of sweeties. Evan carries the ginger bottle and the comics. They take their haul back upstairs to his house to picnic on.

When it gets dark outside and their jaws hurt from chewing, they sit sleepy eyed, twinned together, in the chair beside the unlit fire. Evan flicks through the pages of the comics, but they've already read them twice, until Desperate Dan and cowpie with horns sticking out of the pastry grow humourless.

He untangles his legs from hers. 'I need tae go tae the lavvy. I'm bursting.'

Angela bounces out of the chair. 'I need tae go tae.'

'Well, yeh'll need tae wait.'

'No, I'll go wae yeh!' She grabs his shirt sleeve, letting go when his expression darkens.

'Boys and wee girls cannae go tae the toilet together,' he explains.

'How no?'

'They jist cannae. Yeh can go doon first and I'll wait here.'

'Nah,' she shakes her head. 'I don't want tae.'

'How no?'

'Because of the monsters.'

'Monsters?'

'Aye, in case the monsters get me. Yeh can check the toilet and wait outside when I'm in?'

'Aye,' he replies dismissively. 'I'll dae that, but yeh'll need tae hurry up. I cannae wait.'

Evan darts into the kitchen and comes out armed with a shiny toilet roll. They run downstairs, her hand gripped in his. He pushes open the door and leans in. The toilet bowl is clean, and the place smells of bleach.

His lips smack together as he pronounces, 'Aw clear.'

'Yeh'll wait here?' she asks.

'Aye.'

'Yeh won't go away and leave me?'

'Nah,' he says. 'For god's sake, hurry up.'

Barging against her shoulder, even before she gets out, he tugs at his zip.

He smiles when he comes out, but chews on his bottom lip. 'That was close.'

Chaz, stinking of booze, stumbles backward against the wall. He wears a shiny black leather coat, cinched tight at the waist, and his hand rests on her shoulder. 'Bridget the fucking Midget,' he cackles. 'Get up them stairs and into yer bed. Whit did I tell yeh about playing wae that wee Mickey bastard?'

'And yeh,' Chaz, holding a finger up, pointing it like a gun at Evan, and sniggers. 'You,' he shakes his head, mocks him, but lets nobody else in on his joke.

He slaps the side of Angela's head. 'Move.' He dunts her shoulder, her feet buckle on the final step of the landing.

Evan backs away and shuts the door of the toilet, puts the latch on. He peeks through a gap in the slats until he's sure the monster is away.

Chapter 34

Let your hair down

With no telly to watch, the room feels colder. Evan pulls his jammies over his clothes, and dives under the covers. He sleeps clutching his book of Grimms' fairy tales and wakes, shivering, with a crick on his neck. In his dream, Rapunzel's ethereal singing voice summons him to the dark tower. When he shouts up for her to lower her hair, Angela with her head shaven, screams, 'Run!' Blood and water flood from her mouth.

His feet slow and die in the lobby. The fragrance of ham, the spit of sausages and eggs a shapeshifting religion and memorial to the weekend fry-up. The living-room fire untended. Da's bed empty. A moan escapes from his mouth. All the way to his toes, he knows something has happened, like the slow and silent burn when his mum had died.

Waiting dissolves him. He flits between standing at the window, lying in his bed and bracing himself against the front door. Hunger clocks in with regularity and he gulps water from the tap. His ears become attuned to the flow of traffic. He develops antennae for doors opening and closing in the close, telly and tran-

144

sistor radio noises travelling through the walls from other houses and other lives. The beat of hurried feet on stairs and landing.

His heart races in his chest, sure his da is tromping with his heavy tread up the stairs, but the feet stall at the landing below. He hears the milkman asking for money, and in the gap where loose change falls, Evan listens to his own breathing.

Chapter 35

Power of the stone

On Monday morning, Evan sleeps in. The tenement buzzing with noise and he glances at the clock on the mantelpiece. He works out he's got fifteen minutes to dress, and get to school, or he'll be late and get the belt. He dashes to his room and gets dressed and does everything in regular order before leaving. No cornflakes and no milk and no money for snacks. He puts a tea bag in a cup and fills it with sugar and runs the cold tap and gulps the mix.

High flats throw shadows over him, but his feet ring out on the metallic slope of the dark tunnel, walls run slimy and tendril green with groundwater that stinks of pee. He grows immune to the gloom by shouting 'Daaaaaaaaaaaaaaaad', marvelling at the fusillade.

He bursts out of the darkness into daylight and green grass, ordered park benches and the scent of damp earth. A tall man hurries past him as Evan takes a breather. A short leash of path leads to the Edwardian drinking fountain, a cupola, wrought-iron and painted green, with a white bird with outstretched wings on the top, a monument to the industrial wealth and municipal parks.

Slate-grey step an aid to help small children reach the silver taps. Evan gulps a mouthful of refreshing cold water for luck.

Nearby, a less visible monument. A granite rock by the stream, dedicated to an eighteen-year-old man, Robert Currie, who had tried to save a wee boy from getting hit by a train.

Evan used to pass it with his da when they fed the ducks. 'It's a magic stone,' his da said, 'Cause it's no often in this life somebody does something for somebody else, expects nothing, and dies because he has tae.' And he used to hold his waist and let him rub the tub of the stone.

When his mum died, he was too young to believe in the stone's power. But he hurries towards the memorial and holds his hand on top of the stone. His eyes shut and heaving shoulders, 'Please God!'

Chapter 36

Monday Blues

'Yer drookit,' Pizza Face says, sniggering.

'What time do you call this?' Mrs Thompson's tone arrives at neutral. The quieter pupils in the back desks join in the laughter.

'Dunno,' Evan stares at her, as if she's not there, or he doesn't care.

A few titters from his classmates, which Mrs Thompson silences with a look. 'Well, perhaps I'll need to help you remember.'

She places the chalk in a dusty groove, lodging it beside a stub of broken blue and a dab of pink. Her hands slap together, white dust motes hang in the air. A nervous excitement charges the class when she pulls out her belt from the drawer.

Mrs Thompson steps in front of the blackboard and stands taller and broader by flinging her shoulders back. 'Put your hands up,' she orders Evan.

Drilled in the procedure, elbows in, arms straight out, Evan rests one hand on top of the other. The meat of the hand showing and fingers extended. Whether to tuck the thumb in with the other fingers, or cock it out, and risk it taking the full brunt of the leather strap when Mrs Thompson misjudges the distance is a hard choice. No vote needed in the playground. The belt is much sorer when hands are perishing and cold as his.

Two hard cracks of the belt, both hands stinging. He shoves them under his oxters to settle. He drags his feet over to his desk. Pizza Face glances sideways, his face sympathetic, but waiting to see if his pal bursts out greeting.

Mrs Thompson resumes the lesson. Long-division on the blackboard, chalk workings in a stepwise fashion with 12 on the first step and 1456 sheltering under the box. She holds out a piece of white chalk for him to take. 'Perhaps you would be kind enough to assist us, Evan?'

Evan slips from his seat and stands in front of the blackboard, chalk in hand, fragile and pale, staring at his feet.

'Well?' Mrs Thompson waits. Her bulky presence eats into his confidence, until he lifts his eyes to the blackboard, then to her face and his shoulders sag. 'What is the first thing we do, when we have long division?'

She notices an arm waving in the air. Pizza Face bursting to be noticed.

'Miss, Miss, I know yer answer,' he says. 'Don't I?'

'Better if you learned a little manners. And knew how to wait your turn.'

Pizza Face's eyes narrow. He glances at the pencil marking on his jotter, '121.333,' he says softly and then emphatically. '121.333. That's yer answer.' He grins at Mrs Thompson. His hands clasped behind his neck, making wings of his arms.

Mrs Thompson takes the chalk from Evan's hand. On the blackboard, she runs through routine steps and the answer 121.333 appears on the top line.

Murmuring comes from the back of the class, which she turns to address as the school bell rings for morning playtime.

Desk drawers open and bang shut as workbooks and a blur of blue jotters, pencils and rubbers disappear. Mrs Thompson arrests time. She points an accusatory finger at Pizza Face, 'You boy, out here,' and turns towards Evan. 'And you boy, as well, stick your hands out for not doing as you're told.'

Her eyes swivel around the class. The noise of kids playing outside rises, but she reaches for the drawer and the belt. 'If anybody else wants to join them?'

She pauses, gauging the quality of silence. Pizza Face stands beside Evan, his hands steady. He grins at his pal, and sniggers, giving him courage.

Outside in the playground, with coats and hoods up, Pizza Face playfully punches Evan's shoulder. Older lads congregate nearby to cadge a fly cigarette, pushing and shoving each other towards the reek of toilet stalls. They take turns spying out for the janitor.

'She's fucking shite at the belt,' Pizza Face laughs. 'I could take about six aff her and I wouldnae even blink.'

Evan follows behind him. 'Aye.'

'Where yeh goin?' shouts Pizza Face.

Evan doesn't hear him. He weaves past infants splashing in and out of a puddle and runs towards the school gates. Maybe my da will be home now, he thinks, waiting for me, because I've not done anything wrong. I've been a good boy. He'll be wondering where I am. It always seems to him quicker coming home.

When he charges up the stairs, he glances through the landing window into the back courts. Angela beats a broken branch against the bin lids, her back to him with her hood up. He taps the window, but she can't hear him.

Evan tethers himself to familiar things. He slumps into the chair his da usually sits in, watching the dusty blank screen. When the door chaps, the spell curdling his limbs comes unstuck. But hurrying up the lobby, he already knows it's not his da.

Angela's hair rises into a tuggy stack. 'Whit took yeh so long?'

She brushes past him, stomps into the house and brings it to life. She stops at his room door, peering in at the crumpled blankets. She spins on her heels, studying his face. 'Yeh've been greeting,' she whimpers, her mouth falling open.

Her head whips around. She pushes closer to Evan, clutching his legs. 'Where's da?' Flummoxed, she changes meaning in a whistle of breath to, 'Dermot?'

'Dunno.' Evan sniffs and swallows. Sobs fill his mouth and he can't breathe for greeting. He crumples, sliding down the wall, and sitting on the buckled linoleum. His tears dampen the blue polyester of his school shirt.

'There, there.' Angela plays adult, pats his shoulder, a hitch in her voice and she cries too.

He slaps his arms around her. She leans in and lends childish warmth and cuddles. 'Don't be sad, he'll come back.' Soft splutter of sibilants cling onto the nape of his neck where she presses her face and nose. 'Unless the monsters get him.'

Evan doesn't hear the last part. His head is too busy to listen. 'Is there something wrang wae me?' he chokes up. 'Naebody wants tae be wae me.'

The crowing of Kerry-Ann's cry comes through the walls. 'Angela? Angela? Angela! Where ur yeh? Yeh, better get up here noo, or I'll skelp yer arse bad.'

Angela pulls away from Evan, her cheeks scarlet with heat and her eyes flicker towards the door. 'I better go, or Chaz'll kill me.'

Chapter 37

Ne-no-ne-no-ne-no

EVAN'S FIRST STOP IS MAC'S, HIS DA'S LOCAL. A MAN wearing a denim jacket swaggers out of the pub. The hubbub and the taste of fag smoke, a wavering flag left behind him. Punter's heads turn and gawp at Evan with bemused, glass-eyed expressions when he wedges the door open and scans the room.

'Hi!' the bar woman shouts, good-naturedly, but he runs away.

Evan crosses the road at the traffic lights, heading into the unfamiliar territory of the white houses. He skirts well-lit streets, creeping along fences and bushes and crosses the bridge over the canal. Rancid canal water, whipped by wind and rain, ghosts out to meet him. Everything becomes clearer as he runs in the darkness along the embankment; if he keeps looking, his da will be waiting for him, just around the next bend.

A barking dog rushes towards him, its eyes the only brightness in the night, and he sees Blodger.

A woman wearing a raincoat and plastic hood appears out of the dimness ahead. 'Tito,' she shouts. 'Tito.' The dog slinks back to her side in a way Blodger never would. They stand upon overgrown

153

weeds, abdicating much of the path for him to pass, as if he's liable to bite. Their shivering silence pushes him on.

His duffle coat grows heavy with rain. He continues walking. His heels rub red raw in his wellies. The tenements across from the canal remain a familiar landmark and the main road soon comes into view. Instead of turning back towards home, blinkered, he turns right. He has to keep looking, and close the distance between the next bin, the next lamppost, and set of traffic lights.

Nattering customers outside Connelly's give him the once over. Last orders and going home, but it's not until he leaves behind the entrance to the Yoker Ferry and the chippy and quieter patches of pavement that anyone speaks to him.

'Where yeh goin, wee man?' The voice, a rasp from a black beard. A man steps out of a close and into his path. Head swivelling, the man's eyes jump like brown bugs latching onto his face and body.

'Hame. My da's waiting on me.'

'Where's hame?'

Evan hears the swishing sound of the man's raincoat. A broad stubby hand falls on his shoulder, inside of his thumb, index and middle fingers brown and yellow with nicotine.

'Hing on a minute wee man and I'll take yeh.'

Evan jerks away from his touch. He sprints with his head down. The man's feet clattering to catch up.

'Ya wee bastard,' the man shouts as he's left behind.

Evan glimpses a blue and white Panda car travelling in the other direction, towards home, towards Clydebank and Dalmur. A few minutes later, the police car swerves into the pavement ahead of Evan. The passenger-side door opens. A policeman pulls on his hat as he steps out into the rain. He presents a blue-uniformed barrier in front of Evan.

'Where do you think you're going, this fine evening?' the policeman asks.

Evan shakes his head inside his duffel coat hood. 'Naewhere,' he mumbles. 'I've no done anything.'

The policeman has a big nose and red cheeks and looks cheerful, as if everything he sees wants to make him laugh. He crouches, and large brown eyes study Evan's face. 'I'm no saying you have son. But it's such a horrible night. You'd be daeing me a big favour if you got into the car with us and we gave you a lift.'

Evan nods in agreement and starts greeting. The policeman slides his seat forward. It's warm, a cigarette in the ashtray, and the police walkie-talkie on the dashboard crackles into life. He checks out the back window at the sweep of tenement buildings they pass with a sense of unease, because they are going in the wrong direction, away from Clydebank. He sinks into the padded chair and his eyes close.

'C'mon son.' The engine left running. The heater keeps the car toasty warm, but a draught comes from the open door. 'We're here.' The policeman with the nice brown eyes reaches in and scoops Evan's sleeping body from the seat and lifts him out of the car and onto the pavement in front of Partick Police Station.

Evan whiffs stale aftershave, which reminds him of his da, and the contact makes him feel safe. But he shrinks against his leg as they push through flapping doors into the building. A phone rings on the bar of the front desk. A policeman with a grey side-shed haircut over his pale forehead picks up the receiver.

A hand on Evan's shoulder guides him along corridors. Light bulbs in high roofs illuminate piss-coloured panelled walls, which divide the passages into closed doors.

They come to a kitchen area with a scatter of Formica tables, ashtrays overflowing and tubular grey polyurethane chairs on a tiled floor. Crisp bags and cigarette cartons spill from an over-flowing metal bin situated underneath a sealed window. The radiator on the wall keeps the room stifling.

An officer with ginger hair, his tie askew and the top button of his shirt undone holds court. He sits on the edge of the sink and shares an ashtray with two younger policemen, one with a pimply forehead, the other a crew cut that leaves a bluish stubble like a tattoo on his head.

'I said tae the stupid-looking cunt, "Yeh cannae pish there".' The ginger haired officer glances at Evan but continues with his story.

The punchline follows in a ragged, mocking tone and laughter. Evan's cheeks pink and burn because it's adult and dirty.

The ginger haired cop nods at Evan. 'Scott, whit's the boy's name, anyway?'

'Eh, dunno, he's no said yet. Didn't want to hurry him.' Scott steps into the gap between the fridge, cupboards and the sink. He fills the kettle and plugs it in.

'Fucking hell.' The ginger haired cop struts, pigeon chested. 'A few of the high, heid yins willnae be happy wae that. You've had him in here...' and he winks at his companions, 'all of ten minutes and you've no even got him on a charge sheet and you're offering tea and biscuits! That's an official reprimand in anybody's book.'

Scott rinses matching brown-ringed mugs and pours them tea from an urn. He looks at Evan, keeps it casual 'Whit's your name son, anyway?'

'Evan.'

'You got a second name?'

He answers with adult seriousness. 'Connelly.'

'And what age are you, son?'

'Ten.'

'So what are you here for?'

Evan considers, before answering. 'I was looking for my da. He's no been hame.' His shoulders jerk and he starts crying.

'How long, son?' the ginger haired cops ask.

'Four days and nights.'

'And where do you stay?'

'726 Dumbarton Road.'

Scott's shoulders stoop to keep tea from spilling as he carries their mugs. He guides Evan towards a table at the back, sheltering him from the braying voices of his colleagues speculating about a match with a body they've found.

Scott's knees poke under the table. He blows on his tea, sitting sideways to Evan. 'Sorry, there's no milk.' He pushes the sugar bowl from the centre of the table towards him. A mottled spoon stands upright in the bowl. He takes a deep breath and searches his pockets and lights a Woodbine. Evan sips at the strong tea. 'Don't listen to them.' He takes another drag on his cigarette. 'You're too young to be here on your ain, so we need to get your

157

mum to come and pick you up. Don't suppose you're on the phone?'

'Nah. And my mum's deid.'

'Jesus,' Scott flinches, temporarily beaten. 'What about an auntie or uncle?'

'I dunno where they stay.'

He rests the tip of his Woodbine in the ashtray, acrid smoke between them. 'Well, we'll need to get a social worker here.' He peers across at him. 'You know whit a social worker is?'

'Aye,' a note of defiance in his voice. 'We had wan before.'

Scott watches his colleagues meander away. He leans back in his chair, stretching, makes a sign to the ginger haired cop, gesturing at the ceiling panels and mimics holding a phone to his ear. 'This social worker, don't suppose you remember her name?'

'Marie. That was her name. She was nice.'

'Don't suppose you remember her second name?'

Evan sips at his tea and shoves the mug aside. 'Nah, she didnae huv a second name.'

'Fine. You did good. You did really good. Let's hope we can get Marie here to take care of you.'

Evan squints sideways. 'Whit happens if she cannae, can I come home wae you, or yeh gonnae lock me up in the cells?'

Scott laughs. 'Aye, you could come home with me. I'm sure my wife would love you, but I don't think that's allowed.' He rustles the back of Evan's hair. 'And the only people we put in the cells downstairs are stupid, ignorant people. And you certainly aren't that. You're a very brave wee boy.'

Chapter 38

Risk Street

EVAN SHUTS OUT A PARADE OF UNIFORMS. HE FLAKES OUT IN the back seat of Marie's car, aware of her comforting perfumed presence. The social worker's car splutters into life.

Streetlights and rain freewheel by, but Evan prefers washed and wide streets to porridge-coloured walls.

The Children's Home at Risk Street isn't far from Evan's school. Snobby houses with glass battlements for windows, looking on to the road, protected by high walls, prickly hedges and barking dogs. Gardens where they'd raided apples. Often they were sour, good for only one bite, then flung at your pal's heads. Pizza Face had tripped and skinned his knee. The guy in one of the fancy houses had caught him and dragged him inside. With Pizza Face, it was always a big story, and it ended with the guy washing his knee with a cloth and giving him a shilling and telling him to come and visit anytime. Fat chance.

The house at the top of the street is familiar to Evan. A place where you go when there is nowhere else to go. Now he's been caught. And he promises God he'll be good.

Marie edges the cars through the gates and turns off the engine. It's quiet. Trees creak in the wind. The curlicues and bevels of Victorian architecture adorned by the functional aluminium fire-escapes draped over the back of the house. Their feet crunch on red stone chips which grow thin towards the solid, dark-colour doors. Marie presses the bell on the wall, a monument to history. It buzzes like a child practicing the kazoo.

A large woman opens the door. 'You shouldn't have rung the bell. You'll wake everybody up that way.'

'But how else would we get in?' Marie asks.

'You phone ahead,' says the large woman.

She flashes a quick welcoming smile. They follow her through the outer double doors and a glass-panelled inside door, noise muted by draught excluders.

Chapter 39

The Linen Bank

At 11.45 in the morning, three masked men burst through the door of the Linen Bank on Dumbarton Road. They wear stocking masks over their faces.

'This is a stick-up,' Dougie shouts. The bank shuts at lunch for twelve on Friday, a busy day with customers paying money in and taking money out. It's only later they remember his Irish accent marking him out as foreign because everything happens so quickly. The men carry pistols.

Chaz's gun is a nine millimetre. He loves the heft in his hand. It makes him feel taller. But the matching black costumes and boots they wear already add the appearance of height.

Not that Del needs any help. He vaults the counter. Cashiers cower away from him as if a public monument has dropped from the strip lights. He's quickly followed by Dougie.

Chaz keeps his back to the door and shoots two shots into the ceiling. Plaster falls to the floor but the noise leaves a ringing sound in his ears. 'Face the wall and stay where yeh ur,' he bawls at the customers. 'Or yeh'll get this!'

He glares through the slit in his mask and pushes a middle-aged man in a blue boilersuit, spotted with oil, hard against the wall, and dares him to look at him. A woman with a walking stick and watery eyes takes the longest to comply. The rest of them jump to it.

They've already cut the phone and alarm wires at the rear of the building. Child's play. They also cut the phone wires attached to the chemist shop next door. He owns them.

His comrades quickly fill hessian sacks. Dougie marches the manager to the door, a gun barrel against his bald head. A set of keys dangles limp in the bank employee's hand.

Chaz holds the door open. Del races out to the car, pulls the mask off before he hits the pavement outside and Chaz follows behind. He hears Dougie hissing, 'Which key?' to the manager. 'Don't make me rearrange your brains.'

Del sits in the Triumph, his elbow carelessly perched on the driver-side window. Chaz kicks hessian sacks under the back seat out of sight. *Chirpy Chirpy Cheep Cheep* comes on the radio and Del checks in the rear-view mirror and chortles.

Dougie takes about thirty seconds to lock the bank's doors. He hands Del the keys as the car takes off from the pavement. As they speed along Dumbarton Road, the car skids and makes a quick left and right into Trafalgar Street. Del holds the set of bank keys out of the window and lets them drop.

A woman pushing a pram watches them bounce to the side of the road. Del keeps his speed under thirty and they take the hill on Clark Street like a scrawny kid pushing a bogey. Dougie sparks a fag. By the time Middle of the Road on the radio has finished Chirpy, Chirpy, Cheeping the car is parked on the brow of the Dalmuir Municipal Golf Course. A steep grass embankment on Glenhead Road, shelters them from casual onlookers.

Not even the murder of two men compares to the buzz of the robbery for Chaz. They fling open the doors and get out of the car. Del checks nobody can see them from the road above before he opens the boot.

Chaz wriggles out of his trousers on the back seat, pulls on his denims and a pair of Adidas sannies. He lifts two sacks of money and drops them at his feet. Dougie picks up the other bags and piles them on top. He pulls the black jumper over his head and flings it in the back seat.

Del remains in his black uniform. While they've been getting changed, he's tipped the money into a golf trolley and strapped the guns into the pouch at the front. A driver, a few irons and putter stuck inside for decoration. Gallon petrol canisters are lined up at his feet.

'Here, in case you get cold.' Del flings Chaz an orange cagoule from the boot and a blue-and-white Rangers scarf.

Dougie, wearing a denim shirt and trousers, snatches the car keys of a rust-bucket Mini parked beside them from Del's jacket pocket. His eyes narrow, and before he starts the engine, he gives Chaz a friendly warning. 'Don't even think about playing the fly guy and stealing any of that there money. And don't think we'll not know, because we'll know. You'll get your cut. You'll get your wages. It's for the cause. Let that be enough.'

Chaz doesn't flinch and meets his gaze. 'I wouldnae dae that.'

'Good man. We'll see you the night then.'

Chaz pulls the cagoule hood and ties the drawstring tight under his chin. He doesn't want any of his mates to see him wheeling a trolley and thinking he's one of those old buddies that play golf. He putters along the steep shale path, the slope screened from the greens and grass of the golf course by twelve-foot briar hedging.

A wee boy, near the start of the course, leans over the bridge, grogging into the fast-flowing stream from the Old Kilpatrick Hills. He spins round, open-mouthed, squinting past Chaz's head and up the hill when they hear the muffled explosion.

'Yeh want tae buy any golf balls, mister?'

'Nah,' Chaz ignores the wee boy and keeps walking.

A tartan bunnet, measuring his putt on the first green, pauses, and stands gawping at the black smoke. 'Wonder whit that is?' he cries to his golf companion.

A fuzzy head poking out of the bunker quips, 'Somebody burning their golf clubs, no doubt.'

Chaz wheels his trolley into the park, towards the monument of Robert Currie. He stops at the fountain and drinks a mouthful of cool fresh water, listens to the distant sound of police sirens. He plunges his arm into the trolley and fingers the notes and starts laughing.

In the distance, a woman climbs the hill towards the swings. A wee boy with a white woolly hat on his head reaches up and clasps her hand. They look happy, Chaz thinks, and now I've got money, I could be happy too. I'll maybe even take Kerry-Ann to Blackpool.

He unzips the front of the golf bag and pulls out a pistol. He sticks the .22 Star in his cagoule pocket. The weight feels right and gives him extra swagger as he comes out of the tunnel underneath the railtrack.

Chaz nips into the toilet on the second landing. A thud reverberates through the flats and he splatters his sannies with pish, missing the toilet bowl. He hauls the door open, and the pistol falls from his pocket.

The golf trolley remains where he left it on the landing, and his breathing returns to normal. He tilts and rolls it inside, picks up the gun and snibs the door. Perched on the toilet seat, he reaches back and pulls the cagoule over his head, bunches it and flips it sideways, unravelling as it lies beside the stained ceramic bowl. The gun fits snuggly back in the pouch on the bag. His cock gets hard and he pops the button on his denims and sits wanking, but it quickly goes soft in his hand.

He bumps the trolley through the lobby and into the living room.

'When did yeh take up golf?' Kerry-Ann looks at him with a blank gaze. She gets up from the couch to meet him. He can see she's making an effort, pinning her hair, putting on a skirt and blouse, not drifting through the day in her pyjamas or torn nightgown, but a wisp of hair escapes across her forehead.

Angela sits cross-legged in front of the bubble of light from the new Radio Rentals telly.

Chaz giggles, plays the fool. 'Oh, I've been playing for quite a while m'dear.' He whips a driver out of the bag and holds it horizontal over the couch. Shutting his left eye and looking down the length of it like a rifle.

The club snags a five-pound note, and it flutters onto scuffed linoleum. Angela rolls over and makes a grab for it, her eyes sparkling and mouth open. 'Where did that come fae?' she screams. 'Was it magic?'

'Aye, fucking magic.' Chaz rocks on his heels and laughs. The club drops from his clutch and bounces off a cushion, falling with a clatter. 'And there's fucking plenty mair magic where that came frae.'

'Here!' Angela holds the note for him to take. She doesn't like the way he stares at her.

'Nah, yeh keep it, hen.' Chaz changes his mind, grabs it out of her hand, balls it up, and flings it toward Kerry-Ann to catch.

Kerry-Ann is as astonished as Angela. She looks at the note in her hand and hiccups a laugh through her nose. 'Where did yeh get it?'

'Och, never yeh mind.' Chaz waves her towards the door. 'There's plenty mair where that came fae. Jist yeh go doon tae the shops and get a bottle of whisky and a couple of cans of Pale Ale.' He pulls the trolley towards him and pulls out the golf clubs, tossing them onto the couch. He delves inside the bag and pulls out a handful of notes. 'And go tae the chippy and get us something tae eat.' He picks a tenner from the hive of money. 'Nane of yer usual shite. We want the best fish.'

'But Chaz... I'm no sure the chippy is open.'

'Go on.' Chaz has stopped listening to her. 'Dae as I telt yeh.'

'I'll jist get my coat.'

Angela sits watching the Clangers. The Clangers whistle, don't talk, and live on a moon made of green cheese. The front door bangs shut. She watches him stuffing notes into the lining of the side of the couch. Peering into the trolley, he jiggles it up and down, weighing its worth with his right hand. He sweeps the clubs together and stuffs them back into the bag. Satisfied, he takes a few steps back and peers at the cushions for any evidence of his handiwork.

Angela smells him when he tugs down his zip. She knows what cheese tastes like. It makes her boak. She wishes she could live on the moon with the Clangers.

'Tell anybody and I'll slit yer throat,' Chaz growls.

She shakes her head. The Clangers are going home, clanking shut their lids to go to sleep.

'C'mere.'

'No-oooh,' she whines. 'I don't want tae.'

'Yeh want me tae hurt yeh, bad? Yeh want me tae hurt yer mum? C'mere, I said.'

'No-oooh!'

The Clangers whistle a final goodnight.

When Kerry-Ann comes breezing through the door, her cheeks are crimson and her hands strain with too many bags and she smells of salt and vinegar. She stands in happy disarray on the threshold of the living room, her twinkling eyes taking seconds to adjust.

Chaz lets out a beastly groan. The clatter of bags alerts him to Kerry-Ann's presence.

'Ya, dirty fucking cunt,' Kerry-Ann screams. She goes for him, her hands curved, nails raised to rake across his face. 'Yeh cannae get it up a grown woman.'

He steps back from Angela, sweat on his forehead, his small cock rigid, panting heavily. He lunges and smacks Kerry-Ann across the cheek.

And all the fight goes out of her, but she screams, 'Yer nothing but a fucking pervert.'

He punches her, bloods her nose. 'If yeh werenae such a fucking slut, I wouldnae be reduced tae this.'

He hauls up and buttons his denims to hide his flaccid cock. Rearranges the flap of his shirt. Angela lies curled in a ball.

'Get me a fucking drink, and something tae eat.'

Kerry-Ann backs away from him, falling over the bags, clutching at her nose.

'Look whit yeh done noo,' says Chaz. 'Ya stupid cunt. Yeh could huv broke something.'

Kerry-Ann looks at him, sobbing, and her hands a streaky mess of red. 'Yeh want water in yer whisky?'

'Aye,' he says. 'But jist a wee drop. We don't want tae kill the taste.'

Chapter 40

Tomorrow's World

CHAZ SPRAWLS ON THE COUCH, A SILK CUT IN HIS HAND. HE sparks a can of Pale Ale, leaving it at his feet. Angela, cross-legged in front of the light of the telly, immerses herself in *Tomorrow's World*. A tiny horizontal scab remains on the bridge of Kerry-Ann's nose, and a half-moon under her right eye is purplish. She tries to tempt Angela with a few cold chips, but her daughter leans sideways and turns her head away.

'Jist fucking leave her,' Chaz barks at Kerry-Ann. 'If she wants tae go in a huff for nae reason, that's up tae her. She's jist spoilt rotten. That's whit's wrang wae her.' He lets fag ash topple on to the floor. 'Better get an ashtray,' he tells Kerry-Ann. 'This place is a fucking dump, cause of yeh.'

Kerry-Ann picks at a bit of fish coated in crispy orange batter before giving up. She knocks douts and sludge from the ashtray on the kitchen windowsill into congealed chips, which ooze vinegar and scrunches the contents into a newspaper parcel, abandoned under the sink. Standing with an empty ashtray in her hand, she hears the door being chapped.

'I'll get that,' Chaz cries. He scrambles from his seat. His drink sloshes onto the edge of the couch. The beer smell hangs in the air.

Kerry-Ann holds out the ashtray and, in passing, he stubs his fag out, and brushes his hair off his forehead with the flat of his hand.

On the telly, presenter James Burke witters on about a pocket calculator that meant maths exams in the future will be a dummie's charter.

Chaz quick steps back into the living room. Dougie and Del trail behind him. Their visitors stand corralled between couch and telly.

'Yeh want a drink?' Chaz sweeps a hand through his hair.

Dougie glances at the whisky bottle and Angela in front of the telly. 'No, we're just here to pick up that package.' He looks Chaz in the eye and grins. 'What a lovely wee girl you've got. Watching something educational and so well behaved. If it was mine, they'd be up pestering you like a shot, wanting to know everything about you.'

Del smiles for a different reason. He's checking out Kerry-Ann's short black skirt, tan tights and tight white blouse. The top two buttons undone. The outline of her bra is a reddish colour, and he's almost on tiptoes trying to check out the lace edgings. He notes the bruising around her eye. The way she moves to the side and smiles back at him makes him think she's enjoying the attention.

Del eyes the whisky bottle. 'I'll take a drink.' Everybody laughs, apart from Angela.

Kerry-Ann sashays through to the kitchen to wash a few mugs.

Del says softly to Chaz, 'You've not done anything stupid and been at that money?'

'No,' Chaz shakes his head and shrugs, 'Well, aye.'

Del is no longer watching Kerry-Ann's arse, waiting to see if her skirt rides up her leg. He's weighing up Chaz, waiting for an explanation.

Chaz chuckles, 'The wee yin.' He points at Angela. 'Seen me wae the bag and the golf clubs. And of course she's no content until she gets a shot. I went through tae the kitchen tae get a cuppa tea and when I came back through, she's hacking away wae a putter. And she's got a tenner in her haun. And I asked her "where did yeh get that?" She said it was in the bag. And I told her that was impossible—that it must have been Santa.'

He knows he's got them now and whispers to Dougie, 'Jist take the tenner oot of my cut. I don't want her thinking Santa doesnae exist.'

'Don't worry about it.' Dougie pushes him playfully on the side. 'Where's the bag?'

Chaz drags it into view. 'It's behind the couch.'

Theme music from *Tomorrow's World* blares and Angela spins on her hunkers to face them. 'Yeh talk funny,' she tells Dougie.

'That's right,' Dougie says. 'I'm not from here, I'm from a different country, but I'll tell you this, if I'd a wee girl like you I'd be very proud. Very proud. Your da must love you very much.'

'Aye,' Chaz bites his lip, presenting him with the golf bag. 'And she's pregnant wae another wee yin. I sincerely hope it's another wee girl.' He nods towards Kerry-Ann coming out of the kitchen with the mugs clinking in her hand, and her cheeks glow.

Dougie passes along the golf bag to Del. In Del's big hand it seems smaller, and he hoists it on his back, making Angela laugh.

Chaz pours each of them a good measure. Dougie and Del throw it back and turn to leave. They huddle at the front door, their heads close together in the dim light of the lobby. 'You did well,' says Dougie. 'We'll count the money. You'll get your share. I want you to do a favour for us now. Is there any place you can stash the guns?'

Chaz takes a deep breath, puffs his cheeks. 'Well, aye.' He exhales and tries to hide his delight.

Dougie nods and Del unzips the bag and passes the guns to Chaz, who makes a pouch of his shirt to hold them. Del hitches the bag on his shoulder, pulls open the door and steps onto the landing.

'Good man,' Dougie tells Chaz. 'You'll be hearing from us.'

Chaz imagines ripping up floorboards, stashes beneath the sink and behind bricks levered from the wall in the kitchen cupboard, but the guns are lumped under a soiled dress and pair of striped pyjamas in the smelly cupboard.

Chapter 41

Snookered

WHEN CHAZ GETS UP, KERRY-ANN IS PUTTERING ABOUT IN the kitchen and Angela is watching telly, with the sound muted. He quickly gets dressed for his meeting with Dougie and Del.

He carries the rain in his damp denim jacket into The Royal Snooker Club. The Royal, despite its links to aristocracy is a basement hall scooped out of tenement buildings, near to the Atlantis. It smells rank as public toilets. A popular story was that families had sheltered from the Luftwaffe here during the Clydebank Blitz. The club was still using the same twelve slate-bed snooker tables and pre-war chipped ivory balls.

The guy in charge is ancient. Chaz gazes over the wee man's head. He spots Dougie and Del playing a match on the back tables. Some underage kids whoop and laugh, having a contest on the two front tables near the door. The club doesn't officially sell booze. Chaz buys a Coke from the old guy and walks the dark line of empty tables and carries another two cans for Doug and Del, a lighted fag wedged in his mouth. He sticks the cans near the wooden scoreboard, inlaid with slick brass rails and markers to keep the score.

Doug and Del play in shirt sleeves and are evenly matched. Chaz sips Coke and smiles to himself in the darkness about how seriously they take a daft game. Playing to the rules, they take turns standing out of the opponent's eye line beside Chaz when he takes a shot.

Del whacks the tip of his cue off the end of the table. 'Fuck it,' he says. In the dim light Chaz sees he's raging after missing an easy red ball in the middle bag. He trudges towards the scoreboard.

Dougie chortles at his opponent's puce-faced rage when he takes up the challenge. He peers short-sightedly with a desperate intensity, and cues like he's just worked out his arms and legs connect by jerks of his head. He pots the red, sinks a pink, red and black and then flukes another red and roars, 'Yessss.'

Del pushed the tabs along the board and marks Dougie fifteen ahead. His shoulders slump and he shakes his head. 'You play?' he asks Chaz, but he's not looking at him. He's on the balls of his feet, willing his opponent to miss.

'Nah,' replies Chaz.

Dougie misses his pot but snookers his opponent.

'Fucker,' Del leans sideways, checking the angles on the baize against the white ball, touching the blue ball six-feet away. He picks up the rest from the baulk-end of the table in passing and carries it with him.

Dougie slaps Chaz on the shoulder and sparks his can of Coke in celebration. 'You did well there. And there was more than expected.'

His eyes flicker away from the light on the table to Chaz. He's slow on the uptake. Dougie kicks a red Adidas bag, wedged underneath a stool. 'Your cut's £850. It's all there. But don't do anything stupid and be running about like a fucking eejit, flashing the cash.'

'Nah, I willnae.'

Del using the rest, lines up his shot. The white ball misses the red ball on the baulk line by a foot.

'Yes,' Dougie shouts. 'Play again,' he tells Dell, before turning back towards Chaz. 'We need to go home for a bit of business. Are the guns stashed in a safe place?'

Chaz takes a swig of his can and burps, 'Aye.'

'Grand.'

'Play again!'

Dougie grins and laughs. 'That money will go towards buying arms,' he tells Chaz. 'The thing is, those Republican cunts are pulling all kinds of stunts and even getting fucking arms shipped in from Libya and America. And we're left with the dregs. Every gun we've got is precious. And we might need to use it for more than one job.'

Del misses again. 'That's fucking shite.' He snatches up the white ball and looks over at Dougie. 'Suppose I need to play again?'

Dougie nods, reaches across, marks another four on the score-board, and tortures him with hectoring laughter.

'When yeh goin?' Chaz asks him.

'The night. Ferry from Larne.' He turns his head and scrutinises Chaz. 'In fact, it might be a good idea if you came with us. A wee holiday. A couple of the boys have heard about you and are keen to meet you.'

'Eh, I've no got a passport.'

'Not got a passport? You're fucking good, you are.' Dougie slaps his shoulder again, laughs and wags a finger at Chaz. He turns to watch Del playing another shot. 'In fact, give me a minute, and I'll make a phone call.'

He dodges around Del's outstretched cue and heads towards the gloom. A phone box hangs on the wall across from the concierge's counter and till.

Del plays his shot and puts the rest back in the rack. He comes to stand beside Chaz. 'You seen that, didn't you? I clipped the red.'

'Aye,' Chaz agrees, although he hadn't been watching. He's been looking through the dull shapes and trying to pick out Dougie.

Del leans his cue against the pillar and reaches for his packet of fags. 'Where's Dougie away tae?'

'Make a phone call.'

Del strikes a match and lights an Embassy. 'You want one?'

'Nah, I'll stick tae my ain.' Chaz searches through his pocket and lights a Silk Cut. 'Whit ur yeh gonnae dae wae yer cut of the loot?'

'The usual, wine, women and song,' Del snorts. 'Get my hole. That's the first thing. Your birds a tidy wee thing.'

'You no married?'

'Nah, like to play the field. That's how we need to go back. Somebody's been fucking about wae Dougie's wee sister and we need to get it sorted.'

Chaz shrugs. 'Whit age is she?'

'Twenty.'

'Fuck sake, I'm sure she can take care of herself then.'

They watch Dougie slapping the edge of each snooker table he passes. He checks out how the balls are spread on the green baize.

'You hit it?' he asks Del.

'Aye,' says Del. 'You can ask him if you don't believe me.'

Dougie picks up his cue. 'Millions wouldn't,' he jokes. He turns and grins at Chaz. 'Sorry mate, can't take you this time, but definitely next time.'

'Aye,' says Chaz. 'Great. Don't dae anything I wouldnae.'

Dougie waves a finger and nods towards Chaz. 'Give him that wee package.'

Del hunkers down and pulls out a bag. He unzips it and pulls out a package covered with cloth. Standing up, he slips it into Chaz's midriff and leaves him clutching it.

'Put them with the other guns.' Dougie says. 'You have got them in a safe place, haven't yeh?'

'Oh, aye,' Chaz crouches below the table and puts them in the Adidas bag with the money. 'Safe as houses.' He knew he'd need to move the guns from the smelly cupboard sooner rather than later.

Chaz pulls up his collar against the drizzling rain. Singers to Dalmuir. It's only one stop, hardly worth paying. He stuffs a couple of tenners in his pocket and hoists the bag on his shoulder. Standing in front of the jobsworth, wearing his British Rail uniform, peering through Perspex, and counting out the change of a tenner to him, Chaz realises how easy it would be to stick a gun through the port and take everything. But he's too sharp for that. He sweeps up his change and heads for Platform 2.

He eyes the outlying buildings in Singer's Factory from his heated seat on the train. Thousands on the payroll. More money than any bank in Clydebank. More cash than he'd know what to do with. The Train Inspector, a young guy with shaggy hair, interrupts his reverie by fingering his ticket. 'This is a no smoking carriage, sir,' he points to the NO SMOKING sign on the window.

The train brakes as it enters Dalmuir station. Chaz adjusts his feet to the sway of the carriage, and steps past a woman reading a book in her lap. He sniffs and flicks the lit cigarette towards the Inspector, hitting his uniform jacket above the leather straps, carrying the pouch for change, the dout falling to the corridor floor. 'Why don't yeh fuck off,' he snarls. 'Before I smash yeh wan.' He shoulder-barges past him and out to the concourse.

When he gets home, he hands Kerry-Ann fifty quid. More money than she's ever seen and slaps her on the arse. 'Get yerself something.'

Her eyes glow. 'Yeh sure yeh can afford it?'

'Aye,' he fixes her with an adolescent leer. She's so grateful, he could almost kiss her.

'Whit about Angela, will I buy her something?'

Angela stands at the window, looking into the traffic, picking at a rose flake of discoloured wallpaper. She scuffs a heel and turns when she hears her name.

Chaz's nostrils flare. 'Nah, she's an ungrateful wee cow, gi'e her nothing.'

Chapter 42

Booty

Chaz pushes the door open, and his ma meets him in the lobby. A hairnet protects her curlers and the wave in her greying hair. A dishtowel dangles from her fingers, and her expression is that of a hangman's. 'Whit yeh here tae scrounge noo?' His daft sister is at her back, gawping at him.

'Nothing,' Chaz grins and brushes past them and into the front room. 'Is my da in?'

Wee John sits in his spot by the unlit fire, his shirt undone and a day's growth on his chin. His da's hands rest on his knees and his soft brown eyes turn to meet him. 'Hallo son,' a faint smile on his face.

In the kitchen his brothers Tash and John, called Junior because he's named after his da and granda, are drinking tea and listening to *Love me Do* on the tranny. Tash thinks himself a ladies' man and has even grown a much mocked faint moustache, like Omar Sharif's in *Doctor Zhivago*. Junior, in comparison, is the stocky quiet one, studious even. There was once big talk of him getting an O'Level. Both have straggly shoulder-length hair and the long bone-like family face and they peer at him with their da's eyes.

'Look whit the cat dragged in,' quips the Tash. 'Whit brings yeh tae our capacious abode?' He sweeps a hand out to show the extent of his kingdom.

'Och, nothing,' Chaz peels off a twenty from a roll of notes in the top pocket of his denim jacket. 'Jist thought I'd gi'e the old man a few quid tae get himself a few pints.' He hands the money to his da and turns to confront his ma and the shadowy bulk of his sister at her back.

'Fucking hell,' Tash splutters. 'Where did yeh get that?'

'Had a wee bit of a win on the bookies.'

'Nae good will come of gambling,' his ma hollers, pushing forward to get a better look at hard cash.

'Whit did yeh back?' Junior asks.

'A three-legged donkey.' Chaz answers. And the boys hoot together with laughter.

His ma eyes him like an orphan. 'Don't suppose yeh've got any that money for me?'

Chaz shakes his head and exhales. Plays the gallant. 'Aye, I suppose,' he peels off a twenty and gives it to her. 'That'll shut yer moaning gob up for once.'

'I'll shut my moaning up when yeh get a job.' She turns and sets her sights on the Tash. 'And him as well.'

'See,' the Tash pouts and puts on a coquettish wee girl's voice. 'Never happy.' Fluttering fingers pressed against his pink-boyish cheeks. 'Don't suppose yeh've got any of that money for me, young man?'

'Fuck off,' Chaz guffaws. 'But I'll take yeh for a pint.'

'Jist get my jacket.' The Tash nicks out of the living room, past them and into the lobby. 'I'm oot of here.'

The Tash and Chaz meet Pizza Face coming up the stairs, a burst Adidas ball under his arm. The Tash asks him, 'Whit yeh daeing wae that thing?'

'Gonnae fix it. Wae hot knives.'

'Dae us a favour,' Chaz sounds bored. 'And go up and see if Rab's in and tell him we're in Maggie Scott's.'

'Nah, fuck off.' Pizza Face tries to squeeze past Chaz at the railing.

But Chaz pulls him back by the hood of his duffel coat. Pizza Face braces his arm up over his head, expecting to get a smack, and it drops in stages like a drawbridge. He meets Chaz's gaze through his fingers.

'I'll gi'e yeh a pound.'

Pizza Face looks at the Tash's face for an explanation. When he grins and nods, Pizza Face screeches, 'Too fucking right.' The palm of his hand held out, but he's sure it's a trick, and is ready to whip it away.

Chaz hands him a pound note. He can't quite believe it and his face glows like the bauble on a Christmas tree. The burst ball falls from under his arm and rolls down a few stairs.

Chaz leaves him standing open-mouthed on the landing. 'Mind, Maggie Scott's.'

Chapter 43

Withdrawals

CHAZ NURSES A WARM PINT. THE TASH SUCKS ONE cigarette to death after another. The red Adidas bag, with two Starr pistols and a Beretta, kicked under their table. Chaz has brought nylon stockings to use as masks. He wasn't sure about wire-cutters; he brought a pair of pliers and an axe instead. Neither Del nor Dougie have told him how to disable an alarm.

'Where is that cunt?' Chaz asks.

'Probably smoking that dope,' says the Tash. 'The cunts addicted tae it. He'll end up a junkie, selling his arse.' His foot taps a jig under the table and he squints sideways through a mouthful of snaking smoke at his brother. 'Whit dae yeh want tae dae?'

His nervousness is contagious and makes Chaz wary. 'Whit dae yeh want tae dae?'

'It's up tae yeh, man.'

'Alright then, let's fucking dae it then?' Chaz takes a drink and spits it back into the glass. 'Pish water,' he gives a mocking laugh, and picks up the bag.

Beastie

The Tash's pint remains untouched, and his hands shake when he tries to gulp a final mouthful.

Casually dressed in a uniform of denim jackets and denim flared trousers and sannies, neither of them speaks as they fall into step on the way up Duntocher Road. When they get to the steps at Shakespeare Avenue, they take a fag break. Chaz unzips the bag and checks there's nobody about. He slips the Beretta inside his jacket pocket and stuffs a pair of nylons and a Starr pistol in another. He hands the Tash a Starr pistol and a pair of tan tights.

'I was jist thinking, we should huv got a getaway car,' mutters the Tash. 'Yeh said yeh'd wan for the last job.'

Chaz explains in a monotone voice. 'We huv already went through aw that. That was for a bank. This is a post office. We go in and dae the job, come oot the back door, up through the back lanes and end up here. Through the park. And we'll be hame in jig time before the police even get tae leave the station.'

He picks up the bag. A Panda Police car in its blue and white livery motors downhill from Parkhall shops towards them. Chaz reaches for his gun. Cold sweat on his brother's face tells Chaz he's going to bolt. He turns to leg it, but the Panda car sweeps past him. The Tash flings his right hand against the brick wall, bent over, boaking.

Chaz leaves his brother behind. He's on his own and that's the way he likes it. He strides past Birell's sweetie shop, disappears around the corner, and steps into the lane at the back.

Reconnoitring, he stands on a crumbling wall festooned with household rubbish and peers at the overgrown slope at the back entrances to the shops and post office. No alarms jutting out of the brickwork.

183

He saunters from back-lane exits and lets a woman pulling a tartan trolley pass him on the pavement. He looks through the door of the post office. An old woman in a woolly hat is last in the queue.

Chaz strides into the Post Office pulling the nylons over his face. He turns the *Open* sign to *Closed,* shutting the door and snecking the Yale. A buroo boy getting paid by notes and coins passed through the wicket, cowers, holding his hands up. Chaz jumps onto the counter, a pistol in each hand. 'Any cunt move and I'll shoot yeh.'

He passes the Adidas bag to the postmaster. 'Fill this up with high denomination notes. Any fucking about and I'll shoot yeh. Press any alarm buttons and I'll shoot yeh. Look at me the wrang way and I'll shoot yeh. Got it?'

The postmaster, a middle-aged man with squarish specs and a tight smile on his face, pulls open the wooden drawer beside his stool. He piles notes into the sports bag. A wee girl holding her mother's skirts stares up at Chaz. A customer tries to push the door open. He bangs on it, pushes his nose against the glass panel and peers in. The old woman in the woolly hat sobs, 'Oh my God, Oh my God, Oh my God.'

Chaz hurdles the screen and jumps off the counter. He sticks a gun in the postmaster's temple. He picks up the Adidas bag and warns those in the queue, 'I'm gonnae take this cunt wae me. Anybody says anything oot of turn and I'll fucking kill him stone deid.' He marches him through a dimly lit room to the tradesman's entrance to the post office.

'Open that back door.'

The door opens onto the lane. Light rain falls. 'I'm gonnae play a wee game noo. It's called yeh dae whit I tell yeh.' He switches the bag with the money in it to his other hand. 'See that skip there?' He waves the gun barrel in its direction. 'Let's see how fast yeh can climb intae it. And let me be clear about this, poke yer heid oot, I'll kill yeh.' He boots the postmaster on the arse. 'Go, ya fucker.'

Chaz bangs the barrel of the gun on a metal bin as he passes as a warning. Running, the heavy bag slowing him, he's never felt more alive.

Chapter 44

Hunters and haunted

EVAN SHARES A ROOM AT THE TOP OF THE STAIRS WITH Bruno. It's warm enough to incubate babies. 'He's a bed-wetter,' Julie says in a hushed tone. 'We may get him up during the night to take him to the toilet.' Small, with chestnut-colour hair, Julie's pink open-neck blouse draws Evan's eyes to a gold crucifix at the top of her breasts. A tight skirt hobbles her, but she's breezy and smells nice. She likes to giggle, catches his shoulder as if to stop herself from falling. She fills his silence with explanations: what they are going to have for breakfast; how many rooms there are – seven; how many residents – fourteen, but that doesn't includes Evan, so fifteen, really. And how much great fun he's going to have. 'I'll let you boys get settled.' She swishes her hair and leaves them with a conspiratorial laugh.

Evan listens to her shuffling steps in the corridor, fading on the stairs. A window wedged open ruffles the curtains, but the room stinks of pee. Unsure what to do with his clothes, he leaves them bunched at the foot of the bed. Dressed in his underpants, he hugs himself. A spike of light from the hall allows him to check his roommate isn't feigning sleep.

Near the cupboard and chair, Bruno's head shows, but the rest of him is like Tutankhamun, embalmed in scratchy Clydebank Council blankets. He makes a snorting, snoring sound from the back of his throat. His hair is mousy-brown fluff, unevenly shaved with two bare spots and scabs on his head as if he's been scratching. It reminds Evan when his da shaved his head, and because of that he takes a liking to Bruno.

Evan steals under the covers and stares at the bright colours of the motor-racing posters of Jackie Stewart above Bruno's head.

When Evan wakes, it's the other way about. Bruno is waiting and watching over him, glints of gold in his cat-like eyes. His legs dawdle, his neck lollipops out of his red-striped pyjamas, and he perches on a crumpled waterproof sheet. Bedding peeled off his mattress lie in an unravelled ball and clutters the corridor between their beds. His roommate is thin. The biggest part of him is his grin, with yellowish pointy teeth.

'I got up and checked ages ago. Yeh're the new guy, Evan. I'm Bruno. Whit yeh daeing here?'

Evan returns his gaze but remains tight-lipped. He's wearied answering questions, but Bruno hums to himself and acts unconcerned. He scratches at the back of his head, stands pigeon-toed, and scoops the load of washing to his chest. 'I pee the bed,' he explains, and he doesn't seem fazed, as if it's akin to being cack-handed and pigeon-brained. 'I'll jist go and put this in the washing, but don't worry, I'll come back and get yeh.' He clicks their bedroom door shut behind him when he leaves.

Evan flings on his clothes. He stares out the window at the intimate geography of walls dividing walls, and their back garden from other terraced gardens. He'd read in some book they'd just fling stinky stuff out the window, way back then, and shout

'Gardyloo!' Wonders if he should nick home to use their lavvy, even though he knows his da won't be there. Another part of him thinks he might be waiting. A faraway tree, swaying in the wind, has a rope swing attached to a thick branch. His bed left unmade. He pulls open the door, and Bruno pushes and stumbles into the room. The same daft grin on his face. Evan wonders if he's half-cracked.

'Thought I'd come up and get yeh.' He's breathless, as if he's been running. He changes out of his pyjamas into a T-shirt with hooped red and blue colours. A green and gold snake-belt ties flared denims onto his skimpy frame. 'We've tae go doon and get breakfast.'

He leads the way and gives a running commentary. 'That's Hunter's room.' His fingers brush against wood panelling as they pass a closed bedroom door the same dull blue as their room. 'He's a cunt. Don't mess wae him. He shares wae Simple Simon.' He points at the room nearest the stairs. 'That's Carrot's room. He's awright but can be a bit of a bawbag. He shares wae Drew.' He slaps his hand lightly off the oak finial on the banister and nods, 'Toilet. And up that end, that's where they keep the bitches fae hell.'

The barefoot girl who sweeps out of the toilet is on the cusp of womanhood. A fluffy towel turbans her hair, another towel robes pink skin and hint of breast, and she looks nothing like a bitch from hell. Her blue-green eyes gaze at Evan without blinking. Her face delicate as an Old Master's pencil drawing, but she challenges him. 'Want your eyes back?'

Bruno jumps in to explain. 'He doesnae talk, Norma.'

Evan breezes past her in and into the damp, lush, perfumed heat of the toilet. He checks the door is locked. The water from the bath swirls around black hair in the plughole. Squatted on the pan, he closes his eyes and disappears into himself and cries.

Bruno sits on the stairs waiting for him until he comes out. Evan follows him downstairs, past the office. Two long breakfast tables run parallel. A cornflakes box within hand-reach of each wooden chair with plates, spoons, cups and a jug of milk.

Julie sits with an ashtray at her elbow on the table. She watches them coming in and breaks off her conversation to greet them with a wave. An older girl, round-faced with massive boobs, munches on toast in the chair opposite Julie. Evan looks away when she eyes him up and can't work out whether she's staff or a resident.

Bruno guides him to the table near the windows through which the front and side gardens are visible.

'Hi, I'm Bob,' mutters an older man, who is definitely staff. A cup of tea and a sticky eggshell smashed on a plate at his elbow. He peers through rimless John Lennon glasses at him. His thin face is sand-coloured, with a wispy beard and moustache. He wears a mud-brown cardigan over tan corduroys and sits buttering a slice of toast, pernickety, as if getting the spread consistently right is a matter of physics and not whacking it on with a knife.

'Here, sit here.' Bruno drags out a chair for Evan and one for himself next to it and plonks himself down. 'He doesnae talk,' he tells Bob and grins.

'Really!' Bob leans back, stretching. 'I didn't know that.' He looks over at Julie for confirmation, but she's in conference with the girls at her table. 'You mean he's electively mute or he just can't speak?'

Bruno picks up the cornflakes packet and fills his ceramic bowl to overflowing. 'Aye, he cannae talk.' He pulls another bowl over and fills it with cornflakes for Evan. He hands him a spoon. 'It's great here,' he spills milk onto the oilskin tablecloth. 'We've got a cook. Yeh get as much tae eat as yeh want. Yeh can get sausage and egg and ham when yer finished. Double helpings. And even orange juice!'

A girl not much older than Angela, wears a long flannel dress at the next table, and spoons cornflakes into her mouth. She glances at Evan, and her brown eyes flicker away. He smiles at her, and chokes on cornflakes. Following Bruno's lead, he fills his plate with toast and reaches for the butter. He adds a spread of orange marmalade and sips at his tea.

Bruno works a flanker on the hotplate beside the kitchen door. He slaps square-sliced sausages onto his plate like face-cards but turns around and freezes. Evan follows his gaze.

A boy aged about fifteen swaggers in, a cigarette stub smouldering in the corner of his mouth. Thick, brown, curly hair, a blue hooped top and denims emphasise the wiry and stocky frame of an adult.

'Sit over here.' Bob uses a blokey tone, points with his butter knife to the seat next to Bruno. 'Where I can keep an eye on you.'

'That'll be fucking right! Suck on my knob.' He sticks his tongue, like a gobstopper, into the side of his cheek. He drags the seat out across from Evan, leans across the table and stabs his fag in the mush of discarded cornflakes.

'Language,' Bob chides him, sighs, shakes his head.

'Calm doon,' says the boy. 'I was only spovving yeh,' He looks directly across the table at Evan and kicks his feet.

Bruno slips into the chair next to Evan's, a plate filled with sausage and egg in his hand. The boy leans across, steals a sausage, and masticates with a gaping gob.

'Who's this wee poof?' A flick of the head in Evan's direction. He scrapes a morsel of scrag meat from his discoloured molars with a fingernail.

'Evan,' Bruno grins as he answers. 'He's my mate Hunter and he cannae talk.'

'Fucking great, pissy pants,' mouths Hunter. 'Another fucking Mongo like you.' He kicks Evan's feet harder this time under the table.

'Watch your language,' Bob's tone is weary. 'There's kids about.'

'Keep yer hair on old man. Pour us a cup of tea and geez wan of yer fags and I'll think about it.'

Evan moves his feet sideways when Hunter tries to clip him again under the table. He chews slowly on a slice of toast and studies the remains of his breakfast.

Hunter fetches breakfast from the hotplate and clatters a plate with sausage and scrambled egg in front of him and slides into the seat facing Evan. He kicks his feet, making the table jump, finding his range. Evan twirls his fork. When Hunter looks at him again, and sneers, he lunges across the table and jabs his fork into the older boy's right eye.

Evan places his fork back on the table beside the butter dish. Hunter staggers backwards, knocking his chair over. Clutching his eye, a colourful arabesque, milky with red veins, he mourns his loss of sight with a keening sound.

Bruno giggles, his pointy teeth show a mouthful of chewed bread and sausage as he watches Hunter dance. 'Yer a psycho,' he says with envy.

Hunter reminds Evan of a childhood toy he used to love, a potbellied green toad. He'd wind it up and watched it jump in no particular direction and croak on the floor. Hunter's hip crashes into the girl's table and the dishes buck. The girl with big boobs picks up two slices of toast and holds them as if marking a glee-club scorecard. Julie catches Hunter and her slight frame wrestles his head down, clutches his curly hair into perfumed blouse and breasts. The foul-mouthed adolescent becomes a snotty compliant child and leans against her and sobs loudly.

'You'll be alright.' She strokes the top of his hair. 'Sshsh, you'll be alright.'

Bob's chair screeches as he abandons his seat and his breakfast. He dunts Evan's shoulder so that he stumbles sideways but regains his feet and his impassive face. 'Move.' Evan is herded towards the door.

In the hallway, Norma comes swanning down the stairs, her black hair in a middle-parting, her red fingertips glide across the rail. Another older girl, about fourteen, with blonde hair, is yakking to her. She sports outsized sunglasses indoors and a lavender scarf. 'What's happening Bob, has somebody been murdered?'

'Nothing to worry about,' Bob's voice is soporific. 'Everything's been taken care of.' He nudges Evan towards the office and bounds ahead of him, opening the door. The girls observe Evan with glinting eyes and renewed interest before he steps inside and the care worker slaps the door shut.

Florescent lighting offers no dark corners to hide. His social worker had sat with him last night in the same worn faux-leather office chairs tight to the wall. Bob follows a snail trail of grey carpet from the door to the desk. Paperwork on it resembles a

Lego-project with silver metallic arms and plastic tier-trays balanced on top of each other.

Bob slumps into the swivel seat behind the desk and pulls the phone across. He takes off his glasses and cleans the lenses. Loosely holding the receiver, he dials nine-nine-nine, and gives the emergency services the location of where to send an ambulance and the police.

Evan chooses the furthest away seat from him, near the filing cabinet.

Bob strokes his wispy beard. 'You do know you're in big trouble, don't you?'

They glance at each other. Evan shrugs and stares at the closed drawers of the filing cabinet.

'It's a lot of work. I'll need to inform the police. You'll be cautioned and need to appear before the Children's Panel.' Bob tries a different tack. 'Hallo-,' he draws the word out, the seriousness in his voice dissipating into mocking laughter. 'You can hear me?' Pauses and segues into pidgin. 'You-can-speak English?'

Evan answers with a slight nod.

'The thing is, I'm not saying Hunter can't be a bit of a horse's ass, but there are ways and means of doing things, and that's not one of them.' Bob feigns concern. 'He could be blind in one eye.' He swivels and stretches his legs in front of him, 'You do understand that don't you?'

He pulls open the top desk drawer. The phone rings and he answers it and a woman opens the door.

'It's for you Alice,' he holds out the receiver, wiggles his eyebrows and scrambles out of the swivel chair. He mouths in an exaggerated manner, 'Social Work Department,' and skits around the desk. 'I'll—' waves his hand to show what he means and slips out the door without finishing what he starts saying.

Alice doesn't look as if she needs any help. With sensible black plimsolls, her movement is operatic. Her rayon dress bulges, her stomach overflows, and meaty thighs are moulded to the swivel chair. The ashtray dragged to her side of the table. She wedges the receiver to her shoulder and fold of skin on her neck, while lighting up. For such a big woman, she moves through the scales in a small soft voice: yielding, good-humoured, put-upon, but sharp and in control.

When she replaces the receiver, she lights another cigarette from the one she puts out. 'Smoking isn't good for you and ruins your life.' Her burble of laughter invites Evan to join her in smiling. 'I've heard a little of what's happened. Look, you're what? Nine-years-old? Maybe ten? You might act tough, but you're only a wee boy. I'd like you to tell me what happened.'

She waits with a smile on her lips. 'OK, here's the deal. I'm not playing down the seriousness of what happened. Hunter has been taken to hospital. We won't know the extent of the damage for at least twenty-four hours. And during that time he'll be in hospital. Then we'll need to decide what to do with him—and you.' Her voice drops and she takes a drag on her cigarette. 'You can stay here in the meantime if that's what you want?' The swivel chair creaks, her hands rest in her lap. 'That what you want, darling?'

Evan's eyes dart to the calendar behind her head. She watches him, the concern in her eyes holding him captive. He melts. All the unsaid worries bubble in his chest and in his tears. He babbles his fears. The rustle of rayon, she steps closer. In a mixture of perfume and cigarette smoke, her firm arms come around his shoulders and she holds him close as if she means it.

Bruno hangs about until Evan comes out of the office. 'An ambulance came and took him away,' he explains. 'Hunter swears he's gonnae kill yeh. Yeh should've stabbed him in both eyes.'

The thought cheers him up and he grabs Evan's arm and guides him to the lounge. White-washed walls, high ceilings with plenty of light. Front and bay windows makes the place feel clean and spacious. A bumblebee buzzes and bumps against the window, trying to gain entry. His feet sink into earth-coloured carpet, not yet scuffed and tarred with feet. Battered leather couches and chairs are arranged around the television.

'This is where yeh go,' he chuckles. 'When yer bored rotten.'

Evan recognises faces from earlier. Girls loll together on a couch, rubbing shoulders, feet tucked under them like mischievous cats, with their jackets on, even though it's not cold and glare at him with cool, disinterested eyes. Others studiously ignore him, including Bob, who is reading the sports pages of the *Daily Record* and smoking a cigarette. A boy, near the unplugged telly, has his hood up, messy ginger hair spilling out, eyes closed, open-mouthed snoring. The chair opposite swallows another boy. He's too tall, too thin, hair too long and uncombed. A pale hand tucked inside his coat pocket; he reads a dog-eared paperback with a fixed intensity.

Bruno seems content to have showed him off. 'Need tae get my school stuff.' He tugs on Evan's wrist expecting him to follow him back to their room.

Bruno shows Evan which steps to avoid because they creak when sneaking up the stairs. His companion chatters about cars and racing drivers. Evan feigns listening, his stomach grumbles and he wonders what will happen to him.

Bruno's mattress remains stripped. He gets ready for school with running feet and a final volley of door banging.

Evan is exempt because he needs to see his social worker. On the ground-floor, far below, a hoover drones. He pokes about underneath the beds, opens and shuts drawers in the pine cabinets. The top drawers contain grubby pants and worn cotton and nylon socks and the third drawer folded T-shirts. Bruno's clothing. The bottom drawers lie empty, except for a broken stick of a purple crayon, waiting for a paper life to fill them. In the cupboard hangs a nylon jacket with a fur-lined hood and a blue school blazer, alongside a pair of neatly pressed grey trousers.

A red Matchstick fire engine is lodged inside a pair of brown brogues. Evan picks it up and scoots the wheels with flat fingers to test if it works. He kneels, rolling it along the carpet, across the stippled white grain of the wall onto the radiator and onto the windowsill chuntering nee-no, nee-no, nee-no fire-engine sounds. A crow calls like a muffled gun from the trees. He ganders out at nodding clumps of daffodils, white and yellow crocuses, colouring the greens and the sticks of wintery-thin bushes. A magpie pokes and stabs its beak into the moss under the tree, adjusting its head as if thinking, bouncing and stabbing anew. It flies onto the swing seat, its call echoing through the gardens, its wings soar over the rooftops into a grey sky.

He sits on his bed with the fire engine in his hand, spinning the wheels, but the magic has disappeared. Falling backwards, he lies on the mattress, holding the fire engine and the world at arm length, conscious of his shoes on top of clean sheets and how his da would kill him for that. His eyes close and his body jerks as he dreams and cries out.

A pair of crows perches patiently on the wire fence, waiting to make a snack of his eyes. Tousled rope from the swing twines around Evan's neck. His eyes bulge and his feet, inches from the grass, dervishly dance. He sees his da and—

Alice shakes him by the shoulder. 'You've been having a nightmare, pet.'

Evan feels groggy and when he rolls over to sit up, the metal of the fire engine digs into his bum.

'You want to come downstairs and get a cuppa and biscuit?' Her tone upbeat. 'Your social worker should be here soon. And we've had a quick confab on the phone and, the good news is, I'm to be your Key Worker.'

He bites his lower lip and nods, not sure what that means.

'We need to buy you some new clothes and shoes. That'll be fun, eh?' Her voice drops to a lower register. 'And we might need to go back to your old house and pick up a few things. You do know you're not going back there?

He cocks his head as he looks at her. A puzzled expression plays on his face and tears form in the corner of his eyes. It hadn't occurred to him he has nothing to wear, or clothes mattered.

She tuts, ruffles his hair, and pats his head. 'Sorry pet, I thought they'd told you. Never mind. We'll discuss it later.' Strokes his shoulder and makes light of it. 'C'mon, there's nothing better than a Custard Cream to cheer you up.'

Evan cries with his eyes shut, blotting out the world. A magpie calls through the glass.

Chapter 45

Cookery lessons

Evan's bored, waiting. He stands inside the kitchen door spying on the cook. The cook splashes dirty pots and rolls her eyes at him. Thick auburn curls tucked inside a hairnet, her wire glasses steamed up. 'You're not supposed to be in here.' She dries her hands on a chequered dishcloth. Up close, she is majestic as a two-legged grand-piano and not much taller. The washing machine drones and vibrates into a spin cycle.

Evan knows he's been staring, feels weird and echoey in his head. He tries not to look sad, cloaks the shadows around his eye and smiles in the way that puts adults at ease.

'It's OK honey, but this place is out of bounds.' She eyes him, critically. 'You hungry? I've got some apple turnovers that are just going to waste.'

She sashays towards the oven, and pulls open the door, pulls out a tray and steps back from the heat. The wafting smell makes Evan's mouth water. Her laughter rings naturally and using the folded end of the dishcloth, she jiggles a pastry and pitches it towards him. 'Better when they're hot.'

He bats it, hand to hand, before taking a bite. Cinnamon mugs his mouth and makes fruit of his senses. He scoffs the lot. Her dark eyes shine. Another snack fresh from the tray. She seems almost as happy watching him eating.

'You're a growing boy,' she laughs. She picks up an apple turnover, takes a nip out of the corner, and bangs the oven door shut with a sideways swipe of her foot. 'You get all sorts here. Some are in for a wee while gi'ing their mum and dad a wee break. And some have been here a wee bit longer.' She dabs and brushes pastry flakes from her chin. 'What's your story then?'

Her innocuous question turns him inside out. His forehead flushes, a wave of vinegar washes through his veins, and he wonders if he can speak. 'My mum's deid.' His voice rises, 'She had cancer.' He finds it hard to speak, impossible to say the words, because it's mum and dad, and there's no going back. 'And my da is deid, murdered, and whoever did it will kill me tae. I jist know. He'll come and get me next. He'll come and get me.'

The cook lets him wrap himself in her doughy body, and he cries into her shoulder. His cheeks feel red as a wonky traffic light. She makes cooing noises and rubs the back of his head. Menthol cigarettes peep from the pocket in her nylon bib, the same brand of cigarette his mum sometimes smoked. The cook smells of home.

'Poor wee soul,' she says. 'There, there, let it all out. You're safe here. If anybody comes to get you, they'll have me to deal with.' Her easy laugh reassures him, and he clings to her warmth for a few seconds before letting go.

'Macaroni and cheese for lunch, with chips,' she says. 'Want to help me make it?'

'Whit's macaroni and cheese?' he scrunches his nose and squints at her.

'You don't know what macaroni and cheese is?' She bats her big boobs as she coughs. 'Well, you're in for the best treat ever. It's scrumptious and it's good for you.'

She whips out her cigarette packet and disposable lighter, giving him time to consider, while she lights up. 'I'm telling you. I wouldn't be this size if I didn't love it.'

'Can I just borrow him from you for a minute?' Alice stands in the hallway between kitchen and dining room, a conspiratorial smile on her face 'She's right, you know, macaroni and cheese is not to be sniffed at.'

Evan shuffles sideways. The cook pats and kneads his shoulders. As he turns to go, the clatter of dishes begins anew.

Alice waits for him. 'Some folk weren't sure you would talk, but I told them to bide their time. You'd speak when you'd something to say.'

Marie sits with a cup of coffee in the office, a sprinkling of biscuits on a plate beside her. She smiles uneasily. 'Sit down, Evan,' she pats the cushioned seat next to her. When he sits, she takes his hand and squeezes it.

Alice tiptoes and sits behind the desk, clasping her hands in front of her, and gives Evan her attention.

'I want you to know that I'm here for you.' Marie looks across at Alice, correcting herself, 'We're both here for you.'

He tugs his hand from her grasp and sits staring at the grey carpet. His gaze shifts to the bin beside the desk. Knowing what she is going to say, his shoulders slump.

'I've got a bit of bad news about your dad... I'm very sorry to have to tell you that he's no longer with us. He's had a very bad accident, and he's, well, he's dead.'

'Can I get my book back?' Evan straightens his shoulders, staring into Marie's dewy eyes.

Marie looks to Alice for guidance.

'You do know what Marie has just told you, Evan?' Alice's boobs flatten on to the desk when she leans across. 'She's just told you, your father, Dermot, is dead.' A slight nod of her head and it's Marie's turn.

Marie tries to take his hand again, but he pulls away. 'We're very, very sorry.'

'Can I get my book back, please?'

'What book is that Evan?' Marie asks.

'It's in my room, *Grimms' Fairy Tales*. I really need tae go there and get it. I really, really need it.'

Alice and Marie's eyes latch onto each other's.

'OK, Evan,' Marie speaks for both of them. 'I think that can be arranged.'

'When? I need it noo.'

'I'm not too sure.' Alice glances at the phone.

'Noo.' Evan rushes away, leaving them sitting.

Chapter 46

Poison

AT BREAKFAST BOB PLONKS HIMSELF BESIDE EVAN, READY TO make a grab at him if he shows any inkling to butcher a resident, or even staff, with a plastic spoon, plastic fork, or paper plate. Bruno sits opposite Evan. He dips with gusto into yolky eggs. He slices through sausage and ham. Metal cutlery on the table placed out of Evan's reach. An intake of breath from the care worker, and a rustle of corduroy, when tea is poured—a splash of milk and four sugars doesn't disguise what a dangerous weapon a hot drink has become.

Bruno, with lip-smacking relish, calls Evan 'Psycho Ward,' and shelters in the notoriety and respect his new roommate has gained among other kids.

Carrot sitting at another table, with his duffle-coat hood up, chooses a fork from the cutlery and mock stabs himself in the eye. Titters of laughter make for a more light-hearted atmosphere. Bob stretches and pushes his chair back. He wanders away, searching for his cigarettes and lighter. Julie dips back into a huddle with the teenage girls. Bruno hauls at Evan's shirt sleeve when breakfast is over. He wants him to follow him to their room, but Evan escapes him and mopes about outside the kitchen.

A stopper wedges the door and the Yale key sticks out of the lock. The cook, flash yellow rubber gloves to her elbows, washes the work surfaces. 'Make yourself useful,' she says, when she spots him. 'Go and get us all the dirty knives and forks and spoons.'

She opens a cupboard under the sink and hauls out a pale-blue plastic bucket. 'Stick them in here, but only the dirty ones,' she warns him with a conspiratorial smile. 'We don't want to be doing double work.'

Evan takes the bucket from her, but before he goes, she pulls out another black plastic bucket and hands him it. 'Scrape the plates with half-chewed stuff: eggs, cornflakes, sausage, tomatoes, toast. It doesn't matter what it is—bung it in here.'

'Here,' she shows him what she means by lifting a plate from the bottom shelf of a metal trolley with wheels near the sink. She bangs a greasy stain of egg and stump of sausage oozing brown sauce off the side of the black bucket he is holding and it slithers into a foul-smelling gunge.

His nose crinkles. 'Whit dae yeh dae wae it when yer finished?'

'I mix it all up with a big spoon and serve it for dinner.'

Caught between almost boaking and suspicion she is having him on, her slow smile arrests his disgust.

'No really,' she admits. 'We stick the slops in the bin.'

'Won't yeh get rats?'

'Aye, we do. I guess they're all God's creatures.' She feels around the space next to the vibrating washing machine, pulling out an opaque brown bottle with a medicinal hue.

Evan recognises the stained markings, yellow skull and crossbones from books about piracy, but he doesn't expect to see it on a label in the kitchen with a red cross, giving off a distinct set of warning and instructions.

'Rats are a lot smarter than some people that work in here,' she reassures him. 'They get a whiff of this and they know.'

'Does it kill them?'

'Aye, sometimes. But then they know to keep away.' A deep belly laugh. 'Scoot! When you come back, I'll gi'e you a bit of tablet. Bad for the teeth, but good for the soul.'

Chairs sit higgledy-piggledy and tables clustered with dirty dishes. Evan hadn't really thought about people's mess until he sorts clean cutlery from dirty and scraping slops into the black bucket.

Spring retreats, a driech view through the window filtered by rain. Hoods and hats hide faces. Coats pulled tight around hunched shoulders, he recognises Bruno's stuttering run as he catches up with the stragglers.

Evan's payment for working is a tray of super-sweet tablet. His blood boils with sugar. Even a cup of milky tea cannot dilute the taste. The cook watches him and laughs, daring him to try another bit, until it becomes a bit of a contest with himself. She takes a slither off him with her tea and a cigarette to take the edge off it.

'How come you're no at school today?' she asks.

'I've got a meeting.'

'Oh, aye, that's one thing they're good at here is meetings. If they drop a pencil off the back of a settee, they need to call the police and bring in all the social workers in the districts, all the high-heid yins, and have a big meeting about it. What's the point?' She grins at him, smoke wafting around her face. 'And I should know because they always want me to get in wee goodies for them. The fancier the cakes and biscuits, the more important the people are. That's how I know there's a big meeting on today.' She waves a finger at the tray of tablet. 'Go on.'

'Nah, couldnae eat another bit,' but he does, picks another square and munches it. 'The meeting's about me. Whether I can stay here. Or, maybe, they're gonnae take me somewhere else, like a prison ship, or something.' He can hardly swallow and tears well up.

'Och, don't be daft.' She slides an arm over his shoulder. 'That lot couldnae organise a menagerie, but course they'll let you stay. Where else would I get such a great wee helper? They know better than to mess with me, or they'll get some of that rat poison in their soup.'

Resting his head, he buries hot pink cheeks in her midriff and sniffles. 'Yeh really think so?'

'Aye, I know so.' She pushes him away, picks a spoon out of the water in the sink and waves it at him. 'Go on, get in there, and make sure there's no dirty dishes left on them tables or it'll be me you've to answer to.'

Chapter 47

Cuban exile

THE SOCIAL-WORK MEETING TAKES PLACE AFTER LUNCH. Evan lies on top of his bed with a bellyache, paging through a stained *Reader's Digest* he'd found on the bathroom windowsill. Alice comes to get him. 'Nothing will be decided today,' she warns him. 'But I think it would be in your best interest to attend. It'll let folk that don't know you see what you're like.' She finishes on an upbeat note, ruffling his hair. 'And they'll see you're no ogre.'

Evan sticks the mouldy book under his bed and follows her downstairs and into the sitting room. Alice squeezes in beside Marie on one of the bigger settees. He glances around but can't find a place to sit. Ashtrays smoulder each end of the mantelpiece and in the shadow of each seat. A mahogany table overloaded with silver service, coffee-stained china cups, plates of pastries and tarts and nibbled tablet makes it seem like a kid's outing.

A mannish woman glances across at him wearing a flowery blouse. She sits on the same couch as Alice, knees and feet pointing at him, dark hair in a middle-parting, opening like curtains showing a horsey face and prominent chin. She's consulting her diary, as are the others, but she has wangled a space for folders and files in the seat beside her.

Evan sits self-consciously, higher than everybody else, on the arm of the chair next to Alice. He is grateful, although his leg brushes her thigh when she shoves along and he can slip and slide and hide behind her bulk.

'I've not got a space for another two weeks.' The mannish woman flicks back and forth through her diary. 'Possibly three.'

'What about next Monday, around 2pm?' Marie taps a pen against her diary entry, 'because I'm going on holiday in three weeks.'

'Lucky old you.' A woman with bright-red lipstick looks up from her diary and picks at the corner of a jam tart with long fingers and pink nail varnish. She flicks it into her mouth and glows with a guilty smile. 'Going anywhere nice?'

'My fiancée's taking me to Los Angeles.' Marie's face flushes, and she looks even prettier. 'But I'd loved to have went to Cuba.'

Bob has commandeered a comfy chair where he can stick his long legs out. He sits a little straighter and cups the cigarette in his hand to speak. 'Aye, I love Cuba. The things they've done there for the working classes. Needs to be seen to be believed.'

He's got everybody's attention. A young cop with a short-back-and-sides stops stirring and gazing into his coffee cup and looks across at him. 'You been there, pal?'

'Not exactly. But they've one of the lowest rates of TB anywhere in the world, ever.' He takes a drag on his fag, clears his throat and stares at his desert boots. 'That's Cuba for you.'

The mannish woman takes a deep breath and sighs. 'OK, Let's get back on track.' She raises her left hand to call for order. 'But that reminds me of a social work report I once scanned for a younger colleague. I'd read this same line about four or five times and I just didn't get it. So I picked up the phone and phoned him—and it was a male—"You've put down here that child X has Alzheimer's".

'I could hear him coughing on the other end of the phone. "Yes," he said. "Well, child X is only eight-years-old; it must be a very rare and malignant variant of the disease."

'He paused and said, "Aye, he's got real problems with his breathing."

'"You mean asthma?" I asked him. "That's what I said," he replied. "And that's what I put in the report and I categorically stand by that" and he put the phone down on me.'

Laughter flew around the room in guffaws, tinkling of cups and shifting of feet. And the women exchange secret nods of recognition and smiles. Even Evan's grinning, although he's not really sure why.

The mannish woman turns her attention to Evan. 'You do know why you're here?'

Evan nods, his face glowing with a pink tinge because everybody gawps at him. He's glad he can hide behind Alice's shoulder and hair.

'Before we come to any kind of decision, we want to involve you in it.' She flutters her eyelids at him.

A gap opens where he can speak. He fidgets, stays silent, figuring it's an adult ruse, like talking to you about Santa, when you've already found the presents, and expecting you to believe in magic reindeers.

The mannish woman gives him an escape route when she turns to question Bob. 'You're Norman Hunter's Key Worker and you were there on the day of the incident. Can you tell us a bit about what happened?'

'Aye, simple, he stabbed him in the eye for no reason.'

'So you can't think of anything at all that could have contributed to the incident?'

'Well, I don't know.' Bob fumbles with the lid of his cigarette packet, aware of the smirks. 'Well, there might have been something. Yon boy's been pretty pally with Bruno.'

'Who's Bruno?'

Alice cuts in. 'He shares a room with Evan.'

'Aye, well,' Bob taps the side of his nose. 'Well, Bruno follows Evan about like a wee dog. And the thing is, I once caught Norman and wee Bruno in a compromising position.'

'What kind of compromising position?' the mannish woman asks.

'Well, basically, he had the wee guy by the hair,' he pauses, aware of the hush and tries to phrase it delicately, but it sounds more stilted, 'and was being orally masturbated, by his, eh, mouth.' He presses his lips together. 'And basically that's why I think Evan attacked him, because they were probably in cahoots and planned it together.'

'I don't believe what I've just heard.' Alice sits forward on the edge of the seat. 'You didn't think to tell your fellow workers of this incident, or log it in a report, or discuss it with a senior?' Her eyes glitter. Words and phrases hard-bitten with contempt.

She turns her attention to the policeman. 'That's a reportable crime. Isn't it?'

'Aye, possibly,' the cop prevaricates. 'Sounds like it to me. But we'd need to know a bit more.'

'But I did ask Hunter about it,' says Bob, flapping. 'And he denied it. Said I'd been seeing things. He wasn't a poof. And I asked wee Bruno about it and he said the same thing.' He pantomimes concern. 'It was dark. So what was I to do? I wasn't that sure myself.'

'You're a blethering idiot.' Alice pats Evan's thigh. 'I can't even bear to look at you. But I guess that makes things easier in the short-term. Evan stays. Under no circumstances can Hunter come back here. And I don't imagine there'll be many tears about that among the staff or residents. And listen,' she looks Bob in the eye. 'Perhaps it isn't my place, but I don't think you should be here either.'

The mannish woman nods in agreement.

Chapter 48

I never get to see anything

Pizza Face sits on the floor in the living room, his back against the wall, gnawing at his thumbnail until his cuticles redden and bleed. His sister slumps on the couch beside his mum. He's in a huff because he wants to watch *Here Comes the Double Deckers*. 'I never get tae see anything,' he complains to his mum.

'Shut up,' she tells him. 'Or yeh'll get Double Deckering!'

His mum is always shouting at him for nothing. His brothers, out of harm's way, snigger in the kitchen, and plan the end of the world, drinking tea, smoking and listening to Radio 1 on the tranny. It's been raining for days and he wants to go out and play, but without Evan, the weather locks him in. He puts on his duffle and tucks his ball under his arm. There's a boy in the next close that wears an eyepatch. They don't like each other much. Pizza Face battered him for looking at him funny, but he is willing to let bygones be bygones.

He bangs the door shut. Angela sits on the top step of the upstairs landing. A hunched posture, limbs flung together like a laundry list. Her anorak hood rests against the close wall, face wan and vacant before her eyes settle on his.

'Whit yeh daeing?' he asks.

'Nothing,' she says through chittering lips.

'Yeh want tae come and play fitba?'

'Nah.'

A car horn toots. Pizza Face bounces the ball, the noise echoing around the landings. 'We could play kerbie. Yeh're rubbish. But I'll let yeh win some.'

She sniffles. 'Can I come intae yer house for a wee bit?'

He considers it. 'No yeh cannae.' The ball almost falls from his grasp, and he clutches it. 'My ma doesnay like anybody coming in. In case they bring in germs, and make a fool of her, cause of her condition.'

Angela stares through him.

He gropes for a half-penny Bazooka in his pocket. He crams a slat in his mouth and climbs the stairs. 'Here.'

She chews gum in companionable silence.

He thrust his tongue into his wad and blows pink. A small bubble appears and bursts with a plip. 'I can dae a lot better than that.'

He sits snug beside her and tries to blow the big one, a pink wobbly mass bigger than his head, which would lift him from his feet and would need to be harvested from his body, but all he manages is wee farters.

'That's shit,' Angela yawns, tucks her hips in tighter to him. 'Yeh think when yeh grow up, and ur really old, like fifteen or something, we'll see Evan again?'

'Aye. He was at school yesterday.' Pizza Face bursts another bubble, looks about as if he is going to appear. 'Why wouldnae we see him?'

She stares at her unbuckled shoe, and pulls the bubble-gum out of her mouth to speak, 'Cause he's been bad?'

He blows a flesh-pink bubble and snaps at it like a dog with his teeth, making her giggle. 'He's staying in a big fancy house jist up the road. And he says it's great. Yeh get tae watch as much telly as yeh like and yeh get pocket money and everything.'

She clutches at his arm. 'We could go see him!'

'Nah,' he swallows his chewing gum. 'It's too wet.'

Angela stands with a determined look on her face. 'He'll want tae see me.' She spits the gum between the railings, and tugs at his coat sleeve.

Slogging up the hill, the wind works against them. Pizza Face tucks the ball securely under his arm as the rain catches them. When they get close to the stone wall, cast-iron gate and driveway, he lets her skip ahead. He nods towards the door of the home. 'It's in there.' A pallid face appears at a downstairs window. He bounces the ball and catches it, bounces it again.

'Urn't yeh coming in as well?'

'Jist tell him tae come oot and play fitba.' The wind catches his hood and he grabs it before it whips backward. He shuffles sideways until anyone looking from the windows is blind to his birthmark. 'I'll wait here.'

Bob answers the door, as a teenage girl sneaks a peek over his shoulder.

Angela voice is tinny, 'I'm here tae see Evan.' And she's suddenly shy.

The teenage girl cups her hand to her mouth and giggles before swanning away.

'Oh, are you?' Bob turns his head and bawls, 'It's for you Evan!'

Angela stands, waiting. Bob shouts again. 'Jesus,' he rants when there's no reply and no sign of footfall. 'You better come in then.'

She cranes her neck to see more of the lobby, and her mouth falls open. Gleaming white rooms, it feels to her like being inside a cosy department store. She spots Evan ambling from the lounge. She runs to meet him, flings her arms around his legs, and presses her face against his thigh. He strokes her wet hair and picks her up. The weight of her seems to hang heaviest in her sopping-wet anorak.

She strokes his hollow cheeks. 'I need tae pee.'

He murmurs, 'Let's get yeh up the stairs. I'll show yeh my room. There's a lavvy beside it.'

Norma mis-steps before strolling past them. Angela recognises her from earlier, standing at the door. 'That your wee sister?'

Angela smiles shyly. 'Nah, I'm urnae. We live next door tae each other.' Remembering they don't, she buries her head in his shoulder.

'She's cute as a button,' Norma tells Evan. 'I've got a wee sister here too.'

Evan nods, 'Who's that?'

'Carla.' She reaches out and tickles the back of Angela's shoulder. 'She's six, about the same age as this one.'

Angela, stiff-necked, fizzes. 'I'm nearly five and I can read. And I'll be goin tae school after the summer.'

Evan avoids meeting her adolescent and knowing eyes. 'Can yeh take her tae the toilet?' He feels the flash of heat in his cheeks. 'She needs tae go.'

'Sure.'

Norma takes Angela's hand. Evan falls in behind them as they bounce up the stairs, at ease in each other's company, Angela chattering away. Norma listening and laughing.

Evan feels like a sitting target on the top step. It's too much of a thoroughfare. Laughter spills from the bathroom. Carrot walks between the lounge and kitchen and gazes at him. Evan meets the challenge, doesn't look away. The bathroom door finally opens and Norma and Angela appear.

Norma explains the delay in a breathy voice. 'I cleaned her up a bit.'

Evan meets her gaze, not sure what to say. 'That's fine.' He blushes and smiles at Angela. 'Say thanks to Norma.'

Angela shakes her head. 'Pizza Face is outside and he wants tae know if yeh want tae play fitba.'

'How did yeh no tell me?'

'I jist did.'

Norma cuts in, 'Who's Chaz?'

Angela's head drops. She looks up at Norma, close to tears.

Evan explains, 'He's Pizza Face's brother.'

Norma's eyes are distant moons. She goes to mouth a reply but doesn't. Whirling on wedged heels, she stomps towards her room.

Evan says, 'We best get goin then, if Pizza Face is waiting.'

Angela offers him a crooked smile. 'Can I see where yeh stay first? Dae yeh sleep in a dungeon, wae big chains on the wall?'

'Aye, c'mon I'll show yeh.'

He nods towards rows of shut doors. She sidles up beside him as they creep along the hall. He pushes his room door slowly open. She springs back against his legs when wind dashes rain against the window.

Evan giggles, shuffles inside and sits on his bed. She takes it in her stride and follows him. Her presence seems to alter the space between the two narrow beds and fill the room in a way neither Bruno nor anyone else could.

'Gimme yer jacket,' Evan holds out his hand. 'And I'll hing it on the radiator.'

She twirls out of her anorak and skirts past him, pulling open the cupboard door and takes a gander inside. Nothing grabs her attention. She briefly looks at the racing posters. Her anorak steams and fills the room with a damp doggy presence. Under his bed she finds something she can hold on to, pulling out the cover of a hardback book. She sounds out the name by finger pointing in the way Evan had taught her, but it is familiar as the word 'cheese' to a wedding photographer, *The Big Book of Grimms' Fairy Tales*.

He makes encouraging noises, his smile off kilter. 'That's right.' His social worker, Marie, had presented it to him in the office downstairs. Wrapped in brown paper, he was unsure. Weighty in his hands. The title—familiar. But not the same book, with the stained and ragged spine, not his book with crinkled and torn pages, but the stories familiar to him as his feet.

'I bought that with my own money,' Marie said.

The bin had rung when he tossed the expensive volume into it, but later it had turned up lying on top of his pillow.

Angela rifles through the pages, her mouth dropping open. When she finds Sleeping Beauty, she sits on the bed beside him.

He puts a hand on her shoulder and kisses her hair; she jerks her face away.

'Once upon a time,' she pushes her shoulder against his chest. She adopts her adult and serious voice, willing him to join in. And he does until words and cadence trace a familiar twisted path through forests and fields and princesses that sleep until passing princes kiss frozen lips. And they entwine their bodies like roots from the same tree and are droopy with sleep. Yawning, he slaps the cover of the book shut.

She holds her hand over her mouth. 'Dae yeh remember, when I was under the water and aw the bells ringing?'

'Yeh mean when yeh were in the canal, drowning?'

'I want yeh tae take me under the water again, tae hear the bells, because I'm sore.'

'Where ur yeh sore?'

'Aw o'er.'

They hear thumping steps. Bruno pokes his head into the room. 'There's somebody outside playing fitba, and he's pretty good at keepy-up, says he knows yeh.'

When she stands, the book falls from Angela's lap and bounces on the floor. Outside, it's getting darker and colder.

Chapter 49

Rent

Pizza Face adjusts his duffle-coat hood to show he is serious about being John Greig. He practices feints and step-overs, even though the rain is coning horizontal. Hitting the ball against the wash-house wall, turning with a slick shake of his hips and getting a shot away into the goals. A dustbin, slightly out of alignment from the others in the uneven cobbled lane, stands in.

'Goal!'

He's won the Scottish Cup in the last minute for Rangers against bitter rivals, Celtic. He holds his arms aloft and he can hear over one-hundred-thousand fans in the stadium screaming the Rangers captain's name: 'Graham-Graham-Graham.' Some of them leap over the barrier to hug him and do a drunken wee dance, bow before him, before getting huckled away by the police.

He spots Chaz, smoking a fag, leaning again the wall of the close and peering through the rain at him. A red Adidas bag at his feet. His older brother flicks his dout away and waves him over.

Pizza Face picks the ball out of a puddle. He wipes wet hands on the side of his duffel. Game over. But the buzz remains, the fans have gone home singing and happy. Plodding towards the close mouth, even from a few yards away, the reek of booze flattens him, but his brother shows no sign of being drunk.

Chaz pulls out a twenty-packet of Silk Cut and shells one towards Pizza Face, 'I need yeh tae dae me a wee favour.' He entrusts him with his heavy gold lighter to spark up first.

Pizza Face toe pokes his ball into the close and steps out of the rain. He catches a whiff of petrol but can't get the flint to work. He looks at Chaz, expecting him to be cranky and cuff his ear, but his brother lights up for both of them and they stand smoking in companionable silence.

Chaz smirks. 'I've got a wee job for yeh. And yeh don't even huv tae dae anything.'

'Whit is it?'

'Och, nothing much worth bothering about. I want yeh tae go somewhere. Huv a quick look. Come back oot and tell me who's about inside.'

Pizza Face coughs, 'Whereabouts?' His brother's ferret eyes glare at him as if he's a white rabbit. He nips the king-size cigarette by rolling the lit end between thumb and finger, as he's seen older guys do, and sticks the dout behind his ear for later.

The rounded toe of Chaz's black leather shoes kicks the zipped holdup. 'See this bag?'

'Aye,' Pizza Face looks at it, puzzled.

Chaz takes a last drag of his fag. 'This is whit we ur gonnae dae.' He lets the cigarette stub fall and crushes it under his heel. 'C'mon and I'll show yeh.' He points upward. 'Gi'e the bag tae my bird. And whatever yeh dae, don't look inside it, or I'll cut yer fucking heid off.'

Pizza Face glances over his shoulder and into the back court. 'Whit if I get caught?'

Chaz chuckles. 'Caught daeing whit?'

'Dunno.'

'Well, then, exactly.' Chaz holds out a fiver. 'Money up front. And another fiver when we're done. Cannae argue wae that. That's mair money than yer da makes in a fortnight.'

He lets it sink in. 'And aw for nothing.'

Pizza Face steps backwards. 'I'm no sure.'

Chaz picks up the bag. Flings his arm around his brother's shoulder, pulls him in tight. 'Let's take a wee stroll.'

'Will I need my baw?'

Chaz doesn't answer. They trek under the tunnel between tenements and into busy Dumbarton Road. Chaz takes an interest in the traffic as it slows and picks up speed, peering at the drivers as if memorising their faces. Chaz's grip loosens as they stand waiting to cross the road.

'I better take the baw back and stick it in the house. Tae keep it safe. Somebody could steal it.'

Chaz laughs. 'Aye, they could.' He urges Pizza Face to cross the road with him as there's a gap in the traffic. 'Jist bring it wae yeh. Mair natural like that way. But whatever yeh dae, don't leave it behind.'

'I wouldnae dae that. It's a good baw!'

Chaz hurries him along past the shops. Their pace slows near the canal at the tenement block with the rent office on the ground floor. He drops the bag, lights a fag, and drags his fingers through his hair, slicking it back from his face. He stands sideways on the pavement and reaches over and pulls Pizza Face's hood up.

'Here's whit yeh dae. Yeh cannae see in cause of that big fucking stupid wall, which is great, because it means they cannae see oot. I want yeh tae kick yer baw up and doon the strip of pavement inside the wall. Natural like. Jist stick yer big heid in the door and huv a quick dekko. Then come back here.' He sniffs. 'Got it?'

'Aye, yeh want me tae kick the baw about and huv a look-see inside?'

'That's right.'

'Whit dae I dae next?'

'Yeh come back here.'

Pizza Face smirks. 'Then yeh gi'e me another fiver?' He'll have enough sweets to last beyond Christmas, or he might even buy a Raleigh racing bike out of Tausney's.

The skelp across his cheek stings his nose and he drops the ball.

'Yeh didnae need tae dae that.'

He picks up his ball and hurries towards the rent office. The metal gate rasps as he pushes it open. Common-red brick worn with age towers twice his height. He drops the ball and boots it to the other end of the passage.

Pizza Face looks through the open door, past a woman with long black hair and a blue scarf who studies the folded cardboard and annotated rent book in her hand. It's a big room with wooden benches along the walls like he'd seen in church. A queue at the windows of the docket stations.

He hurries back to tell Chaz what he's seen. 'Two old fogeys sitting on wan of the benches. And a pregnant woman, so fat she looks as if she could pop any time.'

'OK,' Chaz takes a deep breath. 'Yeh did well.' But he doesn't act like it. Grips him by the shoulder and hustles him back along towards the housing block. He spies through the gate, unlatches it and puts down the bag. Pushes him towards the blind side of the wall.

'Wait here,' he says. 'And when I come oot, I'll haun yeh the bag. Yeh take it up the road.'

He unzips the holdall and pulls out two Starr pistols, a black balaclava and a pair of tights. 'Fuck this up and I'll fuck yeh up.'

Pizza Face nods, his legs shaking. He watches the traffic, expecting police cars and sirens. When he hears a bang, he knows it's a shot from a gun, followed by two other shots. Chaz flies out the gate and passes him the bag and keeps running across the road, tugging the balaclava off his hair and slowing as he hits the other pavement.

Pizza Face's walk home becomes a sprint, even though the bag is heavy—and he's been warned—because he's sure somebody will capture him.

Chapter 50

The wee cow

Bruno perches on the bed in the overheated room with his jacket zipped and the leather strap of his school bag slants over his shoulder. The tip of his tongue pokes out of the left side of his mouth. On his lap is a colouring-in book with pictures of animals and flowers and stars. Using an HB pencil, he copies a clean and sleek looking animal on to the back of the rough blue cover of his math jotter. He quickly hides the colouring-in book under his pillow when he hears Evan coming back from the toilet.

'Look,' he grins, holding out his math jotter to show Evan his drawing. 'Whit dae yeh think it is?'

Evan's smile turns to a frown as he studies the drawing. 'Eh, a wee cow?'

'Nah, that'll be chocolate.'

'A dinosaur?'

'It's a dog.' Bruno bounces off the crumpled top bedsheet and jostles against him. His fingers trace the dachshund's two sharpened and oversized fangs, dripping with blood. 'See its big teeth. Cows don't huv teeth like that.'

Evan looks over to where he's left his school bag beside the window. 'Oh, aye. Yeh're right.' He warms his hands against the radiator before they leave.

Chapter 51

Atheist

Dim classroom lights form a halo around Mrs Thomson's head. She gives Evan two quick licks of the belt for daydreaming during Religious Education. It hurt, but didn't hurt. He's sitting in the classroom and not in the classroom. He lapses into a stupor.

Mrs Thompson enunciates each word as if giving birth to the Bible. 'There is an appointed time for everything, and a time for every affair under the heavens. A time to be born and a time to die; a time to plant and a time to uproot—'

'Whit page is that God's on, again, Miss?' The classroom behind Pizza Face bursts into hoots of laughter.

Mrs Thompson snaps shut the Bible. She gives Pizza Face two of the belt for mocking the good book. He swaggers back to his seat.

She hesitantly picks up where she left off. 'A time to kill and a time to heal; a time to wear down and a time to build. A time to weep and a time to laugh; a time to mourn—'

A powerful realisation shakes Evan's body. There is no god. God does not exist, in the same way that Santa does not exist. People keep wittering on about him to make themselves feel better.

Pizza Face turns the shared text-book pages quicker than him. He nudges his arm with his elbow to pay attention. Mrs Thompson is watching them and ready to pounce. Everybody knows Evan's dad has been murdered. His picture was on the front page of the *Daily Record*, under the headline: 'Manhunt!' A snarling Alsatian police dog straining on a leash is pixelated.

Pizza Face is unwilling to grass to the police, but keen to let others overhear his ideas about who the killer is. 'Someone that owns a lion that accidentally ate him, like in Tarzan, or a big black man wae a spear.'

They crouch hip to hip, with duffle-coat hoods up. They play marbles at playtime with a mixture of ball bearings. Roll them into an overflowing stank water pouring from the kitchen downpipe. Pizza Face, because he has various sized steelies, and shiny ball bearings, wins most of the marbles 18 to 8, but neither will give up. But hungrier than normal, they call it quits.

Pizza Face flings away his dinner ticket and takes him to Blair's. He buys hot pies and cakes. He pays for stacks of swedgers from Jenny's, not normal stuff from the penny tray. Chocolates instead of toffee. A packet of ten Regal and a box of matches with a one-pound note.

They divide their loot at the hairdresser's shop, near the Cressie stairs. Evan dangles a liquorice lace, dripping it into his mouth. 'Where'd yeh get aw the dosh—Chaz?'

Pizza Face checks there are no teachers about before lighting a cigarette.

'Aye.'

'He jist geez yeh it?'

Pizza Face chugs a smoke ring. 'I cannae tell yeh, or he'll kill me.'

Evan turns away and, clutching with his knees, hangs upside down on the top bar of the railing. 'Fuck off, or I'll kill yeh.'

'Sorry, I didnae mean it yon way. It's stupid. He robs things. And I wisnae tae tell anybody. I hang about like a dick outside. It's easy.'

Evan tumbles his wilkies, pulls himself upright. 'Yeh no scared?' His wet arse perched on the bend of the bar.

'Nah!'

'Whit kind of places dae yeh rob?'

'The Rent office is the only wan we've done so far. But it's easy. We're gonnae dae mair, but he's waiting for some boys tae come back o'er from Ulster.'

Evan hadn't paid much attention but heard a report on the radio about it over cornflakes. 'But whit about that pregnant woman that got shot?' The older boys had been talking about it.

Pizza Face hides the cigarette behind his back as a guy in a checked jacket staggers up the stairs. 'Dunno. I never heard anything.'

'But yeh could go tae jail.'

'I willnae. I'd run away, first.' Pizza Face flicks the dout at the side of the broken building. 'They'd never catch us.'

Chapter 52

Rites

ON THE DAY OF HIS DA'S FUNERAL, EVAN GETS HIMSELF
ready early. Staffs busy themselves having a meeting to decide
who is to accompany him. They prioritise and get everybody to
leave for school. Evan skips breakfast and sits on his bed, waiting.

He nips in and out of the toilet because his tongue seems to swell
in his mouth, it blocks his throat and he feels sick. Someone rattles
the door. He shouts, 'There's somebody in.'

'Well, hurry up then,' a girl's voice and lilting laughter drifts
further away. 'What you daeing in there, anyway?'

His reflection stares back at him from the cracked mirror mottled
with flyspeck. He trudges back to his room and climbs into bed
fully clothed in school tie and blazer, grey flannels. He doesn't
even take off his shiny black shoes. Cocooned under the blanket,
he picks at the fringe and hides from daylight.

When he is sure everybody is gone, he surfaces and heads towards
the comforting smell and warmth of the kitchen. The cook's broad
shoulders stoop over a sink awash with soapsuds, smoking, and

looking out the window. Rain belts down outside, but her face is sunny.

She eyes him, critically. 'You look bonny. A real credit to your faither.'

'I'm no well,' he says. 'I cannae go.'

She nods, whether in agreement, he's not sure. Wiping her hand on a dishcloth, she tiptoes across, snuggles him to her with a warm arm, and brushes his hair away from his eyes. 'I've just the thing for you. Andrew's Liver Salts. Never fails.'

The concoction fizzes in a glass and she urges him to drink it.

Tickly on his throat, but he smacks his lips as he puts the glass on the draining board.

'Feel better?' she asks.

'Aye, magic,' he burps loudly.

She draws him in and kisses his forehead before gently pushing him adrift and turns her back, and pots rattle in the sink. 'You better get away, then. No doubt they'll be somebody looking for you.'

He watches through the dining-room window as a long, black, limousine squeezes through the gates and scrunches the stones, reversing and turning, turning and reversing, until it parks parallel with the building and doorstep. The chauffeur gets out of the car and the doorbell echoes in the foyer. A black peaked-cap hides his eyes and he wears funeral colours.

Evan hurries, but Julie answers the door before him. 'You better come in,' she tells the chauffeur, then changes her mind. 'We're a bit pushed for time. Wait there and we'll come out. I'll just get my coat.' She doesn't wait for a reply, yattering over her shoulder as she retreats. 'I had to borrow one because mine isn't black, and it's a bit too big for me.'

The chauffeur fiddles with his leather driving gloves and goes and sits in the car.

When Julie returns she is aflutter, gathering Evan and checking her purse, perfume, cigarettes, keys and diary are safely inside her bag.

'Hold this,' she tuts, handing Evan her bag and rushes away again, having forgotten something.

The limousine parks behind the hearse, outside Dalmuir Parish Church. Evan stares across at his old house from the car window, looking for his da's face. The chauffeur holds the door open for him to step out.

He marches to the other side of the car and holds the door open. A black brolly appears, and he tilts it high over Julie's head.

Evan tags on behind them. Clusters of tight-lipped men, stooping and dragging hard on their fags. A sprinkling of women, in ill-fitting clobber, stand black against the wall and fence. Julie's pallid prettiness, turkey-red lipstick and nails pink as semi-precious stones seem out of place among such sombre faces. Douts flicked into the gutter, washed away by rainwater. Church goers straighten up and fall into weary step. The opening bars of *Abide with Me* strikes God's last waltz on the organ pipes.

Julie squeezes Evan's hand as they sit in the front row. They share a hymn book with a glazed look and their lips frozen. The woman next to Julie makes an awful fuss. Top heavy with a curly mop, flushed face and broad shoulders, Evan looks away because he's embarrassed for her. Arms flapping, a marionette, lilting an out-of-tune rendition of the hymn, 'Whit am I gonnae dae, Lord?'

An older man's voice wheezes, 'That was his bit of stuff, wae a bun in the oven. Wee cow'll know aw about it, noo.'

Reverend Soutar, a tall cadaverous man with a pointy grey beard, hurries through the service. He stares over the head of the congregation and recites prayers in a monotone voice, punctuated by morbid hymns with the glory sucked out. He mentions Dermot's age, a young Roman Catholic wife that has gone before him. And he has a young son, Evan. He delivers God's words of consolation as a list of telegram messages.

Pallbearers sneak up the side aisles of the church, broad and familiar florid faces. His dad had worked with big men, sure stepped, shouldering the coffin, carrying his dad out to his final resting place.

Julie sniffles and cries into her hanky, throughout *Amazing Grace*. The bit of stuff outbid her. A fainting fit. She is carried out of the church feet first, much like Dermot's body.

Outside, Evan shakes hands with people he doesn't know, dry-eyed among all that sobbing. He wants to go home, but he doesn't know where home is now.

Chapter 53

Torture

KERRY-ANN ANSWERS THE DOOR, TUGGING THE BELT OF HER flowery nightgown tighter, smiling, and giving a little wiggle as Del towers over her and ogles the top of her breasts.

'Your man in?' he asks.

She loves his accent. 'Yeh want tae come in?'

'Nah,' Del winks at her. 'Would love to, but you know.' His clean-shaved jaw leans in close enough for her to whiff musty Hi Karate and ingrained cigarette smoke on his jacket. He grins at her. 'Just ask him to come down and see us.' He nods towards the dimly lit landing and stairs. 'We've a car, waiting.'

Angela stands by the window, hand cool against the pane, breathing on the glass and searching for rainbows. She turns when her mum comes into the living room. Two mugs of tea lie beside the bed. Chaz stinks the place up with his booze and farting. Kerry-Ann gently shakes his bare shoulder to waken him.

Chaz snarls, 'Whit?'

She says, 'That Irish boy is at the door for yeh.'

He whips the bedding back and jumps out of bed naked. Angela turns away, rests her head against the window, humming a tune she's made up.

'Yeh never told him I was in, did yeh?'

'Aye,' Kerry-Ann takes a step backward. 'Course I did. I thought he was yer pal.'

'Stupid cow!' Scanning the burst couch, he searches the floor for his trousers. He hurries to pull them on but the zip catches on the foreskin of his penis. He cries out and hops from foot to foot.

Denim shirt and brown brogues lie pooled at the foot of the bed. 'Whit exactly did he say?' He searches Kerry-Ann's face, dresses quickly and sits on the couch to pull on his shoes and lights a fag before going out to face them.

Chaz slicks back his hair and ambles towards the Ford, the red Adidas bag in his right hand. He flings the holdall into the back seat and gets into the car. 'Alright lads. Enjoy yer wee holiday?'

Dougie remains po-faced. 'Well, you could say that.'

Del turns the ignition key and the engine stutters into life. Less than ten-minutes later, the car passes Drumchapel Baths.

Foreign and gangland territory for Chaz. His only visit to the pool was with his wee brothers, when he was about ten-years old, had ended with them getting mugged by bigger boys and handing over the few pennies they had.

A sharp left, sloshing through puddles and grey streets. Kinfauns Drive, the main artery of the scheme spiralling off into the scheme's nervous system. Pedestrians shabbier than those in Clydebank. The car jolts to a halt.

They'd passed Merryton Avenue, which didn't look very merry to Chaz. All the drab blocks of houses look interchangeable. He reaches across and picks up the holdall, hugging it to his chest. Dougie and Del stand on the pavement, smoking a fag and wait for him to join them. Across the road, a woman in a blue triangle headscarf grips an infant's pudgy hand and pulls her one step forward, and two sideways, dancing towards a distant bus stop.

Chaz knows it's too late to run. Loaded guns weigh down the bag he carries. He keeps his movements slow and tries to keep the tremor in his hand from showing when he lights a Silk Cut. He forces a smile on to his lip before going to stand beside them. 'I done a wee job when yeh were away.'

Dougie drops his lit cigarette on to broken paving, scrunches it with his heel and there is a glimmer in his eyes. 'Yeh, we heard all about it.'

Chaz blinks and looks away. 'Aw the money's here.' He holds the Adidas bag out like a parcel.

Dougie nods towards the rows of dull windows. 'We'll talk about it inside.' He leads the way to the top landing. *Fuck the Pope* is sprayed in black paint on the walls. *Up the UDA.*

They left the front door unlocked, which surprises Chaz. The lobby is full of shadows, ready to make him jump. From the living room uncertain sounds and a whiff of cigarette smoke. When Dougie pushes the door open, a single wall light glows. The room is bright and airy. A cheap transistor radio on the windowsill blaring, Dawn's *Knock Three Times on the ceiling and I'll love you.* But their presence seems like an act of male violence.

A girl stands chaste in a white bra and skirt in front of the fire. 'Give me a minute.' Her Irish accent is as natural as freckles on her silken white skin. A glimpse of her forehead and the skin around her eyes crinkles, with a faint aquamarine cast squinting sideways at them in amusement. She irons her hair over the ironing board, uses a brown paper bag sheath as a guard, and sizzles it into straight straps with a whiff of burning copper wire.

Del jokes, 'For God's sake, Lizzie put some clothes on. You'll be giving us all palpitations.'

Dougie speaks in a soft burr, 'Aye hen, that would be an idea.' He reaches behind the telly and pulls the plug for the iron out of the double socket. 'Then you can nip across the road and see your Auntie Ina. We've a few things we need to get sorted here.'

He reaches over and takes the Adidas bag out of Chaz's hand and gives it to Del, who takes it through to the kitchen and unzips it. The money is tied in hundreds.

Dougie tells Lizzie. 'Don't hurry back until I come over and get you.'

Lizzie flushes and pulls on a blouse. 'You're always trying to get rid of me, You said we were going to the La Scala,' but she's already flouncing out of the room.

Chaz slides into the nearest seat on a musty couch as Dougie turns his attention from her to him and his eyes narrow.

Del scoots in behind the couch and draws the chintz curtains. On the windowsill, an aerial spikes out on the radio, a pathfinder, George Harrison and the plaintive tones of *My Sweet Lord*. Chaz feels Del's bulk standing behind him.

Fear has a focus, and it's Dougie, drumming his fingers on the ironing board. His light blue eyes float around the room as if he doesn't recognise him, or anybody in it. He follows the cable, tugging it towards him. A metallic horse's hoof in his fist. He brings it, in a flash of silver, above Chaz's knee, branding his thigh. The iron has lost heat, but Chaz's writhing matches the smell of burnt flesh. Del puts him in a headlock. His screams ricochet and seep through breeze-block walls. The edge of the iron catches him across the nose and it flattens above his other knee.

Clumps of hair come away in Del's fist as Chaz's squirming allows him a second of relief. He scrambles to the far side of the couch. Cowering, his hands flapping. 'Don't hurt me,' he pleads, bawling. 'I gave yeh aw the money. Whit mair dae yeh want me tae dae? Tell me!' His arms gesture surrender. 'I'll dae it. Jist don't hurt us.'

Del stands beside Dougie at the door, like human barbed wire.

Chaz glances behind him weighing the window as an escape route. His mind tumbles to mental gymnastics, thinks about a third-floor fall onto municipal grass turned to hay, assorted cheese and onion and salt and vinegar crisp packets and his body in bloom like a used condom wrapper.

Dougie sighs. 'Look son, I don't really want to hurt you. Don't need all this fuss. You think you're a hard man, but you're about as hard as Ginger Rogers without the tits. But that's not what it's all about. It's all about trust. And it's about the cause. I've got things to do and you're pulling strokes. I need to come fucking back here to run after you, ya fucking clown.'

Dougie turns to Del. 'Was the guns there?'

'Aye.'

'Much was in the bag?'

'About £1800'

He gazes at Chaz, who has taken a step sideways and backwards.

'Aye, well,' Dougie's expression softens a little. 'Not bad. I'm going to ask you a few questions and for your sake, I better get the answer I'm looking for.'

Blood splatters from Chaz's nose onto his denim jacket and he swipes it away. 'I widnae tell yeh any lies, Dougie.'

Dougie snorts, 'You're a fucking liar.' He puts the iron face down on the ironing board. 'I see I'll need to cut a wee bit rough with you.'

Del edges round the side of the couch to flush Chaz out. It's like a playground game of British Bulldog. Chaz feints one way towards Dougie and his left knee knocks against the telly, and he's ready to cut across the fireplace and try to get past Dougie in a lopsided sway. Bits of his body are on fire. His cheek swells and grows purplish and his nose makes snorting noises like a blowhole. An eye puffed and closed. But with sharper vision, he checks for space to dart into and escape through.

Dougie waves a weary hand, and Del stops slinking nearer. Chaz stands shivering beside the mantelpiece, a gilt-frame picture of a younger Dougie and a wee girl in school uniform, white socks a tide mark above her skinny wee legs. Red hair in a frizz that frames a heart-shaped face that is all smiling white teeth the camera locks in.

'Yon pregnant lassie in the papers, you killed,' Dougie says. 'What did you shoot her for?'

There's desperation in the way that Chaz speaks, acknowledgement of the terror he feels. 'Her boyfriend tried tae grab the gun off me and I panicked.' He almost believes it himself.

'So you're saying it was collateral damage?'

'Aye,' Chaz clings to that notion. 'Collateral damage.'

Del chips in with a quip. 'She was a fucking Pape, anyway. And that's two less of the wee bastards to worry about.'

Chaz is aware of his slowed breathing and the sudden, unexpected, silence on the radio slot between songs.

Dougie challenges him again. 'What about that post office in Parkhall?'

Chaz acts affronted, becomes a tad more upright and confident. 'That's nothing tae dae wae me.'

'That'd be fucking two jobs in a week,' Del says. 'You'd need to be the worst kind of fucking idiot to try that.'

Chaz agrees, 'Exactly.'

'I'll need to make a phone call,' Dougie says. 'Keep him here. And if he makes any attempt to leave, break his legs and cut his balls off.'

Del scratches his head. 'Sure, no bother.'

But when Dougie leaves, Del isn't sure what to do next. 'Sit down there,' he tells Chaz, pointing at the couch and a seat near the telly.

He wanders into the kitchen. Chaz hears cupboards opening and closing, and the sound of water running. He knows he can make a run for it but stays put. Del comes lumbering back into the living room, grinning like a crocodile, waving a bottle of Eldorado and two glazed brown mugs.

He plonks himself beside Chaz. 'Thought we might as well have a wee drink while we're waiting.' He puts the mugs on the edge of the rug and fills them.

Chaz tries to keep his hands from shaking when he's handed his measure, but he needs to use both hands. His bruised lips jerk away from contact with the rim and his teeth clatter off the enamel. He gulps it to calm his nerves.

Del doesn't seem to notice, he's too busy scoffing his own drink and smacks his lips. 'She's some bit of stuff, that Lizzie.'

'Aye,' Chaz answers tentatively, wondering if it's a trick question. 'Very nice. Is that Dougie's daughter?'

'Fuck off, ya stupid cunt. Better not let him hear you saying that. That's his wife.'

Chaz tries to erase the memory of the snivelling shadowy self by tearing into the booze. But Del isn't hanging about either. They match each other drink for drink. When the bottle is empty, Del goes to the kitchen, brings back another and cracks it open. The room hangs heavy with cigarette smoke and the ashtray on the table in front of them brims with douts.

'She's some girl that Lizzie, you know,' Del's slightly awry smile carved into his jaw, like a watermelon with its eyes lit up. 'She hates those Fenian bastards more than anyone I know. If you gave her a gun she'd take over Dublin.' He knocks over his mug, reaching for the bottle. The dregs soak into the flowery petals of the carpet, leaving a damp spot and stench of booze. Shoulder to shoulder with Chaz in a drunken haze, he confides in him. 'The thing about her was she was my wee sister's pal and used to knock about our house. You know how it is when you're young and you're trying to impress the girls.'

'Aye,' Chaz nods his head in solemn agreement.

'Well, she was always there, egging you on. The 12th of July, you'd have The Walk. Try and see who'd the biggest bonfire. And you'd scavenge stuff from everywhere and even the boys up the road would need to watch out for you, because you'd steal their stuff quicker than look at them, or set it alight, to fuck them up. There was all that growing up stuff. But you know Lizzie would be out helping you. I mean, she was a scraggy wee thing. Not up to much, but the next thing you'd look round, and she'd be looking at you, with thon big eyes. She set a car on fire for a laugh. Plum crazy. And if you set a bonfire off, she'd be fucking sitting on top of it like Guy Fawkes, daring you to—'

He shakes his head, slaps Chaz's shoulder, and drapes his arm around him. 'I suppose you're lucky. You've got a bit of stuff.'

Chaz takes a mouthful of wine, ignoring the reference to Kerry-Ann. 'Whit's she daeing o'er here then?'

Del's cheeks pink and redden. 'Fuck knows. I'm just a number.' He blows out his exasperation in a long breath. 'The cunts never tell me fuck all.'

When Dougie and Lizzie breenge into the living room, they look at Del and Chaz as if they'd been holding hands and she giggles.

'I telt you to keep an eye on him,' Dougie growls. 'Not treat him to a party.'

'Hi,' Del replies. 'I'm not a dog at your beck and call.'

The ugly twist of her mouth disfigures her pretty face. 'Godsake, boys, don't start fighting over nothing. Let's all just be friends.' She turns to Dougie and takes the heat out of his eyes by rubbing his arm.

Dougie shrugs, 'I suppose.'

Del relaxes and takes another belt of wine. 'I didn't know when youed come back, right enough. So I just thought I'd have a wee drink.' He includes Chaz in the nod of his head. 'We'd have a wee drink. But I'm alright to drive,' Del burps and Lizzie smiles at him. 'I've just had a couple.'

Dougie holds out the palm of his hand for the car keys and Del dives into his pocket and hands them over.

Chaz sits in the passenger seat looking straight ahead and feels for the outline of his razor. It reassures him he might have a fighting chance if something else happens.

Dougie is a more cautious driver than Del. The car slows on the hill by the public baths, windscreen wipers batting away the rain, cigarette burning in the pulled-out ashtray before Dougie speaks. 'You're lucky the guns were all there, and you'd the common sense, and the common decency, to put the money from the job in the bag or you wouldn't be sitting here now, but it wasn't up to me. It was up to the boys back home. They said "youed showed commendable initiative."' He lets that sink in, flicking the indicator on. 'I thought you were a sensible lad. What were you thinking of?'

'I jist saw a chance and I took it.'

'Without backup?'

'Aye.' Chaz doesn't mention his wee brother's role.

They overtake a dark coloured Vauxhall Viva and Dougie shakes his head, whether at the slow speed of the woman driver, or at Chaz himself, he's not sure.

Dougie's verdict; 'Stupid. What if you'd got caught? All our good work down the swanny. Not to mention all the guns and ammos we have in Glasgow.'

'But I didnae.' Chaz quickly changes the subject. A note of merri-
ment in his voice. 'I think Del's got a wee thing for yer wife,
Lizzie.'

The car swerves at the roundabout. Dougie grips the wheel hard,
'How, what'd he say, like?' He squints at him, a cheek muscle
twitching.

'Och, nothing much.' Chaz keeps it casual, stubs out his cigarette.
'He jist said they'd grown up together and they went back a long
way.'

'What else?'

'Nothing.'

Dougie slaloms into an uncharacteristic U-turn manoeuvre,
cutting off a van, something that Del would have done without
thinking about. He parks in front of the Kippen dairy and turns
the engine off, ignoring the blaring horns.

Dougie reaches across and grabs his wrist before he can get out.
'What else?'

'Nothing. He jist said she was very pretty. Yeh know what he's
like.'

'Aye, I've a fair idea what he's like.'

Chaz steps out of the car and onto the wet pavement. He's money
in his pocket and he needs a drink. The car stutters into the line of
traffic. Chaz sniggers, thinking Dougie looks like he might need a
good hard drinking session too.

Chapter 54

Cooked

SEAGULLS SCREECH ABOVE ANGELA'S HEAD, CONVERGING around the bins ranged along the top of Risk Street. A blackbird underneath a fuchsia, tucks in beside the wall, falters in song and falls silent as she gets closer to the Home. Her hair raffishly cut in a bowl shape. She blows gold tresses off her forehead.

She finds home in the kitchen's warmth. She shares hot fudge from the oven that scalds her mouth. Angela's bright eyes darken like a shadow over water when she stands still, and she blinks rapidly when she forgets and talks about Chaz.

The cook scours the pots in the sink. 'Is he your da?' A burnt pastry smell lingers in the air.

Evan answers for her. 'Nah, he's jist somebody her mum knows.'

'He's no my real da,' Angela avoids the cook's intense gaze. 'But we're gonnae huv a little sister, or brother, soon. And I've tae help take care of the baby.' She swells up with the responsibility.

'Uhu,' the cook dries her hands on a dishcloth. 'Sometimes we don't like talking about some things. My da was a bit like that. He wasn't much use.'

Angela giggles and as the cook bends to put a blackened frying pan beneath the sink, she rushes over and briefly hugs her leg and is hugged back.

The cook turns and pats Evan's shoulder. 'Better keep an eye on her,' she laughs. 'Before she gets into some kind of mischief. There's a bit of the devil in her, yet.'

Evan grins. 'I will.'

Wellies keep their feet dry. Duffle coats keep them well wrapped against the cold, but they wander aimlessly around the back of the house, making tracks as grass peeks through unseasonable grey slush.

'Whit's that?' Angela points to an old-fashioned stand-up-and-beg bike, with high handlebars pushed against the wall. Steam from the storage-room vent at the back of the kitchen swirls above their heads. She yanks the handlebars away from the wall, almost toppling it. 'It's a bike!' A note of awe in her voice. 'We could... we could go on it.'

Evan replies, 'It's ancient. And it's got a flat front tyre.'

'But it still goes.'

The bike falls sideways as she tries to scramble onto the saddle.

'Whit yeh daeing? It's broke.'

She ignores him. 'Help me up on tae the saddle. Push me! I'll guide.'

She grabs the handlebars as he hauls her up, but her legs straddle the metal bar from saddle to front column, and she can't reach the pedals. The bike wobbles as she jockeys it. Evan digs his feet into the stone chips and pushes, trying to keep it from tilting and falling. The bike and its passenger reach pavement and open road. Her cheeks glow apple red and she cries with delight. 'See, I told yeh I could go a bike.'

His back sore and arms weary, the bike tilts and falls.

'Put me back on,' she demands. 'I was jist getting the hang of it.'

'Nah, I'm no daeing it. It's jist stupid.'

Bruno bounces out of the front door and comes towards them. 'I was looking everywhere for yeh.'

Angela pipes up. 'We're taking shots of goin on a real bike.'

'Great,' Bruno claps his hands. 'Gi'e me a shot.'

Angela declares, 'Yeh need tae hold me up on the bar and push me. Evan'll show yeh how tae dae it.' She points imperiously towards where she wants to be wheeled. The slope where deciduous hedges spun with crumpled gold leaves poking through mark the boundary of hill, road and pavement.

'Nah,' Bruno tells Evan. 'She's too wee. I'll huv a go first.'

'I'm no,' Angela shouts. 'I'll be at school soon, like yeh.'

'Push,' she tells Evan. The bike wobbles sideways into the wall at the bottom of the street. She falls but is quickly on her feet and giggles. 'Let's dae it again.'

Chapter 55

Gouching

Enclosed in the front-seat bubble of a red Volkswagen, and stuck in traffic, Chaz snoozes. Del is driving. They tag behind a security van as it picks up and drops off money. The route takes it from Paisley Road West through the Clyde Tunnel onto Dumbarton Road to Dumbarton, near the Sheriff Court and back along to Partick. It's boring. They've been following the schedule for about a fortnight and it's the nearest thing Chaz got to a real job. He knows exactly where the white van is going to stop. How long the security guards will take. He can even pick out which security guard is doing the delivery from behind by the way he walks.

'Drop me off here,' he tells Del, passing his house, as they shadow the van coming through Dalmuir. 'I'm gonnae go for a pint. Fancy it?'

The security van stops next to the pavement at the Linen Bank and the bigger of the two security guards gets out. It's next to Maggie Scott's and too good an opportunity to miss. They watch as the security guard strolls to the door of the bank.

'Nah,' Del sticks on the handbrake. Parks beside the chip shop at the canal. 'You batter in,' he jokes. 'And have one for me. You know what Dougie's like, he'll quiz me. Want to know what colour of knickers those playboys are wearing.' He nods towards the humph-shouldered security guard, carrying his satchel. 'It's a fucking lark.' He takes a deep drag of his fag, glancing sideways at the mirror and through the side window into the traffic.

Chaz scoots out of the passenger door and pulls his denim jacket tight against the rain. They've a fleet of four cars they use in different lockups. He feels little sympathy for Del, his chauffeur and their wheelman, but the growing elation of a man sneaking away from work early.

Chaz does what he's required. He supposes his growing ability to ease the dial through the hicks and shrieks of white noise, cut through dissonance, and pick out police frequencies on the radio receiver installed in the car, will later be a more useful tool than swapping channels between Radio 1 and Radio Clyde.

The same old faces in the pub when he pushes through the door. A pint waiting for him. The barman limps over with his hand out, waiting to get paid. 'Huv wan for yerself.'

The pint tumbler near the till dings with Drew's tip money. 'Cheers.'

Chaz lights a Silk Cut. Tired jokes flutter into life from the tables close by and burn out quicker than the Bluebell match he uses. Cliff Richard and the Shadows from the transistor on the bar leave him unmoved in a fug of smoke.

Rab sits with dregs of lager in front of him. From where Chaz stands, he is on the nod. A coughing spell brings him out of it. His eyes startled but unaware. He rocks backwards and forward. His lips crinkle as he tries to put a roll-up into his mouth, but a hacking cough defeats his effort. His head turns, his plukey face has waged a war with blackheads and his hair hangs lank as greaseproof paper.

'Chaz,' Rab shouts in recognition. 'Is that yeh? C'mon o'er here, my man.' His bony hips move sideways and he lifts his pint and puts it to his lips. His eyes flicker towards the bar.

'Whit's wrang wae yeh?' Chaz wanders over and settles his bum on a three-legged stool across from Rab and puts his pint beside the ashtray.

'Jist too much tae drink.'

'That's no drink. Whit yeh on? Hash?'

'Nah, I'm jist tired.'

'I hear shite talking. Whit ur yeh in here for, exactly?'

'I thought I'd come and see my best mate. Nae harm in that, is there?'

Chaz leans across the table. 'Whit is it? That LSD? Yeh seeing wee green men?' He flutters bent fingertips in front of Rab's face.

'It's heroin,' Rab whispers. 'I was hoping yeh'd lend me twenty-five quid tae gi'e tae Tam Daly, or he said he's gonnae break my legs.'

'Fuck off.' Chaz takes a sip of his pint. His uncle Tam Daly lends money out of the Atlantis. He'd come home with his da at New Year and had a drink in his house to welcome the bells. Meant to be a hard nut. But he doesn't like Daly threatening his mate, and how that reflects on him.

Rab's apologetic tone works as a plea bargain. 'The Tash owes at least double that amount. Yer brother's on the gear as well.'

Chaz swivels on the stool. 'Wait and I'll get yeh a pint.' Nobody messes with his brothers.

Chapter 56

Carry out

ANGELA LIES SCRUNCHED LIKE A QUESTION MARK AT THE bottom of the bed, blankets halter tight around her shoulders, not just to keep out the cold. A fire smoulders in the ashes of the grate throwing off heat, making the room too warm, adds a gleam of light and the scent of burning clinkers. Kerry-Ann sits on the edge of the couch, wrapped in a nightgown. A lit cigarette burns in the ashtray at her feet among blackened douts. She picks at the pink nail polish on her fingers, but like Angela, she is waiting for Chaz. The uproar of the pubs at closing time, babbling men milling about on Dumbarton Road, tells them how late he is. It's better than the Westclox's alarm clock, its illuminated hands ticking on the mantelpiece.

The heavy footsteps on the stairs, Angela hazards a look from her hidey-hole. Kerry-Ann rubs the bulge of her stomach, and she holds herself and rocks from side to side. She covers the strain of waiting, and no longer waiting, by staring straight ahead at the Test Card on the telly. She flutters up. 'Is that yeh, Chaz?'

He bounces against the lobby wall. A can of McEwan Pale Ale peeks out of each side pocket. His fingers clench into a fist carrying a white plastic bag. His eyes flicker like candles. He swerves past her and sways towards the kitchen.

His head buckles and he closes his eyes but holds the bag up in triumph as if it appeared on his wrist. 'I could fair go something tae eat.'

'I'll get it.' She prises the plastic bag away from his floppy hand. It's like peeling a jumper from a wain holding onto her sleeve. An unopened can spills from his jacket pocket and rolls beside the leg of the wooden chair.

'Put some music on. I want tae hear some of my records. Some Faces.'

'It's too late.'

'Put some music on.' Chaz lifts his droopy head as if seeing her for the first time. 'Want tae hear some of my records.'

'It's too late.'

'Don't fucking tell me about fucking too late.'

Kerry-Ann takes a step back, tries a different tack. Curry sauce pools in the bag. Grey rice soaks into it. She turns her back on him, searching on the top shelf of the cupboard for a clean plate. Rattling through the drawer at the sink for a knife and fork. Banging the two trays on to the plate, she minces them together with a wooden spoon.

Picking up the fork, he spears cubes of chicken in curry sauce into his gob, standing and swaying to the music in his head. 'Huv some,' he says. 'It's good.'

'I don't like that foreign muck.'

'Look at the state of this place.' His glance takes in the dishes in the sink, the cupboard door with a hole where he'd punched it, and rests back on her. 'Look at the state of yeh. Fat as fuck and good for fuck aw.'

He points the prongs of the fork at her nose. 'I bought this Chinky for yeh. Yeh better take a bit.'

She veers around him and takes a fork from the murky water in the sink and runs it under the tap. Through the window, a full moon hangs in the sky, resting in blackness and far pinpricks of light.

'Better get tae yer bed,' he mutters. 'And get tae sleep.' Rouses himself. 'Where's Bridget the Midget?'

'Sleeping.'

'That's good. I'll need somebody tae coorie up tae. Yer fucking useless.'

'But Chaz—' her voice a fragile thread.

'But Chaz, fucking nothing. Dae as I telt yeh.'

Angela waits for the sickly stench of boozy breath to possess her. His weight to roll onto her and prick her. She remembers the time she was under the water in the canal, the bells peeling and everyone cheering.

'Yer lucky, yeh cannae get pregnant and yeh'll be well broken in for the boys when yer older.'

Her mother has her back to them and feigns sleep, but Angela hears muted sobbing.

Chaz's snoring is a mark of departure. Angela doesn't feel her mother rising from the bed but hears her cold feet tapping on the linoleum. Kerry-Ann staring out of the kitchen window into the hostile night.

Chapter 57

Withdrawal

DEL FITS NUMBER PLATES TO THE WHITE VOLVO, STOLEN TO order for the job, in the early hours of Friday morning. Dougie lounges against the wall smoking a Capstan. He plays lookout and peers into the blur of cold rain. But there's nothing to see. The council lock-ups at Kirksowald are built tight together like a communal magnet with a narrow entrance. They're hidden from the high flats. The boulevard runs parallel and takes five minutes from their safe house in Drumchapel.

Del gets soppy-eyed with a love song on Radio 1, but gets back to work, tuning the scanner into police frequencies. The Irish boys dress in military fatigues. An Armalite assault rifle lies on the back seat, and they carry a Starr pistol.

They laugh as they put on wigs and false moustaches. Each of them has a beard. Dougie's straggly and peppered with grey. They weave bandages over their fingers and palms to avoid leaving prints.

Chaz sits in the gloom of the garage with his shoes off, his hands and fingers bare. 'I canny pull,' he moans. His bum slides along the dusty floor, trying to fit his legs into a pair of dark, acrylic trousers.

Dougie gets in on the joke, winks at Del. 'Canny pull, what?'

Del chokes with laughter. 'It might get sore.' He slaps Dougie's shoulder as he passes him and slips into the driver's seat, his pistol in his lap. He smiles at his reflection and at how ridiculous he looks and adjusts the rear-view mirror.

Dougie checks his pistol before sliding into the front seat, keeps it tucked between his legs, out of sight. Their good humour spills over to Chaz who settles into the back seat, dressed in the livery of a postman, a cap pulled over his forehead, his eyes show as slits. He adjusts the postbag, the sawn-off shotgun hidden.

They drop Chaz off beside the postbox on the hill at Apsley Street. He checks his canvas sack as he meanders along the pavement towards the Post Office where the Securicor van makes the last pickup. Partick is busy with shoppers, pedestrians and students from Glasgow University slacking off.

The Volvo turns the corner and overtakes him. The boys have placed traffic cones on the road outside the Post Office, leaving a bay into which the car edges into the pavement and parks near the double doors. Curly wigs touch heads, listening to the police channels, the engine ticks over and the smell of diesel fumes hangs in the air. In the rear-view mirror, Del watches Chaz adjust the slanting strap on his bag as the Securicor van comes along Dumbarton Road to pick up the last money-bag of the day. Chaz stands beside the Volvo, not looking at them, but once more inspects the contents of his sack.

The Securicor van double parks, as it usually does, with hazard lights flashing, holding up traffic. The beefy security guard jumps out, leaves the van door open and car horns start tooting. He hurries through the double doors, almost home, his job done for the day.

Chaz finger on the trigger sticks a sawn-off shotgun, both barrels, in the security guard's face as he comes out of the Post Office. 'Gi'e me the bag, or I'll blow yer fucking head clean aff.'

'Get out,' Dougie stares down the driver of the Securicor van. He points the Armalite rifle at his face and tells him, 'Leave the keys on the seat.'

Wild-eyed, the driver's hands shakes, keys jangle and chime as he tries to separate himself from them and drops them onto the worn-out passenger seats. He falls out the door, almost getting hit by a Corporation bus as he scrambles across the road.

Dougie boosts himself up into the van, lays the rifle on the floor, and picks up the keys, checking the side mirror, before turning the key in the ignition barrel.

Del waits for the van engine to start before slapping the security door three times in quick succession, a code the workers used to show the coast is clear. The door opens and a white face looks into a Starr pistol. Del reaches in and pulls the older man by his shirt collar, sandbags him to the ground and kicks him in the ribs. 'Move from there and I'll shoot you.' The older security guard holds his arms out, shielding his face and sobbing.

Chaz runs from behind Del and leaps into the back of the security van. The Irishman bangs shut the security door with him inside. A driver of a Ford Cortina two cars back in the queue of traffic gets out of his car to get a better view. Del points the gun at him and he skulks behind the open door.

Del jumps behind the wheel of the Volvo and drives off. The Securicor van tucks in behind him and traffic ebbs forward and car horns stop tooting.

Twelve minutes later, the Securicor van parks on Cochino Road near the woods. They wrap their guns in towels, unload the bags of cash and torch the van with their disguises inside it. Nine minutes later, they park the BMW they use to courier them outside Drumchapel Baths and swap it for a lime-green Volkswagen. Four minutes later, they are in the safe house's bedroom, counting the loot piled on a double bed. That task takes much longer than the robbery. Thumbs sore, the tip of lips chafed. Counting and recounting scuffed notes. Blues, greens, browns, pinks: £38 882 in piles of one hundred.

Del punches the air. 'We'll need to celebrate.'

Dougie lets himself be hugged by his Irish partner 'Fucking, too right.' He sticks a hand out, pulls Chaz across, sweeps him into the embrace of the Irish brotherhood, dancing and jigging together. 'Think how many weapons we can get with this fucking haul.'

Chapter 58

Bone shaker

Bob rolls up the sleeves of his frayed, checked shirt, and uses the side window of the dining room as a seat. No wind, slow-moving clouds and sunshine gilding the bark of a birch tree offers a pleasant morning before lunch. He fouters with the wheel. When any of the kids come close, the flatness of his stare through rimless glasses lets them know he wants to be alone. A cup of cold tea lies on the sill beside him. Five or six douts at his feet speckle the grass. He uses soup spoons from the kitchen to lever the tyre off the frame of the wheel. A cigarette dangles from his mouth, nicotine-stained fingers tug and stretch the inner-tube. He eyes his kit, and a plastic basin of water. It doesn't take him long to mark the punctures with yellow crayon. Patching takes as long as it takes and eats into the working day.

Angela appears at lunchtime as she often does on weekends. Her hair is as dirty as her mouth. But her clothes and shoes are shiny and new. A thick, brown cardigan under her duffle and she kicks off Clarks shoes under the chair. Bruno has given up his usual seat beside Evan to her.

Bob mutters, 'It's like dining in an off-site caravan.' Lukewarm Smash potatoes grow cold in a bowl, left untouched, beside a plastic dish of HP baked beans. Sandwiches offer a sliver of cheap orange cheese on Sunblest bread. A plateful of look-warm sausage rolls on each table are scoffed. 'Any chance of getting some more?' He affects a jocular tone when the new cook appears to clear the tables.

Carrot and Doc stop bickering with their mouths open, chewing on white bread and beans and gaze at her. Girls at the other tables look on with interest.

The new cook's hair is wrapped in a cloth turban and her uniform of wraparound floral crackles with nylon static. She points a ladle in the general direction of Angela. 'There would be enough for everybody, but I cannae be expected tae feed every waif and stray that wanders in off the street. That's not in my job description.' She picks up the bowl of Smash. 'Besides,' she adds, 'I cannae cater for everybody's taste.'

Bob snaps, 'Oh, for goodness' sake!'

Angela puts on her shoes. They push their chairs back and get up to leave. Bruno bumps into Evan and giggles.

Carrot laughs, 'Look at the wee bum boy go.' He waits for others as his table to join in.

Angela slows before the front door. 'Whit's a bum boy?' Older children hurry up the stairs to their rooms.

'Dunno,' Evan knows from her tone, she's likely to go on and on until she gets an answer. 'Maybe yeh should ask him.'

Bruno's grin shows sharp and discoloured teeth. 'I guess it's cause I like boys.'

'Whit's wrong wae that?' she says. 'I like boys too. I'd much rather be a boy than a girl. Yeh don't get people grabbing yeh aw the time.'

Bruno shapes his hands into claws and clomps towards Angela. 'I want tae be a vampire when I grow up. Aw yeh huv tae dae is sleep in a coffin during the day and bite people at night. I'd be good at that.'

'Chaz sleeps aw day,' Angela declares. 'And goes oot all night. But he doesnae sleep in a coffin. He sleeps beside me and my mum, which is worse.'

Before they can escape outside, Alice appears in the office doorway. 'Can I have a word, with you Evan?' He shakes his head, not sure what he's done now. 'You too, Angela.'

Bruno shouts, 'Whit about me?'

Alice shakes her head and smiles. 'No, your presence won't be required, Bruno.'

A cigarette burns in the ashtray on the desk. Alice sits on the swivel chair facing them. Evan sprawls in the seat next to Angela, a bored look on his face.

'I don't know how to tell you this.' Alice sighs. 'I've had a complaint that food has been wasted because we're feeding non-residents.'

Evan translates for Angela. 'That means you.'

A hitch catches in Alice's throat. 'The thing is, the said person has got a point. And even though it's stupid and petty and absurd, there's really nothing I can do about it. Angela, I'm sorry to say, you can no longer have meals here.'

Angela's sobs and sniffles as she draws breath. 'Does that mean I cannae come here again?'

Alice moves quickly from behind the desk, drawing her into her soft body and lifts her on to her knee. 'Oh, no, darling. You can come visit anytime. It's just... Sshh,' she whispers. 'It's all right, darling.'

Evan whacks his hand against the chair. 'I hate that cook. She cannae cook for toffee. How come we don't get the other wan back?'

Alice strokes Angela's hair. 'It's not as simple as that. Short of poisoning the lot of us, she'll be here for a while.'

Chapter 59

Race

Bruno picks up the letters in the doorway and takes the mail through to the office. Evan brushes past him to join Angela outside.

Angela kicks at the stone chips. 'I liked the other woman. She was nice.'

Evan makes a cap of his fingers over his eyelashes against the glare of the sun. 'Don't worry. She's jist a fucking stupid cow.'

He edges closer to Angela and rests his hand on her shoulder. The postman hurries down Risk Street. Pizza Face wobbles on the razor seat of his bike as he tries to change gear and turn the corner.

'Maybe she'll come back.'

'Maybe she will.'

Pizza Face wheezes to a halt outside the gates. His hands knuckled gripping the Raleigh's handlebars. 'Chaz bought it for me,' he explains. 'It's twelve-speed gear.'

He crouches to show them, his long trousers tucked into grey socks and black sannies— the uniform of a professional cyclist.

Evan edges closer, squats beside Pizza Face to get a better look. 'That's a bumper.'

Angela says, 'It's crap.'

They ignore her. Delight in a boyish way Pizza Face can pick up the frame with one hand and spin the front wheel. The way the gears are flickable. The way the bike comes to an instant stop on the hill.

'Can I get a shot?' asks Evan.

Pizza Face smells of fag smoke and sweat. 'It's maybe a bit too big for yeh.'

'But I'm bigger than yeh.'

'Aye, but yeh've got wee-er skinner legs—and it's my bike.'

Angela disappears round the side of the home. She appears wheeling the old bone-shaker through the loose stones and lets the bike topple to the ground in front of them. 'I'll go this bike and yeh've got that wan.' She points at the bone-shaker. 'Help me on it, Evan. And we can huv a race.'

Pizza Face and Evan exchange bemused glances.

She has trouble wrestling the handlebars, getting the bike upright. Evan helps her prop it against the weathered wall. Her hand grips a rod of the rusted iron fence and she pulls her body up onto the brick shelf.

Evan grabs her and the bike, keeping both upright. 'Whoa.'

Pizza Face whinnies with laughter. 'Yer fucking nuts.'

Angela's face remains solemn. 'Push me.'

Evan holds her and the bike. An anxious gasp escapes from her mouth as the wheels pick up speed and she clutches the handlebar and smiles awkwardly.

'Faster,' she shouts.

Pizza Face follows on his bike in slow arabesque outside their juddering run.

A green Ford speeds past on Duntocher Road on the curve of the hill, followed by the roar of an SMT bus. Evan scuffs his shoes and slides, grapples with the handlebars and pulls the bike and Angela sharply towards him.

Evan looks up at Pizza Face from the scrum of bikes and bodies. 'The brakes didnae work too well.'

'Yeh alright?' Evan asks Angela as she wiggles from under him and stands up.

'No,' she whimpers, greeting. 'Yeh made me hurt my wrist.' She clutches her wrist with her left hand to show what she means.

Pizza Face abandons his Raleigh on the road and hurries across to help her. 'Yeh'll be alright, pet.'

Evan scrambles to his feet, his mouth slack and a guilty look in his eyes. 'Don't worry, I'll kiss it better.'

She holds her floppy wrist. He makes smacking sounds with each kiss, dots her arm from the pale beat of blue veins to her elbow.

'I want tae go hame.' But she lets herself be comforted, drawn in, hugged tight. She clutches him and smiles.

Evan strokes the crown of her hair. 'There, there.'

'That bike's a death trap,' declares Pizza Face.

'Nah, it's no that bad. She's jist too wee tae go on it.'

'Well, yeh go on it. And we'll see.'

'I will.'

Evan's brisk with Angela, brushing her aside, guides her towards the high kerb and pavement. The handlebars and the front wheel of the heavy bike dragged into position. Branches and beech leaves rustle and offer temporary shade. 'Up and back tae Parkhall shops. And we'll see who wins.'

'Yeh goin on that thing?' Pizza Face lifts his bike with one hand. 'Up and back? First back here?' He wheels his bike up beside Evan's, the toes of his sannie on the road, holding it upright. He studies the gears as if memorising them.

'Right,' says Evan. 'Angela will countdoon, wan, two, three, go.' He twists his torso around to look at her while holding the boneshaker. 'Won't yeh?'

'Nah,' she replies, folding her arms.

'Fuck it,' Pizza Face balances on his toes. 'Yeh dae it.'

'Wan, two, three, go!' Evan gets an early lead with his bluff tactics. He stands upright as a jockey, arse in the air, pedalling. The bike wearies his legs. After the initial jump-start, his bum falls back and settles on the saddle. A whirr of wheels behind him, the sound nips at his back like an angry wasp. He hears Pizza Face's ragged breathing.

Clutching ram's head handlebars, Pizza Face overtakes him before the Parkhall shops.

An Austin horn blares and it brakes with a screech and smell of burning rubber. The car speeds along Duntocher Road without stopping. Pizza Face jerks his handlebars sideways and cuts inside. His back wheel clips the old bike. He brakes and his bike wobbles. And he falls off.

The bone-shaker skids. Evan leans into it, foot scraping, he makes the turn across the road, without looking back. It's downhill and the weight of the bike is no longer a hindrance. He cuts across the corner of Risk Street. Momentum takes his bike juddering over cobbles up the hill. He doesn't need to pedal until the last few yards Ticker-tape in his head as he wheels to the gate.

Minutes later, Pizza Face slumps over the handlebars of his racer like roadkill. 'Yeh fucking cheated!'

'No, I fucking never.'

'We'll race again.'

'OK.'

'OK.' Pizza Face turns his head and squints his eyes. His sweaty face making his birthmark a deeper plum colour. 'Where's Angela?'

'Dunno.' Evan rubs sweat from his forehead. 'She might be inside. Yeh want me tae check. I'm gonnae get a drink of water, anyway.' He glances at his pal. 'Yeh want a drink?'

Pizza Face hums and haws, 'Nah, the wee shites probably away withoot me. Yeh know whit she's like.' He balances on one leg and tap-dances his way around until his front wheel faces downhill. 'See yeh.' He holds his hand up in salute as the bike picks up speed.

Chapter 60

Aggro

EVAN LEANS THE BONESHAKER AGAINST THE WALL. THE COOK is outside the kitchen door having a smoke in the sunshine.

He angles his body so he can step past her. 'Jist gonnae get a drink of water.'

'The kitchen is out of bounds,' she declares in a bored tone. 'You want a drink of water, go to one of the toilets, or ask a member of staff to get you it.'

She blocks his way, their bodies almost touching, and eyeball each other.

'Yeh only work here—yer a fucking rotten cook. I live here.'

'You're just a cheeky wee bastard. Nae wonder your parents dumped you here.'

He brushes past her. His eyes adjust to the shut blinds. The two sinks are piled with dishes and pots. He dips his hand into the scummy water and pulls out a green glazed mug, running it under the hot tap to clean it, and filling it with cold water. He drinks it and refills another mugful. It touches him to think how clean the old cook had kept the place.

Reaching into the gap between the sink and cupboard, he fishes for the bottle of poison. He hears her footsteps and sticks it inside the front of his trousers, covering the bottle with his T-shirt. The keys hang in the door and he unlocks it and makes his escape through the dining room.

Evan dashes up the stairs and dives into his room. Bruno spots him from the lobby and tags after him, with the usual jaggy grin on his face. Evan searches for a place to stash the bottle. He kneels and bangs it against the bed leg nearest the back wall and window. Rolling sideways, he sits up as Bruno slopes in the door.

'Whit yeh been daeing?' Bruno drops his shoulder, angles his head to one side, reading his face, but squinting past him and under the bed.

'Nothing.' Evan quickly stands, going toe to toe, getting in his way.

Bruno steps backwards and smirks. 'Yeh'd something up yer duke. I seen yeh. Whit is it? Bottle of ginger?'

'Nah.'

'Whit then? Yeh don't huv tae gi'e me a drink if yeh don't want tae.'

'Nothing.'

'Is it whisky?' Bruno whoops. 'I'll no tell anybody. My da made me drink whisky wance, but I didnae like it, and he said I was a wee poof.'

'Mind yer ain business.'

'I can drink bevvy—but prefer Irn Bru.'

'It's nothing for nosey pokes.'

Bruno chortles, tries to dodge past Evan to take a look, but a hard dunt on the shoulder stops him and he takes a step back. Flummoxed. The hurt lies in his eyes and he's close to tears.

'It's no that I don't want tae tell yeh,' Evan whispers in a conciliatory tone. 'It's jist that yeh always blab about everything and yeh cannae keep a secret for toffee.'

'Honest, I'll never tell anybody. Never-ever-ever.'

Evan frowns and picks at the grit on his elbow. 'Say, Dib, Dib. Cross my heart and hope tae die.'

'Dib, Dib,' Bruno slaps his hand against his striped, blue T-shirt and bony chest. 'Cross my heart and hope tae die.'

'OK then. I believe yeh, but first yeh've got tae tell me a secret. So that's us even.'

'Eh?' Bruno scrunches up his face. 'I stole money, a lighter and fags oot of Bob's pocket in the staffroom.' Colour reddens his cheeks as if he's been running and he sniggers.

'Much?'

'About ninety-two pence.'

'But yeh don't smoke. Whit did yeh dae wae the fags and lighter.'

'Gave them tae Carrot.'

'Whit did yeh dae that for?'

'Dunno. So-es he'd like me.' Bruno is quick to correct himself. 'I'd huv gi'en them tae yeh first, but yeh don't smoke either.'

'Aye, that's true. But yeh could huv gi'en me the lighter.' He shoves his pillow to one side and sits on the bed. 'Yeh can huv a look, but if yeh tell anybody—'

Bruno drops to his knees and wriggles under the bed. He surfaces holding the bottle, his cheeky smile once more in place. He sniffs and unscrews the lid. 'Whit is it?'

Evan grabs it. 'Whit yeh daeing? It's poisonous, no for playing wae.' He cradles it in his lap. Bruno flings himself on to the bed beside him. 'Mind noo, yeh've no tae tell anybody. Yeh swore on it.'

'Aye, but whit ur yeh gonnae dae with it?' Bruno's foot taps and his knee bops away from Evan's. 'Yeh could kill everybody in the world by putting it in their pudding.' He holds his throat, makes gurgling noises, and crosses his eyes, sinking between the beds and closing his eyes.

Death doesn't linger. Bruno springs up, and he leans over and feints and makes a playful grab for the brown bottle.

Evan pulls it away. 'Don't fucking touch it. And stop playing the cunt. We need tae find somewhere tae put it. Somewhere safe?'

'If yeh'd a wooden leg, yeh could stick it inside it.' Bruno clumps about in half-circles to show what he means.

Evan chews the inside of his cheek. 'Somewhere outside,' he pronounces, as if speaking to himself. 'It wouldnae be safe in here. Staff root through yer stuff. Kidding on they didnae mean it. And when yeh catch them oot, they say it's aw for yer ain good.'

'I maybe know somewhere.' Bruno stays silent, the way he usually goes after he's been blubbering and kids on he hasn't. 'It's where I keep my stuff.'

'OK.' Evan gets off the bed. He tugs out his T-shirt, unbuttons his trousers, and wiggles his hips to make a gap to hide the bottle without it slipping too much.

'Let me dae it.' Bruno puts a hand on his arm. 'Gi'e me a heid start. People notice yeh, but whenever they see me, they look the other way. I'll get yeh outside by the tree and I'll show yeh.'

Evan waits impatiently, his scalp tingling, wondering why he'd taken the poison from the kitchen. He hears a faltering laugh coming from the other rooms. It sounds like Carrot messing about. And a crash against his wall.

He stares out the window and sighs. Bruno trudges close to the wall and between overgrown bushes.

Evan gives his roommate another few minutes before tiptoeing down the stairs to catch up with him.

Julie, crossing from the telly room to the office, waits for him, smiling. 'Where're you skulking off to?'

'Jist oot.'

'Don't do anything I wouldn't do.' She pats his shoulder and heads into the office, smiling.

Bruno crouches behind the tree trunk with the rope tassel hanging on its limbs. He's unscrewed the bottle lid. 'I tried a wee bit on the weeds o'er there.' He nods towards some yellow buttercups, 'but it didnae dae anything.'

'Gi'e me that.' Evan grabs the bottle. 'Where were yeh gonnae show me?'

'It was only a wee bit. Keep yer hair on.'

They check they can't be seen from the road or any of the windows facing them. Bruno burrows into the corner of the garden. Two walls meet at right-angles, and despite the heat in the ground, it feels fusty from the ground elder. Evan clambers underneath a lilac bush. Bruno lifts the curtain of ivy from the bottom. He reaches in and pulls out a brick. A doll's head pokes out. 'That's where I keep my stuff.'

'That's no yer doll. Yeh stole it, ya fucker.'

His eyes flicker away and he caresses Barbie's face. 'She didnae need it. She's got wan already.' He's sure of himself as a feral cat in the overgrown garden with the muted noise of traffic and nobody watching him. 'Yeh want tae keep it here, or no?'

'Aye,' Evan slips him the bottle.

Chapter 61

Driving lessons

CHAZ FIGURES HE'LL NEED TO TAKE DRIVING LESSONS, NOT right away, but soon. He could buy one of those fancy Jaguar cars. He treks up the hill towards the Atlantis, already half-scooped, wide-necked shirt, and denim jacket buttoned tight. In his head he can feel the swell of shock in the car showroom, sees the guy's face when he pulls out a wad of notes and sticks his hand out for the car keys—tells the cunt, any colour but green and to keep the change—that would show him. "That's Chaz Sweeney," one suit would whisper to another.

He swerves a right at the corner, ambles to the chippy and stands anonymously, waiting in the queue, just another punter waiting for a pie supper. Stands outside, his back against a wall, chewing chips. He's bigger fish to fry and taps the hard bump inside his jacket pocket.

He keeps an eye on a young couple as they come out of The Atlantis, arm in arm, laughing. Blonde hair spills over a pink double-breasted frock coat and she's wearing those thigh-high boots Chaz likes. He's a short arse, ink-blue blazer, looks as if he's worth a bob or two.

Behind them, a ragtag group of youngsters spill out of the doors. 'Fuck off Ernie,' one of them cries and throws a punch and they start scrapping. It's pitiful, but enough to make the young couple move on sharpish.

Short arse stands on the road trying to hail a taxi, but the Hackney cab keeps going. His bird ganders at him across the road. Chaz smiles into his chips. Older guys come out of the bar, chuckling, and wave their arms about and break up the youngsters' posturing.

Chaz recognises Tam Daly. His fur-lined, car-coat makes him look brawnier than he remembered. The shirt and thin tie suggest he's a successful businessman, drinking for business, not pleasure.

The backups are late thirties. The nearest flaunts a gut and has a fuzzy ginger beard. The other one taller, with a scar on his cheek, wears a single-breasted checked jacket. Chaz isn't sure how to play it from here.

The lights switch off in the upstairs lounge and downstairs bar. Rain has settled into a constant downpour. Chaz crosses Kilbowie Road, goes for a pee in a close nearby and hurries back, scared he's missed them.

Tam Daly stands with his cronies smoking a cigarette, drunken-ness drawing them into a jabbering, close noose of bodies. Behind them a younger woman with a tight bun and halter-top, locks the main door and waves a set of keys. A black Hackney swoops into the pavement. She clutches her bag as the cab picks her up. An arm waves at the group of men as the taxi passes Chaz.

A dout flicked away, another mashed into the pavement. The two younger guys head up the hill towards Radnor.

His fingers sweep through loose strands of frizz, mussing his hair, not sure if Tam Daly will recognise him. But he shuffles past the close, without looking in his direction.

Chaz follows behind him. He takes a left towards where the sink-hole of the Bannkie's stadium lurks, leaving the bright lights of Kilbowie Road behind. He enters dimly lit shortcuts, cutting through lanes lined with overflowing bins and the stink of decay.

'Tam,' he shouts. 'Hing on.'

Tam Daley wheels around and pushes his chest out to face him.

'It's me,' he says as he gets closer. 'Chaz Sweeney, yeh know my da.'

'Oh, aye, son,' he says automatically, his bullet head leaning forward. A bluff face, pale eyes squinting to get a better look at him. His voice falters, 'I never knew yeh there.'

'Yeh might know my brother, the Tash better.'

The older man's body tightens and the laughter lines in his face disappear. 'Aye, I know that cunt and he owes me money. Yeh fucking following me, ya cunt? Yeh got it?'

'Aye.' Chaz shifts and bobs like a boxer in the ring. The Starr pistol comes up fast, and he shoots him in the head. He traces the contraction of his mouth and the wrinkles of surprise in his face, a child's frightened eyes playing peekaboo at the last.

Chaz pirouettes, job done, not stopping for the encore. He floats away like a philosophy student with a Heidegger dissertation in his back pocket. Stopping to light a cigarette and ponder the bright lights of Kilbowie. Checking left and right, before crossing. Wanting someone to challenge him. A drunken woman staggers crablike up the hill towards the La Scala, shouting and bawling at an invisible enemy.

Chapter 62

Double take

DREW PICKS UP A TUMBLER AT THE TABLE NEAR CHAZ'S. His cloth dabbing at the dregs of spilt drink. Chaz squints at him through fag smoke with bleary eyes and moon of a purple rash on his unwashed neck. He rolls his shoulders as he turns for face him. 'Whit?'

The barman leaves the empties on the circular table. The few afternoon regulars have already left. Drew splashes down a *Daily Record* between beer and whisky glasses. The page unfolded for his perusal hangs over a smoking ashtray.

Chaz glances at the headline. Old news about the brutal murder of Thomas Daly, *a well-loved grandfather and family man*. It's slid from front-page headlines to page five. But a newspaper tag follows with two passport-sized and black-and-white pictures of eyewitnesses. Chaz recognises the nice-looking bint from the Atlantis, with the kohl eyes, who had looked across the street at him. She'd given an artist his description.

The composite sketch is blown-up to half a page and reproduced below their photographs. The police, if headlines are to be

277

believed, urge the man to come forward and eradicate himself from their investigation.

'That looks a bit like you!' Drew fires a friendly warning.

'Away and shite. That cunt looks like Rod Stewart.' Chaz gives a full-throated laugh. 'The cops ur better goin lifting him. They'll get him at the Barrowland this weekend.'

The paper is whisked away from him. Drew bumps backwards, a mock smile of apology on his lips.

Chaz runs his fingers through his hair. 'Aye, that's my uncle, yeh know. Da and the Tash went tae the funeral, said it was a good turnout. A good doo afterwards in The Atlantis. Sausage rolls and pies. A bit cheap if yeh ask me. Nae steak-pie. I would huv went, but I didnae really know him.'

Drew nods. The paper scrunched into a crumpled ball. Empty glasses clink as he picks them up and limps back towards the bar.

'Hi,' Chaz shouts.

Drew turns his body and looks back at him.

'Get me another goldy.' Chaz holds his whisky glass in salute. 'And get wan for yerself.'

Chaz picks up his fags and pockets them. He goes up to the bar and flings back his whisky in a oner.

He picks up his jacket, but he's still got a thirst and ends up in Macintoshes. He spots Rab with his old man, neither of them talking, and nursing near empty lagers. He buys a round of drinks, doubles, and danders across to their corner table. That puts a warm smile on their faces. Rab moves along the wall-seat to make space for him to join them.

Sammy reaches across the table and shakes his hand, tapping underneath his wrist in the Masonic handshake. 'No seen yeh for a while, son.'

'Och, I've been busy, yeh know, wae the Irish boys and the cause. The boys ur away o'er the water'

'Say nae mair,' Sammy winks, and picks up his whisky, looking through it and smiles. 'Wish tae God this wan had been daeing something useful.' He takes a glug and wipes his mouth with the back of his hand. 'Yeh know this wan's been on the drugs.' He squints at his son. 'Yeh know that stuff.' A pull of lager puts him in the frame to get it right. 'The waccy-baccy. I think that's what yeh call it.'

He rolls his eyes and reaches across, lifts his tin and teases tobacco, tapping it, making a smoke one-handed and lifting it to his mouth. 'His mum was goin aff her heid. Fair scunnered wae him. I had tae call in a couple of contacts. Keep him in. Till he got better.'

'Hi, take wan of these.' Chaz digs into his pocket for his packet of Silk Cut, passes one to Sammy, lighting another for himself.

The unlit roll-up put back into the older man's tin, spitting stray bits of tobacco on to the floor.

'Hi, whit about me?' There's a roar of the old defiance in Rab's tone. 'Am I fucking invisible or something?'

'Aye, yeh ur.' But Chaz hands him his packet of Silk Cut and nudges him with his elbow.

Sammy spots an old crony. Chaz slips him a fiver under the table, tells him to go up to the bar and get them both a few drinks on him.

'Yeh sure son?' Sammy tugs at the wrinkled note and hides it away, his dancing eyes sparkled. 'Yeh've always been a good boy.'

Chaz laughs in Rab's face. 'Yeh still on the waccy-baccy?'

'Fuck off,' Rab takes a mouthful of whisky. 'That's kids' stuff.'

'But there's a lot of money in it?'

'Aye, suppose.' Rab averts his eyes from Chaz's gaze, looks across the smoky room to where his da is standing, laughing. He whispers out of the side of his mouth, 'But the real money is in smack.'

'Where dae yeh get that fae?'

Rab sniggers through his nose. 'Whit is this, the fucking Spanish Inquisition?'

Chaz slaps the table. 'Don't fuck me about!'

'The Dunnes.'

'And where dae they get it frae?'

'Manchester. Somewhere in Manchester.'

'Find oot for me.'

Rab studies his face. 'Jist like that?'

'Aye, jist like that.' Chaz finishes his drink and gets up as the last bell sounds. He slaps Rab on the back. 'Don't forget.'

Rab works the odds. 'I'll need cash.'

'Yeh'll get yer money when yeh get me whit I need tae know,' but he peels off a tenner from his bundle and lets it flutter onto his lap.

'That's magic.' Rab's grin reaches his ears.

Chaz takes the razor out of his pocket and taps the base like a finger on the table in front of him. Fear flickers across Rab's face.

'Don't forget!' Chaz sticks the razor back in his jacket pocket.

Chapter 63

Wicked witch

'Hɪ,' Cʜᴀᴢ sᴘʀᴀᴡʟᴇᴅ ᴏɴ ᴛʜᴇ ᴄᴏᴜᴄʜ ᴡɪᴛʜ ʜɪs ᴇʏᴇs sʜᴜᴛ shouts at Angela in their living room, 'Go doon and tell Pizza Face I want a word wae him.'

'Can I get oot tae play, afterwards?' asks Angela.

A flicker of a smile. 'Yeh'll need tae ask yer ma, but it's alright wae me. Although yeh ur a cheeky wee bastard sometimes.'

Angela batters down the stairs, swathed in her nightclothes of pink pyjamas, and out into the heat haze of the back court. The stink of overflowing bins makes her nose crinkle. She hangs back, an audience for Pizza Face's up-swinging arms and step-over tricks with the ball. 'Chaz wants tae see yeh.'

'Whit for?'

Gulling cries war above their heads, winging at each other, and trying to steal a piece of rotted peel. He doesn't hang about, trudging behind Angela to the top landing.

Two flies buzz above Chaz's head. He lolls on the couch smoking a Silk Cut, listening to Radio Clyde. Kerry-Ann sits opposite him, sharing an ashtray. Kitted out in a striped shirt, she looks over the mound of her belly, flicking through a Kensitas catalogue and sighing. She's got her eye on a toaster. All she needs are another 10 000 coupons.

'Here,' Chaz eyes Pizza Face skulking near the door. 'Is Tash in?'

Pizza Face's lips fall open, while he makes his mind up. 'He was in his bed when I left. He's no been that well—aw he does is moan.'

'Can I go oot tae play?' Angela cuts in.

'Can yeh fuck.' Kerry-Ann doesn't bother looking around. She licks her thumb and turns another page. 'Yeh're too cheeky for yer ain good.'

'But Mum...' she whines.

'But Mum, nothing.'

'Och, let her go oot.' Chaz stabs out his fag. 'She's a fucking pain in the arse and I cannae be bothered looking at her.' He exhales as if he's been hard worked, lights another, and gives Pizza Face his marching orders. 'Well, go doon and see. Tell him tae get up here, pronto. I need tae speak tae him about something.'

'Whit if he says he's no wanting tae?'

'Jist away and see.'

Angela is waiting outside the front door for him. 'Yeh want tae go up and see Evan?'

'Nah, no right noo.'

'I'll go myself.'

'Yeh cannae go like that.'

'Whit?'

'Wae yer jammies on.' Pizza Face shakes his head. 'People will think yer a daftie. Why don't yeh go in and get changed?'

'Because they'll change their mind. Keep me in jist tae shout at me.'

She doesn't wait for Pizza Face. The round-faced girl hanging about the front of the Home tells Angela she needs to make a detour to the back garden.

Evan sits reading his Grimms' book of fairy tales in the shade. His back to the wall, he's as far away from the building as he can get without jumping into another garden. Bees buzz inside the purple blooms of a geranium bush, meadow buttercups and cowslip gallop through the overgrown lawn. Bruno is easy to spot with a dark-coloured jacket. He looks over at Angela but ignores her and goes back to bee-a-cide, hitting flying insects with a stick.

Angela edges closer to Evan and jumps in front of him. 'Boo!' The book drops from his hand. She is delighted with her ruse. 'Caught yeh.'

'Ya wee besum.' He mock wrestles and grapples with her and pulls her in close enough to savour her sweet childish breath, cuddling and tickling. They roll over and over in the warm grass.

She relaxes into him, giggles, but struggles to get free. 'Don't,' she cries. 'It hurts.'

He lets her go. 'Whit hurts?'

Greenish eyes flicker away from his face to the terraced garden below. White sheets hang straight on the clotheslines. Wee dresses fastened on the line with clean wooden pegs. Lettuce grows green turbans, each different, but the same, in the ordered muck of a vegetable patch and well-ordered world.

'When aw the magic is tripped oot at night,' Angela squirms and looks away. 'Yeh think there's any left in the morning to waken us up?'

'Suppose so,' replies Evan.

'I jist want tae go under the water again. Will yeh hold my haun and take me?'

Bruno sneaks up on them. 'Yeh don't need tae be that daft and drown yerself. Yeh can drink the poison tae kill yerself.'

Evan scrambles to his feet. 'Shut up!' He shoves him. 'Yer stinking, never wash, always farting on the fly. That's why everybody hates yeh. That was a fucking stupid thing tae say. Fuck off! Why don't yeh? And gi'es peace.'

Bruno drops the stick, steps backwards into the shadow of the tree and into the anonymity of whirring and buzzing sounds. His face beams, ears redden. 'Phew, it's boiling hot.' He fans his cheeks, waving his hand in front of his face.

Evan picks up the stick and pokes at his chest. Bruno doesn't defend himself. 'Why don't yeh cry? Wah, wah, wah, I want my mum. Wah, wah, wah, I wet myself.' He needles him. 'Yer fucking minging and naebody likes yeh. Don't ever forget it.'

'I like him,' Angela pipes up, in her big wee voice. 'He's funny.'

Evan tosses the stick away. A wood pigeon rockets across the treetops. Bruno cups his hand over his eyes to get a better look. Three smokers from the backstairs nip round the side of the house. The flame of Carrot's hair comes into view and his laugh is like the distant clatter of a football rattle. It draws Evan and Angela sideways, hidden by a spur of rhododendron and protected from prying eyes.

'Whit's poison?' Angela enjoys being hidden and playing games.

'It's when—' Bruno crosses his eyes, hands and fingers over his throat and makes strangulated noises 'aaaah, ahh, ah,' while dancing in circles in front of her, falling drunkenly sideways and lying on his back, his legs kicking in the air.

Evan ignores his dramatics. 'Remember when the wicked queen puts poison on wan hauf of the apple? Takes a bite and tries to make Sleeping Beauty bite the other hauf?' He glances at his Grimms' book left lying in the open. 'And she does bite the apple, the poison apple, and falls asleep?'

'Yeh,' Angela looks unconvinced.

'We could show her?' Bruno raises his eyebrows, waiting for Evan to take the lead.

'OK then.'

Bruno beetles away from them into his familiar musty world, stirring leaves underfoot, brittle and broken branches snapping behind him. Angela sucks on her thumb. She watches him take the brick from the wall. He plucks a doll out. Its long straw hair is the colour as her own. Bruno hands the dull brown bottle to Evan.

'That's it,' Evan flashes the bottle. 'Poison.'

Angela gives the bottle a fleeting look. 'Whit was that other thing? Was it a dollie - for me?'

'Nah,' Bruno answers too quickly, flustered. 'I mean, aye it was a doll, but no for yeh.'

Angela laughs and clutches Evan's arm. 'He's funny.'

Evan strokes her hair and cheek. With his other hand, he hides the bottle behind his back. 'The dollie might be for yeh,' his voice rises and he looks at Bruno. 'But yeh'd need tae keep it a big secret.'

Bruno crashes through the branches, returning with the doll. 'Here.'

Angela cuddles the doll, cradles it, and rocks it back and forth like a baby. 'Whit's her name?'

Bruno flees into the sunshine, wiping tears from his eyes as he approaches the smokers.

'Angel,' whispers Evan. 'Aw wee dollies that look like yeh ur called Angel. Don't yeh think?'

'Aye,' she says.

'But yeh need tae take good care of her.' He smiles at the earnest way she fusses with the doll's clothing and coos at it. 'And yeh need tae keep her a secret and thank Bruno for her, the next time yeh see him.'

Chapter 64

Bar-L

CHAZ HEARS THE LOUD SCREECH AND THE RISING HARANGUE which follows. It woke him. It wakes the tenement block. A whiff of cigarette smoke, a reddish dot, and Kerry-Ann rising like a Sphinx beside him with bedclothes around her shoulders. He waits for the climax, recognises his mum's voice.

'Whit time's it?' he feels half-bevvied.

'She's getting worse,' Kerry-Ann mutters in a disembodied voice.

His hand floats in the air and she passes the cigarette she is smoking. Head on the pillow, he takes a few draws and feels her leaning over to retrieve it.

Chaz bumps into Rab outside Maggie Scott's before opening time. He recognises his nervous cough before he sees him. Despite the heat, the round neck of a fawn wool jumper peeks out of a denim jacket buttoned to the neck. He's shivering, shifting from foot to foot. He scratches the back of his neck. His fingers pull and scrape against the outline of his long jaw and fuzzy beard.

'Yeh got a fag?' Rab forces a smile.

'Yer back on that stuff,' Chaz states in a gruff voice. He narrows his eyes but pulls out his twenty packet gives him a fag and lights one for himself.

The door of the pub opens. 'Beautiful day,' Drew favours his better leg, smiling at them.

They follow him inside, blinking away the sunshine. Dust motes and dullness combine with the sour stench of yesterday's booze.

'Two pints.' Chaz holds his fingers in a V-sign. 'And two doubles.' He leaves a pound note on the counter and peels away to take a seat in the corner.

An old regular, with a *Daily Record* under his arm, wanders in. He nods at Chaz before going to the bar and waits. Drew twiddles with the radio, scrolling through the stations before getting to Radio 1 and the upbeat voice of Tony Blackburn.

Rab necks some of his pint. 'That's terrible, whit happened tae yer brother,'

'Whit?' Chaz leans forward, an expression on his face which has Rab measuring the distance to the door.

'Yeh no hear?' Rab gives a nervous cough, takes a mouthful of whisky and gargles with it before swallowing. 'Lifted.'

Chaz puts his glass beside the ashtray, staring ahead, and asks in a hoarse voice, 'Who?'

'The Tash.'

Chaz smiles. 'Stupid cunt.' He sloshes his pint as he lifts it in salute.

Rab takes another nip and becomes talkative. 'Unlucky, caught wae hash and heroin. Wae his record, he'll no get bail. He'll be in the Bar-L.' He lifts a fag from the ashtray and sucks on it. 'Do not pass go. Lucky if he gets oot in a few years.'

'Where'd he get the stuff?'

'I've already told yeh. The Dunnes.' Rab swallows a whisky, followed by a lager chaser, trying to hold himself together, to stop from shivering and the dry boak.

'Don't get fucking cheeky.'

Chaz got another round in. He sprawls back against the chair, legs akimbo, and peers at him through fag smoke and pats at his hair. A woman wearing an eggshell-blue pullover over the top of her shoulders drifts into the bar with an older man.

'The thing is Cha—' Rab starts to say.

'—Fucking shut it.' Chaz digs a roll of notes from the side pocket of his denims and sticks them on the table. Customers glance over but just as quickly look away. 'How dae I get tae the Dunnes?'

Rab slides into the seat facing Chaz and picks up a whisky and downs it in a oner. He bangs down his glass. 'Yeh don't. Invitation only. They're tap of the hill. Holy City. Wan way in and wan way oot. Always got somebody watching, in every one of them closes round about them. They're team-haunded. Even the police cannae get in without getting grief.'

Chaz pulls out the pearl-handled razor and puts it on the table beside the money. He flings back a whisky and bangs the glass on the table. 'If the mountain won't come tae Mohammed... how dae yeh get yer stuff?'

Rab's hand trembles as he reaches for the packet of Silk Cut. A packet of Swan Vestas skitters across the table in his direction. He lights up, takes a deep drag. 'I've got contacts.' He sniffs, and a mouthful of lager clears his throat.

'Nah, nah, nah,' Chaz points the finger. 'We've got contacts.' He leans across the table. 'Who ur they and where will they be, round about noo?'

'Eh?' Rab takes a drink of lager to buy time to think.

'Don't fuck me about,' Chaz growls. 'Where would yeh go noo, if yeh wanted something?'

Rab knows he's been caught out. 'I'd go doon tae The Bisley bar. There's two guys in there, I kinda know. Usually got something. But yer best bet is The Cleddens. That's home territory. Always somebody hings about. Dealing.'

The wad of cash swept off the table and into Chaz's pocket. The razor tucks into his inside left. He finishes his lager. 'Leave that pishwater,' he tells Rab. 'We'll get a pint in The Bisley then The Cleddens.'

Rab's mouth falls open. 'Fuck sake Chaz, ur yeh mad?' One glance at his face and he knows the answer. The pupils in his eyes are black holes.

Chaz grins at him. 'Hurry up, ya stupid cunt.'

Chapter 65

Scars

WITH ALL THE CASH CHAZ CARRIES, AND THE HURRY-SCURRY, Rab is surprised to be standing beside him at a bus stop. Chaz brought a bottle of VAT 69 to keep them lubricated. A bus comes before they can finish the bottle and Chaz leaves it half-empty on the pavement. They sit on the top deck of the bus, smoking. When they pass Kilbowie Road. Rab gestures, 'That's the pub there.'

Chaz drops his cigarette out of his mouth and it rolls under the back seat. He leaps up and pulls the cord, alerting the driver they are getting off. 'I thought yeh said the Bisley Bar.'

'Aye, I did,' says Rab. 'But I meant that wan.'

'Yer a fucking roaster.' A shuffle of feet. Chaz nips along the aisle, swaying as the bus stops before Dees, the clothes shop. Rab clumps behind him, the conductor smiling ruefully at him, and bending backwards to step out of his way.

The heat hits them. They get their breath on the pavement and wait for the traffic on Dumbarton Road to slow before crossing and walking back towards the ground floor of the blackened tenement block. The Regal Bar and Off Sales. Clanging metal

292

screeches from the yard behind them. A beacon for mums and kids hanging about outside Woolie's doors. A more public place than Chaz would like. He feels sober now, wired. Ready for action, he fingers the top of his razor.

He follows Rab inside for a quick dekko. The size of two big living rooms. The pub's yellow facade appears as inviting as a cage door plummeting into a coal mine. Head-height windows, like skid marks in the snow. The Regal Bar sells itself as a working-man's pub but remains empty of working bodies.

The barman in a striped shirt and wide patterned tie hurries across to serve them. A solitary customer in a tartan shirt, dark flared trousers worn high, stares into his pint at the bar, ashtray beside him full of douts.

'Two lager,' Chaz spit out his order to the barman through clenched lips. He turns to face Rab, sharp cheekbones and down-turned mouth shape into a warning. 'Don't fuck me about.'

'It's alright,' Rab whispers out of the side of his mouth. 'That's him.'

The barman wanders to the other end of the bar. Chaz turns his back on the company and sips at his lager, pocketing his change. 'Whit dae yeh come in here for?' He laughs, dryly. 'This place is such a shitehole, it's worse than my house.'

'It's near the buroo.'

'Right,' Chaz concedes the point. 'Whit dae yeh dae next?' He takes out his cigarettes and offers Rab one. He lights his Silk Cut, waits for Rab to spark his fag, and the silence deepens and draws them in.

Rab gulps at his pint and looks away. 'It's pretty easy. I walk past him, gi'e him the nod and he follows me intae the toilet.'

'Like a couple of benders. I don't like the sound of that.'

'No-oo... well, aye, but no like that.'

Chaz swallows a drink and considers. 'Is he carrying?'

'He doesnae need tae. That's Frank Dunne, the baby of the family. Touch him and...' he makes a phewrr sound, and he glances at Chaz. 'Yer no gonnae. Ur yeh?'

'Nah, nah, I didnae know it was Frank Dunne.' Chaz sniggers and speaks in a braying and loud voice. The slight frame of the youth stops spinning the box of Vulcan matches he's toying with on the bar and glances towards Chaz's frizzy hair and at Rab's face. 'Aw I need is some weed tae help me sleep.' He dips into his pocket and passes, underhand, a ten-pound note. 'Get something nice for yerself.' He grins and takes another mouthful of beer. 'Jist tell him tae wait for me in the toilet cubicle like a good boy.'

Rab bites his underlip. He doesn't trust him, but his body's quivering like a tuning fork. Money grasped in his hand, he feels buoyant. Frank Dunne ganders at him, his face broad and white as marshmallow. He has the weird sensation of having been here before. Striding past him, he heads towards the toilets at the top end of the bar.

Rab sits on the edge of the lavatory pan, disinfectant fumes cling to him. The cubicle walls decorated with fuck the popes and fuck king billy and celtic and rangers forever. Some carved, some inked, all poorly spelled. There's a scrawled phone number for Sindy and a drawing of an open mouth, penned in red ink. He hears feet shuffling closer, and three sharp raps on the panelling. The tenner is in his hand, he cracks open the door.

Frank Dunne squeezes in beside him, his eyes zeroing in on the money. 'Who's that prick wae yeh?'

Footsteps scurry. The bathroom door bangs open. Chaz's razor cuts across Frank's cheek, then the other and digs deep into his forehead. He falls backwards into Rab, his hands held flat in self-defence. The tip of his ring finger almost slices off. Deep tram-lines in his other hand leave him bleeding and crying. He feels his jacket being tugged away from him, and his pockets being emptied.

'Don't kill me,' he squirms and begs.

'I'm no gonnae kill yeh. This is jist a warning. As of noo, I'm taking o'er the drug trade in my toon.' The razor slices into Frank's big nose and breaks the blade. 'Cunt,' Chaz kicks him in the ribs.

He reaches a hand out and helps Rab up and laughs. 'Yeh better wash yer face. Yer covered in blood. Look at yeh, I cannae take yeh anywhere.'

Chapter 66

Fair Friday

COCKTAILS OF CHAZ'S OWN DEVISING. AWASH WITH PINTS, even mouth-puckering gin, with a slice of lemon and whisky in the same glass. The circadian rhythms of liquor licensing hours flung in. He stumbles out of Maggie Scott's into stinging afternoon sunlight. He's thinking ahead and of The Pine Trees Hotel, the extra two hours of freedom to drink that gives him. But he needs his bed more. Waiting to cross the road at the junction of Duntocher Road, a taxi passes going up the hill, and he sticks his arm up and it stops with the engine running. He's meeting Del later and the blonde with the tits. He tells the driver where he's going and falls back into the seat.

A clapped-out Vauxhall Viktor passes the taxi on the junction of the hill at Risk Street. He ducks his head. There's something vaguely familiar about the driver and in the back seat Frank Dunne, gauze bandages, and his face a fair imitation of an Egyptian mummy.

Chaz clears his throat, addresses the driver, 'Mate.'

The beefy driver takes his arm off the window, foot off the accelerator, shifts gear and the old diesel engine rattles like it has loose change in the tank. His brown eyes shift from the road and he momentarily studies his passenger in the rear-view mirror.

Chaz looks out, but he can no longer see the Vauxhall and shakes his head, fumbles in his pocket for his packet of cigarettes. 'Nothing,' he mutters, staring straight ahead.

The driver's elbow returns to roost on the window inside and outside the cab. 'Nice weather for Clydebank Fair,' the driver says. 'Yeh on holiday?'

Chapter 67

You know the score

Burst bags and overflowing bins from the last bin-strike no longer register with Pizza Face. 'Goal!' He retrieves the ball. Short anthems of glory proclaimed to shining tenement windows, but no one watching him. He mops his face with his strip and the adulation of thousands of fans chanting his name at Hampden Park washes through him.

A man appears out of the shadow of the tenement. Two, three, or more men follow him into the sunlight. And a man with bandages on his face scurries from the close next door. They gander up at the windows but slant their gaze towards Pizza Face. He bounces his ball, shifts his feet. They amble towards him with the rehearsed quality of men looking for something. He smiles at the older man.

'Watch this.' Pizza Face flicks up the ball and counts out loud as he plays keepie-up. 'Wan, two, three, four, five,' he lunges, but the ball rolls away from his right foot.

'That's great.' The older man shuffles nearer. A scalped head with long ginger hair around his ears and black NHS specs perched on a beak of a nose. 'Dae yeh know who Chaz is?'

'Aye, that's my brother.' He bounces the ball. 'I can dae a lot better than that, yeh know. I can keep it up tae a hunner, or even mair.'

The younger bloke steps in and puts the leather sole of a shoe on the ball after Pizza Face flick it up.

'Wee man, we hear Chaz lives in the top flat. Which wan is it?' His eye twitches on and off like a duff light switch so that Pizza Face feels sorry for him. He's got the same sharp beak as the others, but less sunburnt.

'It's that wan there.' He points at the windows of the wrong flat where Evan and his dad used to stay. 'But Chaz is away oot in a taxi. He's never in at this time.'

The posse of bodies turn to look where he is pointing. Pizza Face makes a grab for his ball under the twitching man's boot.

'Hi, wee man,' the twitching man drags the ball left and right with his foot and does the same trick with the other. He flicks it with insouciant ease into his hands. 'Yeh sure he's away oot?'

The tallest and thinnest brother pushes past the man with bandages and grabs Pizza Face's wrist. He rasps, 'Yeh wouldnae be fucking telling us porkie pies, would yeh?'

Bluebottles buzz around their heads. He wants to run, but the thin man shakes his wrist and arm. His body jolts as if an electrical charge passes through him.

'We aw make mistakes, eh?' The older man leans over him. 'Maybe yer brother is still up there, waiting for yeh tae come in fae playing fitba. Maybe yeh should shout up at him, telling him yer doon here. It would be a terrible shame tae miss him.'

'Nah mister, he's no in.' Pizza Faces stares at the ground, a fly buzzing in front of him and his mouth feels hot and dry. 'I seen him goin oot myself.'

'Well, shout up then,' the old man urges him. 'Nae harm done. And then we'll be sure.'

Pizza Face's lips twitch. He looks at the semicircle of men facing him but says nothing.

The man with the bandaged face and hands barges through them. 'Let him go a minute,' he hisses. The thin man lets go of his wrist.

'Yeh the youngest?' the man with the bandages glares at Pizza Face, his chin jutting, sharp with anger.

'Aye,' Pizza Face starts greeting.

He doesn't feel the razor slashing both his cheeks, tramlines. His fingers hold his face together, blotching blood red.

'Tell him I'm gonnae kill him,' growls the man with the bandages. 'Nae question.' He's first to walk away. The other men follow behind him. No hurry. Hands screen their eyes as if in salute as they look up at the windows above them.

Pizza Face's squeals hit the high notes. He chokes on blood and snot and tears, gasping for breath. He staggers towards the close mouth and home. His feet toil to lift over worn stone step like an old drunk. Leaning against the banister for support, he pulls himself along with two hands, a terrible tiredness in his legs. He hangs onto a metal railing to keep upright and rests, greeting.

Chapter 68

Getting the message

JUNIOR HURRIES HOME, TIRED AND HUNGRY. HIS HAIR SUN-washed and steel toe-cap boots chalky from the cement he handles every day, which gives him the appearance of a grey ghost.

In the dimness of the close, a metallic scent like loose change hangs in the air and the hairs on his arms prickle in warning. His hazel eyes dart to his brother curled like an unwanted embryo on the landing below their home. His brain disconnects and brings together the hair and the football strip, shiny football boots matted with gore, childish groans, but it is the familiar voice that fixes the horror of who it is in his head. 'I never telt,' Pizza Face whimpers. 'Never grassed.'

'Never telt who?' Junior doesn't wait for an answer. Blubbering with tears, Junior scoops him into a bear hug and leaps up the remaining stairs. He kicks the door until his mum answers. Her goldfish-shape mouth sucks on indignation, with a dustpan and brush in her hands. His sister hulking behind her.

'Oh, my God,' shrieks his ma. 'Somebody phone an ambulance.' The cleaning utensils clatter onto the linoleum.

'Oh, my God,' his sister echoes, with hands flapping. 'Somebody phone an ambulance.'

Nobody usually takes any notice of her wittering, but his da's frowning face appears in the lobby, sports pages folded in his hand. Three older brothers ripple out of the kitchen in their vests, cigarettes jammed at jaunty angles in their mouths. They crowd in, eager to help, but getting in Junior's way as he barges past them. Blood sticking to his hands, he places Pizza Face on their ratty couch, plumps a cushion behind his head and watches it turning crimson.

'Get hot water and a facecloth,' cries his ma.

Her son's eyes glint as they follow the path of blood dripping from Pizza Face's chin. They dance as a war party in front of the couch, raining fag ash. Curse among themselves, swear oaths to kill and maim, plan revenge on whoever, or whatever, had done such a thing.

'Get the boy a cuppa tea, cup of water, or something,' his da shouts and swears at his ma. 'Son, yeh'll be alright,' he bows his head to tell Pizza Face.

Eric, the bookish and sensible son in the family, takes charge. His experience of putting on a plummy accent on the telephone and dealing with his mother's committals to Gartnavel gives him seniority over his father and brothers. 'Fucking get a clean cloth and hold it to his face to stop it bleeding.' He gives his sister's fleshy arm a hard stinging slap, tells her to stop squealing. The clamour settles and begins again. He slaps her face, which shuts her up.

Reassurance radiates from his unhurried movements, in the way he pats and checks his pockets, before quickly disappearing to summon an ambulance.

His ma sits sobbing on the couch. She gathers herself together and pulls her youngest son roughly across her aproned lap. Rocks him back and forth as she makes cooing noises.

'Won't be long. Won't be long.' His da's faux cheery tone fools nobody but lends assurance.

'Where's Chaz?' Junior looks about. 'That bastard 'll know something about this. I'm gonnae go up tae see that cunt.'

'He's no in,' Pizza Face murmurs from the couch.

And they gaze at him as if the corpse of Lazarus has spoken.

'Wheesht, wee yin,' says his da. 'Haud yer strength, son. Haud yer strength. No be long noo.' And he glances at the window and cocks his head. 'Save yer breath, son. Save yer breath.' His hand covers his mouth. He coughs and splutters and rubs at his eyes, trying not to cry, but his eyes welling. Brothers restrict their field of vision to avoid wet, red-rimmed eyes staring back at them.

Chapter 69

Playing for Rangers

CIGARETTE SMOKE DRIFTS ABOVE PIZZA FACE'S HEAD. HIS IS a dumb, frightened silence amid bickering conversation and accusations of neglect. Flashing lights and the klaxon of sirens rises above the traffic. Ambulance men tackle the stairs. A medic puffing loudly, a bit overweight, with a moustache. His younger colleague carries the stretcher like a portable ladder, finding the centre and swinging the weight upward. His ma is ready for them, framed in the door. She recognises the oldest of the pair of ambulance men and steps aside. 'He's in there.'

Pizza Face looks at the older guy with panicky eyes as he unrolls a gauze white bandage. Pressed against sundered flesh, it smells clean as the dentist's surgery. Another layer added. A patchwork quilt.

'Haud that tight, son,' the bearish ambulance man's eyes crinkle with good humour. He guides Pizza Face's fingers to a pad near his ear, 'And we'll soon huv yeh right as rain.'

The younger ambulance man lays the stretcher parallel with the couch on faded linoleum diamond prints. An arm snakes under

Pizza Faces back. He whiffs the beefy guy's smoky breath as he grips him under the oxter to ease him upward. His colleague bends over the side of the couch, ready to lift his feet.

A deep breath and Pizza Face sits up and proclaims, 'I'll jist walk.' He looks at his da and then at his ma's face. His sister's pumpkin grin behind them.

'Yeh will no,' his ma's cigarette ash falls to the floor. 'The very idea. Yeh'll dae as yer telt.'

'No, it's alright Mrs,' says the younger ambulance man. 'If he can walk that's a good sign.' He helps Pizza Face straighten into a standing position and supports his weight.

Pizza Face's fingertips glide over the bloody bandages. 'Will I still be able tae play for Rangers wae my face like this?' He looks to the senior ambulance man for an answer.

Junior guffaws. 'Course yeh will, wee man. Yeh play wae yer feet.'

'Na son, yeh play wae yer heart.' His old man slaps the shirt buttons on his chest and coughs. 'And yeh've got that in spades. Yer a stick on tae play for Rangers, son. Don't yeh worry about that. And we'll aw be there tae cheer yeh on.'

A murmur of agreement and good-natured smiles encircle him and eases his exit. The ambulance men, hats fixed firmly in place, lean into Pizza Face and escort him like a celebrity to the door. His ma picks up her coat and clutches her bag like a shield behind him.

Chapter 70

Frankenstein

CHAZ STUMBLES UP THE STAIRS, A PLASTIC BAG TIED TO HIS hand with a chicken curry sloshing inside. His shirt reeks of spilled lager, sweat and fag smoke.

He breezes past Kerry-Ann and slumps in the armchair opposite the light of the flickering telly. Angela sleeps at the bottom of their bed. He could reach out to touch and waken her. Lights flash on the telly and a crowd of peasants brandishing flaming torches, and with a rising music crescendo, rush towards the castle gates. In the flagstones of the dungeon, Frankenstein is strapped to a gurney. Liquid in retorts bubble and hiss along glass tubes, sparks fly and the bolts in his neck jolt and the monster's eyes open. The peasants are almost upon them. Square- jawed Peter Cushing has a decision to make. The door handle rattles, but it's locked, but it won't hold out for long. It takes Chaz an age to realise that somebody is banging on their front door. Kerry-Ann goes to answer it.

Chaz isn't really sure what happened to Peter Cushing or Frankenstein. He must have shut his eyes for a jiffy. His brother Junior is standing staring at him, square-jawed, swaying from side to side, his fists clenched.

'Pizza Face is in the hospital. And it's yer fault. I don't know whit it's got tae dae wae yeh, but it's got something tae dae wae yeh.'

Chaz waves a beckoning hand at Kerry-Ann, who is standing behind Junior. 'Light us a fag,' he tells her. Rioting peasants on the telly flood the basement with a dam of water, but Frankenstein is made of sterner stuff. Chaz puffs on his cigarette. Angela's bright eyes stare at him, but she pulls the bedclothes over her head and disappears. 'Whit was it yeh said was wrang wae him, again?'

'Somebody slashed his face tae fuck.'

Chaz sniggers. 'Well, nae harm done. I mean, he'd that big monstrosity on his face. And he'd never huv got a bird looking like that. They've probably done him a big favour. And he'll be able tae get fucking plastic surgery noo.'

A fist crashes into Chaz's cheekbone and he falls sideways. Another hits his nose and mouth and against his forehead. His feeble attempts to get up are like an umbrella trying to stave off forked lightning.

'Fucking aye playing the big man,' Junior, with bruised knuckles, holds off Kerry-Ann with his other hand.

'Where's the fucking gun yeh use, cause yeh cannae use yer fists?' Junior hits him another smack, but it's diverted by her shoving him.

'They're in the hall cupboard,' Kerry-Ann bawls at the back of his head. 'Don't hurt him.'

Junior stops pummelling him. He registers her dishevelled appearance, swerves around Kerry-Ann and goes to search.

'Fucking bitch,' snarls Chaz, tilting his head, blood running into his throat. Sprawled over the side of the couch, he gags. Booze and blood spilling onto the floor beside the window leaves a splattered mess and stink.

On the telly, the happy Eastern European peasants whoop, men hug and kiss and drink from flagons. They engage in a traditional folk dance with the prettiest girls with flashing white teeth and big boobs. Chaz finally gets up. He staggers into the hall. The dirty washing pulled out. The guns missing. Kerry-Ann watches him. He holds his head and groans. 'Ya fucking stupid cow. Yeh've jist signed my death warrant.'

Chapter 71

Gone missing

Marie waits for Evan in the office. Julie flustered, leaves her sitting alone, because there's nothing in the diary and they can't find Evan. She paddles through the contents of her bag, pulls out her perfume, sprays her wrist and sniffs, turning her head sideways to check that nobody has seen her. She doodles on her notepad, lists the things she has to pick up for dinner.

Dayshift-staff circle around. 'If you wouldnae leave everything at your arse,' Bob bawls at a seven-year-old kid in the hallway and begins searching for Evan on the ground-floor.

Evan yawns, legs dangling, bides his time until lunch. Cloudless, blue skies, the smell of newly cut grass and soporific heat. Bruno sits beside him in the branches of the tree with the swing below them.

Bruno grins and points towards Angela's blonde thatch of hair, Pizza Face behind her. He holds a finger to his lips. 'Shush.' They watch them silently from above.

Bruno giggles as he clambers down. He creeps behind Angela, who squeals when he jumps out on her. Pizza Face nearly drops the bottle of poison.

Evan joins the huddle under the canopy of leaves. 'I thought I told yeh no tae tell anybody.'

'I never,' cries Angela. 'I only told Pizza Face, and he wanted tae see.' She sticks her tongue out. 'So there.'

'Yeh know what she's like. I thought she was kidding on.' Pizza Face bats away a daddy-longlegs, which darts across his wounded face. 'Don't worry, I'll stick it back where I got it.'

He slinks away and puts the bottle back in the hole in the wall, carefully replacing the brick.

'I'm bored outa my box,' announces Bruno, rocking on his heels.

Angela ignores him and edges beside Evan. He winks at her. A droning insect rising and falling in Pizza Face's wake makes him jump out of the shadows.

'I heard about whit happened,' Evan whispers.

He examines the black stitches and the alternative routes they create across the florid splash of birthmark. The way they extend across his other cheek and bisect his shaved left eyebrow. Pizza Face flinches when Evan's fingertips brush the knots of threads and trace a line of x-x-x-x. Evan snivels.

Pizza Face flings his arm over Evan's shoulder, pulls him into a brief hug, before he lets go. His eyes redden. Angela crowds in to be comforted.

Bruno sits apart, cross-legged, and digs with a stick. 'Watch it,' he warns them. 'Somebody's coming.'

310

The boys wipe at their eyes and Angela pushes against Evan's leg. Twigs snap underfoot and a waft of perfume. Norma comes out of the light. A bit of greenery stuck to her plaited black hair. She stoops to join them behind the tree trunk. 'They're all going nuts in there looking for you,' she tells Evan. 'You running away?'

'Nah, no really,' he replies. 'How did yeh know we were here?'

'Can see you lot sneaking about from my room. Always wondered what you were up to.' She looks about and seems disappointed that they're not up to much. 'I've got some Irn Bru, but it's a bit warm.' She flashes the bottle in her hand.

Pizza Face takes a quick dekko at her tanned legs in fraying cut-down denim and bumps of small breasts in a V of white cheese-cloth. Her tomboyish actions a weird pleasure, although his expression doesn't change, the way she screws the lid off and swallows a drink straight from the bottle without wiping it, before passing it around.

Pizza Face hands her the empty bottle. 'That was great.' He burps and blushes.

She lobs the bottle into the bushes. 'What happened to your face?'

'I got attacked by a gang of bad bastards.'

She squints her eyes and peers at his face. 'It's pretty cool, in a way. Nobody will mess with you now.'

Bruno dodges away and brings back the Irn Bru bottle. 'Finders keepers, losers weepers. Nae back backers'

'That's a total reddy.' Norma turns her head, following the drone as wasp nips behind her. 'I better go. What happened to the men that did that?'

'His brother killed them,' hoots Bruno. 'Bang! Bang! Bang!' He crooks his fingers into the shape of a gun and turns his sights on her. 'Bang! Bang! Bang!'

Norma blushes. 'Saw his picture in the paper.' She swats midges away from the corners of her eyes. 'He's quite cute. Has he got a girlfriend?'

'Nah,' Pizza Face answers on his brother's behalf. 'But he killed a guy and wounded another two fuckers. And they took him away and put him in Barlinnie. And I'm gonnae go up and visit him in High Security.'

'Got to go,' Norma looks towards the house. 'My wee sister will be looking for me.' She holds out her hand and asks Angela, 'You want to come and play?'

Angela shakes her head, 'Nah. Don't like her.'

Chapter 72

The crack

'WHAT'S BEEN THE CRACK, THEN?' DEL LEANS ON THE doorjamb, a cigarette jammed between his lips. Tan on his muscled arms contrast with a clean, white, open-necked shirt. It's marching season, and he smells of booze and is in holiday mode. Smooth-faced, features raw and blunt as a snouted animal, eyeing Chaz and smiling. He exudes good will, his bulky body blocking off landing and stairwell.

Chaz unshaven and bleary-eyed mopes in a trapped silence and rolls on the back of his heels as if ready for flight. He composes his face and launches into a story. 'It's been a fucking nightmare tae be honest, Del.' Slaps himself a smack on the chest. 'Here's my house, here's my heart. Come in, Del. Don't jist be standing there.' He points at the ghost of a yellow bruise above his eye. 'See that! Had a bit of a run in when yeh boys were away.'

He turns to Kerry-Ann, 'Get him a cup of tea.'

She shuffles up the lobby. They follow her into the kitchen. Her chiffon dress too tight at the waist. She pats her round belly before turning to put the kettle on. 'Get in there,' she tells Angela. 'Stop hinging about. Stop annoying folk.'

Chaz goes through the ritual of searching for his cigarette, finds the packet of Silk Cut in his top pocket, flips it open and flicks the lid of his brass lighter.

Anger flashes across Del's face. 'Who did that to you?'

'Wan of they Dunne boys. Papes.' He spits a bit of tobacco onto the floor. 'Yeh know whit they're like, sneaky bastards. Blindsides yeh.'

'I hope you gave him what for.'

Chaz shrugs. 'Look it wisnae like that. Yeh know how it is when yeh go tae take somebody a square-go?'

Del follows Chaz into the living room. They sit opposite ends of the couch, an overflowing ashtray at their feet. Angela shifts from her berth and stands by the window. Chaz continues talking. 'Yeh know whit it's like. Guy punches yeh. And yeh punch him back and yer rolling about the floor, getting the better of him. And then he pulls out a blade... I mean, fuck sake, whit would yeh dae?'

Del's jaw quivers. 'I'd fucking kill him.' He chain smokes, lighting one fag from the carcass of another.

'Aye, well, I admit I cut him up a bit, but the most annoying thing was it wasnae even my fight. Yeh know Rab?'

Del's upturned lip shows he doesn't like to remember.

Kerry-Ann interrupts them. 'How many sugar dae yeh take in yer tea?'

'Three,' Del offers a whimsical smile. 'I'm sweet enough.'

A thumping sound comes from their downstairs neighbour's. When Kerry-Ann returns, mugs clink against each other. Del sweeps the glazed mug from her hand and sips sugared tea with lip-smacking noises of appreciation. 'Yeh want any biscuits?'

'Aye, that'd be grand,' Del raises his eyebrows in mock surprise. 'I'm partial to a biscuit of two. Can't you tell?'

Kerry-Ann offers Del a tight-lipped smile. Worn slippers with a small heel, scuff across linoleum but soon hurry back. 'There's nae biscuits.' She stares at Angela. 'That wee bastard ate them aw.'

'No, I never,' Angela cries.

Del snorts and sips at his tea. 'Doesn't matter.'

Kerry-Ann goes into the kitchen and returns with a Silk Cut in her mouth. She leans into Del's shoulder to get a light off him.

'I wouldnae huv minded if they'd been man enough about it.' Chaz sprawls back on the couch, glances at the side of Del's face. 'Four or five of those Fenian bastards came here and carved my wee brother's face up. It was touch and go. He was in Yorkhill for well o'er a week.'

'For fuck sake,' Del jumps up, tea sloshing onto the lino. 'How did you not tell me? The bastards. I'd fucking shoot them dead.' He studies the wet stain, mouths 'Sorry,' to Kerry-Ann and swipes a big hand across the tea splashed onto his flares above the left knee.

Chaz cackles, 'I would tae, but my wee brother beat me tae the punch. He went up tae the pub they drink in, the Cleddens. Shot wan or two of them bastards deid.'

'For fuck sake.' Del checks for dampness. His gaze circles the room, glances across at Angela and at Kerry-Ann. He mutters as he turns to face Chaz, 'Where did he get the gun?'

'That's whit I was trying tae tell yeh. There was nae way of contacting yeh. He got the guns from here. I don't know how he knew they were here, but he did. And he jist took them.' He can't read what Del is thinking, but his glower deepens. Chaz blushes slightly and blunders on. 'I mean, I wasnae here. Kerry-Ann couldn't keep him out. Could yeh, babe?' He nods at her, a cigarette at the corner of her mouth, encouraging her not to speak by prattling on. 'Yeh know whit they're like, these pregnant women? Can't tell up fae doon. Always sitting wae their mouths open and their legs shut.'

'Dougie won't be best pleased. We best go and see him now.' He stands, leaving the mug cooling at his feet.

'Thanks for the tea.' He nods at Kerry-Ann and winkles out a smile for the little girl watching him.

Chaz has a haunted look but brazens it out. He kisses the side of Kerry-Ann's cheek. 'No be that long, hen.'

Chapter 73

Something important came up

LIZZIE LIES CURLED UP ON THE COUCH, TOP BUTTON ON HER denims popped, white blouse, and hint of breast. Her bare feet stretching over Dougie's lap, they watch *Coronation Street*. Her eyes flicker to Del standing behind Chaz and then back to Hilda Ogden. Two-bar setting on the electric fire, an overflowing ashtray on the knee-high table makes a stuffy room. The perfume and heat of sex clings to their faces.

'Sorry to interrupt,' Del's gaze lingers on Lizzie, but he addresses Dougie. 'But something important came up.'

'True,' Dougie smiles. 'Something important always does.'

Del slopes off to the kitchen. Chaz listens to the traffic and rain falling. He is careful not to give anything away. Sliding into the seat opposite them, he pulls his cigarettes out of his denim jacket. Taps one out of the packet. 'Yeh want wan, hen?'

'No thanks,' Lizzie shakes her head, eyes returning to the small screen.

'Dougie?'

He looks through him. Eyes sympathetic as pebbles. 'What's the game?'

Del bumbles back into the living room, squeezing through the gap between chair and couch, holding the bottle and four teacups. 'It's all I could find?' he apologises. He wedges his stocky body onto the couch beside them. A cup on the floor at his feet, he hands out the other cups to Dougie and Lizzie and stretches, passing one across to Chaz. He cracks the seal on the bottle of Glenfiddich. Pours himself a good measure and holds the bottle up as if to warm their eyes. The theme music of *Coronation Street* a background noise, but with whisky in their hands, Del has their full attention.

'I'll kill two birds with one stone. Chaz isn't here for a social visit.' He swills his whisky and drinks it in a gulp and pours himself another. 'But if you ask me, it wasn't his fault.'

Dougie notices him looking at Lizzie's painted toenails. 'What wasn't his fault?' He lifts her legs off his lap and jounces her feet onto the floor, so they sit like three passengers on the same bus.

Chaz gulps a mouthful of whisky. 'My wee brother, Junior, killed wan or two Papes and noo he's in Barlinnie.'

Dougie grunts and lifts a drink to his lips. 'It would be pleasant if we talked in English now and again.'

Lizzie laughs and reaches for her gold Dunhill lighter. Her fingers disappear and come back from the side of the couch with a packet of Menthol cigarettes. 'He can be sweet, but usually he's a crabbit old bastard.' She lights a cigarette, all eyes on her, but she is used to that and a minty smell hangs in the air between them.

Del holds up the bottle, an offer of another drink. He pours himself a treble since nobody else has taken one. 'The thing is...

the gun he used was one of ours. In fact, I think we're pretty much fucked and they've got all our cache of weapons.' He makes it sound like aircraft, tanks and bazookas. 'But as I said, fair's fair I don't think it was his fault.' He looks into his drink. 'I'd have done the same thing.'

Chaz considers his options, get treated as the retard in the corner, and grovel, or bite back. 'It's true maist of the guns ur gone.'

Dougie reacts angrily, but he's listening.

'We've still got a Starr Pistol and some ammo.'

'How come the bizzies never cleaned you out, shook you down?'

'They did, but the stupid bastards went doonstairs tae my ma's house. That's where Junior stays.'

'Have you brought the pistol with you?'

Chaz shakes his head. He finishes his drink and holds the cup out for Del to fill.

'Is it safe?'

'I don't know.' Chaz tries to appear concerned. His gaze shifts to Lizzie. 'But when yer wee brother, who's still in his school shorts, is slashed tae fuck for nae good reason. And is on life support— that was the least of my worries. I joined the UDA cause I'm a patriot, but when yer ain family is maimed—' He trails off, glancing at the window behind Lizzie's hair.

Lizzie gives him a tight smile. 'What age is your wee brother?'

'Seven.' Chaz wonders if he's a bit older but figuring younger plays better. Flings back his drink and holds out his cup for a refill. 'Cunts,' he adds.

'I'd a wee brother killed by the IRA.' Lizzie's voice wavers and she swishes her legs together.

'Aye, he was a grand lad.' Dougie pats the top of her thigh. He stares at Chaz and shakes his head. 'OK, the clock's ticking. I'd a few angles I was looking at. A few jobs planned. We'll need to move everything forward and we'll come back to this later. Right now, I want that gun and ammunition. We'll be moving to a new safe house to—'

'I'm not going anywhere until I've had a bath and washed my hair.' Lizzie stands and wiggles her way past Dougie, taking the long route.

Del watches her ass and his face turns soft.

Dougie gives Chaz a blank look. 'Del will take you home.' He takes a drink of whisky and motions with his hands and says to no one in particular. 'You know something. Sometimes I get a gut feeling about things—'

Chapter 74

Hard times

Chaz sits at his usual table in the corner of Maggie Scott's, nursing a warm pint. At home, mooching about in his Y-fronts, four-day beard, watching telly, cashing his Giro and reduced to smoking shitty roll ups. Even Kerry-Ann has been giving him snash about needing stuff for the wain starting school, and he had to give her a slap or two. He takes a sip of his beer. Work can't come quick enough.

He checks his pockets for his pouch of Old Holborn, the rattle of Bluebell matches, and feels for the weight of the gun and ammo. Under starter orders.

Leather seats, radio blaring and ashtrays in the new Volvo aren't yet filled with gunk. Usually that's enough to get Del excited and talking about cars, but he answers questions in monosyllables and smokes one cigarette after another. They pass through Dumbarton Town Centre, the hollow bump over the bridge, the taste of water and the dull bronze of sunlight coming off the embrace of cool green hills. They've done the journey stacks of times, shadowing a Securicor van, moving easily with the flow of traffic.

'I meant tae say tae yeh,' Chaz licks the edge of his roll-up paper to seal tobacco inside and tamps it before he's satisfied, 'Close wan, eh?' He searches his side pockets for matches, puts the cigarette behind his ear. 'We nearly caught them at it.'

'Too right, we nearly did.' Del slaps the wheel and grins like a wee boy. 'She's some girl.'

Chaz lights his cigarette and puffs contentedly and squints sideways. It's easy to figure out what he's thinking. Del's eyes are chock full of Lizzie. He chuckles and turns the transistor up. Diana Ross warbling *I'm Still Waiting*.

Just before Balloch, they double back on themselves and follow a single line track. Dougie sits high in the cab of a flatbed truck with a metal girder welded onto the back. A V-shaped lance hangs over the top of the cab, and hanging from the front bumper, grappling hooks.

'Whit's that for?' Chaz jokes. 'It fucking looks totally fucking mad.'

'To ram into the back of a Securicor van. It'll open it like a tin opener.'

'When?'

Del leans across, pops open the glove compartment. He pulls out two orange wigs and two pairs of tights. Fiddles about and yanks out a pistol and puts it on his lap. Stretches the denier on the tights and pulls it over his face. Plonks the wig at a raffish angle on his head. 'Round about now,' he laughs.

'Yeh should huv told me.'

'You never asked.' Del looks over his shoulder as he reverses. He guns the Volvo engine until it roars and the flatbed truck follows at a steady pace behind them.

Chaz pulls the tights over his head and puts on the wig. He checks the gun is loaded before sitting it in his lap. 'I didnae think yeh had any guns.'

'Don't be so fucking stupid,' Del keeps the Volvo at a steady thirty, following the winding roads. 'Nearly every lorry driver that comes across can be leant on to bring us what we need. We're not going to fucking advertise that fact, now, are we?'

'How is this gonnae work? I mean, it seems a bit slapdash for our Dougie.'

'Ours not to reason why.' Del takes a gloved hand off the wheel. He taps a finger against the side of his temple. 'He's got the smarts. This is a big job. Straightforward, estimated, one-hundred grand. Maybe more. And it couldn't be easier. In these wee back roads, there's only one place to pass. We overtake the van with the money in it and park in the middle of the road. It can't get past us. Dougie's waiting with the lorry behind it and comes up and smashes right into its shiter. We can be back in our cars and back in Drumchapel within half-an-hour and we've got a lock up ready.'

He puts his foot down and speeds up. Over the hump of the hill they see the white of a Securicor van lower down, green fields and empty space on either side of it.

Chaz snorts with laughter. 'That's fucking brilliant. Tae think about an hour ago, I was a worthless piece of shit that was thinking about a spot of burglary tae keep me goin. Noo, I'm gonnae be loaded again.'

'Too right,' says Del.

The Volvo darts forward and overtakes the van.

Chapter 75

Missing in action

CHAZ DOESN'T REALISE HE'S PEED THE BED. KERRY-ANN wakes in the morning and pulls away from him. She points to the mattress stain and the damp patch on her nightie. He sniggers, flings his arm around her shoulder, rubs his unshaven chin against her cheek, and includes her in his drunken humour. 'We'll buy a hunner mattresses if that keeps yeh happy. Who gi'es a fuck?' He glances around. 'Where's Bridget the Midget?'

'She's away oot.' Kerry-Ann tries to smile. 'Don't yeh member? Yeh hurt her. We might need tae take her tae a doctor.'

'No fucking doctors, ya stupid cow.'

Chapter 76

Kick starts

'I huv tae see Evan,' cries Angela.

Bob stands elephantine in the doorway. 'He's still in bed,' his breath vapour visible as he speaks. 'Most of the kids are. It's a bit too early for visitors.'

'Is Evan no in?' Angela asks.

Julie brushes past Bob. She crouches and takes Angela's hands in hers and pulls her into a cuddle. 'You've not got a jacket on and it's not the weather to be out on your own.'

'Is Evan no in?'

'Has something happened to you, pet?' Julie strokes Angela's bedraggled hair and ghost-white face, trying to elicit a response. Her fingertips brush against a damp stain on the backside of her blue nylon dress. She flinches at the reek from her. 'It is a bit early—'

'Is Evan no in?'

'Oh, for god's sake,' Bob mutters. He turns and clumps away, leaving them to it with his parting remark. 'He's up the stairs. Why don't you go and annoy him? Gi'e us all peace.'

Angela draws away from Julie and weaves past Bob, not looking back, resolutely climbing the stairs.

Angela barges into the boys' bedroom, the lustrous reds of the racing posters on one wall in the dull light making the room seem lopsided. She stands in the passageway between beds, listening to the distinct sounds of their breathing. She kicks off her shoes and slips under the covers and piles into the bed beside Evan. He murmurs but doesn't waken. The snuggled heat of his skin from his arm and leg soothes and settles her and draws her into slumber and sleep.

Bruno wakens first. He wafts his blankets, up and down as if checking. 'That wasnae me.'

If surprised to see Angela in bed beside him, Evan doesn't show it, but his arms feel slightly dead under her neck. He slides away from her clammy warmth, sitting against the headboard and shakes his wrist and the feeling back into his hand 'Whit wasn't yeh?'

'That's pooey,' Bruno sniggers.

Evan sneaks a look at Angela. 'Don't smell anything.'

She squirms beneath the blankets. Her long eyelashes flicker and there's a coy expression on her face. Her hand brushes the nylon of his pyjamas at the top of his thigh, which makes him jerk his leg away from her.

'Whit yeh daeing, Angel?

'Nothing,' she whimpers, her gaze fixed on his face. She buries her face in the blankets, a blob of blonde hair. 'I didnae dae anything. It wasnae me.'

Evan rubs and pats the top of her shoulder as she rocks back and forth crying. 'It's OK... Yeh never did anything. Yer alright.'

Bruno drags the sheets and undercover off his bed, leaving the foam-rubber mat and undercover bare. He squints at Evan. 'Yeh'll probably need tae put yer stuff in the washing tae, cause she's minging.' He bundles his dirty washing into a tightly hugged ball.

'Am not,' Angela snorts from beneath the blanket. Her head appears. 'Yer jist stupid.' She rolls her eyes.

Bruno gives her a broken-toothed grin. He doesn't hang about hauling away his laundry with a grunt, a coverlet hanging and sweeping the carpet. The racket of other children stomping along and laughing in the corridor grows louder when he opens the door and fades.

Angela looks at Evan. 'Yeh want tae go oot and play?'

Evan hesitates. 'I'm no sure. It's still a bit early.'

Her gaze drops, she pushes her legs out of the covers and stands, wobbling a little. 'I hate yeh. My daddy would get mad and come and kill yeh. He'd stomp on yeh like a bug. And rip yer clothes off.' She leaps between the beds, ripping the top of her dress. 'And hit yeh on the heid. And. And. And. Split yeh in two by ripping his Y-fronts off and putting his cock inside yeh. Aw the way up, so it comes oot everywhere, makes yeh bleed, and spits on yeh.'

'Yeh've no got a da.' Evan's cheeks burn. He hops out of bed. 'And if yeh did, he'd batter yeh for talking like a wee cow. Where did yeh hear aw that stuff? I thought yeh were a nice wee thing.'

Bruno bounces back into the room. 'Yeh gonnae go for breakfast?'

'In a minute,' Evan replies.

'Whit's she greeting for?' Bruno nods in Angela's direction.

Evan shakes his head. 'Dunno.' He nods towards the door. 'Yeh go doon first and I'll get yeh doon there.'

'Nae danger, I'll jist wait for yeh.' Bruno avoids Evan's gaze. He brushes past Angela and sits on his bare mattress. 'She cannae go for breakfast anyway because she's no allowed.'

'Shut up.'

'I was jist saying.' Bruno leans sideways and gets down on one knee. Scans the darkness beneath the bed and pulls out his drawing pad and a plastic dish with crayons and coloured pencils and marker pens. He flips through the drawings on his lap.

'Whit's that?' Angela rubs her eyes and points to the top of a page, showing the outline of a purple box with a green crayon roof and red and orange squiggles.

'That's where I used tae stay, but it was in the sky.' Bruno uses the end of a brown colouring-in pencil to tap the red and orange marks. 'That's the stars.'

Angela sidles closer, her knee brushes against his kneecap. She peers at his drawing. 'Where's yer mum and dad?'

A harrumphing sound and Bruno's pencil taps against two tiny black stick figures enclosed in bubbles. 'They don't live in the sky, but sometimes they float up when they want tae see me—well, my mum sometimes does.'

'Wow,' says Angela.

Julie raps the frame of the door and sticks her head in. Her hair falling over her face, she sweeps it back. 'C'mon you two, breakfast.' She does a double-take and laughs. 'I was wondering where you got to. I thought I might have had to call the police.'

'Can Angela come for breakfast too?' Evan pulls a V-neck jumper from the pile of clothes on the bottom of his bed and drags it over his head.

'Yes, of course,' Julie turns away, but leaves a parting remark. 'I used to have friends over for breakfast when I was young.'

Evan laughs, finding it difficult to imagine Julie being young. They hear Julie rapping on the bedroom door next to their room and her sing-song voice, 'Lazy-bones...'

Bruno flips over another page to show Angela. It's full of blobby shapes of different colours. 'That's wizards. They can see everything and go anywhere.'

Angela wrinkles her nose. 'Can yeh draw fish?'

'Easy-peasy.' Bruno grabs waxy orange and green crayons and quickly dashes the curves and the crossover triangular tails on the corner of a page. He dots the eyes. 'So they can see where they're goin.'

'I want tae go under the water in the canal,' says Angela. 'Can yeh dae the big bells ringing in yer ear? And angels singing?'

'Aye, I think so.' Bruno goes to the back of his book and puts the edge of the orange crayon against a blank sheet. 'But yeh don't need tae go under the water. Yeh can go and live in the sky wae me.'

'No. I'm goin under the water in the canal and Evan's gonnae take me. Urn't yeh Evan?'

Chapter 77

Child's Play

DEL AND DOUGIE WAIT OUTSIDE CHAZ'S HOUSE AT lunchtime, car engine running. Hungover, Chaz almost boaks as he pulls a mask over his ruddy-red cheeks and face. Del jokes with him from the driver's seat, 'Ford Cortinas are so easy to steal, even with a pair of kid's scissors, it's almost criminal not to.'

Dougie studies a folded-up street guide, mapping out a marriage of convenience, which he fills Chaz in on as they motor past the chippie. West End branches of Bank of Scotland and Royal Bank of Scotland face each other across the road staggered by shops and a pub. Banks ideally situated for withdrawals with a sawn-off shotgun and two handguns.

The first bank is a study in time and motion. They're outside in less than six minutes with sacks of money.

The Cortina double parks outside the Royal Bank. A have-a-go hero at the counter, an elderly man with a walking stick proves more of a nuisance. Chaz is near enough to force the barrel of his gun against his ear. Del, with a flick of his wrist, wrestles the old codger to the ground. He laughs at his audacity, and his Fu

Manchu moustache falls off. They leave the bank in their bright wigs like a girly gang giggling and drive off at high speed for a few hundred yards and swerve around the corner to Otago Lane, leaving the Cortina burnt out.

Chaz jokes about the switch to a lime-green Lada where they stash the money and weapons in the boot. 'I'd rather walk than get in that thing.'

'Aye,' Dougie doesn't miss a beat. 'But it's raining and beggars can't be choosers. Call it progress, or call it Russia's fuck you to Western civilisation, but the police never stop a Lada because they're too embarrassed for the driver.'

Chapter 78

Jackpot

CHAZ HAS A FEW DRINKS IN MACS. HIS BODY STILL ANTSY with adrenalin, Del picks him up. The safe house is a top-floor flat in Kinfauns, the snobby bit of Drumchapel, near the road that cuts off to Bearsden, giving twin points of departure and arrival. A nice enough two-bedroom house, with a newish lounge settee, a television and a potted geranium at the window.

They follow indistinct sounds, the up-and-down drone of Northern Ireland accents of a man and woman and back-and-forth bantering. Cash litters the bed and floor. Chaz and Del step lightly into the room, a plush landing for their plodding feet.

Dougie and Lizzie sit facing each other, knees touching. An old-fashioned chest of drawer leaves an indent in the carpet where they've pushed it away from the window and made more space to work. They bundle loose notes into currency of the same denomination: pound notes, five-pound notes, ten-pound notes and fifty-pound notes for sorting later and to make counting easier. Red elastic bands and clear plastic bags splashed at their feet. A transistor, an ashtray, two ceramic mugs and a pink plastic rattle clutter the chest of drawers dusty surface.

'Turn that shite off,' Dougie gestures towards the radio. 'I can't concentrate with it on.'

'Och, going raffle yourself.' Lizzie laughs, her breasts jumping like salmon in her man's loose shirt. She looks through Chaz and smiles at Del standing in the doorway. 'We'll put it to the vote. On or off?'

'Eh, on,' says Del.

'Off,' cries Chaz. 'I cannae stand that cunt Tony Blackburn. Yeh jist want tae put his face in a blender tae get him tae fucking shut up.' His face scrunches up as he reconsiders. 'I'm no even sure that would fucking work.'

'You don't get Tony Blackburn on the tranny at night,' says Lizzie.

Chaz remains dour-faced. 'But yeh never know wae that cunt.'

'Well,' Dougie pats his pockets. 'Two votes each. We'll need to toss a coin. All this money and I've not got a coin.'

Chaz ferrets in his pockets and comes out with a handful of change. He kicks over a wad of notes and flicks Dougie fifty-pence. 'Mind I want it back.'

Dougie smirks. 'Heads or tails?'

'Tails,' shrieks Lizzie.

The coin somersaults in the air. Dougie catches it and smacks it unseen on the back of his left hand. 'Heads.' He pulls his fingers away and shows Lizzie.

'Fuck,' she quickly recovers her brio. 'Best of three!'

She watches the coin spin through the air twice more and Del watches her watching. 'Yes!' Lizzie punches the air triumphant. 'The tranny stays on.'

Going back to sorting out the money, Dougie laughs through his nose and doesn't seem too bothered,

At the end of the night, the bedroom breeds cigarette smoke and mugs of cold tea. After a few false starts, Dougie takes a deep breath. 'I reckon we've made £172 221.'

'Fuck me,' Lizzie's eyes twinkle. 'That's enough cash to buy the whole of Northern Ireland and still have some change to buy that shitebox Dublin too.'

'Yeh,' says Dougie. He rolls his neck and stretches his back. 'There'll be a few investments made over the next few days, that's for sure.'

Del grins. 'Time for a drink.'

'Too fucking right,' Chaz laughs, and sticks his hand out to get his fifty-pence back. 'That might even get me wan of them Ladas, even though I cannae drive.'

Del wiggles the car keys. 'I'll take you home, son.' He gets Chaz in a playful headlock. 'But I'm sorry it's not a Lada. There's certain fucking standards a man won't go below.'

Chapter 79

Judgement Day

'This big, gigantic guy wae wan eye is trying tae kill him,' Bruno's voice rises in exaggerated fashion. 'So he can eat him.' His arms sweep like a crab's pincers to show what he means. In a world full of blood and gore and monsters, he's the tanned heroic hero. Evan takes his hands out of his denim pockets to bat midges away. They trek back to the house, following a path they'd made earlier through uncut grass.

'Haa-Aargh,' Bruno roars. 'And then he stabs it in the eye.'

Evan stops to let him catch up. 'Then whit happens?'

'Och, nothing much.' Bruno stares at the ground and notices a horned grey snail. He squats on his heels and picks up a twig and spears its slimy body. 'It looks different when it's deid.' He holds it out as evidence.

'Whit did yeh dae that for?'

'It's only a slug.' Bruno drops the stick and stands up, looking towards the house. 'Soon be lunch time. I'm starving. Could eat a horse.' His grin shows discoloured teeth. 'Yeh know the French eat slugs?'

'Shut up,' Evan bumps his shoulder against Bruno's. 'No even yeh would eat a slug.'

'Want tae bet?'

Bruno giggles. 'Yeh want tae go up the Park?'

'Nah, it's boring when yeh've nae money for sweets.'

'We could go up the golfie and look for golf balls. And sell them.'

'Nah.'

'How no?'

Evan ambles towards the house. 'I don't play golf.'

Pizza Face, with rolled-up sleeves, sprints around the corner. He takes a breather, shoulders heaving. His face glazed with sweat and his skin blooms pink and purple patches. He stinks of cigarette smoke. 'It's Angel. She's fucking doowally. And is talking about flinging herself in the canal and drooning herself, again. She wants yeh tae go wae her. And kill yerself tae.'

Evan shakes his head. 'Well, I'll no.'

'Fuck sake, I know that. But I couldnae stop her. She's already away doon the canal. Yeh know whit's she's like.' He grabs his arm, and they break into a run. 'C'mon, yer the only wan she'll listen tae.'

Traffic slows them at Dumbarton Road. Pizza Face sprints and catches up with him. They weave in and out of the slow-moving cars and buses, horns blaring, and face a motor bike which swerves around them.

When Bruno catches up with them, they stand together on the bevel of the footbridge scanning the murky water.

'Angel's no here,' cries Evan.

Pizza Face continues studying watery reeds and cow parsley and the stretch of canal that runs to Bowling, the unpeopled side.

'O'er there!' Evan points a wavering finger at a white squib submerged in tender green roots, but partially floating free. He clambers over the railing. 'It's a plastic bag, I think.'

'Aye,' says Pizza Face. 'But that's whit we thought the last time.'

Bruno sidles up behind them and looks over their shoulders. 'Maybe she went hame?'

Pizza Face takes a hard look at him, a nip in his voice. 'Who fucking asked yer opinion?'

'I was jist saying.'

'Well don't.' Pizza Face slaps him hard across the cheek. 'In fact, fuck off!'

Bruno's hand cups his reddened cheek. He looks at Evan, his eyes petitioning, but he is staring at the water. His right leg buckles when Pizza Face takes a swipe and boots his arse, but he regains his balance and runs with his head down and blinkered, so nobody can see his tears.

Evan hisses, 'Whit did yeh dae that for?'

Pizza Face squares up to him. 'Whit?'

'Shut up,' Evan looks again at the waterlogged plastic bag. 'We'll need tae go and tell Angel's mum that she's drowned herself.'

Pizza Face snorts, 'I'm no telling her that.'

'Somebody will need tae.'

They cross the bridge and meander the short distance towards Kerry-Ann's house. When they get to the tenement block their feet slow.

On the top landing, Pizza Face sniffles and stands behind Evan, mopping at his eyes. Silence stitches them together. Evan flicks the letter box, once, twice, three times. He retreats, staring at his feet.

The clatter of shoes in the hall getting nearer becomes a relief. Evan looks at Kerry-Ann with a duck's egg of a bump poking out of her pinny. Angela stands behind her.

'Whit is it?' Kerry-Ann looks at Evan, then at Pizza Face, suspiciously.

Pizza Face smirks. 'Is Angel coming oot tae play?'

'No, she's a cheeky wee bastard. I've grounded her. Her da says the same thing.' Kerry-Ann looks around at Angela and frowns. 'Urn't yeh?'

'He's no my da,' screams Angela. 'And yeh urnae my real mum.'

Kerry-Ann shakes her head and flings the front door shut in their faces.

Chapter 80

Truth or lies?

RAB STUMBLES INTO MAGGIE SCOTT'S AND STANDS DRIPPING wet at the table in front of Chaz.

'Holiday weather?' Chaz swigs his whisky, holding in a belly laugh, and keeps a straight face. 'Yeh're wetter than Maggie Dunphy's fanny.'

Rab shakes his head and his eyes crinkle. 'Dunno about that.'

Behind him a fat elderly couple argues, and the man's voice takes on a hectoring tone. Rab wets his dry lips with the tip of his tongue. 'Yeh want a drink?'

Chaz holds out a spirit's glass of whisky. 'Wouldnae say no.'

Drew stops nattering to a squat, grey-haired man with faded RFC tattoos on his right shoulder, standing at the bar, a Woodbine behind his left ear. He watches as Rab picks his way through empty tables and chairs and rewards him with a smile.

Rab fingers the change in his pocket, pulling it out and carefully counting it. 'A whisky and water.'

'Chaz doesnae take water in his whisky, son.'

'Nah, I mean a glass of whisky and a glass of water.'

'You taking the piss? This is a pub son. You want water, go outside to the canal and open that big fat gub of yours. We sell booze.'

'I've only got enough for a wee whisky,' mumbles Rab, fingering loose change.

'That's alright son.' Drew swivels, picks a glass from a tray below the gantry and sets it under a bottle of Whyte and Mackay. 'You should have said,' he adds. 'You want ice wae yer water?'

'Eh, nah.' Rab turns, makes space for Chaz beside him.

Chaz leans against the bar, a cigarette dangles in the corner of his mouth. 'Whit's he drinking?'

Drew delicately places the whisky glass on a Tennent's beer mat. He smirks and places a half-pint glass filled with tap water and a pink straw in the glass beside it. 'He's gonnae go dry.' Nods towards Rab. 'Says he wants water.'

'Don't be so fucking daft.' Chaz pulls out a wad of five and ten and fifty-pound notes and wangles a pound. 'Get him a pint. And keep the change.' He jiggles his drink and saunters back to the table. He takes a seat, looks around the room, waiting for Rab to follow him.

Rab puts his pint on the table. 'Cheers Chaz.'

'Aye, cheers.' Chaz picks up his glass and toasts his companion by reaching across, clinking his glass against the bottom of the pint tumbler. 'Yeh've been avoiding me, pal. And I don't like that.'

'Nah, I huvnae Chaz, I've jist been dead busy.'

Chaz watches Rab's hand shaking as he takes a drink. 'Daeing whit?'

340

'Nothing much, yeh know. This and that.'

'Shite.'

'No, honest Chaz.' Rab gulps a mouthful of lager. 'Honest.'

'Yeh still on that stuff?'

Rab scratches the flaky scales at the back of his neck. 'Whit stuff?' He plays for time. 'Eh, aye,' he admits. 'That's whit I'm here for.'

'Yeh want tae take some of my hard-earned cash?' Chaz, an amused look on his face, shells a Silk Cut towards Rab.

'Nah, I wouldnae dae that Chaz.' Rab catches the cigarette. 'But I've got a message for yeh.'

Smoke curls around Chaz's face. 'Who fae?'

'Frank Dunne.'

'Oh, aye,' Chaz sniggers through his nose. 'Whit does that wee prick want?'

'They want tae call a truce.'

'Fuck off. A fucking truce. Whit ur we playing, cowboys and Indians? My wee brother's in prison because of they cunts. And Pizza Face—'

'Aye, but Chaz, it's no as if they got aff Scot free.'

Chaz leans across the table. 'Yeh taking they cunts' side?'

'Nah Chaz, it's no like that. They know about yer back up. The boys fae Ireland. And they know there's nae way round it. They need tae cut a deal. Business is business. Naebody is making money wae aw this shite. And wae yer contacts they can move on and take oot Drumchapel. Then Maryhill. And that's hauf of Glesga—'

'Whit's in it for me?'

'Yeh get fifty percent and yeh don't need tae lift a finger until it gets doon tae the nitty-gritty wae the competition.'

Chaz laughs into his drink. 'Fuck off. I want wan-hundred percent. But let's say I play ball. How dae I know yer no a fucking Judas and it's a trap?' He growls, 'Whit's in it for yeh, ya stupid cunt?'

'Look Chaz, I'm no gonnae lie tae yeh. If we pull this off, I'll huv a regular supply of the good stuff and we'll be rolling in cash.' He takes a quick mouthful of lager, his Adam's apple jiggles as he swallows and watches Chaz's face. 'They've got it aw planned, a big shipment, flood the market. Gi'e oot free samples wae a bit of hash. I know how that works. It happened tae me. Yeh never think yeh'll get hooked, but soon yer scratching. And yeh'd sell yer granny for the next fix. We cannae lose.'

Chaz shrugs. 'Yer poor granny is deid. Yeh wouldnae get much for her.'

'Aye, but yeh know whit I mean.'

'I'll think about it.'

Rab slumps back in his chair and wipes at his forehead. 'Please Chaz,' his fingers entwined into a prayer steeple. 'I'm begging yeh.'

A woman with fat dimpled arms and holding a shopping bag scrapes back the chair. She knocks into the back of Rab's seat and clumps sideways with unsteady feet. A man's voice rises in anger, 'Sit doon, I'm no finished wae yeh.'

'But I'm finished wae you, ya bampot.' She threads her way through the bar to the door.

Chapter 81

Trick or treat?

RAB FINISHES HIS PINT AND FOLLOWS CHAZ OUT OF THE PUB. 'Where does that cunt Frank Dunne want tae meet?' Chaz's lip curls when he mentions his name.

'Wherever yeh want. It's yer shout. But they want tae get things sorted, pronto.'

Chaz weaves past a woman on the pavement. She grasps a toddler's maroon woollen cap. Chaz turns into his close. 'Yeh think I'm fucking daft? I'm no meeting nae cunt until I'm carrying some serious shit.'

He clatters up the stairs, taking them two at a time. Rab slides the palm of his hand along the banister, wheezing, trying to keep up. Chaz jiggles house keys in the lock when the door to the landing below opens.

Chaz's mum and sister peer out at him. 'I thought that might be yeh,' his mum's voice shrewish. 'Yeh no spare yer family a minute of yer precious time. We're huving a wee get together for yer faither's birthday.' She smacks her thin lips together. 'I already told yeh about it.'

'Aye, that's right.' Chaz pats his jacket pocket for his cigarettes and feigns a smile, taps a Silk Cut out and searches for his matches. 'It slipped my mind, tae be honest.' His fingers trail through his hair. 'And yeh can see I'm in a bit of a hurry.'

'Yeh can never be in too much of a hurry for yer ain faither.'

'For yer ain faither,' his sister echoes her, wrings her hand and laughs in a high-pitch.

'And there's cake,' his mum adds.

'But Ma—'

Her front door left open, and her slippers slap on the linoleum in the hall followed by the heavier thud of his sister. The lit cigarette at a jaunty angle in the corner of Chaz's mouth and narrowed eyes doesn't fool Rab. He grins at his friend's embarrassment and sneaks away.

A shoogly three-legged table has been pushed against the sagging couch. A cake sitting on top of it. His da, with a glass of Pale Ale in his hand, sprawls on top of a candlewick cover thrown over burst cushions, staring at the sticks of candles with bloodshot eyes.

'Has anybody got a light?' his mum whimpers. 'Then yeh can blow them oot—forty-three-years young and handsomer than the day I met yeh.'

Chaz fishes his lighter out of his pocket. Flicks it open. Small flames wiggle as they catch on the candles and move together and hold something beautiful. His attention shifts to his da's wheezing breath.

Chaz drops a fifty-quid note onto the couch. 'Sorry, I didnae get yeh a card.' It settles beside the brown cardigan and the box of Panatella cigars. 'Take that and get yerself something.'

Duty done, but he feels a surge of anger. He stares out the window, remembers how he could tell how drunk his da was by his footfall in the lobby and what kind of beating to expect.

'Blow oot the candles,' shrieks his sister, clapping her hands together, and her cheeks rosy with warmth. 'Happy birthday tae yeh, happy birthday tae—'

'Happybirthdaytaeyeh,' shouts his mum.

His da breathes out a couple of candles on the side nearest him and shakes his head. 'That's enough.' He swallows a drink and slaps the glass on the table. Opening the packet of cigars, he uses candlelight to suck smoke into his lungs and blows out a small cloud that fills the room with cheap cigar fumes.

'Make a wee wish, John,' his mum sounds coyish.

'Cheers,' his da mumbles, winking at Chaz and slips the fifty-pound note into his trouser pocket, ignoring her.

'Whit about the rest of us?' says Eric. 'Dae we no get any thanks? Or is it jist for the blue-eyed boy that gets aw the praise for swanning in and dropping a few quid in yer tail?'

'Blow oot the candles.' His mum bends over the icing on the cake. Her daughter waddles in beside her and, ruby cheeked, they make a game out of extinguishing the flames.

'Stop yer whining,' Chaz sneers at Eric over the women's heads. 'Naebody asked for yer opinion. Whit did yeh get the old man? A fucking cardigan?'

'Aye, a cardigan. Bought wae my ain money. Yeh always were a selfish wee bastard, even as a kid. Yeh always did whit yeh were gonnae dae. And yeh'd walk away without a scratch, and never gi'e a thought tae anybody else. Never ask. Always expect. Nothing changes.'

'Right boys, that's enough,' his da takes another puff of his cigar.

'I'm no asking yeh for anything.' Chaz puts a hand to his ear. 'Yeh hear me asking for anything?'

'Oh, but yeh ur,' says Eric. 'Yeh don't even need tae ask and we acquiesce—'

'—Oh, acquiesce is it? That's a big word. Sounds like yeh've got a poker stuck up yer arse. Wouldnae surprise me if yer wan of them trendy hom-oh-sexuals.'

Eric surges forward and throws a punch, hitting Chaz on the bridge of the nose. He follows it with a volley to the right eye. Chaz grabs at his torso, and they wrestle and fall into their da's lap, knocking the cake to the ground.

'Happy Birthday!' their sister cries, laughing and clapping her hands.

Chapter 82

Café life

CHAZ SQUATS AT THE DOOR TO THE SMELLY CUPBOARD. A thirty-watt bulb allows him to inspect the Starr pistol in his hand. Cocking the gun, looking over the composite steel. Fingering the bullets. Placing one in the chamber and snicking the gun closed. Loaded. Sitting at the shiny bottom of a rifled tube waiting to explode into Frank Dunne's scarred face. He places the gun in the inside pocket of his denim jacket and stands up, feeling the comforting weight next to his striped shirt.

He plans to walk to Simeone's Café to clear his head, but it looks like rain. He waves down a Hackney and steps inside.

The driver spins his cab into the traffic. The cabbie runs a commentary out of the side of his mutton-chop mouth about the changeable weather and bangs on, about Rangers' next clash with Celtic.

Chaz lets him witter on. Simeone's quickly comes into side-view, Café sign at the front, imperial red stencil against the white-washed walls on a single-storey building at the corner, once the social hub of Whitecrook. He only offers the driver a ten pence tip.

Penniless teenagers hang about on the corner. Del sits at a Formica table near the window. His knife and fork clatter on an empty plate. He picks batter from between his teeth with the edge of a menu and takes a drag from his cigarette.

Chaz knows he carries insurance credentials: a sawn-off shotgun in the boot of a car parked in a side street.

The waitress yawns behind the counter and plops a dollop of ice cream into a glass of lemonade. A boy with slicked back hair stands waiting at the till.

Chaz signals to the waitress he doesn't want served, and squeezes into a seat beside the wall. He lights a fag while Del sips at his tea and drums his fingertip on the table.

'What's the plan then?' Del asks.

'The plan?' Chaz clears his throat.

'Aye, the plan,' Del chuckles. 'Maybe I've been spending too much time with Dougie, who tells you how long it's gonnae take, who's gonnae be there. And when you can fart and when you should hold it in, but you get the drift?'

'I never thought of that.' Chaz smacks his lips together.

'You want a cuppa tea?' Del points at his empty mug. 'I'm having another one.' He edges sideways, squeezing between the table and the wall.

'Nah,' Chaz waves him away, toying with his cigarette lighter. 'I'm fine.'

Del chats-up the fat counter assistant, which puts a smile on her glum face. Unasked, she adds a bit of shortbread to his plate.

'I've no got a plan,' Chaz watches Del scooping spoonfuls of sugar into his tea. 'I thought we'd jist go up and hear whit the fuck they've got tae say. And if they gi'e us any shite we jist shoot them up tae fuck.' 'Let's face it. I never asked for this meeting. They did. And Frank knows I'm no tae be fucked about. The scars ur there on his face tae prove it.'

'Hmmm,' Del says. 'That's a kinda plan, but not the kinda plan Dougie would like.' His face becoming shy but sly. 'But he's not here, so fuck him.' He wipes his mouth and swallows a mouthful of tea. 'You did well not to involve him. He doesn't mind getting his hands dirty at home, taxing drug dealers and the like. And I'm sure he thinks, like the rest of us, all junkies are scum of the earth and better off dead. So we would be providing a kind of public service. But he wouldn't be happy.'

'Aye, I appreciate that.'

'But you don't want to get on the wrong side of him.' He waves a teaspoon in Chaz's direction. 'And another thing. If this comes off, you'll owe me big time.'

'I know that. I'll make sure yeh get a cut of whatever's goin.'

Del nods in agreement and grows meditative. 'I didn't mind a regular rammy with bottle and blades. It gets you involved in things. And you're right fucking up for it. Us against them there Papish bastards. You know you're doing something. And you're something. And if you're feeling a bit weak, or are a bit off the boil, you pay for it. But you know, with all these guns, it's more like office work. You load the gun and point it and if they're frightened enough, they'll give you what you want.'

'And if they urnae,' Chaz laughs. 'Yeh shoot them anyway.'

'Aye, that's about the height of it.' Del swirls and gargles a mouthful of tea and pushes the mug across the table. 'You up for it, then?'

'Aye,' Chaz gets up and heads towards the door.

'I'll just go and pay yon wee woman.' Del adopts an impish smile. He turns to Chaz, 'Where is it we're going, again?'

'No far.' Chaz pushes open the door, wind breezing in. 'Tap of the hill. Cleddens. It's a shithole. But we'll be back for dinner time.'

Chapter 83

Spats

DEL PARKS THE JAGUAR ON THE HILL ACROSS FROM Clydebank College and pulls the handbrake. 'How many doors in the pub?'

'Two.' Chaz traces the shape of the gun in his inside pocket as he considers. 'Main entrance off the main road.' He glances out the side window at the rear end of the pub, checking. 'And wan beside the chippy.'

'Right,' Del turns to have a look. 'How do you want to play it?' He waggles a finger towards the double doors off Kilbowie Road. 'You go in that way, and I'll get tooled up. And I'll give you a few minutes and I'll come in that other way.'

Chaz rubs at his chin. 'Sounds alright tae me.' He smacks his lips together. 'I'll get cracking.'

'Listen,' Del stops him. 'We've rode our luck a bit. Too many bizzies cutting about for our liking. So we're going home in a few days for a bit. Until things cool down.'

Chaz checks Del's face to see if he's going to say more, but he looks straight ahead.

'Aye, that's understandable.'

'No, but you're coming with us.'

'I'd love tae, but—'

'Dougie insists.' Del raises his brow and smiles in a concerned way. 'You don't want to be pissing him off. Not now.'

'Aye, alright then,' Chaz says. 'We'll see.'

He is glad to push the car door shut and stand on the pavement in light rain. A man in a long coat and Houndstooth deerstalker staggers towards the chippy. Sweetie papers ride on the wind and pick themselves up and dance ahead of Chaz, washing up against the cul-de-sac and pub wall.

He pushes against the flapping double-doors. Holding his breath until the familiar odour of fag smoke, whisky and beer assail him and make his eyes crinkle. His gaze sweeps a long barn of a room. Hairs on the back of his neck prickle from sweat stains. The jukebox rifts a melancholic *Lighter Shade of Pale*. An older man in a tan raincoat addresses the barmaid in a mock English accent. 'A few pints of your local anaesthetic, dear.' He jingles his coins and laughs. 'And don't spare the horses.'

The barmaid, a half-pint of permed orange hair, laughs. She watches the old man fiddle with the loose change in his hand before spilling it onto the counter for her to count.

Snatches of conversations in the hubbub seem to grow dimmer around the cordon of wooden chairs and tables set aside for the bunkered Dunne clan. Identikits, ginger hair, scuffed denim jacket, checked shirt and wide-cut trousers worn high with wedge-platform shoes. A uniform Chaz also sported with a casual ease. He recognised the sense of energy and the sense of themselves that had taken root and grown beyond the rough plaster of the walls and his mark in it, the livid scars of Frank standing out like lightning bolts as he glares at him.

A balding brother, seated to Frank's right, squints at Chaz through NHS specs, white sleeves on his shirt rolled up as if ready to go navvying. He raises an arm and waves him across. 'O'er here,' he shouts, nods pleasantly and smiles, nudging a face to his left to make room. Lifting his pint and his packet of cigarettes and placing them at another chair.

Chaz waves back. 'Can I buy yous lot a round?' he hollers, letting his hand slide from the gun and trying to attract the attention of the barmaid. She stands chatting to a man in an open-necked tartan shirt at the far end of the bar. The jolt of somebody bumping into him from the side is unexpected.

A pockmarked face with pleasant green eyes gazes at him. Chaz feels a liquid tipped over his head, soaking his hair, jacket and shirt and smells petrol. 'I don't suppose yeh've got a light, bud?' The man with the pockmarked face cackles, flicking the throw-away lighter flint and lighting his cigarette.

Chaz scrambles for his gun, but another man with reddish hair and shoulders like billboards pins him squirming to the bar.

'Bert,' the man with NHS specs shouts to the guy holding the lit flame. 'Don't want an audience. Take the cunt ootside, for fuck sake.'

The shotgun detonation hits the man waving the lighter in the chest. It carries him across the room. His body buckles and comes to a halt against the panel of the door as if arguing with a Guinness poster.

Chaz feels the blast and smells cordite as the man with the wide shoulder's head disintegrates beside him, his hair matted with blood. He gets his hand on the gun and points it downwards, shooting the guy holding him below the thigh. He brings the gun up and shoots into the scrum of Dunne brothers, dodging and trying to scramble away on their knees, tables tipping sideways and glasses smashing. A woman, with shopping bags at her feet, screams from her seat at the corner table.

Del stands with his back propping open the side door. His shotgun covers the centre of the room. Hands held up as if auditioning for a cowboy movie.

Chaz, ears ringing, can't hear his feet smacking the floor as he runs towards the door. He runs out into the rain and barges into an old man.

'Jesus, where's the fire, son?' the old man stares at him from the pavement, and scrambles for his deerstalker.

A stilted walk to the car, flared denim flapping in the wind, their guns pressed one-handed, hard, against their bodies and concealed in their coats. Del tosses the shotgun in the back seat, takes off his jacket and flings it over the gun. He slips into the front seat and starts the engine. Chaz shrinks into the passenger seat beside him, picking goo from his hair. The Jaguar built for speed flirts with second gear and they tail behind the bubble of a red Volkswagen before taking a right at Clydebank College and getting off the main roads.

'That was a close call, eh?' Chaz listens for sirens. They coast sedately past church and school. He pulls out his packet of Silk Cut, tamps out a cigarette. Sticking it in his gob, he searches his pockets for his lighter.

Del swats the cigarette from his mouth. 'Are you fucking crazy?' He checks the rear-view mirror. 'You're covered in petrol, ya daft cunt.'

Chaz, startled, adopts a hangdog expression. He glances at his right shoulder and his left and sniffs the air, as if checking it's not somebody else been talked about. 'Yeh, that fucking smoking is way bad for yeh, anyway.'

He rolls down the top of the window and stuffs his packet of Silk Cut outside, caught in the slipstream it bounces along the road as the car makes a left turn and heads towards Drumchapel.

Del fumbles for his cigarette packet in the glove compartment and leans forward using the car lighter. He blows smoke sideways towards Chaz. 'We fucked up there. I mean, I fucking love this car, but we'll need to ditch it. In fact, Dougie will be fucking pissed, big time, with the hassle and so many bizzies floating about. And there'll be hell to pay.' He hits the horn as a young boy on a bicycle coming from the swimming baths peddles across the road in front of the car and mounts kerb and pavement.

'Aye,' Chaz nods in agreement. 'It's jist wan of these things, I suppose. Cannae be helped.'

'Aye, I suppose,' says Del, eyeing him. 'I'll drop you at the station. You'll need to get a train home.' Del sneaks another look at him. 'You missed a bit there.' He tilts his head and taps his own cheek below his left eye to act as a mirror, to show his passenger where to wipe away the smear of gore beneath his eye. 'No doubt we'll be on that fucking Larne ferry, pronto.' He mashes his cigarette out in the ashtray. 'And we'll be in touch.'

The engine idles, and they sit in the shadows of high walls enclosing the church grounds outside the station.

'Hi,' Del taps him on the shoulder. 'You can't go with that jacket on. And anyway, it'll save me fucking looking for petrol to torch the car.'

Chaz wriggles out of his jacket, reaches for the butt of the gun, and stuffs the barrel inside the band of high-waisted denim. 'But I'll huv naewhere tae hide it, noo.'

'Don't be worrying about that. Fling it in the back seat.' He jerks his head towards his jacket and the shotgun beneath it. 'And I'll get rid of it. You'll not be needing it now, anyway, will you?'

Chaz tosses the gun into the back seat and gets out of the car. 'I'll catch yeh later.'

Del mouths a reply, but Chaz isn't really listening, waving his arm in farewell. He hears a train speeding towards the station and he makes a run to catch it, dodging past the guard, trying to usher him into buying a ticket before getting on the train.

Back in Dalmuir he knows he'll need to keep his head down and get cleaned up, get himself tooled up with a replacement gun and go gunning for Rab, but coming out of the station he heads in the opposite direction toward Maggie Scott's pub. Most of all he needs a couple of pints to settle his head.

Across the road from the hairdressers, he swaggers down the hill, when a dark-coloured car overtakes him and brakes suddenly. Chaz spins to make a run for it. Doors in the car open like shields and big men emerge in a scrum. He sees a flash of hazard lights, a Ford van parked further up the hill, its back door open. Rough hands grab him. He feels himself being torn one way, then tossed another, lifted, his face rammed against the rough stone walls of Dalmuir Primary school. He fights against nausea, his body dragged and flung into the back of the van.

Chapter 84

School ways

ANGELA SITS ON THE TOP STEPS ON THE LANDING, WAITING. Tugs have been pulled and combed from her blonde hair. Her skin scrubbed pink in the kitchen sink. Her deep blue, almost black, school uniform is not a regular hand-me-down, but bought in the big store in Clydebank and the blue shirt and grey skirt are a snug fit. The triangular badge sewn on to her blazer pocket by her mum is a source of pride and wonder. She stares at the golden threads of a sailing ship on a silver ocean and the legend Dalmuir Primary, black runes, in a golden scroll. The shimmer of gold hangs from her neck, a loose knot in the school tie, making a zebra of her with its brown diagonals from neck to hips.

Dinner money, family silver, clasped in her hot little hand. She's starting school, her knees chapping and feet tapping time on cold steps. Toys lined up and drilled, stories told, and harangued about how they better behave—or else. The tenement building shakes with the harried running feet of tribes of children getting ready. She grabs the strap of her new leather satchel.

Kerry-Ann plays peek-a-boo from the dim lobby, a fag dangling from her lips. She holds her hand over her mouth as she coughs. Jerks her head in the direction of the living room.

'Angela, pet,' she softens her tone. 'Yeh can go tae school another day.' She takes another drag on her fag, followed by an extended bout of coughing. 'Yer da never came in last night. And I've no been that well. And I cannae go oot in case he comes back and if I'm no here... there'll be hell tae pay.'

The school bag drops from Angela's hand. Coins bounce onto the stairs. Her shoulders jerk as she cries, hair drooping and partially covering her face. Her body slumps in defeat.

'Whit's wrang wae yeh?' Kerry-Ann screeches. 'I'll write yeh a note and yeh can go tae school the morrow. Then that'll be you. Gonnae be goin for at least the next ten years. Whether yeh want tae or no. And yeh'll hate it, anyway.'

'Whit did I do-o-o. It's not fair-rrr.'

Pizza Face saunters out of the door below them. He spots the shiny two-bob sitting on the stairs and he looks beyond it, taking in Angela and her mother. He skips up the stairs and picks up the coin. 'Yeh drapped this.'

His mum, Senga, and sister stand witness at his back. 'Whit's the matter wae her?' Senga asks.

'Och, it's nothing.' Kerry-Ann's right hand cups the mound of her belly. 'She's supposed tae be starting school, but Chaz didnae come hame last night—'

'He's jist like the rest of them,' mutters Senga. 'Useless. It'll not be the first and it'll not be the last.'

'—and she's no been feeling that great.'

'I'm fine,' Angela blurts out. She wipes her nose on her sleeve. 'It's you that said yeh werenae well.'

'Well, anyway,' crumbling cigarette ash falls between Kerry-Ann's fingers. 'She can go the morrow.'

Senga skelps Pizza Face on the side of the head. 'Gi'e her the money back,' she warns him, before her unblinking attention turns to Kerry-Ann. 'I'll take the wee lassie tae school,' and receiving no acknowledgement, adds, 'If yer not that well?'

'Well, I'm no sure.' Kerry-Ann asks Angela. 'Whit about that tickly bad cough, yeh had? Ur yeh well enough tae go?'

Senga snorts at asking a child's opinion. 'Get my coat,' she tells her daughter.

Pizza Face slinks away. The thought of going to school with his mum, his daft sister and a wee girl trailing beside him, and his pals seeing him, laughing at him, brings the worst kind of reddy, and it blooms on his cheeks.

Outside their close, Senga clutches Angela's hand firmly. She ties the triangle of headscarf tighter around her neck and frowns. Her daughter's firm step lurks behind them. Younger mothers walking to school make a detour around the windbreak of her wide back and step further into the rain.

'I can already read and count tae wan-hunner.' Angela squints at Senga, her face beaming.

'Can yeh dear?' Senga gives her wee fingers an extra squeeze. 'I'm sure yeh'll be a smart wee cookie.'

A mother with a pram and a baby tucked inside and two older children passengers, riding shotgun, passes them. Another girl, with ringlets and olive skin, about the same age as Angela and wearing the same uniform, but with white socks that stay up her legs, pushes a pram the same colour as the bigger pram with a baby dolly tucked inside it. Angela gawps and reaches her hand out to touch it, before pulling away. They cross Duntocher Road together in a group and fall into step, walking up the hill. As they get closer to the school and pass the first of the big playgrounds. Children bombing about inside and the ululating noises grow louder.

Angela holds on tighter to Senga's hands and starts blubbering. 'I want tae go hame. I want my mum.'

The other little girl looks over at her, imperiously, with hazel-green eyes, but before they get to the school gates, her lips tremble. 'You can get a shot of my dolly. Her name's Molly.' She shakes her head. 'I'm not allowed to take her inside because she's only a baby. And she's not real.' She holds out her hand and Angela slips away from Senga and fastens on tight to her fingers. Both girls sob on each other's shoulder.

Chapter 85

Taxing

CHAZ FEIGNS UNCONSCIOUSNESS. WITH A STIFF BODY AND A head vaguely attached to his senses, it's not too taxing. He feels the floor moving and the van performing a U-turn. Voices gab over him in English accents, one of them recognisably Geordie. It unsettles him. He remembers the North of England is roughly the place where the Dunnes buy their drugs wholesale. Out of the side of his swollen, Panda eyes, he notices khaki uniforms. Their haircuts are a throwback to the fifties, no-nonsense short-back-and-sides, and boyish, innocent, clean-shaven faces. They josh with each other in a bantering tone. Sharp turns, the van throws them from side to side. A lad prods at him with the toe of his boot. Chaz coughs, a whirlpool of phlegm and watery blood. He lifts his head, bobbing up and down, as he turns to grog and spits broken teeth out of his burst lips, which brings laughs and jeers. His fingertips run over his face and it feels like the mush of an overripe banana.

'Cunt,' remarks one of them

Chaz flinches and holds his arms out protecting his face and head, expecting to be hit and mauled, but the fresh faces study him with curiosity and detachment, which worries him more. The van comes to an abrupt stop. They pile out. The stink of sweat from so many bodies eases. Chaz tries looking around corners, hoping for the chance to escape, but windmills of arms reach in and hands tug him out and bundle him to the ground.

They park the Audi in front of a child's drawing of a cottage with rough white walls. Cattle graze in nearby fields, their lowing a dumb presence. The van blocks off the entrance to the lane. The front of the homestead nestles in the Old Kilpatrick hills, screened by dry-stone walls and overgrown fir trees. Proximity and anonymity points to professionalism that even Dougie would have been proud.

Someone grabs his elbow, pushes him along the short path towards the cottage. Chaz makes a run for it, twisting one way and another. His legs are kicked from under him. Pain in his face and shoulders spreads across his back. His escape attempt causes great hilarity among his captors, who whoop and cheer and call the man that let him go 'a fucking nugget' and curse him, good-naturedly, in a medley of English accents.

Two men leave bruises on Chaz's arm, as they grip and flank each side of him. They propel him towards the cottage door. Inside, the stench of damp and mould inflame his crusted nostrils. Basic furniture. An unlit Calor Gas fire. Camp beds line the white-washed walls. Wooden chairs and a table claim the centre of the room.

A big man, with a paunch belly, instructs the men to stick Chaz in a chair. An upper-class accent, he is used to being heard and obeyed. He sits facing Chaz across the table. A weathered face gazes at him, leather patches on the elbows of his jacket. Behind his grey hair hangs an old photograph on the wall, faded sepia, father, mother and son, falling into the darkness of forgotten people that had once lived in the cottage.

'You've led us a merry chase.' He strokes his long chin. 'Running about like a windy-up Action Man. But careless with the casualties. Careless with the fingerprints. They seem to be all over the place. And your brother—'he cocks his head and seems to listen— 'John, we had a cosy little chat, didn't we?'

It's not a question Chaz can answer. The old man's eyes are watchful as an alligator and a matching smile.

'I'm going to ask you some questions and I want straight answers.' He chortles. 'All off the record, of course.'

Chaz sneers, 'Yeh want me tae grass?'

The old man gives a nod. Chaz is head-locked and his arms held. Four or five punches hit him on the face, harder than he has been punched before and it flattens his nose towards his cheek and pain radiates across his head and neck. Another nod and Chaz is let go.

His captors watch him going from shock to anger. He attempts to get out of the chair before slumping backwards. Chaz closes his eyes, remains still as an ornament.

A broad shadowy presence appears in front of him and he feels the blood being wiped gently from his face. He is handed a tea-towel to clean himself up, and he looks at the gloop from his nose, blood-red centre in the shape of the Japanese flag.

The old man picks up their earlier conversation. 'We're not buying bullshit, son. We're selling. I want you to tell us everything you know about your Irish connections.'

'Fuck you!' Chaz spits a spray of blood towards the old man and quietly laughs. 'Yeh're gonnae kill me, anyway.'

Only a little phlegm reaches the old man's jacket, which he ignores. 'Yes, we can kill you. And believe me, there is more than one way to die. Some of them, one finds, very unpleasant indeed.' His eyebrows twitch and he swallows a smile. 'There's certainly the option of being shot in the head and being buried in some out-of-the-way place, as you well know. But we're waging a war and there's going to be some casualties. Your bosom friends Del and Dougie, for example, might not be here for much longer. They've been making some very unrealistic demands. We have some very good information that you are going to get a foot up. When you come back from Ulster, you'll be in charge of operations in Scotland, which opens up a whole new ball game for us.' His laugh is like the bark of a distant border collie.

Chaz sits straighter in his seat, wiping at his bloody nose. 'Whit dae I need tae dae?'

'We want you to be our eyes and ears.' The old man points across the room to a man with bushy eyebrows watching them. 'Report in once a week to Mr Hawkins over there.'

'Is that aw?' grunts Chaz.

'Don't be so downbeat,' the old man smiles pleasantly. 'We'll give you all the help we can.'

Chapter 86

The sash my father wore

CHAZ IS A RELIGIOUS MAN ON THE LARNE FERRY, A BELIEVER in the hereafter. The smart gilt lapel badges on drab uniforms show how shipshape they are. Even the guy with anchors tattooed on his forearms behind the bar, selling watery pints of stout, is an Admiral, and with a wink to his captive audience he talks about a promotion being in the pipeline. Dougie and Del lap it up. Lizzie sits between them and settles for vodka and coke and Golden Wonder cheese and onion crisps. She laughs when waves hit the windows and lift the ship and the Artic currents of the Irish Sea drag it back down again. Chaz's face is buried deep in the curved bowl of the lavvy pan. No rationing of water and nobody counting how many times he's spewed on a short crossing. His eyes are watery and old, his throat raw, his denims and shirt crumpled and damp. Handholds on the urinals. The thrum of the walls close in on him and his body takes on the characteristics of the bilge, the stink of diesel, rubber boots and the spit of boiled veg and a spiteful spirit, the attar of the deep sea. Carpets in the alcoves are a marshy sick colour to camouflage stains. Chaz finds it difficult to find the line of his feet. He swears he'll never get on another ship as long as he lives, if he lives.

'It's a cold one.' Dougie leans into the wind in the grey light, and rubs the sleep out of his eyes, his arm around Lizzie's back.

The gantry cranes of Harland and Wolff silhouette East Belfast beside the chimney stacks sheltering railway trucks. Del coughs and reaches for a cigarette. He stands beside Chaz, the bustle of the boat coming alive. The gulls screeching, merging with a metallic voice over the tannoy as they enter the Lough and the arms of land jutting out to meet them, its lights twinkling in welcome.

The enclosed worlds of West Belfast, the Falls and the Shankhill, in which Chaz plays tourist, entail a car journey. His clothes are noticeably too hip and modern, and a Glaswegian accent marks him out as being a foreigner. Soldiers and B-Specials stand beside checkpoints. Lippy teenagers at the shop in the lower end of Dover Street joke when Del stops to buy cigarettes and Chaz runs the gauntlet of catcalls, wondering, aloud, if he's a Fenian bastard.

'I'll fucking Fenian, you.' Dougie stands in the shop doorway, his eyes glinting. 'I'll drop the whole fucking lot of you over the other side of the wall and there'll be no coming back.'

The boy with a pudding haircut and sloppy-joe T-shirt keeps his eyes downcast and his mates trudge out into the rain at his back. 'We're only playing a joke, mister. Nah, he doesn't look Catholic at all.'

They billeted Chaz upstairs in a house on Scarfield Street. The mattress has a hollow ridge, he rolls into as if replacing another dank body. During the night, he hears gunfire but turns over and goes back to sleep.

A knock on the front door in the morning. Del shouts a greeting and Chaz hears stamping feet in the hall. He stands beside the landlady in the kitchen's cosy glow with a cigarette in his mouth.

'You fit?' Del smiles, almost shyly, at Chaz in his new surroundings.

Chaz gets his coat. They walk along the road to an oddly shaped bar, the size of a living room, packed with a crowd of drinkers and the blue haze of cigarette smoke. Del goes to the bar and nods over to the corner table where Dougie is sitting, glasses of Irish whiskey in front of him. Beside him, sporting a khaki jacket, a middle-aged man with long stringy hair. Chaz sees he's watching him, as are the others in the pub, but there's a depth in his grey eyes, a small, disquieting gleam that flickers and vanishes that makes him feel uneasy.

Dougie pushes up to give Chaz a seat beside him. 'This is Bri.' And he nods at Chaz and introduces him.

'Get another round of drinks in,' Bri shouts.

Dougie wrangles his way to the bar and Bri pushes in to sit beside Chaz. He holds his hand out for Chaz to shake. 'Heard a lot about you,' he says. Up close, his breath is eighty-percent proof and his nose is the colour of fine wine, but his hands are small, soft and white and his knee presses against Chaz's. 'The thing is, I need to know if I can trust you.' A flicker of those eyes again. 'Can I trust you?'

'Aye, aye, course yeh can.' Chaz breaks eye contact; Del and Dougie elbow past customers with glasses of whiskey in their hands. The first short glass hits the table. The hot spike in Chaz's stomach as he swallows it gives him renewed confidence. 'Ask these boys. They'll vouch for me.'

Bri picks up a glass of whiskey and holds it to his lips. 'I have asked them, right enough.' He flings it back and wipes at his mouth. 'But tell me this, who will guard the guards?'

Dougie glances over at the bar. Del's eyes glint as he rolls his eyes. Bri holds his glass up like a candle in the dim light. 'Who will fucking guard the guards?'

Chaz tries to ease his way out of the seat and buy a round. A hand sits on his shoulder and Bri, in a voice that merges pity with outrage, shouts him down and tells him to behave himself as he's their guest. He bows with a smile in acknowledgement of their common tradition, which reminds him of home.

When Del goes to the bar, a short, balding man with a smudge of moustache trails behind him. At each step, his body sags and pulls him to the side threatening to spill the drinks. Loose skin at his neck overflows his starched collar, and he wears a shiny blue tie. 'Get out the way,' he demands in an angry voice, rising above the din. Customers step, sheep-like, out of his way and fill the gap his body has left.

Del places the drinks on the table. He waits for the older man behind him to do likewise. 'I'll get you a seat, Da,' he looks over the heads of the punters in the crowded bar.

Dougie holds onto his chair and scrapes its wooden legs backward. 'Take my seat, Craigie.'

Chaz pulls his chair closer to the table and Dougie shuffles behind him and presses against the stained wall.

The little man sticks out his chest, and his eyes tighten. 'You'll need to move son.'

Chaz scrambles out of his seat, 'Sorry.'

Craigie makes a wide-angle approach. His left shoulder slopes lower than the right and he taps the ground with his right foot, before testing the weight of his body and swinging his left leg forward. He flops into the seat with an 'Ahh' sound. Glancing left and right, he looks surprised to be sitting in company. Bri looks at him sympathetically and nudges a whiskey glass towards his shaky hand.

Dougie wanders away to claim another chair and for a moment Craigie sits rigid, his lower jaw moving. When he raises the glass of amber fluid to his lips, his face softens. 'What's the crack then?' he says with a thin smile, his eyes aglow.

Their group splutter laughter into their drinks. Craigie enjoys the attention, which allows him to re-tell old tales. 'Some people you give them a house and you try thim a job, but as God is my witness, they'd have you bowing to Papish beliefs. I was brought up Protestant.' He bangs the table with his fist, making the empty glasses and the ashtray jump. 'We read our Bible in the front parlour and went to Sunday school. Those Papes aren't allowed to read the Bible. The Papish tradition is yon here priests have to read it for them.'

'You're right there, Craigie boy,' Bri slaps his shoulder. 'We're having nun o' that.' He laughs with discoloured teeth. Those facing him smile politely.

'They always brought trouble, you know,' Craigie carries on, without seeming to have heard him. 'They're like children. You got to keep thim in place. And we'd a particular way of dealing with it in the yards. A foreman, you wouldn't want to be getting your hands dirty with the likes of thim. So you'd wait a while and push one of thim into the lough.' He smacks his lips, sips at his whiskey, and tasting the past. 'Well, you know what they're like, always dobbing themselves with holy water. So, of course, they can swim like a fish. You'd need to be cute enough. Get a pole and when he tries to scramble up the embankment, prod him down again.' Bri laughs, the others join in. Craigie soaks up the attention. 'And when he gets to the other side of the river, you've got to have a man positioned with an even longer pole.'

'Aye,' shouts Bri, slapping the table. 'Drowning is too good for likes o' thim. You want thim to suffer a bit first.'

'What about you, son?' Craigie takes a mouthful of whiskey and turns his attention to Chaz. 'It must be hell over there with all the Papists taking all the good housing and all the jobs.'

'Aye, it's pretty hard,' Chaz answers with a hitch in his voice. 'I even had wan touching up my handicapped wee sister.'

'Fucking Jesus.' Craigie shakes his head. His hand shakes as he holds a glass to his lips. 'It doesn't surprise me. Incestuous, they are. They think that kind of thing is alright.' He sniffs, weighing his words. 'The only answer is leaving thim in the middle of the river.'

'Aye,' Chaz smiles. He glances around at Dougie and Del hunched over the table, listening. 'That's whit we did.'

Craigie slaps his shoulder. 'Good man.'

Chaz knows he's one of them now, and he's passed a test. 'I'll get this round,' he shouts, doesn't take no for an answer. He winds his way through thin spaces and makes his way to the bar. The barmaid with dishevelled hair and thick arms puffed out of a dress too tight for her smiles at him. Chaz feels he's not left home.

Chapter 87

Dirty

At the top of the Cressie Stairs, Angela bends away from the straight road to school. She skips past the mazy groups of boys and girls in uniform. School bag beating against her knee, not sure which direction her feet are taking her, she finds herself in Dalmuir Park. The railway station lies below her. Metal lines sing and the overhead lines spark lightning as a train speeds along the track. She recognises the swings and roundabout and tucks her hands into her pocket to keep them warm, trying to work out how she's walked so far and came back to where she started. Dark tenement windows glisten. Her forehead furrows, she peers along the rows trying to pick out the rectangle of glass through which her mum will be watching her. She cries, 'I'm running away and yeh'll be sorry.'

She spots Bruno, on the path near the railway line and tunnel, waving back at her. She runs down the hill to meet him.

Bruno seems delighted to see her. 'Yeh dogging it tae?'

'Nah, I'm running away.'

His mouth settles into a crooked smile. 'Yeh'll no get very far like that. Yeh need sandwiches and juice and a stick to beat away mad wolves.' He sucks in his breath and sniffs as he ponders. He tilts his head and gawks into the blackness under the bushes and trees screening the railway track. 'We could get yeh a stick in there. But it needs tae be a big wan.'

'My da, I mean, Chaz, has got a gun.'

Bruno puckers his lips, eyes glistening and leans forward. 'That's even better. I could show yeh how tae shoot.' He shuts an eye and sights his fingers at a bench halfway up the hill. 'Pow. Pow.' He grows serious. 'Where does he keep it?'

She shivers, lets her school bag drop and sticks her hands under her ochters to warm them. 'Under the dirty washing.'

'Em,' Bruno takes a deep breath as he weighs up their options. 'I could tell yer mum that yeh'd been hit by a massive truck and she needs tae come right away. And then yeh could sneak inside and get the gun?'

Angela treats her near fatal demise and the deception it entails with a crinkle of her nose. 'But whit about Chaz?'

'Yer da? Doesnae he go tae work?'

'Nah.' Angela shakes her head. 'He jist lies about aw day telling everybody whit tae dae and punching them when they don't. And then he goes tae the pub, comes back drunk and batters everybody. That's aw he ever does.'

Bruno hesitates and rolls his shoulders, looking behind him. 'Where is he noo?'

'He's in the house. Back fae his holidays tae Ireland.'

Bruno darts away and picks up a rain blackened stick. 'If yeh ever get attacked by a wolf, yeh know what tae dae?' He whips off his duffel and wraps it around his left arm, pantomimes hitting a wolf on the head, swooshing, breaking its forelegs and comments on his masterful, finishing, stroke, 'Yeh poke both its eyes oot as a lesson for messing wae yeh.'

Angela grows breathless with all the swishing, hitting, and killing.

'Well,' Bruno takes a step back, glowers at any suggestion of retreat. 'But there's probably a pack of them. And yeh cannae kill them aw. So yeh need tae run away and hide up a tree and light a fire.'

Angela steps closer and tugs his jacket. 'Maybe yeh should come wae me.'

Bruno hands her the stick to hold. He unwinds his jacket from his forearm and puts it back on, but avoiding Angela's eyes. 'I will, wan day.' He bites his chapped lips and straightens up. 'No right noo.' He brightens immediately. 'But I could teach yeh how tae drink from a stream and catch fish and light a fire withoot matches.'

'I'm cauld.' The stick drops from her fingers to the ground and lies on the frosty grass.

A man wrapped in a scarf and long coat wearing a flat cap walks out of the tunnel into the park, his breath a cloudy plume. Bruno and Angela take a step backwards to let him pass, even though the man doesn't seem to see them.

Bruno unbuttons his coat and drapes it over Angela's shoulders. He brushes it with his hands for a better fit and pulls up the over-sized hood. Her head and face look out at him like a dandelion clock.

'Whit yeh running away fae anyway?' he asks. 'Yeh stay wae yer ma and da.'

'He hurts me.'

'How?'

'It's alright,' he closes his eyes, and wraps his arms around her because she can't answer. 'Someone hurt me there tae.'

He waits until her body softens and she stops greeting before playing a trick on her and trumpeting a fart sound in her ear. She laughs when he picks her up by the hood and holds her dangling in the air.

'Look, whit I caught!' Her feet touch the ground. 'Yeh look like a wee—' His hand falls on her head and he rubs her blonde hair awkwardly. 'Yeh'll be alright, sometime.'

'But I'm freezing,' says Angela.

Bruno pulls her towards him. 'That's easy sorted. I'll take yeh back tae school. It's always boiling hot in there.'

Angela holds his hand and leans into his side. He does a funny whistle as they run through the tunnel, to scare away the ghosts. When they get to the school gates, he unpicks his coat from her shoulders and puts it on. Shivering, he pats her head. 'In yeh go. Nae harm done. Yer no even that late.'

She trots forward toward the side door but stops and shouts back. 'Whit about you?'

He shakes his head. 'Nah, naebody cares about me.'

Chapter 88

Emergency Services

CHAZ, A HALF WHISKY IN FRONT OF HIM, SHOUTS ACROSS AT the barman, 'Is that phone in the corner still working?'

'Aye,' Drew snorts. 'As far as I know. You want me to check?'

Chaz looks at the phone number in his hand. He was supposed to memorise it. 'Nah, don't bother, I think I've got a couple of tuppences, I'll check myself in a minute.'

Three boys shuffle into the pub. A cortege of platform shoes and flared trousers with high-waist bands bigger than their heads. They look nervously about.

Drew looks up from the racing tips in the *Daily Record* at the leader of the group, a pallbearer's complexion, small, with a freckled nose. The biggest of the small fry searches for money. His hand digging into the top denim-jacket pocket and his side trouser pockets.

The barman takes a deep breath and flips over another page in his paper, shakes his head. 'Nah,' he says to the boy before he can speak. He exchanges a wink with one of his regulars—who had nipped in and forgot to nip out again—a blousy blonde in a satin dress sitting on a barstool, a cigarette in her mouth.

'Three lager,' the boy's momentum overrides the warning and blank face staring back at him.

'Beat it,' says Drew.

'We're eighteen, mister,' the leader pipes up. The pound note, as evidence, held up like a birthday card in his hand.

Chaz laughs from his spot at the corner table. He shouts over the heads of regular customers, glad of the entertainment. 'Fuck sake Drew, jist serve them. I'll pay for it.'

'Nah, cannae,' Drew shakes his head.

Chaz shuffles forward in his seat, takes a quick drag of his cigarette and takes a roll of notes from his pocket, an elastic band holding them together. 'Look, get them wan, and get yerself a wee double for the trouble. Yeh cannae say any fairer than that.'

The barman's cheeks suck in gravity. He turns and glances at the clock above the gantry, which is set ten-minutes fast and calculates closing time for the afternoon shift in twenty minutes. 'Just the wan.'

A thickset man sitting at a table near the door shakes his head. Three empty quarter-gill glasses, a jug of water, an ashtray, and a packet of Capstan Full Strength and another glass with a smidgen of White Horse at the bottom sit on the table in front of him. He waits until Drew looks around the pub and meets his eyes before he speaks. 'They're underage. Don't serve them. Yeh're no daeing anybody a favour here.'

'Whit the fuck's it got tae dae wae yeh, pal?' Chaz shouts.

The man sits motionless under Chaz's stare. There is no rancour in his voice when he addresses him. 'I wasnae talking tae yeh.' A bob of his head towards Drew. 'I was talking tae that good gentleman o'er there.'

'Who ur yeh talking tae, ya bampot?' Chaz pokes out his chest. 'Dae yeh know who I'm ur? This is my pub. Serve them their drinks, Drew.'

The freckled-faced boy's voice cuts through the hush. 'It's alright mister, we'll jist go.'

Chaz's knees batter the underside of the table as he jumps up. 'Yeh'll take a pint, ya wee prick, and like it, whether yeh want wan or no. And so will yer wee pals.' He lifts a beer glass from his table.

Drew flips the lager tab to top up slops at the bottom of the glass. 'One drink and you're out,' he warns the boys, watching him.

'I widnae dae that,' says the thickset man.

Drew shrugs. 'My pub. My rules.' His eyebrows shoot up. 'They look at least eighteen to me. What you want me to dae, phone the police to check?'

'Nae chance,' says the thickset man. 'I wouldnae gi'e police the time of day.'

The pint tumbler smashes into the thickset man's head, cutting near his earlobe and the side of his head. Chaz looks at the base of his thumb, which is also bleeding. The thickset man blinks, looks at him with cool grey eyes. Nervous laughter ripples from a nearby table when he stands up because he's so tall. He blocks the door and the room shrinks. 'There's naewhere yeh can hide, noo.'

The blousey blond edges from her seat, scuttles around the side of the bar and picks up the phone. She dials 999 and waits for the phone to ring and operator to ask in a robotic voice which service she wants. 'Police, Ambulance or Fire Service?'

She cups the reciver and ponders the menu. She watches Chaz getting punched, picked up and punched again, ragdolled over and under tables. The thickset man apologising to customers whose tables he'd knocked over and promising to pay for any spilt drinks.

'Eh, police and ambulance.' She pronounces the pub's name out of the side of her mouth and where it was situated on Dumbarton Road with gusto. 'Oh, fuck it, send the fire brigade as well. He's hell of a big chappie.'

'My name? Oh, it's Princess Anne,' she tells the operator.

'Yer on yer way,' she slurs. 'That's nice. I better be going then.' She combs her tousled hair with her fingers, steps daintily around the debris at the bar, tucks her bag under her arm and makes her way out the door.

Three teenage boys look at her. 'There's a riot in there, missus,' says a bright-eyed adolescent.

'Is there?' she holds her head up, a carmine-lipstick smile, as if he is about to take her picture, high heels clicking along the pavement.

Chapter 89

Weet-weet

'Weet, weet,' says a drunk man at the bar. The cuffs of his gabardine coat fall over his thin wrist as he necks the last of a Grouse whisky.

'Aye,' laughs his pal, standing beside him and a few of the old guys nearby chuckle and stare into their pint. 'She's a cracker.'

Chaz inhales a mouthful of the ambulance woman's perfume. 'I don't need any help,' he splutters. 'I'm no an invalid.' It seems offensive to him being tended by someone so young and pretty. He looks into her dark eyes. She is unfazed by his outburst. Cradling his wrist, she pulls him towards the shiny seats by the door.

Two policemen totter into the pub, their eyes sweeping the room and quickly settle on Chaz's bloodied face.

'Does this hurt?' She prods him into sitting. Her fingers poke and prod, running over Chaz's face and body like a lawn aerator. 'Here? Here? Or here?'

'Nah,' Chaz spits from burst lips. A disjointed nose and fresh blood runs over encrusted scabbing and his eye shaded a turnip purple. His jaw aches. He's not sure if it's also broken. His breathing is ragged and audible in his ears. 'I jist need tae go and lie doon for a bit.'

The senior ambulance man hovers behind her. 'He might be suffering concussion,' he offers advice in a parental tone. 'We should take him in.'

'Nah,' Chaz flops backwards onto the cushioned rest of the seat. He sits straighter and shakes his head. 'I'm awright.'

The policeman at the door holds the crown of his hat and feeds it between finger and thumb. 'Can I have a word, sir?'

'Eh, nah.' Chaz's knees hit the underside of the table with a dull thud as he gets up. But he slumps back into the seat.

'We just need to check out a few things.'

The ambulance crew step aside and the jowly policeman towers over Chaz. 'Can you tell me your name, address and date of birth?'

'I'm no sure I can remember aw that, whit wae yer concussion.'

He slides in next to Chaz, pulling him into a standing position and patting him down. His cigarettes and brass lighter appear on the table. Toilet roll from his back pocket and a cigarette coupon. Some loose change. Pound note. A fiver. A roll of ten and twenty-pound notes draws everybody's eyes to it.

The jowly cop smacks his lips. 'That's quite a bit of money, sir,' he declares. 'Do you mind telling us where you got it from, or are you too knocked out to remember that too?'

'Eh, that's mine,' says the man with the gabardine coat. 'I jist gave him a loan of it for a minute.'

His pals snigger, until the two cops look over at them and fall into silence, shirking away from their gaze.

Chaz grins. 'I won it at the bookies.'

'Oh, aye, which horses did you back?' The senior policeman eyeballs him, sticks a forefinger out and pushes him on the breastbone. Chaz falls backwards and sits down.

Chaz wipes blood and snot on the denim sleeve of his jacket. 'Cannae member.'

'We're taking him in.' The jowly cop looks around at the ambulance crew. 'One of us will travel with him in the ambulance and escort him to hospital.' He turns to look around at Chaz's face. 'Until he's been treated and stops gabbing shite.' He pulls out a set of cuffs. 'You don't mind if I cuff him, do you?'

He doesn't wait for an answer, already lifting a wrist and applying the bracelet to his left hand. He ratchets up his right wrist until the flesh puckers.

'That's sore,' says Chaz.

'We need to be safe, sir,' replies the jowly cop.

The ambulance man grimaces but stays silent. The policeman hauls Chaz to his feet and pushes him towards the door.

The younger policeman steps into the back of the ambulance. He sits tight to Chaz, thighs touching on a gurney that rolls and wobbles when the engine kicks in.

Across from them sits the pretty medic. She waits until the ambulance is in traffic before she speaks. 'Can't you take his handcuffs off?'

'Don't have a key.' The policeman smiles at her to lessen the blow. 'My partner's got it. We'll get him up there.'

'I'm dying for a pish.' Chaz shoogles his wrist in protest.

'Oh, well, if you're dying, I better ask Jimmy to turn the siren on,' she says, but her gaze isn't for him.

The young policeman becomes detached and professional outside Casualty at the Western. He waits for his senior partner and they push Chaz ahead of them into reception. A nurse with scarlet beneath her apron patrols the aisles and bays. They're given precedence over a woman with stringy hair double-parked in a wheelchair near a door that flaps open and shut as the medical staff passes through it. Other patients wait quietly, smoking and sharing ashtrays. The young cop talks to a charge-nurse through the aperture of a plastic screen.

'Look,' Chaz eyeballs the older cop. 'I'm dying for a pish. If yeh don't let me go, I'm jist gonnae sit here and pee myself.' Up close under the sodium lights, he can see the beginning of a monk's crown when the policeman takes off his cap and sits it in his lap.

'Suit yourself.'

'Nurse, nurse,' Chaz shrieks. 'I need the toilet.'

The nurse bustles across and stands in front of them. 'There's a toilet this way.'

The jowly cop helps Chaz up and guides him by the elbow. The nurse leads them outside the bay and along a corridor. When they reach a bottleneck of milling patients hanging about, she points to the toilets, and turns back, leaving them standing together.

The policeman drags him by the cuff into the men's toilet, barging his shoulder through the door. The middle cubicle has water-logged toilet roll soaked in excrement stinking and littering the floor. The policeman pushes Chaz towards the loo next to it, and turns his head slightly, to give him privacy.

'Yeh'll need tae uncuff me,' Chaz holds out his manacled arms. 'I need a shite. Or ur yeh wan of those types that likes taking a man's zip doon and hauding his cock?'

'Fuck off,' the policeman pushes Chaz hard, until he trips and batters against the flimsy cubicle wall. 'I don't need to do anything. Whether you pish, or shite yourself in there has nothing to do with me.'

'Hi, wait a wee minute.' Chaz pulls himself upright. 'We've got off on the wrang foot. I want to tell yeh something that might interest yeh. I'm in the same Lodge as yer Chief Superintendent.'

The jowly cop stares at him blankly.

Chaz adopts a beseeching manner. 'I don't want tae waste yer time. Yeh've got aw my money and yeh've got my fags, which is fine. But yeh'll find a phone number among the other stuff. I'd suggest yeh phone it.'

'You're in no position to suggest anything,' but he reaches for the keys and pulls Chaz roughly towards him to unlock them. 'You're in luck. But if you're bullshitting me, I'll smash you all o'er the place.'

Chaz rubs his wrists. 'Nae bullshit mate. Phone that number and the army boys will put yeh right.' He pulls the door towards him and locks it.

Chapter 90

Running away

KIDS CRASH OUT IN THE DAYROOM AFTER BREAKFAST, watching some crap about religion on the telly. Evan perches on a wooden chair, his pale face mirrored by the windowpane. He looks outside as snow falls. The wind whips it upward and drifts and eddies and disappears into damp spots on the uneven road and pavement. Snow creates little kingdoms of whiteness and wilderness.

Angela in a duffle coat and wellies treks through it toward the Home, Bruno behind her. Telly watchers turn from the screen and stand at the windows, mouths open and gawping in reverence at the snow.

'I'm gonnae make you a snowman,' whoops Norma to her wee sister, her hand briefly rests on Evan's shoulder. His face flushes, but other kids don't seem to notice.

Evan waits until Angela and Bruno stomp through the gate and into the hall before he goes to meet them.

'Brrrr.' Bruno wears an Aran jumper under his anorak and he shakes himself like a mangy dog.

Angela stands beside him. She gazes at Evan, almost in a shy way. He grabs her, pulling her in close. 'I feel the freezing cauld off yeh, my wee Angel!'

'Don't,' she cries with petted underlip. 'It hurts.'

'Whit hurts?' Evan's hands drop away from her.

She trembles and looks at him with teary eyes.

Bruno mutters, 'We're gonnae run away!' Grinning. 'We're jist here tae get some stuff before we go.'

Evan replies, 'But it's snowing.'

He heads towards the stairs. 'Doesnae matter.' Angela tags on behind him with her hood up. 'That'll cover oor tracks.'

Evan falls into step behind them. When he gets to his room, Bruno kneels and keeks under his bed. Angela stands behind him, with a snottery nose. He pulls out a plastic shopping bag, pulls it open, and peers inside.

Evan asks, 'Whit huv yeh got?'

Bruno lifts out the items and places them on the blue matting of the bed. A torch, a packet of matches, a lighter, a packet of Digestive biscuits, a bottle of Lucozade and a long white candle. 'I've got some money and we'll get food on the way.'

'Much?'

'Seventy-two pence. And I know where a gingy bottle is.'

'That's never enough.'

'Well, we would huv had a gun, but Angela said she couldnae get it.'

'That wasnae my fault,' Angela cuts in. 'He takes a gun everywhere wae him noo, says he's like the police and if anybody annoys him, he can jist shoot them.'

Evan shakes his head. 'The police urnae allowed tae carry guns. Only soldiers are allowed tae carry guns.'

'Well, he does.' She stares at her wellies, and her chin drops onto her chest. 'And he hurts me.'

Bruno's eyes glisten. 'We're gonnae take the poison instead.'

'Shut up,' Evan sneers. 'If somebody is gonnae hurt yeh, yeh shoot them. Yeh cannae jist hold their mouth open and pour poison doon their gob.'

Bruno stuffs his haul from the bed into the plastic bag. 'Aye, but we wouldnae tell them we had the poison. They'd maybe be holding us as slaves. Make us work in the kitchen. Or something. So when they werenae looking I'd get the poison oot and pour it into their cup of tea, or their dinner, and serve it to them. Then we'd run away.'

Evan takes a sideways and backwards step, bumping into Angela. 'Whit of instead of taking a chance of getting caught and poisoning everybody and anybody, we put the poison in Chaz's tea. Then yeh'll no need tae run away.'

Bruno nods in agreement and grins. 'Suppose we could. And I could buy sweeties wae the money instead.' He drops the bag on the floor and turns his attention to Angela. 'Whit does he eat?'

Angela's head falls under the weight of attention. 'He doesnae eat anything much. Maybe a fry up in the morning and chicken curry and chips at night, but I'm meant tae be sleeping, though he mings the place oot.'

Bruno starts laughing. 'If yeh stick it in curry, yeh wouldnae taste a thing.'

Evan stumbles to one side. 'Especially if yeh were like my da when he used tae come hame blootered.' Then he falls to the other, bouncing off Bruno's shoulder.

He play-grabs Angela, grapples and tickles her as they fall sideways onto his bed. With her choking laugher, wisps of hair stick to her mouth.

'How ur we gonnae dae it?' Bruno's seriousness sobers them. 'I mean, how ur we gonnae poison Chaz if he's got a big, massive gun?'

Angela pulls free of Evan. Her mouth hangs open as she considers. 'Sometimes he sticks it under the bed when he goes tae sleep.'

Evan pats her on the head. 'Yeh can take aff yer jacket, pet, and fling it on the bed. It's boiling in here.' He glances at the window, the snow's drifting light.

Angela unpicks the toggles on her jacket and a flouncy white dress pokes through. She hands her duffle to Evan. She wiggles her hips but refuses to sit on the bed. 'It's too sore,' she shivers and dances away from his outstretched hand.

Evan gives in and flings her coat on top of his bed and flops down beside it. He picks up the book of *Grimms' Fairy Tales* by the cover and flicks through it. 'If we could jist make ourselves invisible.' He stares at a wood-cut drawing of a woman with golden hair, her face pressed to the side of a spinning wheel. 'We could nip in and oot and nobody would ever know.'

Bruno looks over his shoulder. 'We could hide under the bed. Wait until he's sleeping and then poison him.'

Evan feels it's his job to come up with the right way of doing things. 'If he's too drunk and sleeping he'll no be hungry.'

Bruno yawns. 'I'm always hungry. We could maybe hold his nose and glug the poison doon him before he wakes up.'

Evan slams the book shut. 'Shut up.'

Bruno spins, 'Or shoot him?' He crooks his fingers into the shape of a gun. 'Bang, bang. Cause the gun will be lying about and we could steal it and take it under the bed wae us and hide it.'

Evan stares out the window. 'Let's go oot and play. We could make a slide from the top of the street tae the bottom. Maybe even go up the park and see if we can make a sleigh and slide doon the slope beside the duckie. That's whit aw the big boys dae.'

Angela cries, 'I want on a slate!'

'It's a sledge,' Bruno giggles. 'Not a slate.'

Evan laughs too. 'Put yer jacket back on Angel, and we'll see if we can find yeh a slate tae play on. I'm sure there'll be something lying about we can use. We should go and get Pizza Face. He's good at finding that kind of thing.'

He chews a half-moon of skin and spits a splinter of nail. 'It's Pizza Face's birthday on Monday. We could take the poison tae the house then and sneak it upstairs.' His voice seesaws up and down. 'Yer mum would let us play in the house if it's Pizza Face's birthday party, wouldn't she?'

Angela considers it. 'Only if Chaz isnae there.'

'But he willnae be there,' Bruno dunts her shoulder to help her remember. 'He's always at the pub, getting steaming.' He chuckles with his false laugh but shuts up when nobody joins in.

Evan grows serious. Bruno avoids his eyes. 'Then wan of us could hide under the bed and wait for him tae get in? But yeh'd need tae be dead quiet. Yeh'd hardly be able tae breathe.' He stands quiet and still as if he's already under that bed. Bruno and Angela cock their heads and listen and wait. 'And if yeh got caught, then yeh could jist say yeh were playing hide and seek and fell asleep.'

'I could lie under the bed wae yeh,' screeches Angela. 'Kid on, I'm invisible too.'

'Nah,' Bruno sighs. 'Yeh cannae dae that. Yeh've got tae act aw normal. And wait till night-time until Evan sneaks oot. Then yeh can keep watch for him.'

Angela repeats what he's said with a breathy flourish. 'I can keep watch and act aw normal,' nodding her head in agreement.

'Nah,' Evan yanks his duffel coat out of the wardrobe, pulls it over his shoulders and wrestles it on. 'Would never work.'

Bruno voice is overly cheery, 'We could still run away,' but it doesn't stretch to his eyes.

'Shut up, wae the running away. It's freezing oot there and yeh wouldnae last five minutes.'

Angela peeks at Evan. 'We could go under the water.' Her blonde eyelashes blinking and eyes filled with tears. 'Where it doesnae hurt.'

Evan kneels on one knee and pulls her in close. 'No goin under the water, pet. It's too cauld,' and his eyes brim with tears.

'My social worker, Marie, said it must have been four days, or longer, when it was cold and he was on his own.'

He remembers her crying and having a hanky ready to share. But he didn't know how to share. And the smell of his da, the sense of his da, and him just being out of reach. He was sure he'd heard him whispering to his mum. He'd never told her that. Those were secrets he can't tell adults.

'I'll lie under the bed wae the poison. I know I can dae it. And I'll put it in his curry when he's no looking. I'll make myself invisible again.'

'I'll help yeh,' Bruno says. 'I'll haud ontae the gun. I was only gonnae run away a wee bit, anyway.'

Chapter 91

The Intensive Care Unit

FROM DALMUIR TRAIN STATION TO GLASGOW IS A DISTANCE between not far and life changing, the High Court an Intensive Care Unit of the Criminal Justice system. Nobody visits it by accident. Outside Glasgow Central Station, near Boots dispensary, Senga absent-mindedly pulls a hanky from her coat sleeve and waves the white cloth in front of Pizza Face. She wipes his nose as if it's her own and shoves it back in her bag. He has taken a bit of a stretch in the last few months. His neck juts out of his smart school blazer, clean and buttoned-up white shirt and school-tie choking his neck. Weegin black shoes are buffed at the toes to shine beneath the shelter of grey flared trousers.

Senga gets her bearings in the drizzling rain on the concourse, pigeons circling above her head. Heading towards Argyle Street she clutches her son's hand, ignores his protests, the slow-moving double-decker buses and black Hackneys choking the air. She quickly establishes her right of way on wide city-centre pavements. A nylon blue hat, the size of a saucer, pinned forcibly to her grey hair and pressed over her forehead. A heavy dark coat falls below the knee and is good for any weather, from tinkling her white toes and paddling in the sea at Rothesay in sunny weather to attending the High Court in Glasgow.

As they get nearer to the High Court, they hear his cries before they see him. The wee man parading with twin billboards tied with string that chops his body off at the neck. A scrawled Bible tract declaims: 'Let Jesus into your life. Open the door to a new life. Open the door of your heart and let Him in.'

'This way,' Pizza Face dips his shoulder, bearing the weight of responsibility. He's practiced in how his mum's crabbit face goes vacant.

The High Court in Glasgow hits them square in the face. Its architectural roots in murky and damp subterranean cells. Cold stone darkened by soot, fashioned in neoclassical style with porticos and pillars, made to tower and intimidate. They get nearer and the past meets the present. Wind whips off the Clyde and through the dreich wide-open spaces of Glasgow Green and brings the tang of river life. It brings on a case of the shivers into high walls and men dressed in old-fashioned wigs and courtly gowns.

Pizza Face dithers whether he wants Kerry-Ann to hang. That's what his da and brothers want. The *Daily Record* cites Maisie, the shopkeeper at the bottom of their close, in an exclusive interview that adds local colour. The report's illustration is a black-and-white picture of Kerry-Ann in a summer dress, with bobble sleeves, laughing and eating an ice-cream cone. Splash headlines in bold black-block ink lead with how Kerry-Ann became a bloody butcher twice. Once for poisoning her partner and the other for murdering the innocent child inside her. Comparisons are drawn with child-killer Myra Hindley, who also had dyed blonde hair.

Pizza Face knows they no longer hang people in Scotland. Neither his da nor brothers mention if they hanged Myra Hindley and Kerry-Ann, they'd also need to hang Junior, even though he'd done nothing much wrong. The next best thing is rotting in prison. He imagines her in a metal cage, attached to the walls outside Corton Vale Prison, soaking in the rain and bits of her falling off and thudding to the ground: a hand, an arm, a leg landing with a satisfying splat.

Unwashed bodies block their passage to the courtroom. Someone lights a cigarette while waiting for the trial to begin. A reporter breaks rank with his colleague, a connoisseur of misery. He edges closer for the kill. 'Mrs Sweeney, any comment?' he barks in her ear, 'to set the record straight?'

Senga looks through him and marches on. She pays more attention to finding a seat for Pizza Face and herself. The galley quickly fills and slopes behind the prosecutor and defence lawyer's desks. Senga and Pizza Face sit, about twelve-feet away, behind the prosecution team. The jury team of fifteen honest men and women, but mainly women, sits to the side, elevated above the proceedings.

Pizza Face enjoyed time off school but gets bored. Old folk mope about searching for hankies or cigarettes with distracted fingers.

Kerry-Ann, flanked by two prison guards, is brought from the cells below. She shows little inquisitiveness, does not glance around to see Senga and Pizza Face sitting in the visitor's gallery. She doesn't look like a murderer. Tangle of hair and pallid hollowed-out face with sad eyes.

Kerry-Ann's face flushes. She places her hand on the Bible as the clerk of the judiciary swears her in on the witness stand. 'I swear by Almighty God that I will tell the truth, the whole truth and nothing but the truth.'

Judge Lord Drummond Brodie with kissing-squirrel tails of eyebrows that seem attached to his wig, peers at her and reminds her, 'You have to answer.'

'I dae.'

The charge is read out and her hand trembles as she takes a sip of water.

'On the 31st October 1971 at a house in 176 Dumbarton Road, Clydebank, you Kerry-Ann Boyd Orr did assault Charles Sweeney by causing him to ingest paraquat or other similar toxic substances and you did murder him.'

'How do you plead?' the clerk asks, looking up at her. 'Guilty or not guilty?'

'Not guilty.'

Representing the Crown and prosecuting for the Fiscal Office, Queen's Counsel Montrose appears born to the era of wigs. He absentmindedly fingers the gown commonly known as silk. He's tall and sharp beaked, with a tendency to lean towards those he cross-examines. His hazel eyes flicker over Kerry-Ann slumped in the witness box. The defence team's case is built around a prepared statement, which he reads. His sonorous voice, old school, artlessly sure of its place in the world, clipped vowels, each word enunciated like new-minted coin.

'That on the 31st October 1971, the ambulance services had called at Kerry-Ann Orr's flat around three a.m. Her daughter was in attendance. Kerry-Ann Orr said that Charles Sweeney had forced her to eat part of a chicken curry "that was not quite right" which she pointed to. The accused was vomiting and in considerable pain. Charles Sweeney was lying in bed with bedclothes pulled over him. It was clear to the ambulance services that he was already dead. The accused was taken away by the ambulance service and subsequently suffered a miscarriage causing her to lose her child.'

'You say in a statement given to the police that your partner abused you?' Montrose raises his eyebrows and offers her a chance to comment. He shares a rueful smile with Judge Drummond Brodie when she doesn't.

Lord Brodie prompts her in a gruff voice, 'The witness has been asked a question.'

Kerry-Ann looks at him, eyes blinking and baffled. The judge gives a slight nod, a cue that Montrose picks up immediately and he repeats his question.

She looks from the polished hardwood floor at the rows of name-less people watching her and the prosecutor smirking at her. 'Whit was the question again?'

His eyes lock on hers. 'In what way did your partner abuse you?'

'He beat me.'

'He beat you?' Although Montrose and his team have carefully read through and annotated the police report and the psychiatric reports prepared for the court, he gives a boyish grin and acts surprised.

'Yeh.'

'Anything else?'

Her shoulders slump. 'He raped us—I mean me!'

'He raped you.' Montrose turns towards the bench behind him and his grin grows wings, big enough to fill the court, letting them in on the joke she presents by her appearance – her common-law husband would need to rape a common woman like that. 'Anything else?'

Her small mouth opens and her lips move as if offering a prayer, 'Nah.'

'So in your belief your partner beat and raped you, you hatched a plan to poison and murder him, which you did. Is that not correct?'

'Nah.'

'If he beat and raped you, as you allege,' Montrose sighs and shakes his head. 'Why didn't you simply walk away and leave him?' He pauses and smiles at her. 'After all, it's not as if you were married to him. You already had a child out of wedlock and presumably walked away quite readily from that relationship.'

Kerry-Ann's hand trembles, tapping fingers on the oak stand. She quells the movement with her other hand, but her body takes up the beat and trembles. When she answers, it's a stuttered, 'I don't know.'

'I think you do know. Let me take you back to the night of 31st October last year. It's the early hours of the morning and your partner is found dead. Laboratory reports suggest that he has been poisoned. You, yourself, pointed to chicken curry which you said he'd consumed. And a bottle containing paraquat was found at the scene. How do you explain that?'

Judge Brodie frowns. 'Witness must answer.'

'I don't know,' she replies.

'You don't know.' The prosecutor holds up her statement for the court to examine. A frail, elderly man sitting in the jury coughs. A woman juror with permed hair, seated beside him, hands him a paper hanky. The Queen's Counsel waits for the bout of coughing to end, the elderly man to sip a glass of water, before continuing, and once more turns his attention to Kerry-Ann in the dock. 'Is it not true that you waited until your partner was suitably intoxicated that his taste buds were impaired and you mixed a poison that is commonly available in any high street with his food and thereby killed him?'

Kerry-Ann shakes her head. 'Nah.'

Her answer seems to amuse the Queen's Counsel. He flashes his teeth in a smile and offers her another option. 'Perhaps you didn't mean to kill him? Perhaps,' he pauses, leans towards her and lowers his voice, 'You only meant to give him a fright. To warn him off, but you got a bit mixed up with what you were doing. A perfectly understandable mistake?'

Kerry-Ann shakes her head. 'Nah, I'd hardly poison myself tae, noo would I?'

'Can you speak a little louder and a little clearer?' the judge reminds her. 'For the benefit of the stenographer and the jury.'

A faint flush travels across Kerry-Ann's face. She tries not to look at the jurors, ordinary looking people, as she repeats herself in case something in their passive expressions changes and hints they don't believe her. The Queen's Counsel doesn't give her time to think.

'As you well know, your partner Charles Sweeney's death was hardly instantaneous. He would have had difficulty breathing. His throat would have been burning and there was a hole in his oesophagus that shows he would have been in considerable pain.

He would have been physically sick. We can only surmise that he cried out for help, but you chose to ignore those cries. Instead, you let him lie in his own filth and hatched a plot to douse yourself with the self-same poison in order to give yourself an alibi, but here you made a terrible misjudgement and overdosed. Is it not true there were two innocent victims here, Charles Sweeney, and the child you miscarried, and you were responsible for both of them?'

Kerry-Ann blinks rapidly as she looks at him, shifts her feet, and holds her hand over her mouth. 'I don't know.'

Judge Brodie regards the witness with concern as she sobs. 'Take your time,' he advises her. 'Perhaps a drink of water?'

Kerry-Ann shakes her head and tries to compose herself.

The defence and prosecution teams shuffle papers. Montrose waits until her sombre and tearful face once more looks across at him. 'You made a statement to the police in which you said,' he glances at the paper in his hand to remind him and allows a winning smile to shape his profile as he changes register, "That you were glad he was dead and hoped he was rotting in hell?" Come now, is it not true that you had the motive and helped him on his way?'

The jury waits for the cross-examination to cease and for Kerry-Ann to reach a verdict for them.

'Nah.' Kerry-Ann's body trembles and her quavering voice settles into a crying out. 'After aw he's done, I hated him and I'm glad he's deid, but I didnae kill him, although I wish I had killed the bastard.'

Chapter 92

Good cop–bad cop

Detective Inspector Grier knows his place. He sits smoking in the largely soundproofed room, away from the stage of the courtroom. He becomes nostalgic for simpler times when he was facing a gang of neds armed with razors at Glasgow Cross and he had to stand by himself with a bit of wood, a truncheon.

When he is called as the next witness in proceedings, he follows behind the macer. He is on nodding terms with those that wear fancy costumes of robes and wigs in the High Court. He knows their routines and the jargon. As a senior officer, he believes part of his job is to explain to rookie detectives where to go, what to expect, and most importantly for any cop what *not* to admit.

Even in dress uniform, his appearance is roughhewn, bald, tall and bulky as a wonky set of double wardrobes. Plodding up the stairs and putting on his public face in the dock, he promises to tell the truth, the whole truth and nothing but the truth, so help him god.

He clutches the ledge around the jury box to stop his hand from shaking. Rows of faces roll downward on him like a wave and,

399

gawping, rake over his every movement. He keeps his eyes on the stenographer, pale sweater and skirt, with imitation pearls at the throat and long fingers primed and at the ready. The double door to the court opens. There's nervous laughter at the back and around the aisles as a stiff-legged shadowy presence is escorted out, stumbling and cursing. All the seats have been long taken by family members of the murder victim, fresh-faced lawyers, government councillors and worthies in bespoke pinstripe suits from the same tailors, so expensive they might well have sewn fifty-pound notes to their backs. Tweed coats with leather elbow patches occupy other seats. Shetland sweaters. Charcoal grey wool, three buttons and waistcoats. A lime-green blouse, frilly at the breast and loose in the midriff and light-blue bellbottoms. Journalists sit in clusters near the doors, ready to buck and stampede to get first to the public phones at the entrance and file copy of the evidence so far. The odd barrel shaped Glasgow woman, provides ballast, in her best finery, coat and gloves, who would have won the day at the Battle of Flodden Field and kept going until she got to London, but has taken a day off from the picture halls to view real live entertainment and waits expectantly chewing a Polo mint and with a packet of paper hankies in hand.

Kerry-Ann's legal representative, Barclay, is the kind of QC the public and tabloids love because he's a winner. He talks like a commoner, but with a slight Highland lilt. A poplin robe flows behind him like a cape when he struts into view, but more often is dowdy with falling cigarette ash. The wool wig sits on his head like a stray cat with its tail hanging over his back and liable to shift and go walkabouts. A twisted tomahawk for a nose. All over Glasgow and beyond its porous borders, his fame has soared so that paperboys dipping a newsagent shop's takings, to the aristocracy of the criminal world, sing from the same crime sheet, 'Get me Barclay!'

'M'Lord,' Barclay nods at the judge, before he turns and as he begins his cross-examination of the man in the dock. Chairs creak and squeak in the gallery, followed by a rustle of clothing as they lean forward. 'Detective Inspector Grier, it seems to me like an open and shut case. You have your timeline and you have your killer?'

Barclay's eyes crinkle into a smile when he pronounces his name and addresses him like an old friend. They have previous in High Courts and low.

Grier hesitates before opening his mouth. 'That's true.'

'Well, I won't keep you long.' Barclay points towards the evidence table. 'You've got some lurid snapshots of the deceased for the jury to examine. Did you take them yourself?'

Titters of laughter come from the back of the court. The judge's frown is directed towards Barclay.

Grier massages his neck with his big fingers and rubs at the sweat stain at the back of his collar before answering. 'No.'

'Then who took them?'

'My colleagues.'

'Did they take them at the crime scene?'

'Eh, no.'

'Where were they taken?'

Grier turns and looks at those sitting at the prosecutor's table for support. Then he stares steadily back at Barclay. 'You'd need to ask them.'

'No matter, but I think we can safely say, even though Detective Inspector Grier doesn't seem to know who took the photographs presented to this court, it has been well documented that they were taken in the mortuary of the Western Infirmary. Is that correct?'

'No,' Grier shakes his head. 'I mean yes.'

'So it's actually the pathologist and the coroner's office that we should thank for these photographs and for solving the case. Can you tell me what purpose they serve?'

'They serve to show that the murder victim died a painful and awful death.'

'Yes, but we already know that. We're not disputing that. So did the coroner's office instruct you to arrest the deceased's common-law wife, or did you make that decision on your own?'

A bubble of laughter and the stenographer pauses over the keys.

Grier mops at his forehead and averts his eyes from the defence counsel. He takes a sip of water. He pulls out his notebook. The court waits as he flips through page after page. He reads in a monotone voice and stumbles over words. 'We, I mean, I, was informed of the suspicious death of Mr Charles Sweeney at approximately 6.55 a.m. I was also told his girlfriend had been in Casualty. A suspected poisoning of the same toxic substance but was now in Intensive Care. We were not allowed to interview her until the evening of the second day when she was adjudged well-enough to speak to us. When told that her boyfriend had died, she seemed euphoric and said...' He held the notes up closer to his eyes. '"Good riddance, to bad rubbish". 'Upon further investigation, it was decided to take Kerry-Ann Orr into custody for further questioning, where she was then charged with his murder.' He stops as abruptly as he'd begun.

Beastie

'So let me understand this,' Barclay feigns ignorance. 'Miss Orr said to you she had killed Charles Sweeney?'

'No.'

'Then what led you to conclude that she had?'

Grier spends a few moments looking through his notebook. 'She admitted that Charles Sweeney had been alive on the night of his killing. That he'd been in a foul mood, picking faults with everything she did and punching her in the stomach and about the face.'

'Even though she was heavily pregnant?' interjects Barclay.

'Yes.'

Advocate Depute Montrose springs to his feet. 'Hearsay, the deceased is not on trial, neither is he able to defend these absurd allegations.'

Judge Brodie gazes at the jury. 'I believe this jury is mature enough to make their own mind up.' His focus switches to Montrose and his brows crease as he addresses both. 'But the witness has brought into the public domain matters that it might have been judicious not to mention.'

Barclay waits to speak. 'So the defendant Kerry-Ann Orr got herself beaten up, poisoned herself and poisoned her partner and went to hospital and pleaded...' Barclay puts on a booming Glaswegian accent: 'It wasnae me Guv,' and laughter erupts in the gallery.

Judge Lord Brodie bangs his gavel and threatens to clear the court. 'Mr Barclay, this is not a circus, nor an amusement sideshow, but a murder trial. You are flickering on the thin edge of Contempt and all that entails.'

Barclay clutches his hands together and bows to Judge Brodie. 'My apologies, My Lord. It won't happen again.'

'See that it doesn't.'

Chapter 93

Your other national drink

WHEN THE FORENSIC EXPERT IS SWORN IN, HIS VOICE IS A whisper that tickles Judge Brodie's ear and falls deaf to those beyond the second row. But Lord Brodie is so used to seeing Mr Cleary's high pale forehead, in the court circuit, he takes a distant paternal interest and no longer asks him to speak up. The presence, or absence, of a fingerprint at a crime scene is rarely disputed.

Barclay stands before the court. He points at the evidence table where a tagged Irn-Bru bottle with a dark liquid at the bottom. 'Is that the bottle found in Kerry-Ann Orr's house that was dusted for fingerprints?'

'Yes,' says Cleary.

Barclay pauses and smiles, 'Then presumably with all that poisoning, her fingerprints would be all over the bottle?'

'No,' mumbles Cleary.

A hand cups the defence QC's right ear, mimicking an antiquated ear trumpet. He turns to Cleary, but it is the judges 'hrummph' which is most audible under the vaulted ceiling. Barclay acts shocked. 'You didn't find the defendant's fingerprints on the Irn Bru bottle. Then whose fingerprints did you find?'

'We found a small, smudged fingerprint,' admits Cleary. 'But we were not able to match it to any on record.'

'Could this smudged fingerprint have been Kerry-Ann Orr's?'

'Nothing is ever taken for granted.' Cleary perks up and speaks clearer and louder. 'What we are looking at is an individuation in a ten-point pattern of ridges and whorls. There's a protocol which we strictly follow.' Judge Brodie yawns and Cleary stops talking to look at him before continuing. 'So what I'm trying to say is even with the probability of error factored in, and taken as a given, I can say with some certainty that the smudged print is not Kerry-Ann Orr's.'

'There's no doubt then that some other person handled the bottle with poison in it?'

Cleary corrects him. 'There's always room for doubt.'

'Did you find other latent fingerprints at the scene of the crime?'

'Yes. We found a number of other fingerprints.'

'How did you rule them out of the murder inquiry?'

'Well, we don't rule anyone out. What we do is try to pick up fingerprints and identify who they belong to. It's up to detectives to identity who had access to the crime scene so we can rule them out. Then we look for a match between those found at the scene and those on our database.'

'I suppose you'd find the murder victim's prints all over the house?' Barclay looks briefly perplexed. 'What do you call them? A control?'

'Yes, we found them in several locations you'd expect to find them. On door handles, mugs, the television...' Cleary's voice tapers off.

'Not on the bottle of poison?'

'No.'

'This interests me.' Barclay takes a few steps forward towards the dock. The judge watches him closely. Barclay seems lost for words. 'How did you...' he wiggles his fingers and shudders, 'fingerprint a corpse?'

'Oh, no,' says Cleary, correcting him. 'That wasn't necessary. His fingerprints were already on record.'

'So it was quite a simple matter of you taking the murder victim's prints from his criminal record?'

'Yes.'

Montrose proclaims in a weary voice, 'The murder victim is not on trial here,' before sitting down again.

Barclay nods in acknowledgement but turns back to the witness box, and his voice has a renewed vigour. 'Did you find any matches for fingerprints on the handgun or bullets found in the house?'

Cleary knits his hands together. He has to think about this one. Grier had asked him to dust a .22 Starr handgun, but as a favour. He didn't want it logged in any official reports. But Cleary was always meticulous in his paperwork. 'Yes,' he says. 'I did.'

The courtroom sighs like a forest after a high wind has passed through the trees. A reporter from the *Glasgow Herald* tiptoes into the passage with the bank of phones but stands frozen as Judge Brodie stares at him.

'Did you find Charles Sweeney's prints on the handgun?'

'Yes.'

Judge Brodie barks at Barclay before the prosecution team can voice an objection. 'Can the learned counsel reframe the question?'

'Certainly M'Lord,' says Barclay. 'Was the accused Kerry-Ann Orr's fingerprints on the handgun?'

'No.'

'Was the accused Kerry-Ann Orr's fingerprints found on the substantial amount of cash at the scene, I believe it was just under £15 000?'

'No.'

The Advocate Depute consults with his colleagues before pronouncing. 'No questions.'

Judge Brodie thanks the fingerprint expert, Mr Cleary, before dismissing him and calling for a recess. Reporters, first to stand, break ranks like unruly schoolkids with stamping feet towards the double doors when the judge's back is turned. He makes his way at a stately pace towards the door cut into the thick walls behind his bench.

Chapter 94

Unreasonable doubt?

When Pizza Face and Senga took their seats after the adjournment, the jury sat hushed and expectant. Montrose leaves his cigarette smouldering in the ashtray and begins with a plain recapping of the facts. 'Make no mistake, Kerry-Ann Orr is guilty as charged.' He walks back and forth in front of the jury, so their eyes follow him. 'She had the means, a common poison, found in her house, and she had the motive. She watched him die. She let him die. You have seen and heard her over the course of the trial, and not once has she shown an ounce of grief or remorse for her actions. Indeed, our constabulary reported her euphoria when told of his death. You have also seen how she tends to prevaricate. Blame others. She admits she was at home, the front door locked, the only other person being in the house with her, her daughter. Indeed, I think in all my years serving a courtroom, I have never heard of a mother blaming her five-year-old daughter for a murder that she has committed, either directly or indirectly. For me that is a new low.

She showed no remorse. We have seen her dry-eyed, smiling and laughing with her prison escorts. Waving them away like old friends. The truth is, she's a cold-blooded killer, but a first-class actress that poisoned her lover and her child to muddy the waters. I guess she wants us to feel sorry for her, but her acts of violence have resulted in two deaths, but we're here to judge only one of them. Kerry-Ann Orr took an easy-to-obtain poison and killed Charles Sweeney. Gentlemen and Gentlewomen of the jury, I ask only one thing, justice for the deceased and for you to find Kerry-Ann Orr guilty.'

Chapter 95

The loneliest woman in the world

BARCLAY SIDLES UP AND ACTS LIKE AN OLD FRIEND TO THE jury. 'I'll be brief,' he tells them. He smiles and hitches his arms as if he's putting his hands in his pockets, but his gown has no pockets and laughs at the absurdity of his actions. 'Kerry-Ann Orr was the loneliest woman in the world. The architect of her own desolation. She had no real friends and few pastimes. Defenceless against predators in a world such as ours. We have heard her boyfriend beat and raped her and she continually made bad choices. Who among us hasn't made bad choices, done something stupid?' He nods his head and stage whispers. 'We all have.' His voice grows stronger, but more detached. 'The difference is that again and again Kerry-Ann Orr has been punished for her rash choices. She doesn't know who the killer is. Neither does the prosecution. They have trashed what little dignity Kerry-Ann Orr had while not offering an iota of direct evidence that she is a murderer. The case should never have come to trial. Her fingerprints were not on the poison. At least one other person's was. The court does not ask you to decide if she was in the wrong place at the wrong time, because she's one of the people we all know, we are all familiar with, that are always in the wrong place at the wrong

411

time. Kerry-Ann Orr is a victim of poverty. That doesn't make her a murderer. I want you to consider the facts and I'd remind you she's not an innocent babe, but gentlemen and women of the jury, neither are any of us. To find the defendant guilty, you must be sure beyond all reasonable doubt. You alone know the truth and I'm sure if you look inside yourself you'll find the defendant Not Guilty. I only ask you to do your duty.'

Chapter 96

Verdict

KERRY-ANN IS BROUGHT FROM THE CELLS BELOW WHEN THE verdict is reached. She watches the foreman of the jury, almost vaudeville in how he stands, smacks his thick lips together and savours the attention of the courtroom, like an old roué ready to have his day.

The clerk of the judiciary asks, 'Have you reached a verdict?'

'Yes.'

'What is your verdict?'

The foreman of the jury confirms the verdict and sits down. 'Not proven by a majority of eight to seven.'

The gallery shakes off courtroom restraints and conversation burbles into shouts of support as the verdict is transcribed and read back to the jury.

The macer calls for order. Judge Lord Brodie's eyes lock with Montrose's and the Advocate Depute's head drops. One of his colleagues gives him a consolation pat on the back. Judge Brodie's gown rustles as he addresses the court and leans forward to offer his verdict to Kerry-Ann Orr in the dock.

'Not Proven, by a majority verdict of eight to seven. Kerry-Ann Boyd Orr, you are free to go.'

Kerry-Ann is led free from the dock. It seems to her after all the waiting something spontaneous, gracious even, has happened. She was free to go but waited for someone to tell her how she would get there.

Chapter 97

Grimms

'Well, the important thing is you're back now.' Julie perches behind the desk on the swivel-office chair, her pillarbox red lipstick the brightest thing in the room. She picks at fluff on her thick jumper and doles out advice. 'Establish a firm routine. Start as you mean to go on.'

'Yeh,' Kerry-Ann laughs. She fidgets in the seat across from her in a three-quarter length grey padded raincoat and rubs a bit of colour into her cheeks with her fingers. A cup of tea goes cold at her feet. 'I mean, I huv been away for a long time. I brought her something, but she's maybe a bit big for it noo.'

'It's lovely.' Julie smiles at her. 'A girl can never get enough dollies.'

'I need tae go tae the loo.'

Julie waves her hand. 'Oh, it's just the second door on the right at the stairs.'

Kerry-Ann stares at the tangle of phone wire and files on the desk. She has to stop herself from calling Julie, *Mam*. She still expects to hear the jangle of keys and is not yet used to going places unescorted. It was simpler in Corton Vale, being told what to do. Outside, she feels like a tortoise that has been flipped on its back. 'I'm sorry tae be such a pain in the arse.'

'Oh, no, don't be daft. I'll show you.' Julie slips from behind the desk.

Angela bolts the last few stairs, leaving Evan and Bruno behind, and stands in front of Kerry-Ann.

'Yeh've grown.' Kerry-Ann dabs her eyes. She strokes Angela's ponytail, kneels to cuddle her, and squeezes her hand. 'I'm sorry I missed yer birthday, but I sent yeh a card and brought yeh a present.'

The eyes of a stranger stare back at her. Kerry-Ann remembers Angela as a newborn suckling greedily on her breasts. And the ums and ahs and woolly silences of a contented baby.

'Mum,' Angela whispers, 'I want tae tell yeh something.'

Kerry-Ann nuzzles Angela's cheek with her nose and plants a smacker of a kiss on her forehead and holds her tight, so she can't see her crying. 'Whit is it, darling?'

'I want tae go hame.'

'Oh,' Evan breenges past them with Bruno. 'They aw lived happily ever after.'

Printed in Great Britain
by Amazon